THE LAZARUS CONTINUUM

KEN FRY

THE LAZARUS CONTINUUM
Copyright © 2018 by KEN FRY

First Edition

Join Ken Fry's Circle of Readers and Get Free eBooks
www.booksbykenfry.com

Edited by Eeva Lancaster
Cover Design and Book Interior by The Book Khaleesi
www.thebookkhaleesi.com

10 9 8 7 6 5 4 3 2 1

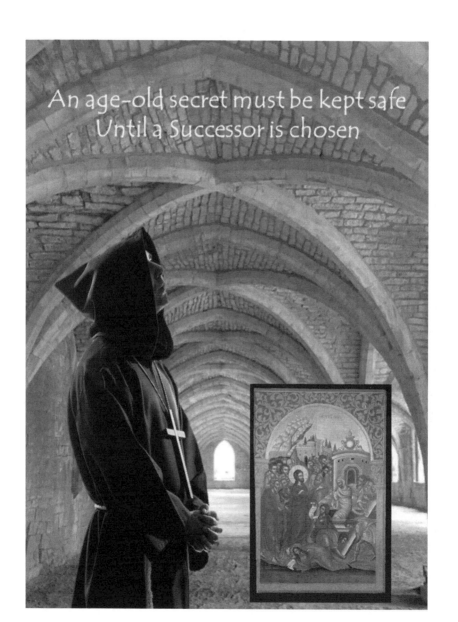

An age-old secret must be kept safe
Until a Successor is chosen

BOOKS by KEN FRY

AUDIOBOOKS

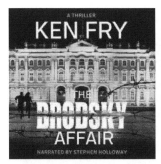
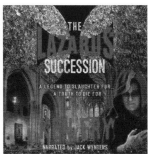
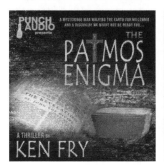

ON AUDIBLE and iTUNES

To all those who seek answers to life,
irrespective of race or religion...

May the universe smile upon you.

Ken Fry
Surrey, UK
2018

PROLOGUE

El Desierto de Tabernas
30 Kilometres North of Almeria, Spain

Raw heat, shimmering sands and scrub, shifted and bent in hopeless supplication before the turbulent zephyr that swirled in undulating rhythms across the tops of semi-submerged rocks and flints. Distant hills blurred in a shifting haze.

Blazing heat.

Nothing moved.

Utter silence.

It caused a stirring in his mind. He didn't know what. But there was a faded familiarity in the panorama around him that draped across his memories … like a worn, ancient, and tattered battle flag. He shielded his eyes to gaze out at the desolation.

This was his choice.

Slowly, Brother Baez, in his monastic attire, alighted from the Land Rover Defender. His emaciated frame creaked from hours behind the wheel. The vehicle was equipped with everything he needed for a prolonged stay; spare clothing, toiletries, tools, shovels, trowels, food supplies, chargers, water, and more importantly, his canvasses, paints and brushes.

Close by, he spotted a rocky outcrop with a small, cave-like structure. *That would help keep my things cool and dry*, he thought.

An hour later, soaked in sweat and his shaven head hot from the sun, he managed to transport most of his gear up the steep slope and into the coolness of the cave. Wonder of wonders, there was water dripping slowly at the rear. *It must be coming from the distant hills.* A small trickle ran further outwards. To where, he knew not, but he uttered a prayer of thanks for the additional water supply.

He paused to sit and survey the pitiless landscape, and his mind scanned back through the years. To the remarkable events that had led him to this point in time.

They had culminated in his request to Abbot Louis for yet another period of reflection. A solitary retreat for forty days and nights to question whether he wished to remain in the Brotherhood or not. Of late, he had felt his faith waver. Not just gently, but with massive vibrations. Over the last year, he had been increasingly troubled by recurring dreams and nightmares. He was unable to ravel their meaning. All he understood was that they went back to the events seventeen years ago, when he had somehow, under a canopy of mystical events, painted an artwork of *The Raising of Lazarus*. It was one of a long line of such works, that at a given point in their time, would vanish … before a new artist was chosen.

He had witnessed his painting demonstrating profound miraculous powers. The cancer-ridden and terminally ill, Condesa Maria Francesca de Toledo, had been cured simply by touching it.

From that point, his life had not been his own. He had reluctantly submitted to the monastery, and to God, who never answered his torments. In the process, he had lost the woman he loved, and had never seen his child come into this world.

His request to the Abbot had been generously accepted. Abbot Louis was not an unreasonable man and had perceived Brother Baez — formerly Broderick 'Brodie' Ladro, eminent historical researcher and TV producer — as a soul in torment, forever bound by the legacy that the painting had laden him with. With that in mind, he agreed that the Brother should spend some time in solitary retreat away from the monastic walls and routines. The only proviso was that he must continue his prayers, and paint for the monastic walls and altars.

It was agreed, and five days later, Brother Baez had driven away from the monastery, and into the desert.

The Abbot understood that his monk was at a decisive crossroads in his life, and that his faith was no longer holding up. He didn't mention it, but of late, he himself had been experiencing a series of strange dreams, and he sensed an odd atmosphere curling around his monastery like a wet tongue.

The heat and the long drive had exhausted Brother Baez. A

deep weariness assaulted him, and using a rucksack as a pillow, he allowed himself to drift into a short, dream-filled slumber.

He dreamt of what had been.

When he awoke, he was an unhappy man. The memories were too much to bear.

That evening, darkness descended quickly, and the temperature began to plummet. He set about making a fire by gathering brushwood, of which there was ample supply. After his prayers, he ate his first and last meal of the day of rice and dried chicken. He had sworn to adhere to this Spartan existence, to himself and to Abbot Louis days ago. As best as he could, he went through the Offices of the day, and finished an early and dark evening with Compline. He accomplished this by using one of his many flashlights.

Later, he found himself awake and unable to sleep. Feeling the cold, he stood and stepped outside. Around the area, he could make out the glinting eyes of nocturnal creatures scuttling about in various directions. He covered his head with his hood and wrapped his arms around himself, as he watched the whiteness of his breath climbing upwards before vanishing into the night air. The sky was clear, and the millions of stars flickering above caused him to gasp in wonder. He imagined how Van Gogh had been moved to paint *The Starry Night* when in the asylum at Saint-Rémy-de-Provence.

The panorama before him made him wonder. *Am I going mad?* It was a frequent thought and one that had been bothering him for the last six months. This was one of the reasons he needed a period away from the monastery. He had to realign his mind and spirit and he knew he would find that elusive peace if he could paint freely.

The image of his hidden work, *The Raising of Lazarus* haunted him. It was almost time for it to be shown to the public. Yet, its secret had to be maintained. There could be no announcement. That was the way it had been done over the centuries and that was the way it will be done until time ceased to exist.

The moon was full, and he made a note to include it in a night painting illuminating the barren wilderness around him. As he took a lungful of pure fresh air, for the first time in years, he felt a sense of freedom ripple through his mind and body. He had to make the most of it. Forty days and nights was all he was allowed. He understood the significance of this well.

CHAPTER 1

The Church of Thomas Reborn
Santa Fe, New Mexico, USA

P astor Shepard brushed off the dab of cream that had dropped from his plastic pot and across his shirtfront. He wiped his hands down the side of his black coat that looked as if it had been poured over him. Sitting down, he lit up a cigarette, which he only ever did when nobody was around to see him. He was a perpetually ambitious, six-foot plus, fifty-one year old, with a skeletal looking disposition enhanced by a mean hard look in his dull grey eyes. He had silver hair and a club foot.

His premises were empty, since his burgeoning congregation of over one hundred souls had long dispersed in a raucous display of hand clapping and shouts of 'Praise The Lord!' He now had dozens of churches across the country, all connected by direct TV relay. Pastor Shepard was quite an inspirational and uplifting speaker. Still, that number was far short of the count he would have liked.

The Santa Fe church was also his home and few knew that he managed to live well. The many thousands of dollars that were lovingly dropped into the service collection bags across the country were deposited to a central bank account of which he had direct access. Funds were no problem.

His lifestyle was a secret. His private quarters were forever locked. On his walls, not seen by a living soul, hung religious pictures of Christ and paintings with religious themes. Mixed in with these were pin-ups of scantily clad and naked women in various poses. He reasoned that God created beauty for men to admire, and there could be no sin in that.

Drawing deep on his Lucky Strike cigarette, he reached across the table and poured himself a three-finger shot of his favourite Bourbon, 'Widow Jane.' Not for the first time, he felt that his true potential had yet to be realised.

He had been an operative in the USSS before his days in the service came to an abrupt halt, with his security clearance revoked. This happened when his affair with a married Russian couple was revealed. It was of course deemed unacceptable and he was fired on the spot, lucky to have escaped charges of espionage and treason.

After that, he was left in a quandary and uncertain of what to do with his life. The existence of his church happened by accident and not by design. One time, he had spoken at a rally and received thunderous applause. He suddenly found himself with a small band of followers which quickly grew into the Church of Thomas Reborn.

Still, he wanted more from his church. It was not satisfying his ambitions.

His thoughts turned to the odd stories that had been brought to his attention by two of his acolytes, Alphonse and Jeremiah. Several days ago, they had told him of a rumour they heard on their recent visit to relatives in Spain. It concerned the existence of a painting, one of a so-called 'successional' series that held the secrets of Christ and the raising of Lazarus. Only one painting with supposed healing powers ever existed at one time, before it would mysteriously vanish and a new version was produced. It was said that a terminally ill noblewoman had been healed just by touching it. That painting, so stories suggested, was concealed somewhere in one of Spain's many monasteries and guarded by monks.

Shepard had the story checked out and it appeared to be the subject of very strong rumours. The woman, it was said, remained alive, and there were hints of a UK connection. It was a powerful story, one he was interested to exploit.

The power to heal! I have never believed such crap, but there are millions out there desperate enough to believe in miracles. Just think if it were true ... or made to appear true.

He took a throatful of Bourbon and welcomed the rush. The woman shouldn't be hard to find, nor the UK connection. His USSS training had taught him a thing or two about tracking people. With modern technology, there were few places to hide these days.

The story fitted in well with an idea that had been brewing in his mind over the last weeks. He had felt restless with the way the church was progressing. In his doubts, he had stumbled across information relating to Layfette Ron Hubbard (LRH), the founder of Scientology. This had prompted further investigation of which he was still in the midst of. The man, at his death, was reported to be worth six hundred million dollars. The Smithsonian magazine considered him to be in the top one hundred influential Americans of all time. He started a 'religion' and became fabulously wealthy.

That story from Spain, whether true or not, could be the catalyst for a similar movement, but with a sacred icon at its core. Shepard's heart started pounding. More research was needed. This could be the start of something big.

If I could bring this story to life, I could transform the planet! Shepard imagined all the wealth and power a sacred icon could bring him. A painting that could heal the sick and dying? Those security bastards who removed him would bend their knees. LRH would be an also ran.

A tremor of excitement passed through him. It was time for a new religion.

One last long draw on the Lucky Strike and he flung the butt into the collection he had amassed in an old corner fire bucket. Pulling out a World Atlas, he opened it up to a map of Europe. He knew the UK well enough, but very little of Spain. He knew there were sacred sites and several monasteries scattered around the country, but that was all.

He opened his laptop and accessed his bank account. Several years of collections and donations accounted for a considerable sum of money. He was not poor by anybody's imagination.

A plan began to germinate. He had enough time and funds to look into a few ideas, and if all went well, maybe begin a new movement.

In six months, he would be attending the bi-annual, six-day, World Charismatic Convention which will be held at the Wembley Stadium in London. From there, he could easily make his way down to Spain and begin his investigations. His deputy, Pastor Michael, could run the church in his absence and look after things.

The more he thought of it, the more he warmed to the idea. At the moment, he had about two churches in each State. This was Mickey Mouse to what could be achieved. A name change would be needed, and with a tangible miracle behind it, everyone would line up to join his church. He had worldwide contacts and these could all be of great benefit to a new movement.

His thoughts were distracted by the sound of boxes falling outside. He looked out at his private, floodlit patio and saw two shaggy-looking brown and black dogs snuffling around the garbage. Shepard let out a low growl.

He stood, and with a jagged limp, moved across to the adjacent wall and unhinged a fully loaded assault rifle he kept for protection or sport. He didn't need a sight. Hadn't he, in spite of his disability, been a crack shot in the service? He propped up his arm and elbow on the verandah support rail, dislodged the safety catch, took aim, and gently squeezed the trigger.

A sharp crack and a single round caused a piteous bellowing moan as one hapless beast fell to the ground with half its head missing. The other attempted to run but another shot brought it down in a welter of blood, before it gave one long last twitch and died..

Praise be to God.

He thought the time was nigh for some serious entertainment.

The Village Outskirts of Uffington Oxfordshire, UK

She never tired of looking at it on the farside scarp of the Berkshire Downs. Cut deeply into the hillside, The White Horse had been there for over three thousand years, since the Bronze Age. It was generally regarded as a masterpiece of minimalist art and protected with loving care. She felt close to it and had felt drawn by its simplicity from the moment she laid eyes on it. Ulla Stuart loved it more than most. For here, she could remember Brodie and how much he loved it whenever they visited.

The years had been kind to Ulla. Her poise and stature remained, and her hair had but a few grey strands. Since the Lazarus episode, she had made a success of her life and prospered in the world of real estate. However, the old yearning to 'liberate' art and precious things never entirely left her. Often, she would be overcome by the desire, the old habit, to walk around at night and release a captive work of art, returning it to its rightful owner. But it was not to be. Her burglary days had died a slow death. The care and welfare of her daughter took center stage.

Gazing upon the horse, she dropped her personal sadness into the green and chalky hillside and pretended that Brodie could return to her life once more. Broderick Ladro had walked out of her life sixteen years ago. The accursed Lazarus painting had broken them up. It divided them like nothing else could, and the strange and mystical events of those days now appeared like ghosts in her dreams and unguarded moments. The entire sequence of events had a momentous dimension that had skewered his life away from her and into the hands of a monastery. God knows where ... in Spain, where the whole business had started.

When he left, she knew she was carrying his child. A child that was now a young woman who had never seen her father ... nor did she know who he was. Ulla had never told her the whole story, which she had written down in a continuous series of sixteen diaries, locked away in the house.

That was about to change.

She had named her daughter Martha for a reason, and it had been an appropriate choice. Not only was she born on the feast day of Saint Martha, July 29, she had grown so like Martha in the New Testament and had developed a very business-like and practical nature. There was something very like Brodie about her. In this, she found comfort that softened the pain in her heart.

In all the time she had known Brodie, she had never thought he would choose the life he was now in. Within her mind, she would attempt to visualise his life and what he could be doing at certain times of the day. She missed him.

Around herself and Martha existed a cohesive link. An understanding that there was, in their natures and lifestyle, a very common bond. It was difficult to define, but many had noticed an unusual grafting of their personalities in a strange way. They would often speak identical sentences at the same time, and their movements would at times appear to be synchronised, almost choreographed.

The following day was to be Marths's seventeenth birthday.

She was mature, far in excess of her years.

Here existed a mystery.

Each year, from the date of her first birthday, a gift had always arrived. It was either blue flowers or a plant. They had never figured out who sent them. No card or address was ever attached. Ulla liked to imagine it was from Brodie, but he would not have known her frequent changes of address, so it couldn't be him.

Over the years, she had written him four letters, care and courtesy of the Condesa Maria Francesca de Toledo, who had figured so prominently in their lives when chasing the Lazarus painting. Ulla had never received a reply from her ... or from Brodie. If the Condesa was still alive, she would know where he was.

Wherever Ulla had been living, and there had been four moves in those sixteen years, the mystery flowers had always arrived on schedule. Somebody out there knew a lot more about her than she felt comfortable with. Tomorrow, she would see if the process would continue.

"Happy Birthday!" Ulla greeted Martha as she descended the stairs, still looking sleepy and wrapped in a large, red dressing gown. College had broken for the summer holidays and she was not in her usual rush.

"Thanks, Mum." Martha leant forward and gave Ulla a big kiss on the cheek. "What did you get me?" She couldn't avoid a giggle.

Martha was a tall and slender girl, and like her mother,

had long blond hair and the same startling green eyes. She had an inquisitive and intelligent attitude to life and was still deciding if she would pursue a degree in art & archaeology, or religion and philosophies, as her potential university studies. She was quite an artist, like her father, and her interest in ancient history was drawing her to the former. Whatever course she chose, she wanted to study at SOAS (The School of Oriental and African Studies) University of London.

"This is for you." Ulla handed her a small, wrapped gift box.

"What's this?"

"You will know if you open it, won't you?"

With care and deliberation, Martha untied the blue ribbon and pulled back the scarlet wrapping paper. Inside was a small silver box. She started to open it, but Ulla's hand pressed down on top of hers.

"Don't be shocked, but it's time you knew a few things. It's your birthright." Ulla withdrew her hand.

Martha, looking puzzled, lifted the lid. Inside was a golden heart-shaped locket. She looked up at her mother and her hand trembled. "I have a funny feeling I know what this is."

"I thought you might."

She unclasped the tiny latch and opened the heart-shaped top. She gasped at what she saw and her hand covered her mouth.

On one side of the locket was a twist of dark hair. On the other, a craggy smiling face beamed up at her from a small photograph.

"That's Broderick Ladro, your dad."

Martha shook. She stared back into her mother's face before

they both burst into tears.

"Sit down, Martha. We need to talk and it's going to be a long story. I'm going to start from the very beginning when I first met your father at the Stephen Chan Museum in New York..."

Two hours later, Ulla had revealed all the details surrounding the Lazarus painting and how it affected their lives and relationship. That included the killings and the miraculous healings that transpired, and the pivotal role Brodie had played in it.

"He," she said, "had been summoned. That was what ended our relationship. I couldn't compete with Christ."

During the conversation, there were several pauses for tears to flow and they hugged each other as only a mother and daughter could.

"Mum, if anybody else had told me that story, I would never have believed it. Coming from you, I know it can only be true. So painful, and you don't even know where he is?"

"No. Somewhere out there in some remote monastery just like Francisco was."

"Do you want to find him?"

"Yes and no ... but the die has been cast. To know he is safe and well would be enough."

A sharp rap on the door interrupted their conversation. They looked at each other and blurted out, "I wonder?"

Ulla rose and strode towards the outer front door. On opening it, she was not surprised at what she saw. A delivery man stood there with an enormous bunch of flowers.

"For a Miss Martha Stuart." His gruff voice seemed oddly reassuring.

"Yes, she lives here. Who are they from?" She knew he wouldn't know.

"No idea, Missus. I'm just told to deliver them."

She signed the delivery ticket and walked back in.

The flowers, as they had always been, were a stunning colour blue.

"*Phacelia Campanularia* or Desert Bluebells if you prefer, and for you, as usual." She smiled and handed them over to Martha.

"Who has been doing this all these years, Mum? It's so touching."

"I don't know. I used to think it was Brodie. But there's no way he could do this."

Martha bent forward to take in its scent, but stopped, knowing bluebells have none. 'Wait, look, there's a small envelope tucked in at the back."

"What?"

She reached in and detached a discreet, cream-coloured envelope. She stared back at Ulla. "Maybe we're about to find out at last." Opening the seal, she reached inside with her fingers and removed a folded note. She handed it to her mother and they read it at the same time.

Written in immaculate, black, cursive calligraphy were the words…

Be happy, for it is almost time.

"What?" They both exclaimed. Their eyes returned to the note and then back at each other.

"I don't like this…" Martha looked disconcerted.

Ulla turned the envelope around and examined it from every direction, even sniffing at it inside and out. "Whoever has been sending these flowers to you for the last seventeen years is a mystery. Why the big secret? And now this? What the hell does this message mean?"

"Should we call the police?"

"What do we tell them? Besides, I don't think your mysterious sender means to harm you. It seems like a promise is hanging around you, though. What that is, who knows?" Ulla sighed. "What a morning for you, Martha. You now know all about your father ... and then you get these. There's just one more thing remaining. Everything that I told you? I wrote them down in my diaries. Let me show you."

"Mum, I don't think I can take much more of this."

"This is the last, I promise you. Follow me."

They went upstairs to Ulla's bedroom and Ulla unlocked the cupboard. Stashed away at the back were sixteen robust leather-bound diaries. "These are now yours to keep. It's our life, sweetheart. Please say you accept."

Martha hugged her mother close. "You know I will, for as long as I live. C'mon, let's get out of here and go for a drink somewhere."

Forty minutes later, at the Fox and Hounds pub, with a view of The White Horse, they ordered lunch and began going through it all over again.

CHAPTER 2

El Desierto de Tabernas
30 Kilometres North of Almeria, Spain

Brother Baez, sitting by the entrance of the cave, wiped away the sweat dripping from his temples using the hem of his cassock. As he did so, he felt the rush of cool air passing up his legs and body. Standing up, he stretched, tugging the heavy, woolly robe off, and sat back in only his light vest and underpants. In front of him stood his extendable easel, with a wide, fully stretched canvas ready and waiting. Arranged in a careful row on a white sheet was his various tubes of oil paints and an array of different brushes, plus water and cloths. Onto his palette he loaded an array of colours. It was almost time to begin.

As had become his custom before commencing to paint, he would spend some time in a mixture of prayer and meditation. This was no exception. He had no idea what he was to paint, relying only on his emotions to guide him through. He opened his eyes and gazed out at the barren landscape and then at the canvas that seemed to contain ideas and promises within its blank whiteness.

Starting with faint charcoal outlines, his strokes became bolder and swifter as he began an unknown construction.

A familiar image started to emerge. Mary the Holy Mother.

Her blue robe flowed and draped down to an unseen floor. Her facial expression had a will of its own and he was unable to prevent the movement of his hand. It swept one way, and then the next, as eyes, cheeks, and lips, took shape.

She had the face of Ulla, his lost partner and lover, and she tenderly held the infant Jesus in her arms. Her green eyes were bright with maternal bliss. He had no idea from where it came. He knew only that it was as it was. His love for Ulla would never die.

As his brush scourged across the canvas, he began to weep.

This new painting would be worthy of the monastery. The Abbot would be pleased.

His hand continued to move quickly across the canvas of its own volition, and his light pencil strokes started to reveal another image. A praying penitent kneeling before the Holy Mother.

Her full profile emerged, and Brother Baez gasped, not knowing why.

Long blonde hair ... a suggestion of green eyes.

He did not know who she was, but it felt right ... and familiar.

His breath descended into short sharp jabs. It was getting difficult. He could not find the clarity and peace he longed for.

In a sense of mounting exasperation, he threw his brushes to the floor. "God, have pity," he yelled out into the unheeding desert.

There was no response … just the whispering of a desert breeze.

Uffington, UK

Martha sat completely still. Of late, The White Horse had become important to her. She would seek its presence and gaze across at its form, and completely lose herself in its grace. It generated a feeling of quietness within her.

On this particular day, she had sat there and had lost all sense of time. It was as if a trance had descended upon her. Ulla's revelations, and what she had written in those diaries, had at first startled her. But those emotions were now replaced with a burning curiosity, an ever-deepening sense of attachment and belonging to a man she would probably never know.

Oh my! What a life they had together. Was it all true? She had no way of knowing. Even her mother, Ulla, had wallowed in an element of disbelief.

The knowledge that her unknown father, Broderick Ladro, was also attached to the artistic symmetry of the chalky horse she was now gazing at, made it all the more poignant. It made her feel close to him. Within her, she felt the stirrings of business unfinished. As if there was something she needed to do. One day, she resolved to discover what that was.

She decided to take a walk, needing to be alone and away from the crowd. Without intending to, her route proceeded up The White Horse hill. Her mind whirled as she considered the endless possibilities. In a world of uncertainties, her recent discoveries hung from her like an injured swan. Her mother's revelations had, indeed, been shocking. Not that she condemned her, far from it. Martha only felt admiration for her mother.

The curvature of the horse became less distinct the closer she got. She paused and rested her qualms into its chalky ridges, which had graced the hillside for three millennia. It oozed mystery that radiated all around. She was alone with its primitive magic and felt the touch of a vanished world, which suited her mood.

The wind whipped up chalky dust particles and Martha shielded her eyes. It was then that she heard it.

A voice…

At first, she thought she had imagined it … but she hadn't. It became clearer and she gripped her fists and closed her eyes tight, lest she offended its presence. It spoke to her in her head. There was no doubting it. She stood, hammered to the spot.

"Martha, you are upset and worried by many things. When the time arrives, you will know. Have no fear, for he is safe." Three times the message was spoken clearly in her mind … and then it was gone.

Martha slowly opened her eyes, only to see she was alone,

as she had been, and gazing across the hill into a small valley. The wind whipped her hair and the grass around her looked wonderfully green.

What happened just then? I heard a voice. I did. I know I did. I heard it three times! He is safe? Who is safe? I must tell Ulla!

Forty minutes later, breathless and with an almost child-like excitement, she found herself blurting out the sequence of events to her mother.

"It called my name and told me that when the time arrived, I would know. The words were just like what's on that note with the flowers. It also said he was safe, and that I shouldn't be afraid. When the voice stopped, and I opened my eyes, everything around me looked and felt so vibrant."

Ulla's expression went from puzzlement to one of worried concern. For several minutes, she refused to speak and just shook her head. What words she managed were almost inaudible. "Please, God. I ask you, not again … please!"

Martha twisted her hair. "What do you mean? What do you mean not again?"

Ulla took a deep breath. "Martha, what you experienced on the hill has an ominous ring about it. It smacks of Brodie, your father. He started having strange and weird moments, like yours, that nobody could explain. I don't know what it means. All I sense is that something is wrong. If it is what I think it is, then strange things will be happening along the way, wherever that is leading. As for him being safe, I guess it would be too easy to think it's referring to your father. I honestly don't know what to think."

"I'm frightened now."

"So am I." Ulla poured out a large scotch and proceeded

to drink it neat.

"What do we do?"

"I don't know. If past events are anything to go by, we won't have to wait too long to find out.

El Desierto de Tabernas

Brother Baez had managed to maintain the order of daily offices with only one or two minor exceptions. There were moments when he recalled the lives of various saints and would begin to paint them for the walls of the monastery. Yet, his heart wasn't in it. He found the exercise mechanical, and almost boring. He needed to feel something, like he had all those years ago, which had culminated in his best work, *The Raising of Lazarus*, the one that had cured the Condesa Maria of her terminal illness. That painting was now a jealously guarded secret.

He knew better. Secrets don't stay secrets and there were others who knew of its existence like the Condesa herself, Ulla, and now several monks. He didn't doubt it.

Those days had changed his life. He had been chosen as a conduit for a greater plan he dared not imagine, and now the official artist to the monastery. Once, he had been Brodie Ladro, but now, he was Brother Baez. He never lost his sense of astonishment at those events and how they railroaded his life forever. The only familiar thing that remained was his painting, his art. Hardly a day passed when he didn't think of *her*.

Ulla, beloved Ulla.
But that, now, could never be.

The next morning, he awoke with a sense of agitation. Something was wrong. He could barely concentrate on his meditations and prayers. In his mind, a strange shape was forming. He couldn't make it out yet. He decided to pick up his brushes, the charcoal, and attempt to formulate what was troubling him. An hour later, with a drawing pad in front of him, he closed his eyes and tried to visualise what he had seen. It didn't take long. A rush of shapes shifted in his mind, and they stayed put. His hand started sketching. At first, he couldn't make out what he had drawn. He stood back and ran his eyes across it … and let out a gasp. He recognised it. It was a sight he hadn't seen since his earlier days with Ulla.

What in heaven's name? Why?

It was The White Horse of Uffington. He had admired it ever since he had first laid eyes on it, but after all these years, he had forgotten. Moving his fingers along its unmistakeable outline and form, he felt pleasure run through him. He sat down a wide rock and a broad smile broke out across his face. *I'll be damned. Why has that surfaced?*

His thoughts returned to the paintings he had done earlier of a blue robed Mary and the penitent woman. Somebody or something had taken over his brushes. Ulla had become Mary and the other seemed so familiar, but he couldn't put his finger on it.

He wiped the sweat from his forehead and decided to get some oils he'd left in the Land Rover nearby. Besides, it needed a start up to keep the engine and battery in good condition.

He stood and turned, and received another shock…

The entire area had somehow transformed, and had become awash with Desert Bluebells – bright, magnificent and glorious. He sank to his knees, his mouth agape with astonishment. He realised in a flash that mysterious things were at work around him.

This was no fluke.

There hadn't been a flower in this part of the world for years, and the last recorded event of rainfall was over six years ago. He bent his head in utter confusion. When he lifted his head, a female figure seemed to appear in the middle of the blooms. He stretched out his hand, reaching for her, but the vision flickered away as quickly as it had appeared.

"No… It's starting again…"

CHAPTER 3

Santa Fe, New Mexico
USA

H is Smith and Wesson, 9mm, M&P M2.0 pistol lay within a hand's breadth away on his desk. Pastor Shepard never took any chances when he sat alone through the late and early hours. It was five minutes past midnight and the church premises were bolted and barred. Nothing but a tank would be able to break in. The once full bottle of 'Widow Jane' was half full, and the pack of 'Lucky Strikes' had twelve remaining. He had surrounded himself with piles of books, and printouts from Google. Occupying his attention was a complete treatise by Roy Wallis, entitled *The Road to Total Freedom: A Social Analysis of Scientology*. Shepard wasn't interested in whether he believed it or not. His area of interest lay in structure, organisation and how to best get a message of hope across to the gullible millions he could foresee flocking to his church.

He allowed himself a brief respite to light up another cigarette, and a few more gulps of bourbon. His clubfoot ached, and he bent down to massage it. As he stroked it, as he had so many times before, he often wondered why his parents had never had it treated. He guessed they were too busy fighting each other and too involved in their extra-marital affairs to really worry about him. The foot had its advantages. There was no way he could be drafted for military service. He'd been wise, though. To offset his lack of a physique suitable for the military, he had joined in promoting the war effort in the Far East via the USSS. His administrative skills and strategies were brought to the notice of military intelligence. From there, he was seconded into raising the morale of troops and preaching a Christian message, to assuage such war crimes as the Mai Lai massacres in Vietnam. He had no problems about that and soon found himself with a powerful and listened-to voice. When he was discharged, he had a notable group of followers, and without even realising it, it had started a church foundation big enough to form a new denomination. Gospels apart, it kept him in a style of living beyond his wildest dreams. He'd never spoken to his dysfunctional parents since.

The Lazarus story compelled him. What he had heard so far, rumours they may be, dazzled him totally. The healed woman, the broken artist, the succession of painters and the myth, if it was that, stretching back to the time of Christ! The story was too powerful to set aside.

It was brought to his attention… surely, he was meant to

do something with this secret.

As Pastor Shepard sat in that small office, amidst bourbon, tobacco, a gun, nude pictures, and his greed and ambition, a revelation descended on him…

The Holy Church of Lazarus. The Lazacrucian movement will be born … and Shepard would be its King.

3 months later

All was in place. Without batting as much as an eyelid, Pastor Shepard told his followers that the Almighty had called to him through a vision and that he, Shepard, was to start a true belief system based on the idea of the dead rising, as demonstrated by Christ's raising of Lazarus. He would be gone for ninety days to meditate, reflect, and structure God's plan. Afterwards, he would return and reveal what God had planned for them all. That got his followers into a high state of excitement.

True to his word, Pastor Shepard did disappear as he said – into the desert – but not for spiritual reasons. He travelled to Nevada's Mojave Desert and booked in at a comfortable hotel on the Las Vegas strip. The church's funds were ample for what he had in mind. To his credit, in between the nightlife, girls, roulette and Black Jack, he did attempt to come up with a viable plan for his new church.

The system would be arranged as a pyramid divided into twelve escalating layers – one for each of Christ's disciples –

before total ascendancy at its peak, where only the chosen few would have access. He, of course, would be at its highest point and known as the Anointed Father, or The Anointed One. There could be no one higher than him. Each member must go through a degree of difficulty in each layer, before access to the next layer could be reached. They would have to prove themselves worthy of the ascension. The degrees of difficulty were to be comprised of scriptural knowledge, intensive doctrinal courses, tests, exams, meditation, severe self-analysis, psychological testing and lengthy community retreats. All would be at ever-increasing expense to the candidates. After all, knowledge and redemption are not free.

There was to be no guarantee of success. A minimum term of one year per layer would be required before access to the next level could be initiated. There would be an escalating fee structure. A postulant, if he ever completed the climb upwards, would have spent thirty thousand dollars, at least, to reach the highest layer.

On top of this, there would be seminars, camps, literature, and any other activity that would earn an income for the Holy Church of Lazarus. Shepard calculated that he could, from the very first year, net an estimated million dollars.

What was needed was a bit of magic, a little trick or two to produce mass hysteria. He thought about this in great detail. If there was truth in the story about the Lazarus painting and he could find it, what a bombshell that would be!

He picked up his Smith & Wesson, balancing it first in one hand and then the other. *We will need lots of these and other weapons. No doubt there will come a time when we will come under attack.*

The new church would have five thousand followers to

begin with. However, an icon rumoured to heal illnesses, even if it was only a rumour, would attract believers from all over the world.

Everyone feared death. Many needed to believe.

He, Pastor Shepard of the Holy Church of Lazarus, would be the embodiment of what most of mankind dreamt and hoped for.

Life.

He would give them something to believe in … Lazarus lived.

Interesting news was not long in reaching him through Alphonse and Jeremiah. In their investigations, they discovered the identity of the woman of noble birth who lived close to Toledo in Spain, the one who had miraculously recovered from advanced terminal cancer. Some were saying Christ had touched her in a vision. Others said she had seen and believed in a picture of Lazarus being raised from the dead, and that had cured her. Local gossip added fuel to the fire. It was said the bleeding figure of the Holy Virgin had led to her recovery. They were stories he had to investigate as soon as possible.

He drafted a statement to his followers, which will be delivered by his deputy. Of how their leader, Pastor Shepard, was experiencing intense spiritual insights and revelations which compelled him to remain in the desert. Shepard read through his prepared statement and it sounded convincing, humble, and even inspirational.

That should get some interest going and the tills ringing.

CHAPTER 4

Martha's dreams had become increasingly worrying and strange for her. There was something about them that she was unable to mention to her mother, Ulla. She felt they held a very personal statement, which in some way reached out to her and her alone. Besides, she didn't want to alarm her.

She had seen knights with red emblazoned tabards, bloody swords and singing a deep guttural chant which she could not understand. A man's face encompassed the entire scene. She knew it was him – her father, Broderick Ladro. It could be no one else. An enormous rush of love had spread through her and she understood why her mother loved him so. He was alive out there somewhere, and she knew now, like she had never known before, that she was going to have to find him.

In the depths of her mind, he was calling to her and was saying, *yes, yes, I will find you.*

A panorama of Desert Bluebells stretched out in front of

her. She saw a man, his arm outstretched, reaching out for her before the vision faded.

She awoke with a deep feeling of peace and comfort.

That afternoon, with a strong sense of something otherworldly, she took a stroll towards The White Horse. She felt her decisions hardening, but not her heart. She would eventually embark on a university course, embracing archaeology and fine art. A difficult combination, she thought, but one that felt totally right for her. Life was meant for challenges.

She knew Ulla would agree even though it would mean she'd be spending most of her time abroad. More reason why she could not tell her of her dream and visions. It was too similar to what Ulla had told her and what her mother had written in those diaries. It could only resurrect her alarms and fears.

That brief, vague vision of him drove her beyond what was expected from academia. But her direction and compass settings were now clear.

A wisp of fear touched her. For in that, her certainty, was contained all the uncertainty of her entire life.

When Martha returned home, there was an envelope waiting for her. "Look, Ma, it's got a London postmark. Oh God, I think it's from SOAS."

Ulla looked anxious. "Well, open it up then!"

Martha ripped it open and quickly read it through. "Yipes! I've been unconditionally accepted. That's unheard of! It says:

Due to your outstanding performance we are prepared to offer

you a graduate course to read both, Medieval European Archae-
ology and Medieval European Fine Art. Please acknowledge
this letter within seven days to hold your place.'"

Ulla gulped. Happiness, for her, was mingled with sadness.
They would not see each other for long periods of time.
"Come here, sweetheart." She hugged her daughter close.

Monasterio de San José de Nazaret
Nr. Segovia, Spain

For the last seventeen years, as was his custom, Abbot Louis,
on this day, every year took special care of his personal hy-
giene. His attire, his habit, and even his sandals had been re-
paired and cleaned of candle wax drippings and incense
burns. He felt like a new man. On this day, all those years
back, it had arrived at the monastery and he had witnessed its
power. He had realised his role as a guardian of Christendom's least known but most potent symbol of Christ's healing
legacy. So secret had it been that even the Vatican knew nothing of it. Nor did his community. Intuitively, he had known
that had to be the way, considering what lengths men were
prepared to go to get their hands on such potent treasures. He
knew of its history and its impermanent nature, which only
became apparent when a new artist was about to appear. As
far as he knew, only four people – including himself – knew
of its existence. The others were Brother Baez – formerly Brodie

Ladro – who had been chosen in a mysterious way to resurrect the work, together with his then partner, Ulla Stuart, and the Condesa, who was living proof of its awesome efficacy.

Also, on this day, she would be visiting the monastery, as she had done every year from when the painting was first deposited here. She was a living testimony to what it could achieve, Condesa Maria Francesca de Toledo, he could testify, had not aged a day in those seventeen years. She came in humility and gratitude, forever asking to be forgiven for all her lifelong sins, to which she open-heartedly and freely confessed.

The great wooden gates had opened, and she arrived in her vintage Delage D6 at a leisurely pace. Once alighted, Abbot Louis saw that she had lost none of her grace and bearing. For a woman just over seventy years, she looked like a fresh fifty-year-old. She dropped to one knee before the Abbot and kissed his hand.

"My Lady, you are most welcome. Your timing is, as always, impeccable. Just in time for tea."

"I was hoping you'd say that. Lead on please, Father."

"This way." He ushered her into the shade of the cloisters and to his office.

"Nothing seems to have changed since I was first here. That gives me a reassuring feeling, Father Abbot."

As usual, on these annual meetings, they reminisced about the events that had brought them all together.

"And where is Brother Baez? He's usually around when I visit, although we never meet."

"I fear that he is in the midst of another spiritual crisis. He has gone to the desert for a while, to pray, meditate, and produce some works of art for the monastery."

"Father, I need to speak to you both, but perhaps you can tell him when he returns. I feel the time has come for the work to be displayed to the public. It need not have a special place but one where it would settle in and blend with all your other art works. Its purpose must be fulfilled, and it cannot do so while it is locked away. It must be found by those who are destined to find it."

"I've had similar thoughts. I agree that it's time it saw the light of day. We need to bring this to Brother Baez's attention. However, its powers must remain secret, and those drawn to it, in their recovery, should never know why or how."

"Agreed. Now, may I sit with it for a while?"

"As always. Follow me."

Locking the metal door behind her, Maria placed the key in her pocket and knelt with reverence before a small altar, on which stood a golden crucifix. She lit two large candles and ignited a minute block of frankincense. Mounted centrally behind the altar was the painting – Brodie's *The Raising of Lazarus*. Something about it reminded her of an English artist she much admired, Sir Stanley Spencer. Whenever she laid her eyes on it, it never failed to make her catch her breath. She made her implorations and prayers for all those who were party to the entire episode, and even for the soul of the man who had all but thwarted the destiny of it all – Sir Maxwell Throgmorton.

As was her custom, she would at first talk to the painting and then meditate on its deeper meaning. This time, she found herself staring at it more intently, drawn into its mystery. The faces, the modernish apparel, and the setting that almost looked like an industrial landscape. Lazarus, looking faceless, expressionless, was emerging from his tomb, surrounded in colours of red and blue. Christ was dressed in black, almost like overalls, and not the traditional white, and his face dripping with sweat. He stood tall amongst his disciples, depicted as artisans, and the many people and faces that surrounded him. His arms were raised but vanished in a glow of yellow and greens. The tomb resembled a dark desert cave. The faces of the twelve apostles stared out of the canvas with expressions of wonderment and astonishment,

It was then she heard a voice, loud and clear in her mind. *It is almost time.* She heard it three times. Her hand flew to cover her mouth and she saw the figure of Christ turn his head for the briefest of moments to look into her eyes. The Condesa passed out in a crumpled heap onto the floor.

Five minutes passed before she recovered.

She sat back up, unafraid and filled with peace. All seemed as it had been, but the realisation was too powerful to dismiss.

Tears flowed.

She reached out and touched the painting with an enormous feeling of gratitude and love.

It is almost time, but she knew no more.

She unlocked the door and headed back to Abbot Louis.

CHAPTER 5

Las Vegas, USA

J ohn D. Bower's psoriasis was giving him trouble on his back and elbows again, but it had begun in childhood and he'd learnt how to handle it. The irritation required minutes of scratching, which his doctors had told him he shouldn't do. He was seated behind a massive, twelve-foot marble and English oak desk, surrounded by an extensive array of CCTV screens.

He paid little attention to them. He was reading Jacobovici and Wilson's *The Lost Gospel* and made frequent notes both in the book and a notebook he kept beside him. Bower was a complete paradox. He delighted in mysteries and conspiracies and had always considered the church as part of a massive cover-up; a scam, and full of untold and unpleasant secrets. His employees knew better than to debate this with him or disparage Bower's point of view. The few that did, had found themselves at the end of his fist and out of a job. His temper was legendary. Being small in stature, and with a soft waistline, his outward appearance detracted from his fists, which were shaped like bunches of bananas.

The paradox?

He operated a flourishing chain of gambling and casino enterprises. It had started when he was twelve years of age, running bets for downtown hoods who wanted to keep a low profile. He never saw a dichotomy between this, when as a young boy, he was also often in the role of a chorister and altar server.

His father scratched a living as a cab driver and his mother took in ironing and washing. A few years later, young Bower was earning more than his parents. He got in early and developed a system whereby expert observers could transmit betting odds to individual bookmakers using a network of clearing houses. The money poured in. He started a small casino and the rest was history.

As a Catholic through habit and upbringing, he used to attend mass every Sunday and on holy days of obligation. He had a secret wish ... that he could use his wealth in some way to discover something that would light up and debunk the world of religion. Like a major discovery that would shake their world and cause everything to be rethought. Not that he believed or disbelieved in God – that had always been an area of uncertainty. But he was convinced that the way the church presented it wasn't right. In some ways, he wanted the whole edifice of the churches to collapse. That this odd desire ran contrary to his profession as the owner of casinos never bothered him. He was regarded as ruthless, more so than his counterparts. But Bower felt a sense of pride that it set him apart from the other slime balls.

In the midst of his musings, a red light flashed on one of the monitors, followed by a bleep. A chip-tracking device had been activated. That meant certain big money chips were micro-chipped and their progress via the big betting games like Craps, Blackjack and Roulette were being monitored. It meant one of two things; either someone was losing big time or winning against the set house odds that never produced a loss.

He forgot about the mysteries of heaven for a while. Switching on a small microphone situated in the centre of his desk, he spoke directly into it, "Focus on that. Table nine."

Table nine was playing Black Jack. A hidden camera zoomed in on the players. Bower noted a tall skinny man, moving with a limp around the tables. He had been marked earlier on and was now placing heavy bets on every game he could.

At least a thousand dollars a hit.

He wasn't doing too well at it either and was looking the worse for wear. The camera moved in for a closer look at him. High rollers were always of interest since they could pour fortunes into his games and machines. Bower gave a start. The man was wearing a clerical collar and around his neck hung a small crucifix.

Well, I'm damned. A holy roller! I thought Einstein said God didn't play dice with the universe?

Bower experienced a curiosity that lit up his money-making and religious boxes. He spoke again into the microphone, "Lorenzo, our man of God out there on table nine, offer him our best deal for the evening and make sure he doesn't refuse."

"Will be done, JB." A disembodied voice echoed around the room.

The 'best deal' was a private room where tables were set for more private play and bets, away from the raucousness of the main rooms and hall.

"What the hell?" Shepard's slurred words sounded lost in the hubbub of the casino's excited cries and groans. A firm grip on each of his elbows by Lorenzo and his counterpart propelled him away from the table and another lost stake.

"We have a better deal for you, sir," Lorenzo whispered into Shepard's ear. "A better chance of winning and free of the hustle around here. This way."

The prospect of a better chance of winning had its appeal. "About time I was treated with some respect around here."

Shepard was aware of having had too much to drink, but as usual, he couldn't bring it entirely under control. He allowed himself to be manoeuvred into a hidden room along the sidewall of the casino. Once inside, he felt himself being pushed forward and facing a large Roulette wheel and a fancy Blackjack table edged in decorative rolled gold ormolu. Standing behind the table and surrounded by a battery of CCTV cameras stood a smallish, slightly rotund, and balding figure of a man wearing a broad silver-striped and ash-grey suit. His face was a fleshy pink, matching the enormity of his hands on which he wore a solitary gold signet ring. Another heavy looking man with a face like a shovel, sporting a ponytail and a tuxedo, stood impassively to one side with arms folded across his chest.

Shepard found himself sobering up fast. "What's going on here? Where are the other players?" His eyes swivelled around the room from left to right, and back to the man in front of him. He felt a flare of uncertainty he had not experienced since he had been confronted by his superiors over his Russian affair.

"My name is John D. Bower and I own this place." His voice was soft and silky. "Welcome sir, or should I say … Father? Please, take a seat." He waved to indicate a spare seat opposite him. "May I get you a drink?"

"Well, yes, but what am I doing here? Where are the other players?"

"All in good time, Father. Now what's it to be?" Bower waved expansively to a glass shelf stacked with every conceivable bottle of spirits one could wish for.

"Straight Bourbon on the rocks." Shepard could feel confusion spreading over him as he watched the man with the ponytail pour him a massive shot over a pyramid of ice cubes. In the brief silence that followed, the only sound was of the crackle of the ice cubes. He held the glass tightly and could feel its coldness spread through his fingertips. He stared directly at Bower.

Bower returned the stare, and then with a nod and a wave of his hand, he dismissed the other men from the room. His voice became sharper once they were alone. "Who are you? What is your name and why is a man of God gambling like crazy in my casino? You've lost over fifty thousand dollars. Did you know that or are you too shot to notice?"

Good God! As much as that? He sipped heavily on the drink and never let his eyes stray from the face of the man sitting opposite him. "My name is Pastor Shepard and I'm from Santa Fe."

"I see. Spending the church funds, are we? It certainly wouldn't be from your stipend, would it?"

Shepard remained silent. He wasn't going to admit to anything.

Bower continued. "If you had won, what were you going to do with the money? Wine, women, and song?"

"I don't know why you're asking me all these questions. I don't have to sit here any longer. I've done nothing wrong in your casino."

"True, Pastor, true, but you intrigue me. Was personal gain your motivation or do you have another motive?" Bower relaxed and leant back into the soft folds of his luxury desk chair.

Shepard took another gulp of Bourbon and for an unknown reason, felt himself relax at Bower's non-threatening posture. "I don't think it's anything you would understand, Mr. Bower."

"Try me."

"I'm attempting to establish a new church and I need funds for it."

"You haven't done too well it seems. Why on earth do we need yet another new church for?"

"I'll tell you why." Shepard felt a fire pass through him as he began speaking of the miraculous stories he had heard surrounding a blessed painting of Lazarus, which was rumoured to heal believers. The original painting created by an artist who had witnessed Christ's greatest miracle. The current artist, it was said, was hiding somewhere in a Spanish monastery. "If it's true and the Vatican is unaware, then it would be the most amazing thing in Christendom and the biggest money spinner the world would have ever known!" He slapped his tumbler down on the desk. He wasn't expecting what happened next.

Bower had leapt to his feet and was leaning forward across the desk with an excited look in his eyes. "Say all that again, Pastor, and say it slowly."

Shepard repeated what he had said at a slower rate. When he finished, Bower sat back down and opened several drawers in his desk, pulling out volumes of books and piles of notes related to Christian mysteries and phenomena. These he thrust at the Pastor.

"Look at these, will you?" His soft voice had transformed into a bellow.

Shepard recoiled. He'd been expecting to see a firearm, not a mess worthy of a literary scholar. He stuttered, "I … I … I don't understand!"

"What is there to understand? A man who comes into a casino wearing his clerical collar and can lay his hands on the sort of money you have lost tonight, might be stupid in one way, but that you got hold of it in the first place says something about you. Don't you see? We have similar ideas, similar ambitions, and I have been haunted by these ever since I can remember. What you have just told me is what I've been studying for the last ten years or more. Am I making myself clear?"

The Pastor's mind somersaulted. A thousand possibilities beckoned to him. "You're making yourself clear, but how on earth can I help you?"

"Think again. We can help each other. This is not the time or place to discuss what I have in mind. I'll get a car to pick you up in the morning. I have a private jet at the airport and I'll fly you to my estate in Sacramento. It's less than four hundred miles so it's not a long flight. You okay for that, Pastor?"

It was music to Shepard's ears. It was as if God had answered his prayers. If Bower was offering help, he was going to take it. That didn't necessarily mean there would be a pay back.

"I'll be packed and ready."

CHAPTER 6

Monasterio de San José de Nazaret
Nr. Segovia, Spain

Abbot Louis, looking older, wiser and more composed than seventeen years ago, pondered over the Condesa's experience. He attempted to piece together all that he knew concerning the history of the Lazarus painting and those before it. He had been privy to all the events and circumstances that had brought Brodie and the Condesa to him, and the sacredness of the unique stewardship they had bestowed him with. The words she had heard spoken, and told him of, *it's almost time,* reverberated in his mind as he silently repeated them.

Maria sat impassively in front of him, her face a mixture of hope and concern. She lifted her head and spoke quietly, almost as if she was afraid of being heard.

"It must be shown. It must be on view."

"I agree." We have both reached the same conclusion at the same time. Abbot Louis nodded. "But it must stay inconspicuous. Just a run-of-the-mill work of art amidst others of similar religious expression. What do you think?"

"I agree, Abbot. Whatever we do, I can't help feeling that something is stirring. You know what happened in the chapel, and I also had a dream last night. There were knights and Crusaders and waving crosses, and I haven't had that since Brodie first came into my life, all those years back."

The Abbot paled and abruptly stood. "Heavens forbid!"

"What?" The Condesa looked startled.

"I had the same dream." He sat back down. "In God's name, what's happening?"

She reached out and grabbed the Abbot's shaking hands. "I think it's starting again. This is how it happened last time. I wish Brodie were here."

"You have not seen Brother Baez for seventeen years as was his wish, although you have been coming here, on this day, ever since. As you know, he's in the desert. He's going to be there a while yet."

"That's a shame. For I am sure, without a doubt, that he is experiencing something similar. I have a feeling we're being forewarned. I think we should move the painting right now, don't you?"

"Yes, I do. We'll get it out, but I don't want the monks to see where we have been keeping it. As far as they're concerned, it's just another painting added to our collection. They must know nothing of its powers."

"It seems the right thing to do, doesn't it?"

"Yes. We both have had similar thoughts and dreams, so

it must be right."

"Let's do it."

"Shouldn't Brother Baez be consulted?"

"I'm certain he would not object."

They proceeded to the back of the monastery and into the Abbot's private room. Pulling back the carpets, they opened the trapdoor and headed underground. It remained as the Condesa had left it. The Abbot produced the key and unlocked the metal gridded gate that led to the wooden door of the small secret chapel. He turned the brass handle and the door creaked open slowly, as if asking for gentleness due to its lack of use.

"You left a light on, Condesa?" The Abbot gestured around the chapel, which glowed with a soft, white-blue light.

She froze mid-step where she stood. "I only used candles. There are no electric lights..." Her voice trailed off into the surrounding silence.

The candles remained unlit and the ambient light shimmered around the painting that faced them both.

Without waiting, Abbot Louis picked up the matches and lit the candles in quick succession, before falling to his knees, bending his head, and making the sign of the cross. The Condesa followed.

They felt no fear, only a reassurance that what they were about to do was correct, and indeed, it was the right time to do so. The light began to fade and before long, they were left only with the soft glow of candlelight. A sense of awe was all they could muster.

"It was a sign." The Abbot arose and again crossed himself.

The Condesa followed suit. "I brought this," she whispered, as she unravelled a broad fold of dark cloth. "I think it should be covered as we move it."

"Of course. Let's do it."

With the greatest of care, they began removing the painting from its attachment. It came away easily. Placing the cloth around it, they moved out of the chapel and ensured it was securely locked.

Fifteen minutes later, they were standing in the monastery's small art gallery. The forty plus art works on display all depicted scenes from the Bible, or portraits of previous Abbots since the place was built in the Middle Ages. There was nothing remarkable about it, and like most rooms in the complex, it was utterly silent. They had decided to place the painting somewhere in the side exhibits, but not too far from the centre. There were plenty of spare hooks and wire. After juggling the displays around the gallery, they hung the painting in an inconspicuous place. It looked ordinary and unremarkable.

They took several backward steps to survey what they had just done.

"Look, I don't remember seeing that before."

In the bottom corner of *The Raising of Lazarus*, she pointed at some very small letters.

✠ KORL

"You wouldn't even know they were there at first glance, would you?" she asked.

"They are quite imperceptible if you didn't know what to

look for."

"I had the oddest thought while we were doing this," the Condesa replied.

"What was that?"

"It seemed that this painting has been here all its life. It looks totally at home."

"I agree. It looks very ordinary and right where it belongs."

"I haven't mentioned that something else kept repeating in my mind. *'They will come ... they will come.'* Who 'they' might be, I have no idea, Father. Have you?"

Abbot Louis paused. "Condesa, I feel we are in the midst of some great mystery here, of which, as yet, we haven't a clue about. You seem to be more attuned than I am."

"All we can do now is wait and see ... and I believe we will get some answers sooner than we think."

Uffington, UK

The dreams persisted. Martha's experiences intensified within them, so much so that her initial fears and anxieties had been replaced with curiosity and a deep yearning to grasp the meaning of it all. She no longer feared them. The bluebells would appear, not every time, but frequently, and the same figure would be there, reaching out for her before fading into a misty haze. If not that, it would be Crusader knights and assortments of monks. She would hear their deep, chanting voices, loud and clear, and behind it all, always the same message, *'Yes, I will find you.'*

She could only think that it was her father calling out to her across time and space. Nothing would convince her otherwise. What the armoured knights and monks had to do with it, she couldn't say. But she knew her mother had experienced the same visions and dreams with Brodie all those years ago.

With everything that was happening, her university acceptance seemed less important now. What was imperative now was to discover what was going on in that unexplained zone of dreams and intuitions.

That morning, she had an overwhelming urge to erect her easel and collect her palette of oils. She hadn't felt the urge to paint for quite a while, and she didn't know why she felt compelled to do so now.

Once assembled, Martha stood back and stared at the blank canvas. *What do I do?* She had no idea. The opening of the door distracted her. It was Ulla.

She saw what Martha was doing and her mouth dropped open. "Oh, my God! Not again." Ulla moaned.

But Martha didn't seem to hear her. She had dipped her fan brush into the green oil and *whoosh*, with several vigorous strokes and some gentle touching, the green of Uffington hill appeared. She snapped out of her trance and turned to face Ulla.

"What's going on, Ma?"

"I don't know, but it worries me. This is how Brodie started. Wonderful in its way, but it broke our relationship. I don't want that to happen again between us. If it does, I will curse the name of Jesus Christ forever more."

"There's nothing religious here, Ma. It's a place we both

love."

"Just wait and see."

Martha returned to her painting and with a few more strokes using a Flake White hue to suggest the oldness of The White Horse, she produced a beautiful impression of what lay beyond their windows.

Ulla could only gulp. The speed and accuracy of Martha's brushstrokes mesmerised her. *How is that possible?* "It's been a long time since you picked up your brushes. Why now?"

"I can't answer that. It's been nagging away at me ever since those flowers arrived."

"I should have known." Ulla's sigh was one of gathering depression.

"Ma." Martha's voice sounded tremulous. "I've been thinking..."

"I can see that, and I know what you're going to say. I am not surprised but it will upset me, I guarantee it. You're going to postpone SOAS, aren't you?"

There was a long pause as they stared quietly at each other.

"Yep. How did you guess?"

"It wasn't difficult. The vibes around you are so potent a child could read them. Are you going to try and find him?"

Martha, her shoulders quivering, began to gently sob into her two hands as she covered her face. "Yes, I am. I have to. He's calling me, Ma. He doesn't know me, but he needs me. He may die without us ever knowing each other. Ma, I have to go to him. Please!"

Ulla, in one moment, felt her heart lurch as it gave a sorrowful, agonising jump. "Listen to me, Martha. No one has a clue where he is. If they have, they are keeping it secret. All I know is that he went back to Spain and entered a monastery somewhere and became a monk. Where, I don't know. But there's one person who might know, although I haven't heard from her since your father disappeared. I had written to her on several occasions, but she never replied. Her name is the Condesa Maria Francisca de Toledo. She has several addresses. We found her in a small place south of a town called Guadamur, a short ride from Toledo. It's written in those diaries. That's all I have to give you. If you go, promise me you will return to me. And if you find him…" Ulla's voice broke off, her head dipped, and then she turned and rushed from the room.

CHAPTER 7

Sacramento, USA

T he flight was proving uneventful. Shepard was impressed with his newfound colleague's wealth and hospitality. Nothing seemed to be too much bother. There was Bourbon and Champagne galore and the interior of the plane was opulent and extravagant. Shepard nurtured a secret thought that things could only get better. *John D. Bower must surely be a gift from God.*

Not dissimilar to his own, he could see the subtle bulge of a shoulder holster beneath Bower's sky-blue sports jacket. Clearly, he was not a man to mess with.

"Well, if what you have been hinting at is true, then there could be substantial rewards for us, eh?"

Shepard hesitated. He hadn't made plans to share anything, but in this situation, it was best to go along with it.

Bower was going to be useful.

"We have to find it first, and everything I know points to Spain. Two of my men are out there right now checking out a few things." Shepard paused as he felt the plane begin its descent and approach run. It was time to be direct. "How do you see yourself helping me?" He noticed Bower nod at his two bodyguards.

"There are ways and means. I have money, rather more than you could stump up. I also have strength, muscle power if you like. Those two," he pointed at the two meat cleaver types nearby, "are just two of many I can call on. Look, I don't piss about, Pastor. You lost an armful of cash the other night. That's how stupid you are. You're never going to pull this off on your own, which I think you're thinking of doing? What's been passing through that tiny brain of yours? I bet it's along the line of, 'I'll use him, then lose him.'" Bower smirked as he slid his M19 Beretta from its holster and tapped Shepard's hand with it. "And don't think I haven't noticed your own pea shooter under that jacket. Whilst you were sleeping, I had my guys run scans and checks on you. There isn't much we don't know, Pastor. I know where you were born, what schools you attended and all your exam results. That dodgy foot of yours held you back here and there, and for a time, you worked for the USSS. They fired you and you were lucky to escape a treason charge for sexing about with Russian men and women. What a naughty boy you are. You then set up a church, 'Thomas Reborn,' is it? You don't mind spending their money, do you? How long do think you can get away with that? You study Scientology and you think you can emulate it. But without my help, you won't have a chance in hell. The IRS will declare your new Holy Church of Lazarus as dissident, and you won't get it off the ground. Now, you see big opportunities with this Lazarus thing. I see the same, too. Let me tell you a few things."

Shepard could feel sweat beginning to trickle uncomfortably across his back and down the crevice of his ass. This wasn't going to plan.

"We'll be at my place soon and then I'll show you what I'm about. We're about the same age and yet our styles are so very different, but we can be useful to each other. I grew up in a shithole basically, and everything I learnt, I learnt there. Others were busy playing tough guys and muscle men, but I used my head and got into the betting and gambling game. Not to play, mind you, that's for mugs like you. I did a three stretch for small time laundering. They couldn't prove the other millions that passed via my setups. Even in jail, I made more money than the staff put together. I saw things you wouldn't want to see or hear about. But there's an odd thing about me in the middle of all that shit … I was interested in the odd, the paranormal, miracles, and religious events. Yes, I even went to Lourdes to see for myself. I think your God is looking after me. Just when I'm wavering, you come along as if you have been sent especially to me. That's how I see it." His next words came out as more menacing. "And that's how it's going to be, preacher man. Got it?" He tapped him again with the gun barrel, but this time with more pressure.

Shepard wrestled with a reply. He was beginning to regret his decision to join the flight. He didn't speak, but nodded, and was glad to note that the plane was about to touch down. It did so with the gentlest of bumps, before slowing and turning in a wide arc to where two large black sedans were parked. Bower put on a very dark pair of Raen 'Parkhurst' sunglasses.

"You're in the front one, Pastor, with my two men to look after you. I'll be following behind. It's about a thirty-five-minute drive from here, so behave yourself. You might be in for a surprise later."

El Desierto de Tabernas

Brother Baez shifted uncomfortably in his sleeping bag. He had had many dreams that night, but The White Horse fed his mind more potently than any other. Riding close across its back, he saw her. Her fair hair flowed from her and he could make out a smile. There was a connection … but he couldn't nail it. Her face was so familiar. So close … so known … but so unknown.

He sat upright. The light of the first dawn waved a weak flutter on the horizon. He reached for his water bottle and gulped rapidly on it. As he wiped his lips dry, memories began passing through his mind like an old movie. He could never free himself from them. He understood that now. Once again, the sword-brandishing knights whispered into his ear and into his mind. They had been absent since he had joined the monastery.

Why is this stirring once again? Oh God, leave me alone! I did what you asked of me. Is that not enough for you?

A sudden blast of moaning wind blew across the barren earth, sending up small pockets of dust all around. Baez pulled his sleeping bag tighter around himself. The air chilled him to the bone.

His mind went back to Ulla and the last time he had seen her, and that last letter she had sent. He knew that he would never see his child. He let out a sigh. Just then, the air appeared to shimmer.

YAAAH!

Without warning, the clash of swords and armour, and the shrieks of terrified horses surrounded him. He leapt to his feet and grabbed a large hammer from the floor close by. He swung it wildly in all directions, but it only swished through empty air. The cacophony of noise ceased as abruptly as it had started, and all he could hear was the panting of his breath and the beating of his heart.

Then he heard it, loud and clear, her unmistakeable voice in his mind chanting the old refrain.

In desert march or battle's flame
In fortress and in field
Our war-cry is thy holy Name.
Deus Vult! Beauséant!

He dropped the hammer as his body crashed to the ground. He covered his ears, but the chant persisted. Finally, after several minutes, the chanting subsided, but it was immediately followed by someone weeping.

That voice ... the accent ... I know it ... I haven't heard it for over seventeen years! It's her. Maria. Condesa Maria Francisca de Toledo. Where is she?

CHAPTER 8

Close to Village 14
Sacramento, CA

Well, Preacher, what do you think of my little place?" Bower waved his hand expansively across one of the biggest houses in the surrounds. "It's my smallest, actually. I've got three more in various parts of this wonderful country of ours. This happens to be the nearest to Vegas, so I often come here. It's got everything I could possibly want. A fully equipped gym, Olympic-size swimming pool, Jacuzzis, six bedrooms, all en suite, and next to the tennis courts, I'll be building a running area complete with woods and a track. Do you like it?"

Shepard couldn't think. He had become overwhelmed at what he was looking at. It was huge. Built in contemporary style, it was more massive than any house he had ever seen up close. It exceeded his wildest dreams. *This is the smallest of three more?* For a moment, his ideas of a new church and a cult following evaporated, but that didn't last long. Right there and then, he realized what real money could achieve. Scientology had done it and so could his Holy Church of Lazarus. *This is what I can look forward to in a few short years.*

"Impressive, John, most impressive." He scanned the property from left to right and back again. The garage, from what he could see, was housing a bright red Ferrari Portofino. There was enough space for at least another six vehicles, with room to spare.

"Well, I haven't brought you here to gawp. It's time to give you a drink and tell you what I have in mind. Let's go to my library."

Several minutes later, Bower was pushing the door knobs on each side of the imposing wooden doors. They swung silently open, and in doing so, they activated an automatic lighting system that lit up the windowless room with a low glow.

"This is my collection, Pastor. There's no natural light here as it causes damage to the books, especially ultra-violet. But it's hard to see the books in a pitch-black room, so the compromise solution was to install diffused lighting, but even that is allowed only for a limited amount of time. It still causes damage, and that can be cumulative, but the alternative is never looking at the books. If that was so, what's the point of collecting, eh?" He pointed to a spacious quilted armchair. "Take a seat."

The library resembled a museum collection. Shepard sat down with care and continued to swivel his eyes around the room. It was about fifteen feet in height and what walls there were, amounted to shelf upon shelf of leather-bound volumes – some of which looked incredibly old. The odd oil painting interspersed the monotony of shelving.

"You look surprised, and so you should be." Bower paused for a moment to dislodge the Beretta from its shoulder holster and placed it on the table in front of him. "Why don't you do the same? Please, Pastor. It will show an element of trust between us."

Shepard didn't hesitate. As he unstrapped the holster, Bower pressed a concealed button.

"Don't get nervous. Your Bourbon is on its way."

Thirty seconds later, the door swung open and a pretty, young, Mexican-looking woman came in with a silver tray. Without asking, she placed ice in Shepard's cut glass tumbler and poured his drink. She left the Champagne.

"Thank you, Valeria. We may need you later. I'll let you know."

She smiled and scuttled from the room with a polite nod of her head.

Bower then directed his stare at Shepard. "I've brought you here for a reason. It's not because of any great liking of you. What you told me about the painting figured exactly into what I've been looking for several years. I want to show you something and you are not to touch it." Opening a drawer, he pulled out a pair of surgical gloves, put them on, and walked over to a wall ladder. He pushed it along a bit, and then climbed to the top. With a slight grunt, he heaved a large volume from the rack and with the greatest of care, descended the ladder and placed the book on the desk. "I repeat, do not touch this. You may regard me as a brash and disreputable casino owner but there is another side to me that few know of, hence, this collection of mine. It's what I spend my money on. No disrespect, but I doubt that you'd know anything of what I am about to show you. This is the jewel of my collection.

"Listen carefully. In 1552, a strange and copiously illustrated book, entitled, *Augsburg Book of Miraculous Signs,* appeared in the Swabian Imperial Free City of Augsburg – then a part of the Holy Roman Empire – located in present-day Germany. It exercised, in remarkable detail and with wildly imaginative artwork, Medieval Europe's growing obsession with signs sent from God. A testament to the basic human yearning for magical thinking, which we often use when explaining feelings and phenomena beyond the grasp of our logic. Known now as The *Book of Miracles,* it first surfaced some years ago, and was auctioned off at great cost, finally making its way into an undisclosed American buyer's private collection. It was one of the most spectacular new discoveries in the field of Renaissance art." He paused. "I was that buyer, and this is the book." Bower caressed the book like a lover.

Shepard thought it odd for such a man to value anything more than money.

Bower continued. "Facsimiles have been produced since that time. There are a few omissions and gaps within its content. Before you ask, it's composed of 169 pages with large-format illustrations in gouache and watercolor, depicting wondrous and often eerie celestial phenomena, constellations, conflagrations, and floods, as well as other catastrophes and occurrences. It deals with events ranging from the creation of the world and incidents drawn from the Old Testament and Christ's miracles in the New Testament. It portrays ancient traditions and medieval chronicles of events that took place in the immediate presence of the book's author. With illustrations from the visionary *Book of Revelation*, it even includes the future end of the world. Absent, most notably, with only captions remaining, are three missing depictions of the raising of Lazarus." Bower paused to wipe a bead of sweat from his top lip. He was clearly animated, if not moved.

"I want this corrupt world of religion to be shaken to its core, and the truth of it revealed, no matter what is required to do so. What you said to me back in Vegas fits in with my plans. A painting or two of Lazarus would complete this priceless work. Your proposed church would make Scientology and the Catholic Church look like long-lost cousins at a wake. The world and its riches would be ours to command. This is not something one man can achieve alone. You will need me and my resources, and I have many. Now, look at these." He began to turn the pages, jabbing his index finger at the various and most amazing examples of medieval artwork Shepard had ever seen. He didn't even know such things existed. It needed no explanation. He saw it clearly. This *Book of Miracles* and the alleged miraculous painting of Lazarus would cause a global revolution, and panic, most definitely panic, amongst mankind's most established religions. The possibility of cheating Death, in this life, had a powerful allure.

Shepard gulped heavily on the Bourbon as Bower sat back and eyed him with what was now an impassive expression. "You'd better start telling me all you know. Before you do, there's something I haven't told you about *The Book of Miracles,* which I think you should understand. I suspect it runs close to what you have in mind."

In spite of the Bourbon, Shepard's hand trembled. Events

were beginning to move at an unexpected pace. "What's that?" he managed to answer. Not certain whether he wanted to hear what's next.

Bower leant forward. "When the manuscript was discovered, it was found amongst a collection of small jewels, weapons, goblets, and so on. I'm sure you can imagine what it might have looked like. Together with these were a number of documents inscribed in Latin. None had any real significance to us in the twenty-first century, apart from their age. There was one manuscript that was worthy of note, and it's in my possession. I have here an enlarged copy of it. How's your Latin, Pastor?" He reached into a drawer and pulled out an A4 sized sheet, inscribed in a beautiful example of medieval calligraphy.

Et cum Lazaro quondam nos coniungit cum magis, et sic falsum est summum hominis ideas et religionum.

"It translates easily, preacher man, but I expect that in your crew of clappies you don't go in for Latin too much. It says: *When Lazarus unites with us once more, so will end mankind's false ideas and religions.* You can read what you like into that, but what is significant is that the painting or paintings of that event are missing from this profound work – all of which must have been known to the compiler of the *Augsburg* work – which commenced in the sixteenth century. Then along came you, who knows nothing about this, but has a story that matches up to what I have here. Like a carpenter's dovetail joint, a missing piece ... and what's more, you're attempting to find it and base a religion on the whole premise. In my world, synchronicity is a fact of life. That's why I'm extremely wealthy. The thing I want to do most is to find that painting or whatever is missing from the book. But until now, I had no clue where to start. Tell me, how rich do you want to be, and how much do you want to run your own worldwide show, eh?"

Shepard realised he hadn't seen the broader picture. He didn't know how to respond.

"C'mon, you little fart!" Bower roared, looking annoyed. "You can do better than that. If we're going to work together, you'd better start talking and fast, because I'm not hanging around here to pussyfoot about. If you don't loosen up, you can walk back to Vegas!" He grabbed his Beretta and slapped it hard on the desk. "Am I making myself clear?"

"What do you want to know?" Shepard felt weak and out of his depth. This wasn't what he had expected.

"Tell me the story about the Lazarus paintings. Everything you know."

Shepard held out his glass for a refill. He noticed the Champagne remained unopened. "I first heard the story from my researchers who had returned from a trip to Italy, France, and Spain, where they heard a story that seemed unbelievable. The story began at the actual raising of Lazarus by Christ over two thousand years ago. A painting of that event was made by a local artist of the time and was reputed to have miraculous healing powers. But over time, it was lost. Centuries later, it was rediscovered ... along with its secret. The work, it is said, somehow self-destructs when a new artist is chosen, and that process has reportedly carried on to the present day. A woman living today in Spain has experienced an amazing recovery from terminal illness after coming into contact with the latest depiction. It all seems very mysterious and I don't quite believe it myself, but it's a money-making opportunity if I ever saw one."

Shepard swallowed hard. He had kept certain facts to himself. He didn't tell him that the woman was possibly of noble birth, maybe a Marchioness, Condesa or a Vizcondesa. Shepard wanted to find her himself. Nor did he share his plans for the twelve-layered pyramid concept. Bower, he surmised, didn't understand religious hierarchies or the need his proposed church would have for weapons to protect themselves. Yet, Bower had one thing that gave him cause to think. The idea of a postulant spending up to thirty thousand dollars to ascend to the highest level began to seem paltry.

Bower responded. "I agree with that. I dabble with painting at times. I see myself like Winston Churchill, running vast and dangerous risky projects – not unlike running my numerous casinos – but relaxing with the finer things of life. Like my book collection and attempts at art."

As they continued their conversation, Shepard thought, *John D Bower is one weird guy. A walking paradox. I wouldn't want to cross him.* This realisation made it more difficult for him to talk. After struggling for five more minutes, Bower held up his hand. "Enough. I get the picture. I couldn't have heard a more compelling answer to my quest."

Bower started Googling a map of Spain and in a short period of time, he had listed all the known monasteries existing there. He printed out several copies and handed three to Shepard.

"Thanks, John." That was only the second time he had used the man's Christian name. "My two researchers, Alphonse and Jeremiah, are due to report to me in more detail soon. I'm hoping they managed to discover more. I'll let you know what they find." He knew that would be a lie.

"Pastor, it's of little use to us charging from one monastery to another. We need to pin down this woman. There must be some information we can go on?"

Shepard didn't think there would be any harm in revealing just a little bit more. "I'm due in London soon for the World Charismatic Convention, where I hope to announce the formation of the Lazacrucian movement. From what my researchers told me, there's a UK connection between an unknown man and woman who were somehow involved in the whole affair. Maybe if news of what I intend to do gets out, someone may lead us to them or better still, the Spanish woman."

"Okay, Shepard, you get to the conference and make an early announcement about the new movement. No doubt, with some sort of fat fee, you'll start recruiting members. At this moment in time, that is your business. But not for long. As soon as I start investing my money, time and effort, then it becomes very much my business." He paused for effect. "Understood?" he bellowed, picked up the Beretta again and pointed it at a startled Shepard.

"Please, don't point that at me. Yes, I understand."

"You will keep me informed every step of the way. If I discover anything new, I will inform you." He lowered the gun. "I shall prepare an agenda and make arrangements for you to meet me either in London or in Spain. I have a few ideas which may be of interest to you. Not now, though. While you are here, you are my guest, and I've laid out some entertainment for you. I'll put this precious book away for now, and then let's go to my private quarters."

Like the rest of the establishment, Bower's quarters were expansive, opulent, almost vulgar. Shepard, looking dazzled, was directed to a massive Jacuzzi and provided with a clean set of clothes and a bathrobe.

Shepard turned his back and undressed, slipping on the bathrobe. Once done, he faced Bower who had a large grin on his face, gesturing to the tub where three beauties, all of whom smiled sweetly as they beckoned him in, waited.

He hesitated, but Bower's shove removed whatever modesty he had, and with one swift tug, Pastor Shepard disrobed and plunged into the warm bubbly water. The three voracious mermaids were upon him in an instant, and after only a short time, Shepard was left feeling and looking like a freshly squeezed tube of toothpaste.

Outside, Bower remained in his seat, impassive, in control, and satisfied to see that the CCTV cameras had recorded the activity and zoomed in on every fleshy move.

CHAPTER 9

Martha stared up at The White Horse and felt her affinity for it. She wondered how long it would be before she saw it again. Ulla stood next to her, checking her watch. The taxi that would take them to Reading railway station was due any time now. Ulla had insisted on accompanying Martha to Gatwick Airport to ensure her safe departure. Martha was headed to Madrid, and from there, she planned to catch a train to Toledo.

The planning had been meticulous, and Ulla told her daughter everything she knew to help her on her quest. Martha was booked at the same quiet hotel she and Brodie had stayed in when they were there – the *Pedro Sanchez*. They had decided not to contact the Condesa immediately. God, they weren't even sure if she was still alive. Martha, her maturity extending far beyond her years, had suggested that a surprise visit might be better than one that was planned. Ulla was sure that if anybody had an idea where Brodie was, and his current identity, it would be the Condesa.

THE LAZARUS CONTINUUM

Martha promised to call her mother every day but couldn't say for sure when she'll be back. There was no shortage of funds and whatever it took, Martha was determined she would locate him. She had seen his form so many times in her dreams, she never doubted it could be anybody else. He was calling to her and she had no other choice but to heed his call.

There came the sound of a car drawing up outside. It was their taxi. Martha gave a little sob from her throat and clasped her mother's hand. With her thoughts, she said farewell to The White Horse, knowing that it might be a while before she saw him again. She felt Ulla's reassuring grip and for a moment ... she doubted the wisdom of her decision. She let it go and directed it into the hillside, which she loved so much.

The train to Gatwick took about an hour and forty-five minutes to arrive at the airport. The journey had been a silent one and neither felt the need to speak. The countryside was barely noticed. They both rested in a private sea of thoughts, some of which overlapped, but each of them aware of a new destiny descending upon them. If Ulla was concerned, she had refused to reveal it. Martha felt excited but also nervous. She had a programme of action to undertake when she arrived, and how that would unfold, she had no idea. She had also promised Ulla that she would visit the Cathedral and follow the route that she and Brodie had taken while searching for Francisco Cortez's painting. But for now, a visit to Guadamur was of the highest priority.

Once off the train and inside the hustle of the airport, Martha sensed Ulla's mixed emotions. She placed her arm hard around her waist as they walked along the travolator.

Ulla hugged her daughter back.

It didn't take long to check the bags in and they made their way to the sitting area to await the flight announcement. In no time, it flashed on the screen and they started walking the short distance to passport control.

"You ring when you get there, okay? Call me every day and whenever you need to. You understand, Martha?"

"Of course, Ma. I'm not a million miles away and you have given me a load of addresses and contacts you trusted. I shall miss you so much!" Her last sentence came out in an emotional gush as they hugged, and their tears flowed.

The flight to Madrid was uneventful and the airplane was only half full. She had an aisle seat and the seat next to her was vacant. That gave her room to place her personal items and room to think about what's going to happen next. A dozen scenarios went through her mind. What will she do when she found him? What will she say?

Martha was so wrapped up in her thoughts that she barely noticed when the plane landed. Once disembarked and through the regulatory procedures, she made her way to *Atocha Renfe* to catch one of the frequent trains into the centre of Toledo, a journey of about an hour and a quarter.

Once on board, Martha felt herself relax and start taking notice of the sights and sounds around her, so different from the gentleness of England's rolling hills. Even where she was in Spain, The White Horse continued to invade her mind ... and she was glad it did. In this strange land, she found its presence reassuring.

Martha had decided that before commencing her search, she would unwind for a day or two, acclimatize a little to her new surroundings, and as promised, visit the Primate Cathedral of Saint Mary of Toledo. It was there, her mother had said, that her and Brodie's search had begun. Martha was hoping that she would find inspiration within its sacred walls, and maybe a clue to lead her further on.

She found the *Hotel Pedro Sanchez* easily, in its narrow medieval street, close to the Cathedral just as Ulla had told her. Sure enough, the walled garden her mother had spoken of was still there, displaying the climbing ranks of roses whose original seeds came from pristine thirteenth century stock. She sat at a secluded table and ordered a tall, white wine spritzer. She was a year over the Spanish legal drinking age and had no qualms about alcohol. A strange emotion passed through her as she realized that in many ways, she was duplicating her parents' original quest. Although this time, a human being was being sought, not a painting.

With care, she spread her research notes across the table. Opening her notebook, she turned the pages to where she had dried and pressed several bluebells before she left home. They were from her birthday gift. As she gazed at them, she gained a sense of security, of balance. They reassured her somehow. Next to them, she had painted a watercolour of The White Horse. As she outlined the activities for the next few days, a deep and unusual tiredness assaulted her. It propelled her to her bedroom and although it was still early evening, she found herself unable to stay awake. Sleep devoured her in an instant and her dream was perforated with bluebells and the inevitable White Horse of Uffington.

✠

5 Miles South of Guadamur
Spain

There had been a time when she had thought of selling her home, which was once the site of a monastery. But now, such a move was unthinkable. Since the Lazarus affair, the Condesa Maria had become deeply attached to its old walls and structures. In particular, the small chapel which she had designed as a miniature replica of the Medici's medieval chapel, part of the Church of Santa Croce in Florence. It was here that she had found hope and had come to associate it with Brodie Ladro. He had proved to be her salvation and for that, she surmised, he was now suffering. The legacy that was bestowed upon him is not an easy yoke to bear. He had to give up everything. Although reluctant, there was simply no way he could have refused. All his predecessors had similar fates, of that she was certain.

Lately, in the coolness of the chapel interior, Maria became more aware of whisperings in her mind. Abbot Louis had also somehow become part of it. As protector of the sacred painting, he bore an enormous responsibility, and she knew he was aware of a rippling in the atmosphere of his monastery.

A crisis was developing, and she didn't doubt that the Lazarus painting was involved. She prayed that Brodie – Brother Baez – would come back soon. She needed to talk to him.

In her prayers, she felt the old chants; the eternal, never ending war cry clashing through her mind.

Deus Vult! Deus Vult! Beauséant!

Danger lurked. She sensed it and had no idea where it was coming from. The painting of Lazarus would soon be under threat. Would Abbot Louis be strong enough to resist an assault?

She doubted it.

She prayed harder, this time sending her thoughts to Brodie.

Brodie, or if you will, Brother Baez, through the power of our Lord Jesus Christ, we call on you once again to do your duty. Save the painting from whatever's coming. We need you. We need your strength, your insight and perceptions.

She repeated her implorations, sending them across the universe and into an unknown desert. When she had completed her prayers, she decided that she would visit the Cathedral the next day to once again give thanks to God for her miraculous deliverance. Her annual pilgrimage to the monastery formed the first part of her obeisance, and the Cathedral would complete her intent.

The following morning, Martha had awoken feeling fresh and ready to start her plan of action. She couldn't wait a day or two to acclimatize. She was ready to go. After breakfast, her first destination was the Gothic structure of the Primate Cathedral of Saint Mary of Toledo.

After a lazy stroll through the narrow streets, she was in

front of the entrance. This is where Ulla and Brodie had started to look for the painting. She paid the fifteen Euros entrance fee and stepped inside. Martha walked around and couldn't help but gawk at the priceless art that festooned the walls. The altar – its sheer size and opulence – dumbfounded her. Her artistic inclinations rose to the surface and she could understand why she had opted for a Fine Art Degree.

The most valuable object in the Cathedral is kept in the Chapel of the Treasure. It is known as the great Monstrance of Arfe or as *La Gran Ostensoria de Toledo*. Made of the finest silver and gold and bejeweled with gems, it measured over ten feet tall and crowned with a seventeenth century cross. This work of art often made an appearance in the annual feast of Corpus Christi of Toledo. It had a hexagonal base and rose on small exquisite columns, with adornments of gems and varied figurines of angels and saints, fleurons, small bells and clappers. Its architectural details – columns, arches, and vaultings – made the whole piece resemble a delicate lacework.

She marveled at it.

Right then, she understood what had compelled her parents to follow this trail so intently. For her, it was becoming a breathtaking and revelatory awakening to the power of art.

The interior was not packed, and she could hear a choir singing from one of the many chapels close by. Their angelic voices blended with the heady and thick presence of incense throughout the cathedral. The whole atmosphere moved Martha, the likes of which she had not experienced before.

There was so much to look at she couldn't take it all in. She'd never been religious but gazing at all the holy art that surrounded her, she wondered if she could have resisted its call, had she been born in a different age.

Her father, Brodie, had submitted. But his circumstances were beyond logic and reason. Ulla had once told her that she thought her father was severely depressed and unhinged. Martha didn't know what to think.

Before settling for a much needed rest, she had promised Ulla she would visit the *Sala Capitular*, The Chapterhouse where the destroyed fresco of *The Raising of Lazarus* by Juan de Borgoña had been a vital clue in their research.

She placed her feet on the marble floor and gazed up to view the *artesonado*, a lacy wooden ceiling that covered the entire area. A tremor rippled through her, and for a reason she was unable to define, she felt strangely at home in this sacred place. The frescos were there as Ulla had said they would be. Small tears filled her eyes.

It was time for a rest.

Her legs were complaining, so she looked around for vacant seats. She found herself heading towards a side chapel with empty pews, drawn to it.

The small chapel was quiet, well-lit and unobtrusive, with a few praying people dotted around. Martha deposited herself on one of the pews and let out a long, quiet sigh. If nothing else, she was overwhelmed. The spectacle gave her a glimpse of a world she had not realised existed. As she sat there, she didn't know what to do next. Martha had never been a praying person.

She opened her shoulder bag, removed her phone and ensured it was switched off. She took out her notebook and a small photograph of Ulla fell out next to her. She picked it up, gave it a small kiss and placed it on the vacant seat next to her. Martha began to record what she had seen and the emotions that had invaded her. She would be relating her experience with Ulla later and she didn't want to forget anything.

At that moment, a tall, statuesque woman, dressed in black, with silvery hair combed back in severe fashion and held in place by two gold clasps, stern chiseled features and clutching a small silver crucifix, took up the vacant seat next to Martha. Making the sign of the cross, she knelt with her head bent and began her devotions. Martha could see her lips moving in silent recitation and could only wonder at how people could do so.

Some time elapsed, and Martha finished writing her notes at the same time as the woman concluded her prayers. She had sat back with a look of contemplation. When her eyes opened, she turned and saw Martha and offered her a tentative smile. Martha smiled back with a slight nod of her head, then she began packing her notes away before standing to leave.

The woman spoke, *"Jovencita, olvidaste tu fotografía."* She picked up the photograph that Martha had left behind, and was about to hand it to Martha, but couldn't resist looking at it first. A startled expression crossed her face as she looked up at Martha and back at the photograph several times.

"Oh, Dios Mio! Es Ulla Stuart!" The woman's hand covered her mouth and her eyes widened like small moons.

It was Martha's turn to look equally astonished. "What? What are you saying? How do you know this? Who are you?"

The woman remained speechless and fumbled behind herself to sit down, her entire body shaking. She muttered several times in English, "Oh, Mother of God! Oh, Mother of God!'

Martha could not comprehend the woman's reaction. She looked as if she had seen her long dead ancestors. "Are you alright? What's wrong?" Martha reached out to her and held her shaking hand. "Who are you? Why did my mother's photo surprise you so?"

The mention of her mother caused the woman to begin weeping. Her accented English added a poignancy to what she said next.

"Tu madre, your mother, she is Señora Ulla…" Her voice broke off and she stared hard into Martha's eyes, as if attempting to make her understand.

Martha tightened her grip on the lady's hand. "Please. Please, don't … this is most strange. Yes, she is my mother and she's in England, Señorita Ulla Stuart. I am her daughter, Martha. How do you know her?" Martha attempted a smile.

The woman lifted her other hand, reaching out to stroke Martha's cheek. "God forbid. Another miracle has arrived."

Martha offered her a tissue to wipe her wet eyes.

The woman graciously accepted and dabbed at her eyes before she said, "I knew your mother and her partner, Señor Brodie Ladro, a long time ago. I am the Condesa Maria Francisca de Toledo."

CHAPTER 10

I t had gone far better than he had dared hope. Pastor Shepard gave rare thanks to God. He had just finished communicating with all his churches and followers.

What he didn't know was that after his speech, his detractors now definitely considered him a complete screwball.

With great and bogus sincerity, he had shared his vision at the World Charismatic Convention, which was covered by the media. Ensuring that his network of churches in the USA heard him too.

"I have spoken with God," he had announced to a startled stadium audience. "Yes, dear friends, I was in the desert doing penance to save my soul and He spoke to me. Do not doubt me, my brethren! He spoke to me. Yes, me, who stands before you now, Pastor Silas Shepard. I cannot lie about such a momentous event lest He strikes me dead where I stand! His voice came as if from behind the clouds, and from the very sands and rocks that were strewn as far as the eye can see. I hid my face from him in fear and shame." At this point,

Shepard made a show of covering his face with his hands before slowly lifting his head skywards. "He told me to prepare the way and commanded me to form a new church, the Holy Church of Lazarus, his one true and final bastion on Earth. Its followers shall be known as Lazacrucians, to commemorate Christ's greatest miracle, and as a reminder that everyone who follows Him will find salvation and life everlasting." Shepard paused, and when he spoke again, he lowered his voice for effect. "With this, God has revealed to me that a painting exists ... its very fabric imbued with the power of Christ's healing ministry." He allowed that piece of news to sink in before he continued. "Yes, beloved friends, it has the power to heal those who believe ... and I, a lowly sinner, have been chosen to establish its potency here upon the planet Earth!"

No one can argue that the Pastor had a flair for drama. All eyes were on him, some faces with their mouths agape.

He continued. "Will you join me on this sacred task by subscribing to our mission?" Soft music gently played across the stadium, and Pastor Silas Shepard fell to his knees. He raised his arms and began a high-pitched rant. "Praise our Lord, for the time is near. The four blood moons have passed, and the great and terrible day of the Lord is almost at hand. By the end of next year, Israel will be no more. The world will be set on fire and the Lord will end this world of sin. The Lazacrucians will be preserved from His wrath, as he had promised me in the desert. When it begins, we must close our windows for three days and not look outside. After three days, we will come out to the new land of God. As Lazacrucians, you and your families will be spared and given access to the healing powers of his sacred painting, which will soon be entrusted in our care."

In the background, a choir began to sing a slow, emotional rendering of *'Gwahoddiad,'* the Welsh inspirational hymn, 'Lord, Here I am!' No tear-jerking opportunity was missed.

"Step forward, my friends, and make your commitment now in front of God."

People poured to his raised dais and knelt in the hundreds. His acolytes began distributing leaflets and booklets which explained the new tenets. Pledges and money began to flood into the numerous and massive collection boxes that had miraculously appeared.

Watching from a safe distance, in a private booth, John D. Bower observed Shepard's phoney but spectacular performance. It had him squirming, but he grudgingly admitted that the man had pulled it off.

They're eating out of his hand. This guy is gonna get rich very quickly if he plays it right. How much richer if the painting is found?

He felt in his pocket for his lucky pack of cards. It was time for a wager. *I'll deal three cards. If the total exceeds fifteen, we will find what we want. Lower than fifteen and we will fail.*

The idea of failure did not sit well with Bower.

He must think I'm stupid. There's stuff he hasn't told me and I'm going to find out what. It might not be a pleasant experience for him when I do.

He shuffled the pack and peeled off the top three cards and turned them over one by one. He was looking at the three of diamonds, then the six of spades. The next had to be a seven at least. It was.

Bower turned to his two bodyguards. "You boys are going

to have to exercise your special skills very soon with that impostor out there. You happy with that?"

They turned to each other and smiled.

"Good. I'll take that as a yes, then. I will let you know when ... but it will be soon."

They had opted to stay overnight at the Hilton Hotel at London Airport, before embarking on a midmorning flight to Valencia's Manises Airport in Spain. Shepard had argued that it was a good place to start making enquiries since Valencia's Cathedral held the alleged Holy Chalice, the very cup that Christ used at the Last Supper.

Shepard was in an expansive mood. The drama of his announcement had sent shockwaves around the religious world. Enquiries continued to pour in from around the planet, together with cash, and bank commitments globally. He had to rename and consolidate his churches soon and give birth to the new Holy Church of Lazarus. In twenty-four hours, he had amassed an extra one hundred thousand dollars and it was only day one.

At this point, Bower realised he had made a poor selection in Shepard. He was becoming too cocky and his stadium performance had gone to his head. The man knew more than he was letting on, although he had verbally agreed to divide the money they obtained by producing miracle cures.

Bower's agenda was different from Shepard's. For him, it wasn't about getting rich in the style of Layfette Ron Hubbard. He was looking at another side of the whole story. There was something about it that he found compelling. He wasn't in it entirely for the money, which to him was quite odd. He was still unsure of the exact reason he was wasting time on this whole affair.

One thing he was certain of ... it was time to put Pastor Shepard, Man of God, and Archbishop of the Lazacrucians, on a tighter leash. He needed some persuasion. Bower could feel his temper rising for he was convinced Shepard was playing a double game.

He called his two musclemen. "Go to his room. When he answers, get inside. I'll be there five minutes after you. You know what to do. Now, go!"

He sat down and clenched his fists. No bible-bashing creep was going to get the better of him. If Shepard didn't cough, then he wouldn't be flying anywhere. The only trip he would be making would be to the hospital ... or maybe the mortuary. *I loathe violence, but sometimes it's the only way.*

A tapping on his door alerted a hyped-up Shepard to visitors. With an expansive gesture, he flung open the door wearing a broad smile. It wasn't Bower, as expected. It was his henchmen. His grin vanished. They pushed him to one side, strode in, and slammed the door.

"Hey, what's going on? Where's Bower?"

A heavy shove sent him crashing to the floor. His first reaction was to grab for his Smith & Wesson, but a fierce stamp on his wrist by a large boot terminated the move. His pistol spun across the room and out of reach.

"Well, Pastor," said Man One. "Mr. Bower thinks you're being, shall we say, economical with the truth. You ain't been telling all you know, he thinks, so we're here to persuade you otherwise. George here," he indicated man two, "he has special skills. Don't you, George?"

George nodded, smiled, and delivered a swift kick into Shepard's crotch.

An agonised screech came from Shepard as he doubled up in agony, clutching at his scrotum with his eyes watering profusely.

"I don't know what you're talking about," Shepard managed to gasp out.

Man One picked up his gun on the floor and emptied all the bullets from the chamber except one. Then, he spun the barrel and forced the muzzle into Shepard's gaping mouth. "Our version of the Deer Hunter's Russian Roulette game. You're a gambling man and not very good at it as we saw. What odds do you want before I pull the trigger?"

Shepard gurgled. Words wouldn't formulate in his drooling mouth. His testicular pain was forgotten as he attempted to push away the man's arm.

"'I think he's trying to say something, George. Let's hear what it is before I pull the trigger."

"Don't do this, please. Don't do this. Get Bower here. Get him here now. I want to talk to him, please!"

Man One pushed his face close to Shepard's. "Well, you lying religious scumbag, I will do as you ask. But any more crap and the game will resume. The only place you will be going to, will be a wooden box." Twice, he slapped the pistol hard, left and right, across Shepard's frightened face, drawing blood from the mouth and nostrils. "Now, get up and sit in that fucking chair, and don't fucking move until you're told to. Move!"

Shepard moved, and fell into the chair, curling his deformed foot underneath. He was shaking as he realised that he had underestimated Bower. An appalling misjudgment that could cost him his life.

He heard another quiet rap on the door. George opened it and John D. Bower entered the room, ignoring Shepard who was quivering in the chair.

"Anything to report, gentlemen?"

"Yes," said George. "I think the toe rag wants to have a chat." He gestured at Shepard.

Bower turned to look at Shepard finally. "You haven't been gambling again, have you, Shepard? Let me guess. High stakes, low returns, and losing as usual. But this time, your life for information. Correct?"

Shepard, to his own amazement, nodded

"Okay. You know things I don't. Get this straight, understand it, or you won't be around to enjoy the fruits of it all. This is what I want to know. How will your new church develop? Without evidence of a miracle, there's nowhere for you to go. I suspect you have something to go on or you wouldn't be dragging your arse across to Spain for nothing. Something has happened somewhere, and you know about it. All that bullshit you spouted out at Wembley was the prelude to some total con. Right?"

Man One slapped Shepard hard across the face, causing him to swing his head around to allow George to slap it viciously back again.

Bower looked at Man One and nodded. The man spun the barrel of the pistol and jerked back Shepard's head.

Shepard knew they weren't playing games. Physical pain and mental terror assaulted his entire being. "Stop! Stop, for the love of God. I'll tell you what you want to know."

Man One and George moved close behind him and placed their hands on his shoulders.

"Well?" said Bower. "I'm waiting." He took out his pack of cards and began a slow shuffle, followed by a series of one-handed false cuts. "Be quick and you might survive this."

Shepard talked like his life depended on it ... and it was. He explained the pyramid structure of his new church and the amount of money that would add to his coffers.

Bower had taken a seat. As Shepard continued, he had a thought. *Seeing his performance at the Stadium and the way people willingly gave him their money, it's a brilliant idea. He can run it, but I want a huge slice. Still, there's an element missing. The painting, if it exists, and the woman who was cured. Without these components, it could all die.*

"Shut up now, Shepard. As I thought, you're a devious scumbag, but not entirely stupid. We're off to Spain, but I've a feeling you haven't told us all you've heard." He turned. "George."

George nodded, and from his pocket, he produced a pair of small, shiny, zinc-plated thumbscrews. In one swift and practiced movement, he had clamped both on Shepard's thumbs. George gave each screw a couple of tight twists, causing tiny spikes to dig into the crevices of each nail.

"For fuck's sake ... stop!" Shepard screamed. What was happening exceeded his wildest nightmares. Exquisite shafts of pain, the likes of which he could never have imagined, cascaded through his hands and pulsated through his skinny body.

"Talk or it will get worse."

"Yes! Yes! I'll tell you more."

"As I thought. You have a hidden agenda. Start spouting, Preacher."

Shepard talked. This time, he didn't miss an iota of what he knew. One mistake and he would be dead meat. He knew that. He talked extensively.

"So ... we're looking for a Spanish woman, allegedly an aristocrat from Valencia, Seville or Toledo. She was terminally ill, but after coming into contact with this Lazarus painting, was restored to full health ... and there were others also. Correct?" Bower confirmed.

"Correct."

"There was a pair of Brits tied up in it, too?"

"Correct."

"Whereabouts unknown?"

"Correct."

"Tell me, Shepard, why shouldn't we waste you away? Now that I know as much as you do, what's the point of you?"

A bolt of panic shot through Shepard. This whole thing had turned very nasty. Only the smartest answer would perhaps save his life.

"My church. You will need it and all its potential followers. Without that, you'll never get this off the ground. And you, a casino owner ... that wouldn't look too good in the media, would it? I'm well-known in this arena and many people believe what I tell them. You've seen that for yourself, haven't you?" Shepard's heart thudded in his chest. He was taking the deadliest gamble of his life.

Bower said nothing. He walked over to the window and stared out at the flat scenery leading across to the distant airport. A silence, akin to that of the ghost of a dead man, hung in the air.

Shepard closed his eyes, and for once in his life, began a silent prayer asking for forgiveness and imploring whoever was listening to spare his life. Sweat broke on his sallow face.

In one swift movement, Bower spun around, his right arm outstretched, and his suppressed Beretta pointed directly at Shepard's head.

CHAPTER 11

El Desierto de Tabernas

The White Horse of Uffington had begun its gallop and drew closer by the day. It had become clearer. Dream after dream confirmed it. A person was mounted upon it, clutching the horse's flowing mane with the other hand swinging a large sword. The same words he'd heard before accompanied his dream.

Deus Vult! Beauséant!

They shall not pass. They shall not!

Brother Baez began reciting the old war cry. Something was telling him the time had come for him to leave.

Please, God, leave me be! Have I not done enough?

There was no reply, only the incessant twitching of emotional strings and words crashing through and upending his rational psyche. He reached for his brushes. *This is my last work in this place. I shall do no more.*

He shut his eyes and it seemed as if Ulla appeared to him. She did not speak but only smiled and nodded. He returned the gesture.

He hadn't felt like this for so many years. The monastery was his physical home, but he had another. It was a realm he could not articulate. In it, was boundless love and compassion. He failed to portray that in paint. Lazarus had beckoned to him since the resurrection of his painting, and he had answered. But now … somehow … he was being summoned again. A voice resonated within him, as if he had known it since time began. The links went into the distant past and were now stretching out to the endless future.

And The White Horse was carrying them.

He set to work … and the hours passed.

The desert vanished.

Horses appeared, galloping.

White and green were spread with enormity and haste. He didn't dare look at what he was painting. It was of no matter. His paints, his strokes were being guided. This way … that way … again and again. He was in a field of bluebells, amidst its heady scent. But they were not supposed to have an aroma. It all became too much for him.

He let out a desperate cry. "It is enough! Enough! It is finished. I am finished. For pity's sake, release me."

The gigantic White Horse of Uffington gazed down upon him.

"My God. Did I paint that?" He heard it snort.

On its back, she sat. It was the female who had been infesting his dreams. He saw her clearly, but he knew her not.

Riding like the wind, she carried a white shield with a red

cross and was waving a sword.

"Ulla? Is that you, Ulla? Or are you Maria?"

There was no reply.

"Who are you?" His tone was edged with desperation. The vision did not answer but faded from view, leaving him with a feeling of despair. However, its edges were fringed with a hopeful note of familiarity. The vague outline of a female figure, warrior-like in her bearing, was all he could discern.

He knew that the time had arrived for him to return to the monastery and the reassuring presence of his old friend and mentor, Abbot Louis. He was being called back. He gazed at the cave, his temporary home. He glanced at the bluebells. Their heads had begun to sag and droop in what seemed like a gesture of farewell.

Even the bluebells are now fading as I'm packing to leave. It's as if they know.

He cleaned up the area of his detritus. If anyone came by, they would not know that someone had lived there for such a time.

The Land Rover fired up for the first time. Before he drove away, Brother Baez, or Brodie Ladro, knelt and gave thanks to his solitary place of refuge. He sensed that something was happening, and it involved himself, but he could not, as yet, get beyond that point. He could only wait and see.

The drive was hot and sticky. He badly needed a warm bath. He could smell his own body odour as his stained, rough-haired cassock stuck to him like a soldier caught on barbed wire. All this seemed trivial to what whirled around in his mind. What was emerging from his thoughts made him edgy.

Concern coursed through him from head to toe, although he knew not its source.

Unknown to him, Broderick Ladro, Brodie, aka Brother Baez, was undergoing a rebirth. Like a gigantic *Attacus Atlas* moth, re-emerging from its cocoon. Once again, forces beyond his understanding were summoning him to do his duty. Only, he didn't know what he was supposed to do yet. His wings began to flutter.

He brought the Land Rover to a sudden halt and switched off the engine. Clasping his hands around his forehead, without warning, he immediately fell into a deep and troubled sleep.

The end had just begun.

On waking, Broderick Ladro had been reborn.

Abbot Louis shielded his eyes with the palm of his hand. Far in the distance, a chalky, yellow plume of sand was heading at speed towards the monastery. He didn't doubt who was driving it. Certain things were about to change. He knew it. Something was amiss. Brother Baez's foray in the desert was more than a search for Christ. It was the man's effort to grasp the circumstances that had propelled him into the monastic life. Brodie Ladro had been deeply shocked and humbled by his experience and had surrendered totally to God. His life had opened up to a miracle that would not let him go. Since he'd arrived at the monastery, his retreats had become more frequent as the years passed. But this one seemed different.

Too many things were converging, and Louis felt he was being drawn into it. God, he thought, was calling him. If anybody asked for what purpose, he would be unable to define it.

The sand cloud plumed higher as the vehicle drew closer. A couple of minutes later, the Land Rover skidded to an uncharacteristic halt outside the main gate.

From it leapt a bustling Brother Baez. Abbot Louis stretched his limbs and went to greet his enigma.

They stared at each other. Nothing was said. Their mutual embrace registered their common understanding.

"Time is pressing upon us, Brother Baez?"

"No longer, Abbot Louis. I'm back. Broderick Ladro is alive and well, older and no wiser. As clandestine monk Baez, with your permission, I wish to remain … maybe. But at this moment, I feel that my former self may soon be needed."

"We sense that, too. When the time arrives, you will have the grace and blessings to do what you must. Your painting, *The Raising of Lazarus*, now hangs with the others in our gallery."

Brodie ignored the implications of what his superior had said.

The Abbot continued, "I see that you have been busy for us." He indicated the assortment of rolled canvases in the vehicle.

"It was difficult, Father. I was besieged by a recurring vision. Known in my country as The White Horse of Uffington, it was always one of my favourite ancient artworks. Are you familiar with it? Its gigantic white form is carved deep into an English hillside. On it, but only in my dream, there was a woman mounted. At first, I thought it was my partner, Ulla.

Then again, it could be my mentor, The Condesa Maria. But it was neither of them. I have no idea who it could be. Father, all around me in a waterless desert, bluebells in the thousands literally sprung up – out of nowhere?" Brodie was babbling, but he needed to share all that had happened to him with someone before it drove him insane. "Look." He unrolled The White Horse painting.

The Abbot looked startled and studied the work for a short while. "That's amazing. Is that the woman in your dream? You have painted her with her hair covering her face. Who could she be?"

"I was hoping you might be able to tell me."

"You haven't seen the Condesa since the day you arrived here with your secret, although each year, on a certain date, she comes to visit. That is the way you both wished it to be. While you were in the desert, the Condesa came here. Like you, she has been having very similar disturbances and visions. We both agreed it was time to move the painting from where it was hidden from general view. It may now continue the work it was meant for. You two are, in some God-given manner, linked … and I don't understand it at all. What do you think is happening? I can feel a stirring here in the monastery as well."

"I have no idea. It's out of our hands. I have done paintings of various scenes for the monastery. Please take a look at them, Father. I have more stories to tell you, but right now, I'd like to see the painting."

Together, they walked into the shady coolness of the gallery. Soon they were both standing in front of it. Brodie reached out to touch it, and as he did, a thousand memories poured into him. It was like yesterday. His hand remained as if glued to the paint. *Deus Vult! Deus Vult!* The words were real, booming and desperate. He heard the voices and there were men with guns. He fell to the floor, his face creased in pain and his teeth bared.

He returned to consciousness to find himself lying in the shade of the cloisters and a small collection of concerned monks tending to him.

"How long have I been here?"

"About five minutes," one monk answered.

"We need to talk urgently, Brother Baez. If you can stand, let's go to my office." Abbot Louis helped haul him up and together, they lurched to his private quarters, leaving a small collection of puzzled monks staring after them.

CHAPTER 12

T hey sat together in a small tapas bar used only by locals. They held hands, unable to articulate, both stunned and speechless by the enormity of the synchronicity that had manoeuvred them together.

Martha Stuart and the Condesa Maria spoke freely, as if they had known each other for years.

Like a mesmerised goldfish, Maria began to speak, in a low hesitant voice as if she was translating from Spanish as she went along.

"Martha, I don't know what to say. I've always suspected the story was incomplete and I wasn't wrong. How did we meet at the Cathedral? How did you walk into my life like that?" She snapped her fingers. "It was meant to be, I feel."

Martha then reiterated the story around the bluebells arriving each birthday. She mentioned the note, '*Be happy, for it is almost time!*' She wove this in with her strange compulsion to find her father and the odd dreams she had been having.

"I've also experienced the same things."

"I'm not surprised. I have to tell you, Maria, I know most of the story concerning the Lazarus paintings; from the days of Annas Zevi, all the way through to my father, Broderick Ladro, and your connection with him." Martha paused, aware of a growing affinity with the proud, but sad-looking woman in front of her. She felt she'd known the Condesa all her life. "My mother, Ulla, who you knew, kept a meticulous record of events, and I suspect that we were meant to find each other. You know where he is. Don't you?"

"Martha, like you, I haven't seen him since he became a monastic and the guardian of his work."

"Where is he?"

"I can't tell you."

"But you know?"

The Condesa nodded.

"I have the right to know. For Christ's sake, he is my father!" Martha's grip tightened on Maria's hand.

"Martha, in the grand scheme of things, you have no right. None of us do."

"What's that supposed to mean?"

"I cannot speak here. Come and stay with me at Guadamur and I will tell you all you need to know." She stood upright with a speed beyond her years and pulled Martha with her. "Follow me."

The GSM Audio Bug, attached to a nearby table, picked up every word of their conversation. Silas Shepard shrugged his shoulders as he looked across at John D. Bower. Behind that look was an appreciation that at the most dangerous moment, just a while back, the trigger had not been pulled.

It had taken surprisingly little to discover through local gossip that a local Condesa had somehow miraculously recovered from cancer many years ago. It seemed the entire city knew the story. Locals had only been too willing to point her out and give them all the information they needed to find her. She had been spotted entering the cathedral. The rest was easy.

The Condesa, it was said, was a very private person. Although news of her recovery had spread, she had steadfastly refused to divulge one scrap of information and rejected every request for an interview. All anybody could deduce was that after touching a painting of Lazarus being raised from the dead, she made an instantaneous recovery.

The bug had confirmed most of these details and it was obvious that the girl called Martha was the daughter of the two Britons who were rumoured to be part of the whole affair.

Bower spoke. "C'mon, we're going to follow them and see where it leads us. That old bat is the key to everything. Your new Holy Church of Lazarus would have to play a role in this … soon." He beckoned to his two bodyguards sitting further away. "Stay close but out of sight."

Thirty minutes later, they came to a halt by a narrow track that twisted its way through the rocky hillside. George switched off the engine, and for a moment, they were lost in the silence of the location. They saw the back of the Condesa's vehicle disappear around a ridge.

"There can't be much up there. She must live a solitary existence. That should do nicely." Bower looked thoughtful.

"It's too early to muscle in. Let's go slowly up there and see what the set-up is. It can't be far."

George restarted the car and set off at a slow pace, careful to keep out of sight. The house came into view and they backed up behind a clump of large boulders.

Shepard shielded his eyes to stare at the manor. "Parts of it look like a converted monastery."

"You should feel at home then, because it won't be long before you'll be paying a visit to the dear lady."

"What?"

"That's right, Pastor. Lazarus and your Church are a match made in heaven, you might say." He sniggered at his own joke. "We need a plan of action and without this painting, your church will lose steam and die. She's the only one who can tell us where this painting could be."

"What about the girl?"

"Not sure, but from what we heard, she's a vital link to this whole process. I'll have them watched round the clock. We need to know where they are going and what for. We have plans to make so let's get on with it. The sooner we do this, the sooner we'll make unheard of sums of money. I think I'm preferring this to running the casinos."

Shepard remained silent. He bit on his lip. The thought that his territory was being invaded gave him cause to fret. This development was okay up to a point. But now that Bower had subtly taken over, he would have to watch what happens more closely.

The London launch of the Holy Church of Lazarus had been a huge success, earning comments from the national press and across the internet. It was moving on the assumption that a miraculous artefact connected to Lazarus was in existence, just as he had envisaged. Bower would be useful, but Shepard knew he could do it on his own. Getting involved with the hooligan had been a mistake. Somewhere in the process, Bower's involvement would have to be terminated.

They sat outside in comfortable wicker chairs under a pergola covered in red and blue bougainvillea. Her maid, Luciana, served iced tea in long, cold glasses. Maria was quiet, saying nothing and just staring at Martha, letting a flow of thoughts take her over. Her eyes began to water, and she barely managed to stifle a sob.

Martha reached out to her. "This must be very painful for you."

"I don't know what to think." She wiped another tear away from her cheek. "He sat in that same chair just as you are now. You are so alike. You sit as he did and you speak like he did, too. It's uncanny. You haven't even met him."

"Is this where he had those strange visions and experiences?"

"Yes. We had a very unusual connection. When he experienced what I had, I knew I was not going mad. He seemed so full of life and I knew at once he was going to be part of my own destiny. When I was healed, it nearly finished him. It seemed like all his vitality had been drained from him like fuel from a tank. He never recovered from the events and had chosen to become a monastic. It was all too much for any man to endure. If only I could give back to him all that he'd lost, I would." The Condesa paused, lost in her memories. "My dreams and visions stopped at that point, and I suppose, that also happened to everyone involved. Yet of late, after all these years, they have returned. Then, you arrive to confirm my deepest feelings and thoughts. That tells me business is unfinished here, and I know now that you are part of it. Our meeting was too remarkable."

Martha gulped on her drink. She had a burning question. "As I said earlier, I've been having dreams too, ever since my birthday. Most strange, and Ma has been getting concerned. Like you, she said it's happening all over again. What visions or dreams have you had?"

"It's difficult to describe. I don't know exactly what I was seeing. It appeared as a strange shape and would only show itself when I get tired. At first, I only saw it occasionally, but now, it's happening several times a week."

"Maria, I paint a bit too and I brought my sketch pad with me. Can I show you something? I had tried to capture what I saw, which is something close to where we live."

"Of course. Luciana, can you get Martha's bags, please? Thank you."

The bags were brought to them and Martha quickly rummaged for her A3 pad, which contained her sketches and artwork. Flicking the pages, she found what she was looking for. She placed her swirling watercolour of The White Horse of Uffington in front of Maria, with several bluebells surrounding it, and off to one side, the figure of a faceless man reaching out with arms outstretched.

Maria stared hard and long at what was in front of her. Her face dissolved into whiteness, like a nun experiencing a spiritual dilemma. Her hand covered the tightness of her mouth. She lifted her head to stare into Martha's enquiring eyes.

"I can't believe it. Identical! Identical!" She repeated the word several times more.

"You're telling me you've had the same dream?"

"Almost exactly."

"Oh, my God! This is unbelievable. What does it mean?"

"I don't know, Martha, but we were led to each other. That, I'm convinced of."

"I must tell Ulla."

"You must. She also has a part in all this. Let me think for a moment." She called Luciana over. "Two large wine glasses and a bottle of my best Rioja Blanco, Luciana. Thank you."

Luciana was quick, and produced a magnificent chilled bottle, from which she half-filled each glass. Without asking, she laid out a plate of olives, prawns sautéed in chilli and garlic, and dishes of small cheeses and picos.

"Martha," continued the Condesa, "enjoy the wine for we have much to discuss. Your painting has stunned me, and I cannot deny that. I need to speak to Abbot Louis, urgently."

"Who is he?"

Maria paused, uncertain of how much she should reveal to the young woman in one sitting. She realised it had to be done in easy stages.

"He is the head of a monastery I know of. I told him I had been troubled by dreams and as he is my spiritual mentor, I trust his advice. He'll know what I should do with these developments. If you don't mind, I'll call him now."

"Use my phone." Martha handed her phone across.

Again, Maria hesitated and stood behind her chair. "It's personal. I'd rather go inside, if you don't mind."

Martha, never short on confidence, responded, "You're

keeping something from me, aren't you?"

The Condesa had seldom felt wrong footed, and certainly never by a young girl. Her eyes flashed with a quick glint of anger. "What?" An exasperated sigh followed. She turned her back and gazed upon the rocky landscape stretching as far as the eye could see, trying to regain her composure. Running a hand through her hair, a rush of thoughts and emotions went through her mind and body. The place whispered to her, as it had all those years ago, and she knew at once that she had to share the secret, because this situation was meant to be. It was no accident, and Martha had every right to know. She swung around and saw Martha standing with her arms folded. She looked uncomfortable.

Maria held out her arms. "You are right, and I was very wrong. Throughout my life, I have never apologised for anything I have said or done. Now, I do to you. The right is undeniably yours, so let us drink our wine and I will tell you more. But first, I'll make that call on your phone and you must listen. I think you may hear a few things you have been so curious about. Abbot Louis heads the *Monasterio de San José de Nazaret*, which is near Segovia. He has been there for many years. Don't speak, just listen.

The call was answered.

"Hello, Father Louis, it's Condesa Maria speaking."

The conversation continued.

"Is Brother Baez there? I think we are all in need of an urgent meeting."

"Of course. He returned yesterday, and he wants to meet with you. You two have not met for seventeen years."

"I can handle that, as I'm sure he can, but it's more than that. I have somebody here he should meet."

"Who? Why?"

Maria breathed in deeply to the full extent of her aged lungs. "Right now, I can't say. But it is deeply important. I will call you again to let you know when we shall arrive."

"Is it his daughter?"

Maria's breath hitched. "How could you guess that? Yes, it is."

There were a few more words and the possibility of meeting very soon. The phone went dead.

Martha, her face strained with an ache of expectancy, was staring at the Condesa. "Is Brother Baez my father?"

Grasping hold of the emotions that threatened to overtake her, Maria breathed deeply to steady herself before replying, "Yes. He was Brodie Ladro."

A silence descended between them, like that which lurks within an empty art gallery.

CHAPTER 13

Uffington, UK

T hat morning, a lengthy feature article in *The Times* newspaper immediately caught Ulla's attention. The strap line ran:

LAZARUS ALIVE AND WELL IN LONDON!

The article concerned the formation of a new church announced at the World Charismatic Convention at Wembley Stadium. It was to be called Holy Church of Lazarus, and its followers known as Lazacrucians. The new church is led by an American named Pastor Silas Shepard, who claimed to have received visions and had conversations with God whilst praying and meditating in the desert. Only those who followed his instructions and the new faith would be saved from

Armageddon. Written in a deeply sardonic style, it was less than complimentary. The writer's name was Ned Garcia.

Ulla felt fazed. It had also mentioned that Pastor Shepard had alluded to the existence of an icon that could bring healing, peace, and joy to humankind.

This could not be a coincidence, thought Ulla. Too many events were stirring around the historical Lazarus. She needed to speak to somebody. Without thinking, she Googled the newspaper, wrote down the phone number, and then picked up the phone and punched the number.

Ten seconds elapsed before a soft voice spoke, "News desk, Ned Garcia speaking."

✠

The Park Lane Hotel
Piccadilly, London
Two days later

Garcia was not the athletic type. Fifty years old and with a florid face, he looked as if he'd been around the block too many times. He wore a worn-out, double-breasted, charcoal-striped suit without a tie, but with a white and red, spotted cravat tucked into a khaki, military-style shirt. The cut of the suit concealed his ample waistline which resembled a loose bag of flour. In his hands, he twirled a large glass containing his favourite drink, a Rusty Nail.

Opposite him sat Ulla Stuart, enjoying her first ever Rusty Nail, and marvelling at the hotel's Art Deco décor. She knew a lot about Garcia's background, courtesy of Google.

He'd been recently voted as the most distinguished investigative journalist of the decade, and that included the TV reporters. One of his controversial revelations concerned a secret paedophile ring that operated within the government, church, and judiciary. It had caused the collapse of the government of the time. Attempts had been made to block his reports and his life had been threatened several times. All had failed. He was dedicated to exposing scams, corruptions, bribery, and cover-ups of all sorts. In some quarters, he was revered almost as a god.

"Ulla, I've listened to your story and it seems like a sack load of rubbish."

She flinched. "I've told you everything I know. The coincidences, everything, and you are the only one I've ever mentioned them to. I don't lie, nor am I a Walter Mitty."

"I appreciate that, but it all sounds unbelievable ... except for one thing." He ordered two more Rusty Nails. Inwardly, Garcia concluded that the woman was dripping with sincerity, and he liked her very much even after such a short time. *You can't invent stories like this ... I wish I'd met her years ago.*

"What's that?" Ulla tilted her head, curious.

"You said something earlier that got my attention. You spoke of Sir Maxwell Throgmorton and his sordid, crooked involvement. What happened to him?"

"I don't know. He just vanished." Ulla lied.

"I ask because when I was a trainee, my mentor, Desmond O'Keefe, who was investigating Throgmorton's corruption, had been found drifting face down in the River Thames. He'd been garrotted and shot through the heart. I swore I'd carry on Desmond's work, and do so to this day.

You couldn't possibly have invented that scumbag. He was real. As for this Pastor Shepard, I've found out a few things more about him. He was discharged from the USSS under a cloud of treason after being caught in a honey trap. My sources said he has a backer by the name of John D. Bower. He is reported to be fabulously wealthy as the owner of several casinos. Rumour has it he was the secret buyer of a priceless sixteenth century folio known as the *Augsburg Book of Miraculous Signs*. I can't prove that, but if it's true, it suggests he has some sort of interest in the world of mysteries. I must admit, with the involvement of these people, there could be a possible scam brewing here."

"You will do this then?"

"It looks like it. I need a new adventure. My editor trusts my judgement and why shouldn't he? Now, I want all the details; names, addresses and every possible connection, locations, etc. You can do that?"

"Of course." A broad smile crossed Ulla's face.

He felt touched. *If only…*

Before he left, she gave him a sealed envelope. "I'll tell Martha about you and I would be grateful if you could give her this when you meet." She handed him a large, thick envelope with the words *'To Martha'* written on the front.

"You were sure I'd bite the bait, huh?"

"No. Hopeful."

He kissed her cheek. "I'll keep in touch."

Thirty-six hours later, he left Gatwick Airport aboard a budget flight via Norwegian Air International to the Barajas Airport in Madrid. Toledo's nearest airport was sixty-nine kilometres away. He'd booked in at the Hotel Abad, a ten-minute walk from the city centre and close to Martha's hotel.

Ulla wasn't slow off the mark. She called her daughter and quickly explained the run of events and in particular, the story of Pastor Shepard. She cautioned her to be on the watch for him. Martha was still talking to the Condesa under the veranda.

"That was Ulla. She's getting concerned with all the events occurring around this Lazarus business. She's spoken to an investigative reporter called Ned Garcia and—"

She got no further. Luciana bustled in, holding a phone. "It's a man from a church and he wants to speak to you, Madam. Shall I tell him you are busy?"

"No, if it's from the church I'll take it." Maria took the phone from her. "Condesa Maria speaking, how may I help you?"

The caller made a reply.

"Where are you then?"

There was another lengthy reply.

"I'm about two kilometres from there. I cannot give you more than ten minutes as I have guests here. I will expect you very soon."

She turned to Martha. "I asked him here out of curiosity ... something to do with a new church called Holy Church of Lazarus. You're right. He is being raised again."

"Is his name Shepard?"

"Why, yes. How did you know that?"

Martha quickly explained. Both looked amazed.

"Leave this to me, Martha. I know how to handle him. I want you out of sight, so get back inside with Luciana. That must be him approaching now." Maria pointed to a billow of dust growing nearer.

Martha looked concerned. "Are you going to be okay?"

"Just you wait and see. I'll be fine. Now, out of sight, please."

It wasn't long before the tall, skinny frame of Pastor Silas Shepard emerged from the SUV to make his way to the seated Condesa.

She refused to stand nor allow him the chance to be seated. She fixed him with a stony stare and ignored his outstretched hand, taking an instant dislike to him. "You are Shepard?"

"Yes, Pastor Shepard. May I take a seat?"

"No, you may not. Stay where you are. Tell me what you have to, I don't have all day."

He began telling her of the Holy Church of Lazarus and the conversation he had with God in the desert.

"*Absoluto sin sentido!* Utter nonsense! So, you have God's phone number? Perhaps you'd like to share it with me?" she snapped. She could see he was not feeling comfortable.

"I heard that you were cured of a serious illness when you touched a painting. I, or we, as a church, are seeking this painting so that we may bless humanity with its powers. Is this true, your … er … er … your Grace?" Shepard wasn't sure how he should address her.

"How dare you waltz in here and ask me such personal questions. What happened to me is my concern and nobody else's, least of all you, and your bogus church. *Usted es un mentiroso!*" The man seemed to understand that she had called him a liar. His face was gradually turning red.

He gained equilibrium. "You have a girl here, I believe, who might know something about this painting. May I speak with her, please?" Shepard knew he was pushing it.

"That is none of your business and the answer is no, you may not. If this is all you came for, there is nothing for you here. It's time for you to leave. Now, get out."

"Now, just a minute, lady. Nobody is going to treat me like—"

He didn't finish. From her pocket, Maria had pulled out her small, silver pistol.

"I've used this before, believe me." She fired a shot into the ground near his shiny, black shoes, covering them with dirt and sand.

"You're mad. Totally mad!" He turned and ran as she fired off another shot that clipped the woodwork near his head. He soon disappeared in a spinning cloud of dust.

Both Martha and Luciana rushed out.

"What's going on?" Martha spotted the gun. "Maria! Are you alright?"

Maria gave a rare smile, tucking the weapon out of sight again. "I enjoyed that, but I don't think we've heard the last of him."

CHAPTER 14

T
he sky was a perfect blue and cloudless, allowing the landscape to glisten in an uncanny display of colour a peacock would have been envious of. It was an artist's dream. He decided to take full advantage of it. Shepard and his two bodyguards were out on a mission to the Condesa's home in Guadamur.

Bower, with a genuine feeling of rare happiness, prepared his seating and arranged his easel, palette, oils and brushes. He contemplated the vista that stretched out before him like a scene from some medieval mystery. The river Tagus glistened like a sheet of tin foil. In his money-making life, the opportunities to indulge himself in this manner were rare.

He had a perfect view of the *Castillo de San Servando*, a former monastery later used by the Knights Templar, and the *Puente de Alcántara*, a bridge that traversed the river. The Romans had built it after they founded the town. In the Middle Ages, it was one of the few entrances for pilgrims into the city.

He looked left, right, then upwards to the blue sky above,

picked up a drawing pencil and made a few swift strokes on his canvas. He was not going to miss this rare opportunity. He'd begin with the castle.

But Bower would experience something different that day. When he tried to paint, his hand and brush seemed to have a life of their own. To his astonishment, he was unable to control them.

What's that noise?

A momentous buzz filled the air around him. The bridge looked so much older ... and full of soldiers, knights and Arabs!

YAAA! A tremendous roar filled the scene as metal, clashing steel, cries of men and dying horses, filled the sky in one terrible instant. Shrieks and curses filled the air.

"What...!" His head was bursting with the clamour of battle noise and the sights of limbs being chopped and heads rolling. Bower stood to his feet, dropped his brush, covered his ears, and then fell to the ground before passing out.

His canvas fluttered in a soft breeze.

When he came to, he had no idea how long he had been unconscious. He stared out at the bridge and nothing had changed. It was a normal day in twenty-first century Spain. Traffic and people looked as they always did.

What the fuck! His jaw hung open. *I saw them ... heard them!* He then received another shock. His hands were covered and dripping with blood.

"AAGGH!" he screamed out loud but there was nobody around to hear him. He held them up and knew it wasn't oil paint ... but he had no wounds. He grabbed his cloth and towel and removed the blood with vigorous wipes. His heart thundered in his chest and his breath came in machine-like staccato bursts. He could not stop himself shaking.

But there was more for him that day...

A quick look at his canvas added to his confusion. He had painted something. A deep green covered its previously blank surface, and in the middle was what looked to him like a great white horse, almost an abstract in its composition.

"I didn't do that!" he exclaimed.

His gaze was transfixed upon it as he slumped back into his seat.

It called to him ... and he had no answer.

Without reason or understanding, his terror began to dissipate, and he became aware of a deep sense of peace descending and enfolding him in an embrace of love, the likes of which he had never known.

But, he resisted.

"I think I need to a see a doctor. This is too damned spooky. I'm out of here!"

Reaching for his hip flask, he took a copious gulp of brandy. Its hot tentacles spread down his chest and stomach, and slowly, he regained his composure. In a state of complete bafflement, he packed up his equipment and headed back at speed to his hotel.

Martha had returned to her hotel, her mind in a turmoil of expectancy. Opening the locket, she touched the lock of hair and gazed on his face – a face full of life and interest. She knew she loved him. The thought of their first ever meeting, which he would know nothing about until they came face to face,

made her tremble. She whispered the word, "Dad." She repeated it to herself, over and over. "Dad. Dad." She had to get
used to the unfamiliar sound, but already, she found herself
liking its resonance.

*How will he react? Will he accept me? Will he love me, or will
he reject me? I'm really scared.*

The room phone rang. She answered, "Martha Stuart,
speaking."

"Señorita Stuart," the receptionist replied, "there is a man
here asking for you."

"Who is he?"

"It is a Señor Ned Garcia."

"Splendid. I was expecting him. I will be about ten
minutes. Please let him know I'll meet him in the bar."

Martha had no difficulty in spotting Garcia sitting at the bar.
In fluent Spanish, he was explaining to the barman the intri-
cacies of making the perfect Rusty Nail. They shook hands
and he ordered a white wine spritzer for her, and then headed
to a quiet table by a corner window.

Martha liked him at once and sensed he was a person she
could trust. *Ma's always been an excellent judge of character.*

"Martha, that was quite a story your mother gave out. I
have a number of leads to follow up on and a whole bunch of
phone calls to make, plus, a mass of Googling to be getting on
with. I guess this is to be a very private and emotional time
for you. I may see you tomorrow or after your reunion. I hope
it will be a happy one. Your mum asked me to give you this."
He handed her the envelope. "Why don't I go back to the bar
and you can read it privately?"

"Thank you, Ned. I appreciate that."

THE LAZARUS CONTINUUM

Once he had left, she unsealed it. Another envelope fell out, addressed to *'Brodie.'* She gazed at it long and hard, aware of a plethora of emotions assaulting her. Placing it to one side, she opened her own.

My dearest Martha,

By the time you read this I truly hope arrangements have been put in place for you to meet your dad, Brodie. I've cried every night since you left, for both you and him. I so much want him back here, so we can all be together.

The years must have worked their changes on him, as they do on all of us. He's carried his burden too long. It's time, surely, for his release. I only hope and pray that he can lay it down and walk away and take rest and comfort for what remains of the remainder of his life.

Tell the Condesa, I think of her often and that she is the most amazing woman I have ever met.

Beware of Silas Shepard and anybody who is involved with him. Trust Ned Garcia. He's a good man and he's on to this scam like a dog with a bone.

Let me know at once how it shapes up and give your dad my letter.

Love you so much … Ma

Martha wiped a small tear from her cheek and thought about

what she had just read. That word 'dad' continued giving her a warm sensation.

She walked back to Garcia.

CHAPTER 15

Shepard experienced an attack of nerves. The encounter with the Condesa had exceeded all that he could have possibly envisaged. He had not been prepared for a gun-toting prima donna. Now, he had to explain his failure to Bower. That in itself was ridiculous. *How had it come to this?*

He knocked timidly on the door. Bower opened it.

"Pastor, just the man I've been thinking of. Step inside, please. How did it go?"

Bower's face had a curious expectancy.

Shepard steeled himself for the oncoming rage and fury, which he had witnessed previously, and which had reinforced his decision to be rid of this man.

"It was difficult." He did not know what else to say.

"Explain." Bower moved over to the drinks cabinet. "From the expression on your face, it looks as if you might need one of these." He poured a generous measure of 'Widow Jane.' "Speak." He handed over the glass.

"She's as crazy as a family of meerkats."

"More, please. Why?"

"When I asked about the girl, I was told to go forth and multiply, and then got shot at twice!" Shepard held his breath for the onslaught. There was none. He looked up and Bower was smiling and chuckling.

"How is it that you can persuade a mass audience that you spoke to God, but fail so catastrophically on a one to one basis, eh? I was wrong in sending you. I'll think of something else. There is more to this than meets the eye. Now, get out and be thankful I'm in a forgiving mood."

Shepard didn't wait. He left his drink, turned, and made a swift retreat, but not before he glimpsed George playing with a military, steel-wire garrotte.

He felt a rush of fear.

Bower sat down and gazed at the panorama of rooftops, chimneys, and the distant rolling hills, his face resembling a half-darkened portrait staring out across a dimly lit art gallery.

Always, in life, he had been certain of what it was all about. Money, power, which gave to him the joys of wine, women and song.

It was for him, a certainty, as leaves falling from trees in autumn.

Now, after his encounter, he was no longer assured. He could not deny or explain what had happened. Any doubts he had about it were dispelled by the evidence of the blood-stained cloth he had used to wipe his hands. It had not been a dream.

He had always considered himself a realist, a practical person, and he wasn't going to abandon the principles that had guided his life so. There were matters that needed attending to and discovering. Obtaining the Lazarus painting was a priority. Without it, the proposed enterprise would be severely hampered.

He began formulating a plan of action … and to hell with what happened out there.

Abbot Louis thought hard about how he would handle the situation concerning the Condesa's visit. He had told Brodie or Brother Baez, whichever role he was acting under, that there were developments afoot, and that the Condesa needed to see him.

Brother Baez was busy framing one of the paintings he had completed in the desert.

"And who is this you have as Our Lady?" The Abbot held up a painting showing a single angel ascending into heaven with the Holy Mother.

"It is the face of my beloved partner, Ulla," Baez replied, not certain if the Abbot would approve.

"I see … and the angel?"

"I don't know, but she rides The White Horse of Uffington. See here." He unrolled his painting of The White Horse.

"Her hair hides her face, but this scene is so similar to what the Condesa had described and what I had a faint glimpse of."

"I know it's vague, but I suspect it will be recognisable once these mysteries are resolved."

"As you know, she'll be arriving soon. I have a feeling it will be quite a meeting."

"After all these years, I suspect we will have a lot to talk about and of recent events. With your permission, Father Abbot, I would like to be excused from the rounds of Offices."

"Of course. She should be here in an hour."

"I can see the main gate from here, so I shall know when she arrives."

Abbot Louis moved away to complete a slow meditational walk around the cloisters.

Brodie was now feeling more like his old self, although Brother Baez would never completely leave him. He found himself unable to concentrate on the framing process. His attention was riveted on the main gates. A surge of nerves hit his stomach, and his mind recalled the events that had brought him and the Condesa Maria together into a spiritual conundrum – a puzzle that had never been entirely unravelled.

It was about an hour later when he heard the main gate bell ring out its echoing chimes. He laid down his tools, rubbed his hands down the side of his cassock, and watched as another monk began to open the solid, wooden double gates. He didn't know what to think and his mind froze.

The splendid white Delage drove in slowly and Brodie smiled. It was typical of her and so in her stylish character. He walked to the shade of the cloister and watched as his Abbot strode across and opened the door for her. She stepped out, dressed as he always remembered her – stately, immaculate in her usual black, and bedecked with the odd diamond and solid silver adornments. She looked no different from the last time he had seen her. His nerves and fears vanished. It was like he had only seen her yesterday. With more life in his step, he strode out to the middle of the cobbled compound and stood still.

The Abbot stood back as she moved forward. When she saw Brodie, she stretched out her hands as she walked closer, reaching out to touch him. Not a word was spoken, and they embraced in complete mutual understanding.

They pulled back and stared at each other.

A tear glistened in her eye. "Brodie, we've missed you all these years. You look older and sadder, my friend. We have much to talk of the years between us. But I fear there will be an attempt to take the painting. We will need you once more."

"There is much we need to discuss."

"Yes, but before we do, there is somebody I would like you to meet." She turned and nodded to Abbot Louis. He retreated back to the car.

"You know I'm not good at meeting strangers and don't enjoy it. Who is it?"

"Wait and see."

She said nothing more and watched as the Abbot opened the door and a young lady stepped out. She was wearing simple sneakers, faded Levis and a bright green T-shirt with an unmistakeable icon emblazoned on the front. Long, blond hair hung on her shoulders. She moved towards them at a steady pace.

Brodie gasped. "Who is this?" His tone was laced with incredulity. He could see The White Horse clearly. "Is this a joke?"

The Condesa said nothing, took several steps back and turned away, knowing this was going to be an extremely private and emotional moment of which she had no part.

The young lady stopped a few feet away from him and they both stared at each other.

"What's going on here? Who are you and what do you want?" His words came out snappier than he had intended. The iconic garment mesmerised him. "Why are you wearing that T-shirt? I know that emblem." He looked around for the Condesa, but she had resolutely moved away and turned her back. "Say something. Are you mute?"

She spoke in a soft, gentle, but tremulous voice ... and her fists tightened.

"Hello, Dad."

"What? Say that again?"

"Hello, Dad." This time, a large, wet tear trickled down her cheek. "I'm Martha Stuart, Ulla's daughter. Your daughter, Dad. Be happy, the time has come."

Brodie's jaw went slack. The numbing, shocking realisation struck him like an electric current. "I know those words." He was unable to say another word. Seeing her simple sincerity, he didn't doubt what she had said was true. He turned to Maria.

"Yes, it's true, and it's a remarkable story."

Brodie began to sob, and Martha moved to embrace him.

When their tears had subsided, he pushed her at arm's length as he regained his composure.

"Let me look at you. You were taken from me and I never

knew you nor saw you growing up." He couldn't take his eyes off her as he ran his hands through her hair. "Oh, sweet Jesus. What can I say? You have her eyes and looks. How is she? Where is she?"

"She's well and will come if you ask her to. We live in Uffington, hence the shirt. She has never stopped loving you and mentions you almost every day. She'll always be waiting for you."

Speechless, Brodie could not stop trembling.

The Abbot approached them. "This is an unprecedented occasion for you all. Let us go to my room and we can have a drink. I understand from Maria, that you are all invited to her home in Guadamur, to stay as long as you wish."

"I need that," Brodie said. "I think we all do."

"Before we have that drink, I would like very much to see the Lazarus painting that has caused such a stir," Martha said, excitement clearly written on her face.

"This way then." The Abbot led them into the gallery.

Martha linked arms with Brodie, who for the first time in many years, felt a long-forgotten sense of pleasure and happiness. He could not stop shaking his head and muttering, "Oh, my God ... Oh, my God. I can't believe it!"

"Many of these were done by your father, Martha. See if you can spot the one we're looking for." Abbot Louis waved her forward.

Martha moved slowly along, looking at each painting in turn. "This is difficult, and here I was planning to take a Fine Art degree." She stopped and looked closer. "Ah, is this it?" She indicated the Spencarian work; contemporary, bursting with energy and power, and almost industrial.

"Clever girl, Martha. What do you think?"

"It's uncanny. It has something, but I can't say exactly what." She reached out to touch it and as she did, she swore a distinct jolt of energy passed through her. "Ooh … what was that?" She stepped back and shook her arm.

Brodie and Maria looked at each other and didn't say a word.

The Abbot raised his eyebrow. "Nothing, probably static from any nylon you might be wearing. C'mon, let's get that celebratory drink. You have to drive back later, and we still have much to discuss. It's been a wonderful moment seeing you all together. I am honoured."

CHAPTER 16

O ne hundred metres outside the monastery and away from the main gates, a darkened Seat Ateca SUV was parked. Leaning against the doors on one side stood Man One. He idly spun the chamber of his revolver and made firing noises to imitate gunshots. Next to him, George was fondly twirling his beloved garrotte, not making gunshot noises, but strangulation sounds. On the other side of the vehicle, Shepard stood tall and motionless, taking care to keep the weight off his damaged foot. He carried, as usual, his Smith & Wesson pistol. He was staring through a large pair of binoculars aimed at the main gate.

"Hold it, guys, there's something happening," Shepard said.

Both men swung around, shielding their eyes to get a better look at the monastery gates that had slowly opened.

"What is it?" Man One asked.

"A man, looks like a senior monk of some sort, has just walked out. There's a girl and another monk behind him.

They are talking ... now shaking hands." He snorted. "That's her alright, the mad cow, and it looks as if they are about to leave. When it moves off, follow that piece of junk, but not too close. Understood?"

"Understood." George got into the driver's seat.

Brodie and Martha sat in the rear seats with Maria driving. They decided to take the A1 Autopista route as it was less wearing on the vintage Delage. They waved goodbye to Abbot Louis who stood motionless as he watched them until they were out of sight. If he saw the SUV go past, he made no note of it.

Brodie remained in his monastic attire. It hadn't occurred to him that he could change clothes. They were all silent as they drove, wrapped in their own private thoughts and memories.

Brodie recognised many of the landmarks. He had travelled this way with Ulla so many years ago. After the sedate pace of the monastery, the speed of events took some getting used to. But already, he could feel old attitudes surfacing and he felt more like his old self.

He found himself looking behind them – an old habit from when he and Ulla were being followed everywhere. A worried frown creased his face.

"Are you ok, Dad?" Martha squeezed his hand.

"I'm not sure. Something's not right."

"What is it?"

He ignored the question. "Condesa, pull over. NOW!"

She looked startled but obeyed. Jerking the Delage to the side, she slammed on the brakes. "Why?"

"We're being followed. Watch out!"

She saw what he meant. The SUV narrowly missed the rear of the Delage and veered violently to the left to avoid a crash. It carried on without stopping.

"Just as I thought. I spotted them as we left. It has matched our every move and speed. Now, let's wait a few minutes before we move off. I guarantee we'll see them again."

"Who can it be?" Maria asked.

"I don't know, but this is about the painting. Someone has their eyes on Lazarus."

Maria looked thoughtful as they waited for a couple of minutes more, before she started the car and drove on as before. As Brodie had said, less than a thousand metres further up the Autopista, the SUV had pulled over, its warning flashers on.

"Ignore them and don't look at them, whatever you do." Brodie's old authority had returned. "Just as I said. It's a bit like old times once more."

"It's pulling out."

"Now, there's a surprise. As long as we're moving, I don't think they'll try any muscle manoeuvres."

Martha spoke with a hint of nervousness. "I never expected anything like this. I'm beginning to understand what you and Ma went through. Wow!"

To his own surprise, Brodie let out an amused laugh. "Well ... there you go."

Bypassing Toledo, they took the road leading to Guadamur. The SUV stayed behind them but when they made the turn to Maria's home, it went straight and out of sight.

As they approached Guadamur, Maria slowed down and then stopped. "Look familiar, Brodie?" She turned to him and reached for his arm.

He gave a deep sigh. "Oh God, it's exactly as I remember it. I don't believe it. Nothing has changed. Nothing."

He stared across at the contours of ancient hills that had dominated this skyline since time immemorial. They were the same hills that had called to him many years back and had begun his quest and transformation. An emotion, immeasurable, rippled through his entire being. Realisation passed like the drawing of a heavy curtain. "The magic and mystery are still here. I can feel it in my flesh and bones." He articulated in a voice broken by a sadness he had never truly comprehended.

Martha and Maria held him tight. His dilemma needed no explanation. It was plain to see.

The moment was broken when Maria suddenly said, "Who's that down there? Look, there's a car parked in front." A solitary figure was standing near the vehicle.

Brodie bristled. "Drive forward and leave this to me."

The Condesa inched closer to the vehicle.

"Now stop, and you two stay put. If you have to, drive off like the wind." Brodie leapt from the car, and at a rapid rate, strode over to the man leaning on the fence, who gave a wave as he approached.

Brodie's old radar system was on full alert. "Who are you?" he demanded, "And what are you doing here?"

"Hi, my name's Garcia, Ned Garcia, and I was hoping to find Martha Stuart here with the Condesa Maria. Her attendant told me she's out and doesn't know what time she'll be back."

Brodie felt wrong footed. "I don't know who you are, but they're in the car." He gave the Condesa a thumbs-up and waved them forward.

As the car stopped, Martha jumped out. "Ned! You found us. Wonderful" They embraced before she introduced him to the others and explained who he was.

They all went inside, and Maria called Luciana over. "I think we need food and drink, lots of it! This could be a long day."

CHAPTER 17

C lack.

The snap of a magazine being loaded into a firearm sounded good to him. There was a satisfying masculinity about the sound, more so when he was able to discharge it. Bower looked at the weapon resting in his hands and positioned his eye down the length of the barrel. *That would do nicely,* he thought. The mad woman would not get the better of him, nor any of the people she had with her. It was amazing how the threat of torture or death to a hostage could loosen tongues into disclosures they wouldn't normally admit to.

Of the people around him, the one he trusted the least was Shepard. He knew the man would double-cross him at the earliest opportunity, and if the artwork was discovered, he would claim it as his own and kill if he had to. Many pastors in the USA used miraculous healings to attract members to their church. They were highly suspect. But the painting would be a visible evidence – a religious icon that can be revered. The legend surrounding it would add to its mystery and allure.

For the time being, he would carry on as normal and Shepard would be dealt with when the time arrived. Right now, there was work to be done.

He called up his bodyguards and Shepard. They were to follow him at a discreet distance to Guadamur, armed and ready.

Moving out of the door, he caught sight of the bloody cloth hanging from his easel. It made him stop, and as he did, his mind was taken over by another vision. It was the image of the strange, white horse that had shown itself to him earlier at the *Puente de Alcantara.*

"God, no!" he shouted. "You're not real. Now, fuck off and leave me alone!" *I don't believe this. I just don't believe it!* He stormed out, slamming the door and rocking it on its hinges.

Guadamur

Luciana had prepared tortillas, rice, chicken, chillies and an array of tapas and varied finger foods, plus several bottles of iced wine.

"Well, this beats monastic gruel by a long measure," Brodie said. "I haven't eaten like this since I can remember."

"Enjoy it while you can, Brodie. You're more than welcome." The Condesa turned to Garcia who was teaching Luciana how to make a Rusty Nail. An absence of Drambuie cancelled out that drink. "Tell us what you know about this Shepard and his followers."

"If it hadn't been for your mother, Martha, I wouldn't be here today. I thought it was a cock and bull story until she mentioned a certain Sir Maxwell Throgmorton."

Brodie caught Maria's pinched expression.

"Whatever happened to him? Do you know?"

There was a pause.

Maria looked up at Garcia, and in a flat monotone voice said, "I shot and killed him."

Silence descended amongst them, so thick it was almost palpable.

Tight-lipped, Garcia drilled his eyes into the Condesa. "I *never* heard you say that … nor did anybody else here. Well, it seems to me the bastard got what he deserved. It should have happened sooner. Well done." He smiled and clasped her hand. "As I told Ulla, Shepard is being backed by a man of vast wealth, who has an interest in the arts and religious artefacts. He's a casino owner named John D. Bower. Believe it or not, he is the owner of the *Augsburg Book of Miraculous Signs.* Have you heard of it?" His eyes turned to Brodie, who nodded. "This Bower had paid a fortune for it. My bet is he's after the Lazarus painting, either to make money from its alleged power, or to add to his collection. A bit like Dr. No in the James Bond film, don't you think?

"To give you some idea of his operation, he employs over eight thousand people, and recently sold off a small chain of casinos to a major media and film production company. That deal netted him billions."

Garcia refilled his wine glass before he continued. He had everyone's attention. "To make life more interesting, a few days ago, I anonymously signed up to one of Shepard's seminars and weekend intensives, which will happen in a few weeks' time. That should reveal a lot. It reminds me very much of the Scientology set up."

Brodie leant forward, his expression one of serious concern. "Mr. Garcia, with respect, you don't know what you're getting yourself into. They'll spot you a mile off, and you'll be roasted alive. This phoney Holy Church of Lazarus and its creepy leader, Shepard, strikes me as no different from our old adversary, Throgmorton. If what you say is true, then he will be back, and it's my bet he won't be alone. He'll have his troops on hand and they will be armed. You'd better believe me." He turned to the Condesa. "What have you got to protect yourself?"

She produced her pistol. "I think you better have this."

Brodie declined. "Technically, I can't. In essence, I'm still a man of God. Anything else?"

"I have an old shotgun that hasn't been used for years, complete with a belt of rounds."

"Okay, do you have wire, axes, gardening tools ... anything we can use to defend ourselves, should we have to?"

"Masses, at the rear of this complex."

"I guarantee if you are left here alone, the worse could happen. The place will be ransacked, and your life would be in danger. Unless you do as I say, you won't have a chance. That pea shooter of yours is no match for what these guys could be carrying."

He turned to Garcia. "I think it's best if you leave before anything happens. There's no obligation for you to stay, and when you leave, take my daughter with you."

Martha stood in haste. "No, Dad. I'm staying with you. I

haven't sacrificed my university place and my heart to find you, just to leave you when we've only met. I'm staying put."

Garcia pushed back his chair and stood, fists tightly clenched and with a fire in eyes that surprised everybody. "I've a feeling that this could get messy. Listen, Brodie, and all of you. What do you think I am … a local junior newspaper reporter? No, I'm bloody well not! I'm an investigative journalist with a worldwide reputation." He banged his fist hard on the table that caused them all to start. "I'm getting pissed off with this and I too haven't travelled all this way to scarper at the first sign of trouble. There's a major story here that could have a global impact, and I'm going to see it through to the end. Get it?" He riveted Brodie with eyes like steel spikes and his voice ascended several pitches. "Request denied!" He stormed off.

Brodie, Maria and Martha were left dumbfounded. What could anyone say?

Martha spoke first and looked at Brodie with a smile, attempting to defuse the tension.

"Dad, I *do* like saying that word, I forgot to give you something. It's a letter from Ma." She reached into her bag and handed him the stiff white envelope.

He took it and stared at the calligraphy style handwriting he had known so well. For a moment, he paused, and his hands trembled.

"I need some space. Excuse me, please." He headed away from them all and found an old bench to sit upon. With care, he unsealed the envelope and swore he could smell her well-remembered perfume wafting from the envelope. He unfolded the paper.

THE LAZARUS CONTINUUM

My dearest Brodie,

I hope this finds you well. If you're reading this, you now know that Martha is our daughter, who I love and cherish as I do you. Even after all these years, there has never been anybody else in my life.

I hope you can love her as I do. She has asked about you so many times and it is only of late that I've told her everything. She is bright, intelligent, and incredibly mature for her age. A wonderful future awaits her, I am sure.

You must also know that the Lazarus painting is at risk from a Pastor Silas Shepard. Speak to Ned Garcia. He is a good man whom I trust, and like, totally.

I want so much to see you again and have you back here at Uffington, with Martha. So that we can all be together, dare I say it, like normal people! We really need that, darling. When you give the word, when you can, I will be there on the first flight.

My darling, Brodie, all my love and more.

Ulla

He held the letter like a crumpled ball in his hands and looked out at the darkening terrain. The rocky, undulating hills that had spoken to him back then, were once again beginning to stir. He felt like an old tree being ripped from the ground.

He took in a deep breath and gave a strangulated sob that breeched his chest and throat, sounding like birds going south to avoid the coming blasts of winter. He wiped the tears from his face. *Oh God, release me from this. Have I not done enough?* There was no answer. Only the feel of a soft arm around his waist.

"Please, Dad, don't be sad. Be happy, as my message told me. We know and love each other. Just leave all this and come home. You don't have to do it anymore."

"Martha, I can't. It's not finished. It's not over by a long way. I need to think. All these dreams, voices, visions, messages, and not forgetting the bluebells ... they are communicating, and I can't walk away. I know I can't."

"We want you home, Dad. Please." She embraced him with all the love she felt in her heart.

Brodie gently pried her away and looked at her with resignation. "My fate is bound up with that painting and it won't let me go. You felt its power when you touched it. That wasn't static as the Abbot wanted you to think. Most people experience nothing ... so I would say that in some way, you are also connected. How? I've no idea. But I don't want you caught up in it. When I leave from here, I want you to go back to Ulla and tell her I will find my way back to you as soon as I am released from this curse."

"But Dad..."

"My lovely daughter, you have brought me happiness I would not have believed possible, and I don't want harm to come to you. I've no right to tell you to leave, but I'm asking ... no, not asking, begging you to leave. Bad things are going to happen again, and soon. I can sense that and so does Maria. We've never been wrong and what she thinks, I know, because I hear her thoughts in my head."

"I told you I'm staying with you, no matter what happens.

Your begging bowl is empty, Dad. You won't change my mind. Let's join the other two."

She steered a confused Brodie back to the veranda.

Maria stood as they approached. "It's getting cooler. Let's step inside where we can feel more comfortable."

"Good idea," Garcia said. He had returned and seemed to have calmed down. "In the car, I've got some photographs of this Shepard weasel, plus, I forgot that I have a bottle of Drambuie somewhere. Rusty Nail, here we come!"

Everyone chuckled as they moved inside.

Garcia headed out to his vehicle, reached inside, grabbed the photograph and then the Drambuie which was wedged in the dashboard locker. He stood, and for a moment, he weighed the situation and events of the last forty-eight hours. He was on to something big … but what? He couldn't figure it out yet.

It was then he caught sight of a balloon of dust, as a vehicle barrelled at some speed towards the property.

Who can that be? He huddled behind the gates and waited to see who it was.

The vehicle, an ageing Land Rover, came to a broadside halt in a shower of gritty dirt and sand. The engine switched off, and a small but powerful man emerged, clutching a clipboard and wearing a denim suit festooned with pens and pencils from the pockets, with two cameras hanging off him.

Garcia moved to meet him as the man approached the gate.

"Hi there." An arm was thrust out and Garcia found himself shaking it. "I'm Luke Majors. I'm doing research on ancient and medieval monasteries of old Spain, for National Geographic Magazine." He waved an ID tag hanging from his neck. "Can I speak to the owner? Is that you?"

Garcia felt an alarm bell give a soft ring in his head. He didn't know why, but his instincts had never failed him yet. Something about the soft West Coast American accent, the missing consonants, the timing of the man's arrival …

"It's not me," he replied. "She's inside and may be sleeping. Let me check." *Why am I saying that?* "If you would care to remain where you are, I'll be back soon."

"Thank you, sir, much appreciated."

Garcia strode quickly into the room where they were all seated. He handed his portfolio to Brodie and placed the Drambuie on the table.

"Outside, we have our first visitor."

"What? Who is it?" The Condesa looked suspicious.

"A guy called Luke Majors. He claims he's from National Geographic and doing research on ancient and medieval monasteries of Spain. He wants to speak with you."

"This is too much of a coincidence. First, Shepard appears, and now this total stranger. What do you think?"

"It's got a smell about it I don't like. I'll tell him you're not available." He turned to leave when they heard a voice behind them.

"Well, well, well … I was hoping it wouldn't be as difficult as this."

The unmistakeable American voice caused them all to swing around. Framed in the doorway and holding a suppressed Beretta in his outstretched hand, stood the man who called himself Luke Major.

CHAPTER 18

Abbot Louis was worried and on edge. As one of the painting's guardians, he was aware that at any moment, someone could come and take it away. The monastery was not a closed order, and parts of it were open to the public, so they could participate in everyday mass and holy days of obligation. The gates opened and were shut at specific times of the day. From this, he calculated that anybody with a view to stealing something would have little trouble entering.

No announcement had been made about the painting, nor would there ever be. He remembered Brodie's words … *'They will come.'* The Abbot truly believed these words came from God. Those in need of its help would be drawn to it and receive its healing grace. That's the way it has always been for more than two thousand years since the original painting was created by Annas Zevi.

Juan de Borgoña's version of *The Raising of Lazarus* had self-destructed, as had all paintings before it. Abbot Louis suspected that Brodie's version would follow the same fate when a new artist has been chosen to create the next version. When this will happen, nobody knew.

He looked at his watch, and true to the minute, the gates were opening and a small flock of the faithful moved inside. The numbers had diminished over the years. For that, he felt sorrow. He recognised most of them by sight, and when mass was over, and farewells were given on departure, he went out of his way to ensure he spoke to everybody.

The Abbot spent more time with new faces. In this secular age, he understood that new blood was always required.

There's a face I don't know.

He saw a tall, thin man with silvery hair and eyes like grey flint stones making his way out into the warmth of the sun. His head was bent, and there appeared to be an air of sadness around him.

"Hello, friend. I haven't seen you before." Abbot Louis extended his hand.

It was firmly taken and shook. "No, Father. I'm a recent convert," lied Shepard in reasonable Spanish. Confident that the Abbot could not have heard of him.

"A convert, eh? That's something we don't often hear around these parts. You are more than welcome. Have you a few spare minutes? We could have coffee and chat."

"Yes, I would like that. Lead on, Father."

Within five minutes, Shepard sat opposite the Abbot, sipping coffee from a delicate porcelain cup and indulging in small talk. He shared the circumstances that led to his conversion.

But as his guest bent forward to place his cup on the table, Abbot Louis caught a glimpse of Shepard's shoulder holster.

A pang of alarm went through him. He decided not to mention it and get the man out of the monastery as soon as possible.

"I hear you have a small art collection here, Father. Depicting various miracles, like Christ's raising of Lazarus and other events. Would it be possible to look at them?"

The Abbot made the pretence of looking at his watch. "Oh dear, not at the moment, I'm afraid. We have the builders in, and I have a meeting in a few minutes. You can return once the builders are done and I would be happy to show you the gallery." He stood, a smile still plastered on his face, but clearly terminating the meeting.

Shepard paused and then he, too, rose to leave. It was as he thought. Once inside the monastery, it wouldn't be difficult to find what he was looking for. The Abbot had not denied the presence of the Lazarus painting. "Another time then." Shepard smiled as the Abbot led him out.

Once outside, Shepard activated his cell phone.

"Who the hell are you? Get out." Maria moved forward but Garcia held her back.

"He's got a gun. Don't be stupid. National Geographic, my arse!"

Brodie pushed Martha behind him. "Who are you? What do you want?"

"Who I am is of no consequence. Just do as I say, and you will not be harmed." He swung his gaze around them all, and his pistol followed his gaze.

Then, it dawned on Garcia. "John D. Bower, I bet. I'd put money on your rigged gaming tables!"

From the expression that crossed the man's face, Garcia knew he had scored a bull's eye.

"Shut the fuck up, whoever you are, or you won't see daylight much longer."

At that moment, Martha moved to one side, away from Brodie. Her stare was fixed on the man and she approached him.

"Come no closer! I abhor violence, if you must know. Don't force me." A tinge of doubt could be heard from his voice, more so when he saw the T-shirt she was wearing. He held up his palm. "Stop where you are! What is that you're wearing and where did you get it? I've seen that image before."

Martha turned to an anxious looking Brodie. "Dad, he's seen this before?" She indicated the logo on her T-shirt.

"Holy Saints!" Brodie looked shaken. "I don't understand what's happening here." He answered for Martha. "That image is carved into the side of an English hillside and it's called The White Horse of Uffington. It's over three thousand years old. Somehow, it's connected us all here. Even though you're threatening us with a pistol, you are part of this story. Where have you seen it?"

Before Bower could reply, the ringtone of his phone cut through the air. "Shit." He glanced at the screen. It was Shepard. "Stay back, all of you." He waved the gun at them.

Brodie gasped as ancient memories surfaced in his mind. *Deus Vult! Beauséant!*

Centuries of history arose once more in his being as he prepared to launch himself at the man.

No, Brodie ... no! He will harm Martha! The Condesa's words ripped into his psyche, stopping him in his tracks. It was like old times and nothing had changed between them. *Not yet! Not yet!*

He pulled back.

Bower continued to talk to Shepard, never taking his eyes off his captives. He spoke rapidly into the phone. "I guess we're getting close. We'll follow it up. I'll see what I can find out here."

Without being seen, Garcia activated his voice recorder. He didn't want to miss any of this.

Bower ended the call and pocketed his phone. However, he didn't know what his next move should be. He got sidetracked and remained transfixed by the horse on Martha's T-shirt. It was exactly like the image depicted on his canvas. An image he had not painted himself! He was inwardly in the grip of a mysterious uncertainty. All his investigations into philosophical and religious conundrums had somehow exemplified themselves in the strange sequence of events that were beginning to surround him. *There's something here I don't understand, and that damned horse is part of it. Yet, I can't waste time on th*at. "I'm here to locate some lost art, but my colleague has just told me that he thinks he's found it."

Brodie looked over to Maria and she gave a slight shake of her head.

Garcia made no movement, but simply said, "Lazarus is alive and well and living in Spain, if you catch my drift."

Bower looked across to the Condesa. "Let me guess. You're the pistol-packing mama who got herself cured by this guy's painting, and she's his daughter. But what fatso next to her does, I have no idea. So, what am I going to do? Let me tell you." He made a one-handed call on his phone. It was answered at once. "Okay, guys, come on down. Everything is under control. Enter through the main door, I'll be waiting." He turned to the four. "My men will be here in a few minutes. They've been waiting up the road a short way back, and they can be very persuasive when put to it. So, you'd better behave yourselves, eh?"

"What is it you want us to do?" Brodie asked.

"We want the painting and we want the whole world to know of its existence. Hiding it away in some crummy little monastery is a waste of its potential. It could be the biggest money-spinner in the religious world, far exceeding fakes like The Shroud of Turin or Lourdes. Already, a vibrant church is being built around it, and followers are lining up to join the Lazacrucian movement. We're going to get exceedingly rich. I bet it wouldn't look out of place in *The Book of Miracles*."

That remark confirmed it for Garcia. This man is Bower and he possessed the ancient book.

Martha spoke, her voice soft, low and aimed at Bower. "I don't know what that book is, but the painting won't work for you right now. I don't know how I know that, but I feel it. Your horse will not let you go yet. You have much to go through."

A look of puzzlement crossed Bower's face. "Rubbish."

"I think she's right." Maria was calm and composed. "What then?"

"Ah, my men have arrived. All of you up against the wall, please."

There was a noise as George, followed by Man One, hustled in looking like two half-chewed beef burgers with the ingredients oozing from them. They both held firearms.

"Did you do as I asked?"

"Yes, boss. We have the keys. We paid three months rental, and all is ready. Who's coming with us?"

A silence descended like a heavy wet blanket.

"What?" Brodie roared. "No one is going anywhere!"

Bower nodded at Man One who strode over and grabbed the Condesa Maria by the arm. Brodie lunged at him but a sharp pistol whip to his head dropped him like brick.

"Dad!" Martha screamed. But before she could reach him, George had hauled her back by her long hair, causing her to crash across an empty table.

Maria was without her pistol and doubted whether it would be of any use in this situation. Brodie was groaning on the floor, a small trickle of blood oozing down his temple.

Man One grabbed a terrified Maria and pulled her towards the door, and George did the same with Martha.

Garcia was frozen to the spot. Rough stuff was out of his league.

Bower looked down at Brodie. "Do as you are told, and they will come to no harm. We've rented a farmhouse in a city north of Madrid, so you can't get too close." He reached out and grabbed Martha by the ear, pulling her close. "I'm certain that you recall the John Paul Getty 111 kidnapping in 1973. Instructions weren't followed, so he didn't look too good when his ear was cut off. Are you following me?"

"Leave her here, please. I beg you, take me instead." Brodie's voice cracked with emotion.

"No chance. Besides, she's prettier than you."

"Why do you need to do this? Why take us?" Maria bristled.

"It will make things easier. With you two as hostages, we

need not worry about the police, do we now?" Bower smirked and aimed his pistol at Brodie's head. "You do understand, don't you?"

"If you so much as harm a hair of her head…"

Bower cut him short. "Losing our saintly perceptions, are we? This is what's going to happen. You will all remain here until you hear from me later. Don't contact anybody, or it will be all the worse for these delightful ladies. You will await my instructions, no matter how long it takes. Understood?"

"Understood."

"Dad, I'll be okay. He won't harm me. Believe me. I don't know how, but I know." Martha's voice trailed away, and her eyes widened in surprise.

"Let them go or I'll blow your head off!" Luciana had entered unseen and forgotten through a side door, and in her hands, she held a large shotgun, pointed directly at Bower.

"No, Luciana. No! Put it down!" Maria's warning came too late.

Man One pulled Maria in front of his body and without taking aim, blasted off a shot at Luciana.

Luciana gave a cry like a wounded animal, and dropped to the floor, as a series of moans rippled through her slim body.

"My God!" Brodie rushed to her, oblivious to the danger and the shrieks from both ladies. The bullet had entered her left shoulder and exited above the collarbone, narrowly missing her neck veins.

Garcia grabbed at a large tablecloth and rushed to Brodie, who immediately began to staunch the blood flow by pressing on the brachial artery opposite the elbow. He turned his head to speak to the intruders, but they had disappeared, together with their hostages. A feeling of sickening despair threatened to overwhelm him. He had to continue.

Garcia sprinted to the bathroom and located a medical kit. It contained gauze pads, bandages and adhesives, which with the tablecloth, would help stem the blood loss.

"Luciana, you're going to be fine. The bleeding is under control. You're going to be okay. Talk to me, Luciana. Talk to me, please. You are a very brave woman. Stay with us. Everything will be fine." Brodie leant in closer, so he could check her wound. He knew he had to stay with her or she could die of shock.

At the same time, his insides were screaming for Martha and Maria. "Please talk, Luciana. Please."

She began to speak, and Brodie brought his ear closer to her mouth, so he could hear what she was saying.

"It hurts, Señor. Where is Maria?"

"She'll be fine. Don't worry now. Stay still. We're going to cover you with a blanket to keep you warm. We won't leave you, I promise. You are safe."

Luciana started shivering. Brodie could do nothing else but pray. He called for help, to anyone who might be listening … but there was no answer.

CHAPTER 19

The City of Pamplona, Spain

The car had bypassed Toledo on its over four-hour drive to the Gothic city of Pamplona, famous for its annual bull run which attracted thousands of tourists.

"Where are we going?" Martha asked.

"Somewhere out of the way," Bower replied.

He'd been uncharacteristically silent during the trip and looked like a troubled man. Both Man One and George, however, looked pleased with their accomplishment.

When they reached the outskirts of the city, the car took a sharp left turn down a small turning, that then became a track leading down to a white, rustic building with large, brown, wooden window shutters. The car slowed to a stop in front of the building. A tall, skinny man wearing a clerical collar but packing a fat shoulder holster opened the front door. Pastor Silas Shepard smirked with an expression of triumph.

"We meet again, my lady, and not so high and haughty this time." Shepard helped to propel her forward.

When Bower stepped out, however, he personally took Martha's arm. Gently and almost protectively, he led her inside the building.

The interior was modest and designed as a family holiday home. Bower had chosen it with some care. They would be hunkering here for several days or more, if needed. There were five bedrooms, all lockable, and to which he had the keys. He had thought it through with care. All had *en suite* facilities, and for the ladies, he had made provisions for changes of clothes. Additionally, the cupboards and freezers were fully stocked. There would be no need for them to leave the building.

"Make yourselves comfortable, ladies. We have satellite TV, so you can watch what you like at any time. George here is a careful man. He has disconnected all phone lines so there's no point in trying to make any calls, and we have your cell phones. Don't attempt to escape or involve the police and you will come to no harm. Understood?"

"Understood," the Condesa replied and glanced over to Martha who nodded.

Shepard spoke, an air of triumph in his voice. "Tomorrow, we contact your father, and all he has to do is bring us the damned painting with no tricks or switches. That's all there is to it. Simple. Once we are on our way, you will be set free." He paused and added with a suggestion of menace. "There is just one thing ... We may need a demonstration of the painting's capabilities."

"Don't be stupid!" Maria rushed at him but was stopped by Man One who stepped between them. "It can't be ordered or compelled."

"Who knows what it might do…" Shepard's grin grew broader, "once it sees what its favourite old firecracker is up against, eh?"

"Shut up all of you." Bower broke his silence. "I've some thinking to do, and you," he pointed at Martha, "I want to speak to you alone. I'm not going to harm you in any way."

"I know you won't."

"That's the second time you said that. You don't know me, so don't get too confident. Let's go into the other room and see what we can make of this."

They sat facing each other. Neither blinked. Bower felt the need to speak before the silence grew uncomfortable.

"I don't know why I'm talking to you like this, but you know something about what's going on with me, don't you?"

"What do you mean?"

"That logo on your sweat shirt."

"You were told what it was."

"Yes, I was. I collect rare books and my big hobby is painting. A few days back, I was trying to paint a view of the *Puenta de Alcantara* bridge across the Tagus river. I then heard the most overwhelming sound of a bloody battle. Men were screaming and dying alongside their horses. I heard and saw the yell of ancient crusaders. *Deus Vult!* they said. Their battle

cry shook me to the core, and then your damned horse galloped into view. I passed out and when I came to, my hands
were covered in blood, but there was nothing around me that
could have caused it. Everything looked normal. And then, I
met you all and that horse is in your T-shirt. It's all very
strange. What can you tell me?"

Martha thought for a while. There was something about
Bower. She trusted him in an indefinable manner, although
his recent actions should put any trust way out into orbit.

"Why are you asking me? It looks as if all of us involved
here are having the same experiences. You should talk to my
father. He'd know." Carefully, she related her own experiences, Maria's, and those of Brodie's in the past. "I would say,
Mr. Bower, that you have a part to play in what's going on
here. I cannot believe you really want to steal this painting so
that other man out there can make a fortune."

"He needs me and don't underestimate him or me, for
that matter. We have our own agendas, which are dropping
into place very nicely. What you have told me confirms one
thing; this is no cock and bull story. There's an element of
truth in it and I'm more than anxious to discover what it is.
Hopefully, that will not be too long now. Once we have this
painting, I'd like to see it perform a miracle cure with my own
eyes. Between us all, we should be able to achieve it like that."
He snapped his fingers.

Martha remained unfazed. "When you first saw me, you
seemed unnerved. You know that what I'm saying is true.
You're in the midst of something you don't fully understand."

"You are a very confident young lady, but I want no part
of this mystical religious nonsense. Now, get back in the other
room with the others. I need to be alone for a few moments."

She turned and left the room. What annoyed him was she seemed completely calm and unruffled. Most people were scared of him.

Bower turned to his easel which he had Shepard set up for him earlier. The last thing he wanted was to be seated in a room with those five all staring at each other.

His canvas beckoned to him and he pulled back the wooden shutters to gaze at the panorama of fields and trees that led further into the city beyond. In the distance, he could see the spires of the imposing *Catedral de Santa Maria la Real Basilica*, which took over one hundred years to build, and not far from the ancient fortress and walls.

Bower was particularly taken by the weathered stone-work. He picked up a pair of binoculars to get a better view and began gauging the perspective he wanted to paint. For a moment, his world of money-making casinos and a miraculous painting were forgotten. Art was his panacea.

He made a soft pencil outline of the scene. The door suddenly swung open and Shepard walked in. Bower glared at him.

"I thought I said I didn't want to be interrupted."

"I know, but I thought you might like this." He handed him a large bourbon in a heavyweight cut glass tumbler. He held another in his other hand.

"Put it on the table, will you? All okay out there?"

"More or less. The old bat is worrying about her maid."

"Too bad. She'll find out when we contact them tomorrow. How's the other one behaving?"

"She's weird … just stares into the distance without an expression on her face. Are you sweet on her or something?"

The stainless-steel palette knife was thrown with such

force it shattered the bourbon glass Shepard had been holding in his hand.

"What the fuck! What did you do that for?" Shepard reached for a handkerchief to mop up the spilt drink. When he looked up at Bower, he found himself staring into the barrel of his Beretta.

"Not another word, not another remark or insinuation, or my finger on this trigger might get jumpy. Piss off out of here, or I'll call in George and Man One who would no doubt enjoy having some recreation with your skinny body. Now get! And before you go, pick up all the broken glass. If there's any left, I'll slice you with it."

Shepard grabbed a roll of kitchen towel, picked up every piece, before retreating at a fast pace.

Bower reached for his drink and took a heavy gulp, running his fingers across his brow. *I'm really beginning to hate that creep.* He paused and thought of Martha and her almost sublime, enigmatic way of dealing with him. As if she was some sort of druidess like Fedelma, a banfili who possessed visionary and weird prophetic abilities.

He gave his drink another pull, took another look through his binoculars and then picked up his brush and commenced with a wide sweeping arc of colour across the canvas.

It happened again…

His brush had its own agenda. It would not go where he directed it.

"My God! What's happening?" he exclaimed. "Martha, quick here!"

Broad, swift strokes … and no matter how hard he tried to stop it, the brush continued of its own volition.

The door burst open with Man One holding on to a wide-eyed Martha's arm and his gun in the other. "Boss, what is it?"

"Never mind that. Leave her here. Get out!"

Man One, used to Bower's outbursts, scuttled from the room.

"What is it?" Martha sounded uneasy.

"Look at that." He pointed to his canvas near the window. With a shaky hand, he swiftly swallowed what was left of his drink. "I picked up my brush and the damned thing painted by itself. I swear to God I didn't do it. It's the same as what happened at that bridge in Toledo, and it's full of red streaks dripping from the person riding that thing that's supposed to be a horse. It was so fast I couldn't control it. You seem to know so much, so tell me … what does it mean?"

Martha gazed long and hard at the work. In one manner, she thought it out of her power to comment. On the other, she had perfect consciousness of Bower's emotions. In spite of his awfulness, she felt compassion for him.

She suddenly wished her father was here. It was only he who had truly undergone what now confronted her. Bower floundered without the relief of inner knowledge. He was being assaulted, indeed, as they all were. But what could his role be in all of this? A crooked casino owner. He was an enigma. He seemed uncertain of what he should be, and now it was beginning to confront him, up close and very personally. She sensed, as she had when she first saw him, that he was a man standing on a crossway and knew not which way to travel.

She stared harder at the work and what she saw made her gasp. She recognised the figure astride the horse.

There was no doubt. It's Spencarian form told her all.

"Listen, Mr. Bower. Don't ask me to explain, but this is

important. You must bring my father here at once. He will know exactly what is happening to you."

CHAPTER 20

Uffington, UK

Ulla Stuart stood looking out at the darkness of the window with her phone pressed to her ear.

There was no reply.

She switched off with a shot of concern passing through her. She had been expecting a call from Martha but had heard nothing for twenty-four hours.

It was 11: 30 p.m. on a Friday evening and she had been unable to sleep. Wide-awake and anxious, she sensed something was wrong. She had called three times, but the result was always the same … zero.

Feeling a chill, she pulled her gown tighter around her and moved away from the window. She reached the drinks cabinet and poured herself another large shot of Jura. A shudder passed through her as she gulped down her drink.

She sat down on the fat, brown leather sofa and felt its coolness around her feet. Ulla curled them up underneath her gown to keep them warm. Grabbing her laptop, she checked her browsing history on Google ... the usual stuff, weather, news, art and antiques, hidden mysteries – all the things that reflected her life. She clicked on 'newspapers.' All the early morning editions paraded before her. It was only when 'The Times' came into view did she realise she had one avenue of exploration left open. One she had forgotten about. *Of course. Ned Garcia.*

Grabbing her cell phone, she scanned her contacts to find his number. "Yes! There it is." She pressed the key and waited. Whatever the time was there, she didn't care. If she persisted, surely, he would answer?

She got the 'Please leave a message' routine.

"Sod that! I'll ring every five minutes 'til I get a reply."

Luciana was stable. From what both Brodie and Garcia could gauge, her wound was superficial, and the main danger was from severe shock and trauma. The bleeding had stopped, and the bullet had exited cleanly and lodged into the adjacent wall. The prospect of calling in doctors or an ambulance would involve a lot of awkward questions ... and lives would be at risk. When they had suggested it to Luciana, she had shaken her head emphatically and whispered a vehement, "No!"

Brodie could not sleep. His mind was awash with a thousand unsolved issues and concerns for his newly found daughter and her mentor, his mystic link, the Condesa.

In that restless parade of memories, he thought he heard Garcia's cell phone ringing. It stopped as soon as he tried to listen harder.

Garcia had fallen asleep and was oblivious to anything.

Brodie was now wide-awake. Five minutes later, he thought he heard it again, and the phone was inside Garcia's pocket, out of immediate reach. There was only one thing to do. He shook him hard by the shoulder.

"Ned! Ned!" He was half shouting. "Wake up, please wake up. Your phone keeps ringing. It could be important."

No response. He shook him harder. This time, Ned's eyes opened but the phone had stopped ringing.

"What? What's the matter?" He looked annoyed as his eyes blinked rapidly, struggling to deal with the light.

"Your phone's been ringing every five minutes or so. Someone is desperate to reach you. It must be important."

"Oh God. Let me have a look." He fumbled around, not remembering quite where he had put it. As he found it, it burst into ringtones again. "Oh, bloody hell, someone is serious." He didn't recognise the number. "Hello? Ned Garcia speaking. Who is this and it had better be good. Do you know what time it is?"

The reply startled him. "Sorry to wake you, Ned. It's Ulla. I'm worried about Martha. I've not heard from her. Where are you? What's going on? Do you know?"

"Jesus, Ulla! What..."

His words went no further. Brodie snatched the phone from his hand.

"Ulla?" he half yelled. Just saying her name caused in him a torrent of raw emotion and his hand, with knuckles turning white, gripped the phone.

"Ned, I can hear you. No need to shout."

Brodie's head tilted backwards. Pain shot through him. The sound of her voice ... he had not heard it for over seventeen years. And with it, in one rush, came in all the memories, hopes and fears ... passing over him like a sunken buoy, its bell ringing a perpetual knell of sadness. He collapsed on the sofa.

Garcia took the phone from him. He had never seen a man sob so.

He could hear Ulla. "Ned, Ned, what's going on?"

"That wasn't me, Ulla."

"Who then?"

Garcia hesitated, and took a deep breath before replying. "It was Brodie. He's too upset right now to speak to you."

Silence.

There was a gasping sound from the other end, followed by a choking cry.

No words.

"Ulla, steady please, I don't need any more waterworks around me. I have something to tell you. Are you listening?"

"I'm listening," she whispered.

"Martha is with the Condesa Maria and she's safe for the moment." As soon as he said that, he wished he hadn't.

His statement sliced through Ulla's spiralling emotions. "What did you say? What do you mean she's safe at the moment? Where is she?" There was alarm in her voice.

Garcia turned his head to look at Brodie who was still slumped on the sofa with his head hanging down. He would be of little help to him in his current state.

"We don't know where they are. It's that phoney Pastor's

backer, who we now know is John D. Bower. They came in here armed, and there was nothing we could do. They took Martha and the Condesa Maria but promised to return them safe after we hand over Brodie's painting." Garcia faltered. He didn't know what else to say. To tell Ulla that the maid had been shot would only compound her distress.

"Enough!" Brodie's voice cut through Garcia's uncertainty like a hot knife through butter. He was standing upright. His eyes, red and raw, glinted dangerously. He looked like a man on fire.

Garcia automatically handed him the phone, turned and walked from the room. This conversation was not for him to hear.

"Ulla, is that really you?" Brodie spoke like a man who had lost and found a beloved and missing pet.

Her voice, choked with emotion, drove into his mind … causing dark corners to come and step out into the light.

"Brodie. Oh, my lovely man. This is all too much. We must leave tears and our sadness behind for another time. We must think of Martha and Maria. Oh God, this is all too much!"

"Ulla, my beloved Ulla, I have always loved you and have never stopped. But you are right, there's a time and place for these things. I promise you that. I also promise we will get them back safe, no matter what it takes. You and Ned have each other's numbers, so keep your line open and keep in touch. We must go now…" His throat tightened. "Your voice. Your voice, Ulla, I've missed you so…"

She interrupted. "I know. I feel the same. To hear you after all these years…"

Before she put down the phone, Brodie heard her sobbing.

The conversation had been brief, but he understood the strength and the emotion behind it. It was all that was needed to resurrect him back from the dead.

CHAPTER 21

Abbot Louis, uncertain of his role in this unfolding episode, sipped gingerly at his black, unsweetened tea. Life was complex as, indeed, were the mysteries of Christ. He had, of late, been troubled by dreams that could challenge his faith. All religious people experienced such things. Yet, underpinning it all was the presence of Brother Baez's artwork of the resurrection of Lazarus. In some way, the painting had driven him into a sacred world that had washed him clean. At times, as he gazed upon it, he had felt its power. He had always turned away before he could know more. Indeed, he thought that attempting to do so was inappropriate. What there was, was what there was. God needed no explanation, no identification.

His tea almost finished, he placed his porcelain cup back on the saucer and felt a compelling urge to visit the gallery and look at the painting.

Breaking the lonely hush of the gallery, his thick, leather sandals slapped on the stone floor, intruding on the surrounding, almost sacred, hushed silence that confronted him as he walked into the area.

Alone.

He could almost swear that the presence of the Lazarus painting had a magnetic force of its own … drawing him inevitably to its presence. So strong was its power, he could have walked to it blindfolded without error.

He guessed that somewhere, somehow, a change was blowing in the breeze of life. He reached the painting and stood stock still as he gazed upon it, and involuntarily knelt on one knee with his head bowed.

After what seemed a respectable moment of time, he lifted his head.

The work shimmered.

He could only gasp.

The truth of it had become undeniable.

"What must I do? What do you want from me?"

There was no reply. Only what he thought was an unexpected slight smile on the face of Christ.

At that moment, he knew he was amongst a very few select people who had an intimate understanding of what might be happening around the work. He knew now that it had its own reason for existing. Life, death rebirth – were one neverending circle throughout the universe, until the Second Law of Thermodynamics gobbled them all up and only God eternally remained, beyond the physics and quantum realms he had created. Brodie's painting said it all. Somehow, beloved Brodie had been chosen – a sinner, a robber, but a man of immense understanding and humility. With those wonderful qualities were reflected the hopes of humankind.

From what he knew, from what he understood, the work

could protect itself. Yet, he sensed danger for all of them – the armed man, his questions, the meeting between Martha, Brodie, Condesa Maria and himself. Somehow, we are all characters destined to play out a mysterious plot.

He arose from his bent knee and stared squarely at Brodie's work. Tentatively, he reached out to touch it.

They connected.

His fingers would not leave. They could not.

Power.

The surge continued. It juddered up his arm and around his spine, before it enveloped his entire body.

He realised that Christ was arming his soldiers.

Then, he collapsed in an ecstatic heap upon the stone floor.

Silas Shepard was beside himself. With the hostages, he knew the painting was almost in his grasp. If anybody was going to get it, it would be him. But how would he eliminate Bower and his cronies? That would take some working out, but as yet, he needed them.

In front of him were his major assets; Martha Stuart, daughter of the Lazarus artist, Ladro, and the Condesa Maria Francesca de Toledo.

They were priceless.

"You two bitches," he commanded. "Here's my phone. I want you to contact those two back at Guadamur. When they're on the line, give the phone back to me. I'll be listening, so no tricks or you know what to expect." He passed the phone across.

Maria took it, punched the number, but handed it to Martha instead. "Brodie will answer."

Shepard removed his Smith & Wesson and pointed it in the direction of the two women. "You say hello and you're safe, and then hand it over to me, or I'll slap this old witch around a bit." He grabbed the Condesa by her neck and held her fast.

Maria made no effort to avoid him but nodded to Martha.

The phone rang a few times before the anxious voice of Brodie answered and asked who was calling.

"Dad, it's me, Martha."

The phone was taken from her and she was waved aside with Maria at gunpoint.

"Martha, are you alright? Where are you?"

"So … there you are, Ladro. We speak at last."

"You're the religious impostor Pastor Silas Shepard, I guess. My daughter, and the Condesa Maria … they've done you no harm. Just let them go. I'll help you get what you want. Where's Bower?"

"No questions. Just listen and do as you are asked. The sooner you do, the sooner these ladies will be released. Got it?"

"Got it."

"I want the Lazarus painting and I want it quick. You are a monk and know the Abbot well. You will persuade him to release it. Then, when you have it, you will send me a video recording of you holding it. When that's done, we can negotiate the next step.

"This could take a day or so."

"I know, so you'd better start moving. Do this if you want

to see your beloved daughter again." He switched off the phone and shoved Maria away.

"I wanted to ask how my maid Luciana was as she was shot."

"Who cares?" He shrugged his shoulders. "We'll find out on the next phone call."

"You're a right bastard. You will never get what you want from this."

"Yes, I will. We need a subject, someone ill or wounded. Since you two are so fond of it, either of you would be ideal. It wouldn't refuse you, would it?"

"You're so sick."

"You'll be sicker if it doesn't work."

CHAPTER 22

**Monasterio de San José de Nazaret
Nr. Segovia, Spain**

Abbot Louis's desk phone gave three sharp rings. For once in his life, he ignored it. He was lost in a reverie of spiritual amazement. His body remained buzzing from the energy the painting had released when he had touched it. He was overawed and continually crossed himself, giving thanks to God and Christ and getting more confused in the process. *So, it is true. It does have divine power. Now I know it to be true. God be praised.*

The phone began ringing again. He managed to refrain from letting out an uncharacteristic curse. "Abbot Louis speaking."

"Father Abbot, it's me, Brother Baez."

"Brother, you sound worried."

"You could say that. Martha and Maria have been taken hostage by an American and two others. Her maid, Luciana, has been shot … but she'll survive. To release the women, they want the Lazarus painting in exchange. If we don't give it to them, I hate to think what might happen. Whatever it takes, Father, we must get them back."

There was a pause. Abbot Louis found it hard to take in. He had just discovered the most wonderful thing he had never known, and now it will be removed from his care. Yet, there was no way he could allow the women to suffer.

"What do you suggest, Brother?"

"I have to collect the painting, video it on a phone, and send that to the man, Pastor Shepard, who is working with a casino owner named John D. Bower. I will then await further instructions, presumably a drop-off point. I have no idea where they might be."

"Then, you'd better get here as quick as you can."

"No, Father Abbot, it will have to be the other way around. You must come here with the painting. We can't leave Luciana. She's not out of the woods yet, and we're taking turns looking after her. As it is, it looks like I might be in for another unknown and possibly long journey. Can you spare the time? We need to do this, Father, so I can try and save the ladies from harm."

Abbot Louis knew he had no choice. He put down the phone with a heavy heart. Ever since his days as a seminarian so many years ago, and as a young man, he had dreamt in the secret confines of his heart for a sign – a miracle from God that he had made the correct choice in his life. Now, just when he had been graced with such a vision, an actual experience, it was about to be taken from him. He placed his head in his hands, removed his steel-rimmed spectacles, and began a prayer. He thanked the Almighty for the one small, but highly significant event He had bestowed upon him after all these years. It was a rare privilege, a bestowal of grace, and he got but only honour from it.

Rare, indeed.

Transitory and without permanence.

Don't dwell on it.

He could only be positive about it, and he swore the memory of what happened in the gallery would never leave him until he died.

Ten minutes later, vowing to be positive, and carrying a large, thick blanket, he walked back into the gallery to stand once more, with a heavy heart, in front of *The Raising of Lazarus*. He said a silent prayer. He could not bring himself to look upon it before covering the frame, removing it from the wall, and carrying it out to his waiting car. He told his deputy that he could be away for several days but would keep in contact.

Guadamur

Brodie checked his watch. He reckoned it would take another four hours before Abbot Louis got to him. Garcia was busy with his voice recorder and making assiduous notes. Luciana had managed to sit up and drink a bowl of chicken soup and was out of danger unless the wound decided to fester.

"Ned, may I borrow your phone?"

"Sure. Who do you want to call?"

"Ulla. I must speak to her, please. Her number's there on your phone, right?"

Garcia handed him the phone and tactfully removed himself from the room.

Brodie paused, trying to work out what he was going to say, but nothing came to mind. He decided to play it by ear. What he didn't want to do was alarm her. There were so many other things he wanted to say … but this was not the time or place. He punched the number.

After several rings, he once again heard Ulla's distinctive voice answer.

"Ned, how are things over there? Do you have any news?"

For a fraction of time, he didn't know what to say.

"Hello?" Ulla repeated.

"Ulla, it's not Ned. It's Brodie."

Her gasp was audible. Her voice, beseeching, was edged with panic. "Oh Brodie, Brodie, what's happening? Is Martha safe?"

Her voice rolled the years back for him, but he had to stay focused for both Martha and Maria's sakes.

"They are safe. I have spoken to their captors and they want the painting in exchange for their freedom. I've a feeling they will be asking me to deliver it soon."

"Is there no other way?"

"No, there isn't. But don't worry, I *know* from what still lurks inside me that the work can look after itself. Another artist is being called upon, Ulla. That's what this is all about. We will know soon enough. But right now, I just want the Condesa back and my newly-found daughter." His voice cracked. "I *will* get them back safe, I promise you. Then, we can be together once more if that's still what you want." It all seemed so rushed, so out of context. But he didn't know what the right words were, if they even existed. As the silence lengthened, he waited with trepidation for her rejection.

Her reply was soft, warm, and emotional. "Brodie, all these years, that is all I have ever, ever wanted – for us three to be together. Can you promise me?"

"I promise you." As he made the promise, he knew deep within he was not as confident as he made her think.

He prayed.

Please, dear God, let it be. I have served you and my sentence has been long enough. What your deeper intention is here, I cannot know ... but I did what you asked of me. I accepted the mantle, the yoke, and have known little happiness since that day. I never want you to leave me, but I want my missing years back. Am I beyond redemption? Beyond forgiveness? Please, keep Martha and the Condesa safe for they have done little wrong.

He let his silent words drift up like wood smoke ascending to the heavens. He said goodbye to Ulla and promised to let her know of any developments. The words *Deus Vult! Beauséant!* without conscious effort or summons, passed through his mind as he relaxed his grip on the phone.

All that could be done now was to wait for Abbot Louis and the painting.

Garcia appeared. "Brodie, when I first heard of this story from Ulla, I thought it was a tub load of poo. Evidently, it's far from it. It's red hot, and some guys out there are prepared to do dreadful things to get hold of the secret. The ladies come first before anything else, we agree on that, don't we?"

"Absolutely."

"While you and Ulla were talking, I found these." He produced Luciana's shotgun and several boxes of cartridges, the Condesa's small silver pistol, a large axe, rolls of wire and a vicious-looking hunting knife.

Memories rushed through Brodie, and his face blanched to the colour of virgin blotting paper. He looked long and hard at the items.

"I thought I could make use of these, but I'm not sure I can do all that again."

"Do what?" Garcia knew nothing of the dark episodes in Brodie's past, that led to the demise of Throgmorton at the hands of Maria.

"That's another story. When this is over, perhaps I'll tell you."

"Okay, that's a deal. Let's check on Luciana, have a drink and wait for our holy courier."

CHAPTER 23

B ower sat alone, glowering into the nearby views of Pamplona. To one side of him sat his easel and paints, which he refused to participate with. He feared something would take over him again if he tried to paint.

That damned horse, and that girl who seems to look into my soul. Now here's Shepard, who I don't trust for one bit. I know his kind. My bet is he'll filch the painting and put a bullet through me if he thinks he can get away with it. I think I'm going to have to beat him to it. All this crap is causing my psoriasis to play up. Goddamn it!

He proceeded to scratch to the edge of bleeding. That thought prompted him to check his Beretta. It was fully-loaded, and he had several magazines to hand. He decided that once the painting arrived, it would be time for action. What puzzled him was, whilst he wanted the painting, desperately so, his desire to make a fortune out of it was waning. It no longer sounded so important. That desire was gently fading like stars when the sun arises in the morning sky. True, it was a contemporary work and totally different from other medieval examples found in the *The Book of Miracles*. He wanted to see it, touch it, and own it … but he no longer shared Shepard's vision.

Bower couldn't understand what was happening to him. These revelations were totally uncharacteristic. Mixed up with these thoughts was a feeling of regret that the maid took a hit. He truly wished it had not happened, but hey, a shotgun pointing at a man with a gun was asking for trouble.

He didn't know what to make of his new emotions. But he was certain that Shepard would have to be eliminated from the equation. He had almost served his purpose. He needed to consult George and Man One on the best course of action.

As yet, no video or photograph had arrived. It was time to speed up the process. He made his way into the other room where Martha and the Condesa were seated.

Martha glanced up at him with a look that reminded him of a child being chastised. The Condesa's gaze was contemptuous, as if she was looking out of her grand window to see what the peasants were up to.

It did not go unnoticed and he felt the full force of it.

Shepard and the others were stationed in various corners around the room.

"Where are we at with Lazarus?" Bower spat his words out to Shepard who looked as if he had been half asleep.

"Still waiting for him to send the video. It may take a few more hours yet. There are distances involved."

"I know that. I'm not stupid." He added his next remark to establish his authority in the room. "We don't want to start chopping off fingertips and ears, do we?" He attempted a smirk as he faced the women, but in his secret self, he knew that was never going to happen. He felt a waft of shame pass through him.

What is going on with me?

Martha stared at Maria, calm and unconcerned. "He wouldn't dare. Believe me."

"I don't trust the flashy trashy worm one bit. He'll do it if he must. If he can't, he'll get his goons to do it." Maria pointed at the two meatballs lounging in the background.

Martha shook her head.

Shepard stood next to Bower to emphasise his agreement, and to show off how much taller he was. "Well, when we get the painting, we could chop off a bit here," he held up his little finger, "or a bit there." He tugged on his earlobe. "Then, we can see if there's any truth in this miraculous artwork. If it's as powerful as we have been led to believe, you should heal at once, eh?" He laughed out loud.

Martha and Maria were not amused.

Bower's insides lurched at his words. "We'll cross that bridge when we get to it."

Abbot Louis didn't drive often, and he found the idea of speeding in his ageing, red Seat Estate more than disconcerting. Everything around him, the cars, lorries, and people, moved many times faster than life at the monastery. Additionally, he had to pull over every so often to check his map and ensure he was heading in the right direction. He knew he had to bypass Toledo, then head down to Guadamur and take a turning along a road that descended into a track. He prayed that his slow progress would not endanger lives.

Wrapped up with his implorations, he repeated several *Hail Marys* but refrained from making the sign of the cross, which entailed taking his hands off the wheel.

The hours passed by and every so often, he would glance at the bundle beside him, as if it was a living, breathing thing that was about to chastise him at any moment. Yet, he recalled his experience and from that, he drew comfort and reassurance. God knew his purpose and would guide him to his destination.

He seemed to do just that.

He found the turning with no trouble, and in no time at all, he closed in on the ancient converted monastery. He had arrived at Guadamur. He pulled up outside the main gates and cut the engine.

Total silence, not even the sound of birds ... only the soft wind on his face as he surveyed the hills and undulations that surrounded the ancient structure.

He felt its past, its spirit, as if it whispered in his ear. His life, his aspirations, his love and hope for mankind, opened up and offered themselves to the awaiting hills. Abbot Louis stood still and absorbed it all and let his gaze flow along and follow the contours of the distant hills and tors that surrounded the place. He understood why they had engendered so much mystery and awe.

His brief contemplation was interrupted by the sound of a slight cough that caused him to start. Turning, he was confronted by Brother Baez, aka Brodie, who was standing firm and cradling a shotgun under his arms.

"That's how it started with me ... gazing at those ageless

hills. Father Abbot, they hold countless mysteries, and I can see by your expression that you feel that too." Brodie smiled. "Welcome to Guadamur."

They embraced.

"You have my painting?"

"I have it. Why the weapon?"

"Luciana's predicament could also be ours. We must take no chances or endanger lives. I'm not sure I could use this gun, but it could be a deterrent."

"How is she?"

"She's doing fine. Come, tear yourself away from those mysterious hills. Ned Garcia, world-renowned investigative journalist, is here with us. You'll like him. He's here to expose the guy called Pastor Silas Shepard, who founded the Holy Church of Lazarus."

"Say that name again," interrupted the Abbot, grabbing hold of Brodie's arm.

"Shepard, Pastor Silas Shepard."

"Sweet Jesus Christ!" Louis blew out his cheeks. "That's the very same man who came to mass recently and tried to get a look at our painting. He was wearing a full shoulder holster. I put him off."

"Well, well! We're beginning to realise what we're up against now, although I know others are involved. I worry for Martha and Maria. We have no other choice but to make the exchange."

They talked for a couple of minutes more before heading inside.

As they entered, Brodie saw Luciana and Garcia sitting very close together and chatting in Spanish.

Looking at them, Brodie was suffused with a good feeling.

A smile passed briefly across his troubled features. He made the introductions.

"We don't have a lot of time, Father Abbot, please unwrap the painting." Brodie got ready with the phone camera.

With the greatest of care and reverence, the Abbot removed all the covering and bubble wrap that protected the painting and positioned it upright against the back wall.

It looked unremarkable.

"Is that what everyone's fussing about?" Garcia quipped. "I was expecting rays of light, blaring trumpets and the odd angel or two flapping about. It's weird, to say the least." He held it up close as if expecting a miracle to occur.

Nothing.

Abbot Louis had already told Brodie of his brief encounter back at the monastery. A knowing look passed between the two.

Using his mobile phone, Brodie took several pictures from various distances and angles and recorded a short video of him standing beside the painting. Once satisfied, he showed them to everybody, checked the recipient's number, and pressed the send key.

Brodie and the Abbot could not explain what happened next, as a wall of sound, heard by them alone, penetrated and thrashed through their minds and bodies … like a full-blown orchestra run riot. Covering their ears, they fell to their knees with gritted teeth and eyes shut tight. A power surged through them both like a raging fire.

It transcended the ethers and the mysteries of cyberspace, knowing its mission would not be for much longer. It could grasp the entire universe and those beyond as it journeyed home to know where it was to return to … and come to eternal rest. Evil was, as it always had been, forever present. The stage was almost complete, and the eternal battle was to begin once more. A new champion was about to be born.

Knights were lined in deep solemn rows. Flags fluttered, men shouted, and the animals were edgy as they began a slow advance to an unseen foe.

In desert march or battle's flame
In fortress and in field
Our war cry is thy Holy name
Deus Vult! Beauséant!

The sound and vision subsided. They were shocked but unharmed.

Abbot Louis was speechless and had turned the colour of chalk. Brodie rubbed at his head and wore an angry expression. He began to stand.

"That was how it was seventeen years ago. Will it never leave me alone?"

His sentence was interrupted by a cry from Luciana who was sitting bolt upright. Her eyes were wide in astonishment and her mouth agape. In her outstretched hand, she held a roll of the bloody bandage that had fallen from her bullet wound.

The wound was gone, and her skin was as unblemished as it was before.

CHAPTER 24

Bower had attempted to pick up his brushes but could find no inspiration. He longed to relax and paint, but his mind was full of other things; the Lazarus painting, a white horse, and the rider of which he was becoming increasingly convinced was Martha. He didn't know why he thought that. But they were connected and in the middle of a mystery he could not comprehend. Bower was, indeed, a troubled man.

His musings were interrupted by a call from Shepard.

"They've sent the video and some pictures. I can see the painting clearly."

Bower moved swiftly across to Shepard's outstretched arm and grabbed at the phone. What he saw was not what he had expected. Instead of a wondrous Renaissance style presentation, he saw a work of almost drab sadness – the Spencarian hallmark of life's tragic realities.

He gasped. "My God! It looks awful. Is this some sort of piss take?" He walked over to Maria and brandished the phone in front of her. "Is this really it? If it's not, then there will be consequences, believe me!"

Maria took the phone, stared at the image, touched it and handed it to Martha – who in turn looked hard at it, touched the screen, raised her eyes, and handed the phone back to Bower. "Yes, it is. Not what you were expecting?"

He swiped the screen, as if there could be another work of more magnificence concealed beneath it.

Nothing.

It began as a low hum, barely perceptible in his ears, causing him to shake his head. He looked at the two women and they had their hands pressed to their ears. Maria had a strange smile on her face and Martha looked confused, her face all scrunched up.

Louder it became, on a brain jarring frequency.

"What is that?" he shouted out, now with his hands pressed tightly to his ears.

"You alright there, boss?" George rushed over but what he saw made no sense. Three people had their heads bent, and their faces indicated they were in the grip of some unknown phenomena.

"Get away from me!" Bower had sunk to his knees on the floor, shaking his head.

A White Horse ... bluebells ... shouts and screams ... Deus Vult! Beauséant!

Martha and the Condesa, both strode towards him with swords in hand and seemed to walk right through him.

He opened his eyes as the sound descended into a quivering silence. He saw them both in front of him, also on the floor. They had all seen and heard the same thing.

Shepard said nothing, but he knew an event of some importance had occurred. It was the evidence he needed, to prove to himself that the painting was authentic. The knowledge gave him a secret thrill. The second weapon he had concealed around his ankle, in addition to his shoulder holster, also reassured him. Nobody was going to know about that until it was too late. There was no way he was going to let Bower be its keeper. He needed to act soon. For a fleeting moment, the tantalising vision of his church holding sway across the globe dared to enter his mind.

"You okay, John?" he lamely asked.

Silence.

He glanced at Man One and George, who only shrugged their shoulders.

"My friends are back," the Condesa whispered. "I never realised I missed them so much."

Martha reached out and touched Bower's arm. His pugnacious expression was absent, replaced by one of perplexity. "You saw and heard, didn't you? Now, can you believe?" In her secret mind, there stirred a lingering notion that there was an innate goodness in the man.

"I don't believe a damned thing! Let's have this crappy-looking daubing delivered fast and see where we go from there." He threw the phone across to Shepard. "Get that monk here with that painting. You know what to say."

CHAPTER 25

Luciana's recovery astonished them all.

Garcia hugged her hard. "It's impossible! One minute you're in pain with a jagged flesh wound and then a second later it's as if nothing has happened. How?"

Luciana looked equally dumbstruck. She was unable to stop rubbing and examining where the wound had been. "God be praised! Christ be praised! Hail Mary, full of grace…" She repeated the words several times, making the sign of the cross each time.

Brodie and the Abbot exchanged glances. They knew how, and both turned to look at the painting. It had a faint but diminishing glow around it.

"Holy Mary," whispered the Abbot. "I actually witnessed a miracle." He fell to his knees, bent his head and began a fervent prayer.

Brodie registered no emotion. He had seen its power before and it was, in some ways, a product of himself … but divinely inspired. He was more worried about his daughter and

Maria.

Stepping backwards, he gathered the material that had been wrapped around the painting. As he did, the phone rang. Everybody went quiet. They knew who it must be.

Brodie snatched the phone. "The painting is here. So, what do you want us to do?"

It was Shepard. "Glad to hear it. Now, we want you to deliver the painting. Alone. Once it's in our hands, the women will be released. No tricks now, mind you. You know what will happen."

"Enough with the threats, Shepard. Those women are more important to me than this painting. We've done what you asked, and I'll deliver it to your location. Where are you?"

"Close to the city of Pamplona. Listen carefully." Shepard gave him clear directions, ensuring there would be no mistake. "You got all that?"

"Got it. I'll be with you sometime tomorrow. It's a long drive."

"It is. Make sure the painting is intact and not switched."

"I understand." The phone went dead before he could enquire about Martha and Maria.

Garcia spoke, "Where are they?"

"The city of running bulls, Pamplona. I'll leave early tomorrow morning. I have a long drive ahead of me."

"I'm coming with you."

"I'm supposed to travel alone."

"I'm not the physical type, but you could do with a bit of backup."

"Okay. Luciana doesn't need us here now. Bring the weapons you found. We might need them."

Luciana did not look happy. "Ned, please be careful. I

would like you back safe."

He gave her a sideways hug. "I'll be back. Don't worry."

"Will we ever see the painting again?" The Abbot looked pained.

"Who knows?" Brodie said. "It has a mind of its own, I believe."

Bower had packed up his easel and his paints. He was now afraid to use them. He could not control what appeared on his canvas. Having no control was an area he was deeply unfamiliar with, and this one was spooky in the extreme.

What concerned him most was the way he seemed to be changing. He almost didn't recognise himself. He was no longer interested in 'ruling the world' with Shepard. Even adding the painting to *The Book of Miracles* had lost its attraction.

I must be going insane. Maybe I have a tumor in my brain.

Bower rationalised ... analysed ... and resisted.

I'm a casino owner, a crook, a hood, a tax evader and criminal for Christ's sake! What am I getting so stupid for? I'm sticking to my original plan. Once Shepard's disposed of, and that crappy little picture performs a documented miracle, then I'll decide what to do next. Religion is not my game!

He called in Man One and George.

They sauntered in with the assured air of a pair who knew they were essential cogs in what could be a greasy business.

"Boss?"

"You two, sit down. I need to discuss things with you.

First, whatever I ask, say or do with those in the other room, are you going to back me up?"

"Haven't we always? What's on your mind?" Man One asked as he proceeded to pick at his teeth with a toothpick.

"I'm thinking of expanding my businesses into other areas."

"Like what?"

"Management ... waste management." He paused for ten seconds. "Am I making myself clear?"

"Cockroach elimination by any chance?" George grinned.

"That comes into it ... yes. I take it you're interested in some promotional opportunities then?"

"When do we start?"

"Soon, I feel. You'll be on special bonuses, you'll be pleased to know. I'll tell you when I'm ready." What Bower said next, surprised him even more. "The ladies out there, I don't want them harmed in any way. You are to protect them at all times. No matter what it takes. Understood?"

Did I just say that? Where did that come from?

The two men looked at each other with raised eyebrows and then back to Bower. "We can do that, boss." George was giving him a funny look.

"I knew I could rely on you. Good. Now, get out and send in the two ladies."

Some minutes later, Martha and the Condesa Maria entered the room, but with Shepard behind them.

Bower sensed an air of suspicion and nervousness emanating from Shepard. He decided to push until his true purpose was revealed. Since the recent events, his dislike and mistrust of the man had increased.

"Sit down, ladies ... but not you." He pointed to Shepard.

"What do you want, Pastor? I didn't ask for you."

"I thought you might need some help."

"You're wrong, I don't. Please go."

"What's going on? I think I have the right to know what you're going to say to them. If it wasn't for me, they wouldn't be here, and you would have never known of them."

"So what? Things are changing around here and what happened when we first met doesn't matter anymore. Now, get out!"

"Now hold on, pal." Shepard had found new courage. "We agreed to act together, and you are clearly not doing so."

Bower experienced an odd calmness. Normally, he would have physically attacked Shepard for contradicting him. He was finding words more effective.

"Perceptive, Pastor. What are you going to do about it?"

Martha and the Condesa looked apprehensively at each other and moved closer to link arms.

"It'll be fine, ladies. You are quite safe unless this bluebottle lands on you." Pointing at Shepard he let out a piercing whistle, and at the same time produced his Beretta.

"Shit!" Shepard turned to go, only to be confronted by George twirling his garrotte and Man One brandishing a pistol. They'd recognised Bower's alarm signal.

"The Pastor here needs to go to the john. Take him there and keep him there until I'm ready. Make sure he doesn't mess himself. I'm not quite ready for a final solution, so hold him there for a while. I still need him. Disarm him also."

They bundled a protesting Silas Shepard out of the room.

"Well, ladies, all we have to do now is wait until the painting arrives and then it can be inspected more closely." He pointed at the Condesa. "You, you've had experience with this painting. What was it like? I mean, how does it work?"

Maria's natural haughtiness had returned. "You really are a *tonto ignorante!* I was told not to suffer ignorant fools gladly, but in your case, I have only the utmost contempt."

He half rose towards her, but Martha was quicker. She stepped in between them.

"No! Leave her. She is who she is, and she is my dear friend. If you're going to hit anybody, let it be me."

"Okay, okay." He held out his hands, palms facing her. "I'll let it be." He sat back down, but with an expression as tight as a knot. "I'm just trying to find out what's going on around here, okay? I'm in the dark, and you two know more about this than I do. I just need to know the truth about this. Ever since I got involved in this, strange things have been happening around me. Let me tell you what."

Martha sat back down next to Maria. "We're listening." She reached for Maria's hand.

Bower began to relate his story, commencing with his meeting with Shepard at the casino, and how for a reason he could not explain, he began to experience things that were beyond his control. The more he spoke, the deeper it went. By the time he reached the part where he had the vision at the bridge, he realised that he had become …

Powerless.

Maria appeared as if in a trance. Her eyes were closed and her body slack.

What was more unnerving was that Martha was saying his words even before he spoke them.

"I sat and looked at the bridge…"

She had said it two words ahead of him. Not only this time, but throughout his discourse.

She's in my mind.

Yes, I'm there. I know you, John D. Bower. I know you well.

"Stop! STOP!" he yelled and held up his hands "That's enough!"

He felt her withdraw.

"What's happening? What have you been doing? Is this a goddamned trick or what?" He demanded with irritation. A deathly pallor like molten wax shone from his face.

"I don't know. It just happened. It was as if I had always known you … from the moment I first saw you." Maria opened her eyes and looked at Martha.

"You have it … as Brodie and I have it." Maria turned to Bower. "You too will know it, for in your heart there is goodness. Just let it out."

"What a load of crap. I didn't become as rich as I am by being a goody two shoes – the opposite in fact. I've had enough of this rubbish." He checked his watch. "That painting should be here soon and then we will really see, won't we? I can't believe that a shitty piece of work like that can hold any special powers." He leered at the Condesa but could not bring himself to look at Martha. There was something there. He knew it wasn't the money, and in his quiet self, it jabbed at him like an aching tooth.

CHAPTER 26

T hey had travelled ten miles in silence before Garcia
spoke.

"What do we do when we get there?" he asked in a
flat tone of voice, as if scared of hearing the answer.

"No idea," Brodie replied. "I promised Father Abbot I
would do everything I can to return with the painting, but
that's number three on my list. My main concern is my daughter and the Condesa."

"What are these guys going to do when they get hold of
it?"

"I suppose they'd want to see if it's authentic. They'll ask
for a demonstration, one way or another. That's the problem.
It doesn't work like that. It can't be expected to perform miracles on command!" Brodie sighed. "If there's rough stuff, I
don't expect you to get involved."

"I'm not supposed to be here, remember?"

"Too well."

Time passed by, as did numerous small towns and villages

before they stopped once for a deserved break of thirty minutes. The closer they got, the faster Brodie drove. His tension rose.

Garcia had the directions Shepard had supplied and there was no problem with them.

"The only mistake they've made is directing us straight to the main door. They obviously don't intend to stay around too long, because they know that once we get out of there, if we ever do, the first thing we'll do is call the police."

"We can't do that." Brodie snorted. "Who would believe a story like we've got? Certainly not a hard-nosed policeman."

Garcia had to agree. He consulted the map. "We're about twenty miles off our next turning. It's a few miles short of Pamplona's city centre, but the road should lead us to the address he's given us. It's a couple of miles long.

Eighteen minutes later, they made the turning. Without warning, Brodie brought the vehicle to a sudden halt and killed the engine.

"What are you doing that for?" Garcia exclaimed.

He got no answer.

Brodie's eyes were shut, with his head tilted back, and his face was the colour of a weathered gravestone.

Garcia whispered, "Are you…?" Something stopped him. Looking closer at Brodie, he guessed the man was in the middle of something he had yet to understand. Either he was praying to God Almighty or he was out of it, in another realm or place known only to him. The entire episode had been so bizarre since he came upon it, he now believed anything was possible.

Right then, Brodie's face muscles began to twitch, and his

lips moved but with no sound coming from them. Brodie then, without opening his eyes, placed his hands over his ears and shook his head from side to side, not violently, but in time with something Garcia couldn't hear.

Then, Garcia clearly heard the words…

The time is near. She sits on *The White Horse of Uffington. Deus Vult! Beauséant!*

Brodie's eyelids fluttered and in an instant, he was back into full consciousness.

Brodie turned to Garcia. "Ned, I'm sorry you saw that, but you should get used to this when you're around me. I can sense it as it's about to happen. I know now that my daughter was meant to be here, and that White Horse was the messenger between us all. It's carried us here one by one. What's ahead of us, I still can't say. That's the way it works. A vision here, a clue there, but it doesn't reveal all." He sighed. "But we both know there will be danger. Martha is, somehow, at the centre of it all."

"I understand. In fact, I think I understand everything. What happened back there with Luciana said it all, believe me. What do we now?"

"We get to the address. When we do, you stay here and out of sight. I'll go in with the painting. We don't know what will happen next, but with the kind of people we're dealing with, it's not going to be good."

Brodie fired up the engine again and they headed to their rendezvous.

Bower no longer felt certain of what he was doing or why. He was a man divided. Part of him was the self he recognised; the man with drive, ambition, a tough, rough hustler in life who had made it good by fair means and foul. He'd done whatever was required to succeed and gone where many would fear to tread. He had created a chilling yet respected persona. He'd lived with that image and reputation for as long as he could remember, and it had suited his aspirations and outlook on life. Yet, beneath all that, he had always felt incomplete. Recent events had highlighted that area of his life. Uncertainty had never bothered him before, but now, it had him by the collar. An alter ego was manifesting, and he had no idea how his familiar persona would handle it. He understood rough stuff, violence and aggression. They had been forever part of his life.

He forced himself to look across to Martha, who was, as usual, staring back at him and into his very soul. *Christ, she's only a teenager yet she makes me feel ashamed. It's like she's trying to get into my mind again.*

"Quit looking at me, will you?" he snapped, completely aware of his rising discomfiture.

Martha said nothing and averted her gaze.

"What are your plans when the painting gets here?" the Condesa asked. "Shoot us, cut pieces off us or something else?"

"We'll sort that out when the time arrives. As you've experienced its alleged powers before, you might just be the perfect candidate."

She turned away from him.

A white horse passed across his mind and seated on it was Martha, her hair flowing behind her, carrying a sword and wearing the cross of a Crusader.

The vision passed in a flash, causing him to gasp out loud, "What in God's name was that?"

"Are you okay, Mr. Bower?" Martha asked, although the look she gave him was far from innocent. "If I didn't know better, I'd say you look as if you've just seen a ghost."

He stood up. "Cut the funny stuff. I don't know what's going on here, but whatever it is I don't believe it." He made a quick check on his Beretta and buttoned his shirt. "You two stay here and don't move. I'm going to check on the others."

Once outside the room, he took a deep breath, counted down from ten, and walked to the bathroom area where Man One and George were keeping watch on Shepard.

The scene inside the bathroom was one of amusement. It took his mind off the strange goings-on in his life. Shepard was seated on the toilet and trussed up with towels, his arms bound behind him and a wedge of gauze stuffed into his mouth from which muffled sounds could be heard. He also had a very black and red eye. Man One was lying in the empty bath and George was sitting on the vanity stool reading a horror comic book, *Tales From the Crypt*. Shepard's Smith & Wesson, with its holster, was visible on the glass shelf.

"You two have been having fun?"

"Yes, boss. He got a bit lively."

"No hard feelings, eh Silas? Untie him, guys, we should be having a visitor soon."

They unknotted him and the gag was removed.

"You scumbag arseholes." Shepard growled, shook his head and lunged for his holster.

"Whoa there, Pastor! Nice and easy now." Bower's Beretta was in his hand in a flash. "We don't want any mishaps, do we?"

Shepard knew when he was outnumbered. He tried to

calm himself but stared daggers at Bower. "You two shits haven't heard the last of this. I promise you that."

"Yeah, we're shaking in our boots. Aren't we, George?"

George pretended to tremble in fear and Bower began laughing.

"Let's go and await our expected guest."

They both saw the house appear about a hundred yards ahead.

"It's time for you to duck down on the back seat, but before you do that, have you got Maria's gun?"

"It's here." Garcia handed him the small pistol and Brodie made sure it was fully loaded.

"I don't know how long this is going to take or what they have in mind for me and the ladies. You may have a long wait. Don't get too curious, okay? You're not in their league and I don't want you getting hurt."

"I'm no hero. I'll stay here and keep my eyes open."

"Good. That's settled. Well, it's now or never." He took a large lungful of air, exhaled, and without thinking said, "May God go with me."

As Garcia moved to the back seat, Brodie stepped out of the car, with the painting clutched tight. He was deeply aware of everything about him. For a moment, he stood motionless and absorbed the warmth of the sun beating down on him. He could hear birds calling as he began the short walk towards the premises. All his senses were on high alert, and the beat of his heart struck heavily in his chest. He hoped they wouldn't conduct a body search.

The stones crunched beneath his feet and he could hear the water from a garden fountain splashing down without enthusiasm.

Butterflies swirled in his stomach. Sweat appeared on his brow, and he could taste the saltiness of it on his lips. He attempted to calm himself but heard only the pounding of his heart.

He reached the brown, wooden door with its massive iron ring knocker, and without waiting, gave it three hefty raps.

The door swung open and the frame of Man One, filling the space like a wide-open barn door, confronted him. In his hand, he held a pistol. "You're expected. Get inside and walk forwards." He stood aside and waved Brodie in.

Here we go. Calmness descended upon him and all tension left. Up ahead was another room. He was ushered through a hallway and through an antiquated Spanish kitchen.

"In there," Man One barked, his gun pointing at the back of Brodie's neck.

Brodie opened the door and what he saw gave him no surprise. Bower and his other goon occupied the centre of the room. Shepard, looking dishevelled and swollen, sat slumped in a chair. At the far end stood both Martha and the Condesa. He could clearly read the situation.

"Dad!" Martha cried out. "I'm okay! Are you?"

Maria held her back before she could rush to Brodie. "Not yet, Martha," she whispered.

"I'm fine!" He moved towards her, but the heavy hand of Bower pushed him back.

"They're both safe. You can chit-chat later. Is that the painting?"

"Yes." He pulled back the covering.

"Stand it on that table. Shepard, get your arse over here now. Everybody stand back."

When Shepard made no move, Bower went over and dragged him to the table. "There it is, Pastor. What are you waiting for, man? It's your baby. Uncover it and be careful."

Brodie glanced at Maria and their eyes met. Maria simply shook her head. He closed his eyes and her faint whisper entered his mind. *Deus Vult! Nos ad id pervenit!*

He agreed and gave a small nod, "Yes, we will prevail."

Martha held her head in her hands. She could make out voices in her head but couldn't understand what was being said.

Shepard reached over to the painting, and with care, removed the covering to reveal *The Raising of Lazarus*.

There were no trumpets or angels, no ethereal lighting, dazzling bursts of sunlight or heavenly choirs.

It was plain and simple.

It did not need pomp or glamour. It had an unassuming power of its own. The room went silent as if anticipating a miracle.

Nothing.

Both Shepard and Bower looked deflated. Shepard placed his hand on the canvas.

Nothing.

"How can this be miraculous? It's a phoney," he declared.

Bower could not bring himself to touch it. That, he couldn't explain.

Maria's voice interjected. "It is not a fake. I can testify to that."

Brodie added, "So can I. You shot and wounded the Condesa's maid, Luciana. I saw it as we all did. What none of you here know was that later, when she gazed at the painting, her wound immediately healed. It was as if the bullet had never gone through her." He turned to Maria and her face had become a picture of joyous wonderment. She held her hand over her mouth, before crossing herself hurriedly many times.

"Is this true, Brodie, or are you attempting to fob us off?"

"It's true. So, what are you going to do now? You have your picture and I want my daughter back and the Condesa with her. I've kept my side of the bargain and done everything you asked."

There was silence.

"I need proof of its abilities."

"I've just given you that and I don't lie. If you're expecting it to deliver a miracle on command, it doesn't work like that. Belief and goodness have a lot to do with it."

"So … you have to be a believer for it to work?" Bower asked.

"Not necessarily, but it helps, I guess."

"I've forever been fascinated by these sorts of stories and this is the most compelling I have seen or heard of. I need to see it work. Who are we going to choose then? We have you, the artist of this weird work … we have her," he pointed at Maria, "and we have the Pastor here. He's a churchman and he's got a puffed-up eye. He sounds like a likely candidate with a ready-made condition. Or maybe, we need something more serious like another bullet wound." He produced his Beretta and waved it at them all, as George and Man One, on cue, moved into position beside him.

"You're making a mistake, Bower. As I said, it can't be made to work by your command. It chooses its moments and could be dormant for years. If you think you can force its hand, you're very much mistaken. It won't happen. It needs to be revered, even loved, and I don't think you're capable of that … are you?"

The simplicity of Brodie's statement unsettled Bower. He didn't know what to do next.

They stared at each other in a dance of undefined assessment.

Everybody was looking at Bower.

The sharp blast of a pistol shot shattered the stalemate.

Man One, with blood spurting from behind his ear, hit the floor like a blacksmith's anvil.

Shepard's voice bellowed across the room. "All of you stand still, exactly where you are, and place your hands above your heads! Anyone who moves even a finger will get the same treatment. Bower and George, drop your weapons. I mean it. Do it now and do it slowly."

Shepard was holding a small Colt Mustang pistol and stood in a classic Weaver firing stance. "I won't ask you again. Do it … NOW!"

Two guns clattered to the floor and hands were raised.

Brodie looked across to Martha and the Condesa. Martha looked shaken and Maria's expression was unreadable.

He heard the Condesa's voice in his head.

Don't do anything.

I won't yet.

"Kick them over to me," Shepard demanded, and George kicked the guns over to him.

Keeping everybody covered, Shepard retrieved and pocketed the weapons.

Bower blazed with a cold vicious rage. An electric charge

zapped through his blood and bones. "Where did you get that, you slimy scumbag?"

"You didn't search me as well as you should have. It was strapped to my ankle." Shepard smirked.

Brodie spoke. "I can guarantee if you take this painting it won't work for you, or anybody else who has anything to do with you and your phoney, so called, Holy Church of Lazarus."

"It doesn't have to, but maybe it just will, on occasions. That's a chance I'm prepared to take. You did say it could well do so. Trust me, I have no shortage of people who would attest to its power. Shame about Man One down there, it hasn't worked for him, has it?" He continued, gesturing towards the Condesa. "You and the old bat there know more about this than anybody else alive. You painted it. She was healed by it. I heard there were earlier versions. What happened and where are they?"

"They – as far as this world is concerned – self-destruct when the time is right, and a new artist is ready. Social and global circumstances come into play. There has been no way of knowing. It could take centuries … it could take a few years. That's the way it has always been since Annas Zevi painted the first ever depiction of the actual event. Each work represents the age and time in which we live."

"You mean it could dissolve or go up in smoke?"

"That's what I mean. Can we cut this crap and do something about that man on the floor?"

"Nothing you can do. He's dead. God be praised!" He turned to Bower who had his eyes closed. "You praying or something, Bower?"

Bower could not hear him.

Brodie furtively glanced over at the ladies to see if they'd noticed. Martha was staring at Bower and Maria was staring back at him.

Communication.

It was hot and sticky sitting inside the car and attempting to keep out of sight. Garcia's patience was not endless. He had heard a gunshot but nothing after that. He had no idea what had happened in the house. He had clear instructions, *do not call the police whatever happens, nor come near the house.* There were no screams or shouts or signs of anybody moving around. Clearly, something bad had happened. For a few minutes, he considered his options. He could sit forevermore in the car, or he could creep up and maybe peek through a window. The thought that he could get shot or injured played a pivotal role in his mind. *C'mon, Garcia, grow some balls! This is not a time to tremble in the back seat of a car. Get in there and see if you can be of use!*

With caution, he inched the door open and picked up the shotgun, aware that he had never fired one before. It had more power than a pistol.

Bent low, he scuttled from bush to bush and inched his way to the back end of the building. He could only guess where they would be … or what he would see. He peered around the corner edging and ducked lower than the window level. Raising his head slowly, he could see he was looking into the kitchen area and it was empty. He moved along further to the next set of windows which were much larger. He raised his head again, hoping he wouldn't be seen. One furtive glance and he knew instantly what had happened.

A man was down, and everybody else was standing with their hands raised. Brodie and the ladies seemed unharmed. *What am I supposed to do? One man had a gun and I don't know how to use this thing!* He lowered himself to the ground, trying to come up with a plan.

Crawling back to the kitchen door entrance, he tried the handle. It wasn't locked, and he pushed it open with caution. He prayed it didn't squeak. Luckily, it swung open with silent ease.

Heart thumping.

Stomach churning.

He was a doorway away from God knows what!

Hesitation.

Brodie's mind was on the pistol he had concealed on himself, but any move to reach it would be fatal. Shepard was not shy in putting bullets into people. It was as easy as double-crossing his partner. What happened next startled him.

From the corner of his eye, he saw the door opening, and the figure of Garcia emerging from behind it … and he was holding the shotgun.

I told him to stay put!

Shepard hadn't seen him and had grabbed hold of a terrified Martha around the neck. Pressing the barrel of his gun against her head, he forced her to hold the painting.

"Keep your hands in the air. Now, no heroics or fancy

work or she will be the worse for wear."

Martha did not put up a fight. In one stroke, Shepard had neutralised them all; her father, her mentor, and Bower who had some sort of link with her. George only acted under orders, and Bower was not giving any. None of them wanted her to come to any harm.

"I'm leaving now. Don't try to follow. I've got more than I want. If you thought for one moment, Bower, that I was going to let you run things and boss me about ... you got that really wrong. No way would I want you pulling strings. No deal ... no way!" He began to back off towards the door, when he caught sight of Garcia pointing a shotgun in his direction. His surprise was one hundred per cent. He didn't hesitate.

Before Garcia could speak, Shepard roared at him. "If you fire that, she's as good as dead! Drop it, whoever you are!" He hauled Martha directly in front of himself as a human shield.

"Ned!" Brodie bellowed. "For God's sake, drop it."

Bower held George back. "It's Fatso! Leave it! She mustn't be hurt!" For a brief second, he thought he could jump Shepard. But the situation was too dangerous.

Garcia lowered the shotgun.

"Empty it now!"

Garcia, looking confused, snapped open the barrels, allowing two cartridges to roll across the floor. He dropped the weapon and raised his hands. *Nice move, Ned.*

Shepard continued to walk backwards towards the door, holding Martha in a tight grip in front of him, with the painting in her hands. "No one needs to get hurt. But if any of you show yourselves at the door, I'll drop you and she will go with you. Got it? Let us leave."

"Got it," Bower spoke first.

"If you so much as bruise her..." Brodie stood upright with fists clenched tight as piano wire.

Shepard ignored them and reached the door, opened it with one hand, and inched out into the sunlight and towards his car.

They were powerless.

Brodie reached for the Condesa's pistol in his belt. He grabbed it, and without knowing why, handed it to Bower.

Bower didn't even look at him. He pushed his arm away. "He'll kill her. No. Forget it for now."

With those words in his mind, a startled and fearful Brodie handed the gun back to Maria, who was standing so still she looked as though she had turned into a pillar of salt.

In all four directions the wind blew ... one for Brodie, one for Martha, another for Maria and one more for Bower. Their message was clear, strong, and reassuring for each of them.

The spell broke.

Martha crashed back through the door in a bundle of jitters

Brodie rushed to her. She was unharmed but in a state of shock. "Dad, I'm okay! I'm safe. He's gone with the painting. What do we do?" She began to shake.

"I've no idea." Brodie stroked her hair and spoke softly, trying to calm her down. "First of all, we have a body here we have to do something about."

Bower, uncertain of where and how he fitted into this scenario, feeling like a fart in an astronaut's space suit, spoke out, "Leave Man One to me. We've no weapons, but we will soon." He glanced at Martha, relieved that she was unharmed. He didn't know why, but he had begun to accept that there was something between them. A white horse that galloped as fast as the four winds.

Somehow, someway, they were connected. All his secret studies and interests in Biblical mysteries and anomalies had come down to this, and in a manner he could not explain. Bower slumped into the sofa, overwhelmed by a force he could not truly comprehend.

George sat down beside him, faithful as ever, and put his arm around him. "Boss, what's happening?"

"I don't know but stay with me." He closed his eyes.

Brodie stood firm with the Condesa Maria beside him, as The White Horse galloped onwards, ridden by the unmistakeable figure of Martha. It was closer, but for now, it was a gap too far.

Bower surrendered.

The Condesa Maria and Brodie knew. They had become as one. Martha was part of it too. Barriers had finally fallen. All the players were in place.

Garcia looked at them all in a mood of expectancy, as if something miraculous was about to occur.

Shepard sped away and his car vanished in a billowing cloud of dust.

CHAPTER 27

Uffington, UK

The sound of the phone ringing gave her a start. Ulla had been expecting a call hours ago and anxiety had her in its grip.

"Yes? Is that you, Martha?" She gabbled out in a hurried gush.

"Ma, it's me. Are you okay?"

"I'm fine. Where are you and Brodie? What's been happening?"

"Sit down, Mum. It's a long story and yes, we are okay … just. The painting has been stolen." Martha then began a lengthy explanation of all the events including the shooting and her near abduction.

"That accursed painting will be the death of us all. As long as you are safe, that's all that matters. I want you to come home. Let me speak to Brodie, please."

Martha handed the phone to her father.

"Brodie?"

"Ulla, we're all fine, but the painting is with that Pastor Shepard. This damned episode won't leave us alone and we are now all caught up in it. Martha won't leave unless I do, but I can't, and you know why."

"I'm coming over. I must see you both. You can't imagine what it's like here for me. I'd rather be there with you."

"Ulla, don't come here, please. The worst is not over yet. Listen and believe me. I will bring Martha back safely, I promise. But please, I beg you, stay put."

They continued talking for another hour, comparing recent events with their experiences in the past.

Finally, with a mutual yearning for each other, they said their goodnights.

Maria, Brodie and Martha were all looking at him, like the scene from John Wyndham's, 'The Midwich Cuckoos.' Bower avoided their communal gaze.

Meanwhile, George had rolled up Man One's body and taken it to his car for disposal later. This was not a matter for the police. He returned with a mop and bucket and proceeded to wash away the drying-up blood. "What next, boss? That bastard's gonna pay for this!"

"I don't know. Do something decent with Man One. Whatever you want to do, you're free to do so. Go back to Vegas, if you want. You have enough funds to do anything you wish. Things have changed here and I'm all over the place, as you may have noticed."

There was a lengthy silence as George sat down beside Bower. "Never did like the food here, boss. No burgers to start with." He patted Bower's shoulders and stood. "I'll see you back in Vegas."

"Keep people in order for me while I'm away, okay?"

"That's what I do best, isn't it?"

"It is. Have a safe trip."

George nodded to the others and left.

They all sat in silence for a while before Brodie retrieved the shotgun and shells and approached Bower.

"It's about time you told us what's been happening here. You're as much to blame for our predicament as that other idiot who had just stolen a priceless artefact. You must have an idea where Shepard's heading. Why are you hanging about here? You could catch up with him."

Bower said nothing. He was lost in his thoughts.

Martha crossed the room and placed herself between them. "No, Dad, no. Whether we like it or not, I believe he is part of this. The four of us … we've all been brought here. Our horse has carried us all, including him." She pointed to Bower. "He's had the same visions we've experienced. Doesn't that strike you as strange? It's compelling for me. If you think about it, Dad, three of us here have plenty in common – we are all artists, painters, and we've all been seeing The White Horse, the bluebells, and receiving the messages." She turned to Bower, whose face had paled, and every ounce of his previous confidence appeared to have left him.

"You are here for a reason, which I feel will unfold very

soon. As soon as I saw you, something flashed into my mind about you and I knew deep within me that you were not capable of harming us. You've played the villain, the tough guy, but I knew it was all an act to be the man you imagined yourself to be. You are meant to be here. We need to talk about this." Martha pleaded, hoping he would open up, or maybe help them find the painting.

"What about me?" Garcia cut into the escalating atmosphere. "I'm not an artist, nor have I had visions like you. But I know I saw a miracle."

Before Brodie answered, he looked at Maria.

She nodded.

"Ned." There was a lengthy pause.

"Ned..."

"What?"

"We need you. You have a part to play here too. Scribes have existed since time began. Without them, we would know nothing. That's why you're here. To witness whatever will come to pass." Garcia scoffed, but Brodie continued. "Your presence is as important as ours. The days of quills and vellum have gone. We now have smart phones, laptops, desktops and you can communicate from any place in the world. You must record everything you see and hear, no matter how bizarre it may appear. Besides, the world needs to know what's been happening over the last of almost two decades. Sooner or later, if we don't catch up with Shepard, something unpleasant will happen. Already, he has an army of adherents who are more than willing to serve him and take on board all the rubbish he will ask them to believe. His wealth will grow and by then, who knows what he'll do?"

Bower stood up and looked around at them all. When he

spoke, his voice was shaky. "I don't understand why I've been brought into this, but since the event at the bridge and in here when I tried to paint, things have not been the same for me. Let me repeat them so your scribe can record what I say. After I'm done, all of you had better relate your experiences. I also need to know."

He spoke at length and when he was finished he was unable to prevent the words *Deus Vult* from spouting from his lips.

"Where the hell did that come from?"

They all knew right then that Bower was about to embark on a long journey.

CHAPTER 28

I t was a long drive – three hundred and ninety kilometres and over four hours at the wheel. He was glad to
get away. Events had escalated way beyond what he
had envisaged. His relationship with Bower was finished.
Something had happened to the man, and he wasn't behaving
normally. Bower was now an unwanted usurper.

Shepard felt he had been more than wise. He had noticed
Bower wobbling in religious uncertainty, which he had been
unable to pin down. Making money was of paramount importance and the Holy Church of Lazarus was the key. Uncertainty had no place in his schemes.

He checked his mirrors constantly to make sure he was
not being followed.

Relax.

He was pleased at the way he had thought the whole
thing through. He was doing okay. He didn't need Bower's
endorsement or money. The guy was an obstacle to what he
wanted to achieve. If anything, it was the other way around.

From his observations, Bower had totally underestimated what he, Shepard, was capable of. He had foreseen events and had made plans to deal with it. He had not been idle, but he encouraged that perception.

His USSS training had been more than useful. He knew the value of being prepared for all outcomes. In his spare time, he had purchased a VIA-2 tag that would allow him to cross the A-2 *carretera de cuoto* (motorway) without having to stop at the toll gates. Speed was of the utmost importance. He had sped from Pamplona, bypassed nearby Zaragoza, and was now heading to Madrid to pick up the signs to the airport. The drive down the A-2 had been smooth and uneventful. He had escaped, and Bower and the others had no idea where he was heading.

The flight from Madrid's Barajas Airport to Jerusalem Airport was clear and open, free from any suspicious terrorist activities. Shepard was booked on it. From there, he had made plans to reach Bethany, fifteen stadia from the Holy City with a view of the Temple Mount. Close by, he planned to visit the reputed Tomb of Lazarus at al-Eizariya, traditionally identified as the Biblical village of Bethany situated in the West Bank. The painting he carried with him was to be instrumental in a major upsurge in his followers, to keep 'the sea of love rolling in,' as he referred to cash contributions. The major question on his mind was whether the painting would be miraculous or not. It seemed authentic, judging from the stories of those fools. But he needed a miracle that will be witnessed by a lot of people.

An idea began formulating in his mind.

Bower sat alone and felt as empty as a church on a Monday morning. There were moments of clarity and moments of desolation. He could not forget that he had held them all at bay with his two men and their guns, and that the maid Luciana had been shot. Now, there wasn't a mark on her. *My God, what was I doing?*

Bower was unable to stop weeping. He experienced a wash of shame that was new to him. "Forgive me. Forgive me, please." His fleshy face trembled.

All present went quiet and still. Seeing a hard man in the throes of redemption was not a sight often seen.

Martha approached him. "John D. Bower, I know you well, and I know you sense this. Don't fight it. Surrender to whatever is happening to you. You are being summoned for a purpose greater than yourself."

Brodie was surprised at the maturity and confidence of his young daughter. Maria held him back as he half-rose from his seat. "No, Brodie. She's moving beyond us. Let it be."

Bower quivered like an aspen tree in the wind. There were no tough guys around him, no CCTV screens, no money-rattling tills, no people he could punch at or roar at – he was alone and exposed. In a few illuminating minutes, he realised that he had lived a lie. His true self lay elsewhere … something he had always suspected.

For minutes on end, nothing was said.

"No, I don't believe this. It's a load of hogwash." Bower resumed his tough expression.

"Well … what're you going to do? Stay here with us and

help us trace what you originally came for – or run back to your money and the life you have up to now been most happy with?"

"That phoney scumbag has double crossed me and when I find him, he'll pray to his God he wished he hadn't."

"So, by that … are you going to help us find him?"

"He could be anywhere or hightailing it back to the States."

Garcia interrupted. "I don't think he'll do that. I've seen the likes of him over the years. My bet is he's going to be lying low for a while and gathering his followers. He's got the means to draw down as much cash as he needs, and my research showed that his Holy Church of Lazarus already has a considerable number of supporters."

"Leave me alone, you lot. I need to rest and think about what I'm going to do next. I need to paint something and it's not going to be some stupid white horse either. My paints are in my car. I suggest you all choose a room and get some rest, too. Then we can decide what to do." He walked away.

"He's right," Maria added. "We all need a break to gather our thoughts. I'm going to rest up for a while."

"Great. That'll give me time to update my report and speak to my editor." Garcia left to get his laptop.

"I'll do some sketches, Dad. What about you? Maybe John has some extra materials we can use."

"Not a bad idea. It's been a while since I picked up a pen or brush. Who knows? We might get some inspiration."

Martha followed Bower to his car. "John, do you have an extra easel or two or some sketch pads we can use? It'll help pass the time." She smiled at him.

Bower looked up from his trunk, surprised. "Why yes, I

do. I always keep my painting stuff here, so I can work wherever I want to. Help yourself." He gestured towards the trunk, returning her smile. He could refuse her nothing.

Martha peered into the trunk and was filled with joy. It was an artist's dream. There were painting and sketching supplies, even watercolours. *Clearly, this man loved to do this.*

A couple of minutes later, they walked into the house carrying easels, pads, brushes and paints.

Jerusalem

That the painting had worked before, Shepard had no doubt. The same was true in Lourdes. Ever since pilgrims and the sick – by the millions – had visited the grotto, there had been sixty-nine healings officially declared as genuine, lasting miracles. The cures by the paintings of Lazarus – since the year he had been raised from the dead – had never been counted. Who knows how many have occurred since then? From this painting alone, he could testify to two miracles ... the cranky Condesa and her maid, Luciana. A good percentage that sure as hell put Lourdes to shame.

If it didn't work, he reckoned he'd have little difficulty in finding people who would be more than willing to attest to its authenticity. With some gentle lubrication, of course. But, if people could witness an actual miracle ... Shepard sighed at the thought. He could almost see the number of people clamoring to join his church.

First, he had to absorb the atmosphere of Bethany and the Tomb of Lazarus. It wasn't going to be easy, but there had to be a way. This pilgrimage site could exceed Lourdes if played with care and detail. Of that, he had no doubt.

Bower was now history. Shepard could succeed on his own, as he had for most of his life.

It was blisteringly hot and the heat oppressive. Shepard checked in at the American Colony Hotel. After a much-needed rest, he began plotting out his agenda for the coming days. The first item he attended to was to transfer funds from the church account to his personal account.

He ordered some food from room service and as he waited, he scoured the fat information pack in his room. He soon found what he was looking for … details of how to get to the Tomb of Lazarus. What disturbed him was that he hadn't considered the on-going conflict between Israel and Palestine. A very high security wall had been built to separate the two. The area surrounding the tomb was now under the jurisdiction of the Palestinian authorities, and a Palestinian taxi driver would be needed to visit the site or the use of public transport.

That put a damper on his plans.

CHAPTER 29

Maria slept on in one of the guest bedrooms, her advancing years succumbing to the assaults of time and longevity. A hush had descended on the property as if awaiting a sign or signal.

Martha was aware of its presence. As she began her sketch, she knew that this was not normal. She looked to Brodie. His face was contorted in concentration – of things discovered yet unknown. His arms were moving swiftly across his paper.

Outside, the wind intensified.

She closed her eyes and was assailed by visions at once.

Crucem Sanctam Subiit.

He carries the Holy Cross.

Deus Vult!

Omnes habitatores Lazarum.

Lazarus lives in all men.

Using charcoal, pencil, pen and ink, she drew exactly what came into her mind.

Brodie seemed to follow and had lapsed into a flurry of sweeping strokes and marks, as if possessed by an outside force.

The spell broke.

They moved around to look at what the other had produced.

"My God!" Brodie clasped at his daughter.

She responded and held him tight.

They were identical.

The easel seemed unwilling as he erected its structure. Once in place, he sat down with a heavy sigh. He felt as if he was being absorbed, taken over in some way. His casinos had no connection with him or his current predicament. It felt a million miles away.

The killing of Man One had quietly shocked him. So much so that he offered up a prayer even in his disbelief. He used Voltaire, changing the wording very slightly…

"Oh my God, if there is a God, save his soul, if he has a soul."

It pacified him that he was able to offer a prayer for his dead comrade.

Staring at the blank canvas, he felt the full extent of his corrupt life parade through his senses and the neurons of his memory. He reached for his brushes and filled his palette with different colours. *Please, no more white horses.*

He dipped a brush into the colour nearest to him.

Black.

Specks of light and of red.

A dark and ancient structure began to form, and he had no idea what he was creating.

Working at speed, another hour passed by before he had rendered what was in his mind. He stepped away from what he had painted, not certain if he had been responsible for it. At first, he could not identify what he was looking at, but it became apparent as his body and mind returned to normal.

I have to show this to Martha!

He didn't know why he had to show her ... but she was part of it.

Shepard regarded al-Eizariya with dismay. It looked as if God had abandoned it. Everything was small and hovel-like, not a place where something grand and wonderful could happen. Tourists sat everywhere, and it was not looking good.

He found it uninspiring.

The presence of a thirty-foot high wall behind the tomb – separating the Israelis and the Palestinians – increased his gloom. This was beginning to look less and less appropriate as a place to present his miracle to the adoring masses. It would probably not be allowed, nor was the location suitable at all.

He decided to check out the tomb to see if it had a redeeming value.

The entrance to the tomb was down via a flight of uneven rock-cut steps from the street. As it was described in 1896, there were twenty-four steps from the then-modern street level, leading to a square chamber serving as a place of prayer, from which more steps led to a lower chamber believed to have been the tomb of Lazarus.

Shepard could barely move, and the miniature space made it necessary for him to crawl.

Three steps connected the antechamber with the inner burial chamber (which measured a little more than two square metres in size). It contained three funerary niches (*arcosolia*), now mostly hidden by the Crusader masonry. According to tradition, Jesus was standing in this antechamber when he called Lazarus from the grave.

Shepard found himself disbelieving that a man could be buried in such a tiny space. How on earth was he able to stand and walk out?

Once out of the tomb and standing in bright sunlight, Shepard knew for certain that this was not the place to present his painting to the world.

He could hear a guide describing the raising of Lazarus as the last miracle before the crucifixion.

"Lazarus, as a friend of Jesus, was also under threat and was forced to flee from the authorities and certain death because his story was spreading throughout the region ... and as a friend of Jesus, many Jews were rallying around him."

What the guide said next got Shepard excited.

"According to ancient Cypriot tradition, Lazarus went to Kition, Larnaca, Cyprus, where later, he was met by the Apostles Paul and Barnabas on their missionary journey through Cyprus and was ordained by them as the first Bishop of Kition.

Cypriot tradition was not the only source of information about Lazarus. The discovery of his already ancient sarcophagus was made in 890 AD.

Lazarus had a unique claim to fame. He was buried twice. Here at Bethany and a second time beneath a tiny church on the site of the present Ayios Lazaros church in Larnaca. His sarcophagus is inscribed with these words:

"Lazarus, four days dead and friend of Christ."

Twenty-four hours later, Shepard sat aboard a Cyprus Airways flight to Larnaca.

CHAPTER 30

Larnaca, Cyprus
Grecian Park Hotel
25 Miles from City Centre

Something about the warm sun and lying on the sun-
bed of his porch overlooking the pool of the Grecian
Park Hotel took his mind away from the true reason
he was there. The girls looked fit too. He could have booked
a hotel close to the Church of Saint Lazarus near the city centre, but there was far too much noise and bustle for him to
concentrate on what he had in mind.

The city was perfect and expansive. It had all the attrac-
tions and diversions anyone could wish for. A second
Lourdes or Turin was more than possible. There didn't appear to be any casinos to have fun in nearby, but that could be

a blessing in one way or another. The casinos were situated in the Turkish northern part of the island, such as the Grand Pasha, and The Golden Tulip in Nicosia. Since the recent financial crisis, gamblers were taking their money and using it in the north, much to the Greek Cypriot's chagrin. Plans were under way to construct the first legitimate casino in the city or close by, to rectify that situation.

Nobody knew where Shepard was, so he could take as long as he wished. *Tomorrow, I'll check out the Church of Saint Lazarus and see how it can accommodate what I've got in mind. The guy has been buried twice and with his bones here, it sounds like the perfect place to get a miracle or two on the go.*

He had a bottle of Bourbon in an ice bucket nearby, and he reached for it to pour himself another three-finger shot. A satisfying glow of relaxation passed through his mind and body. Life could be sweet.

The following morning, he checked out the painting as he made a point of doing. It looked no different from the previous day, so he wrapped it and placed it back in the cupboard. Before setting out, he ensured he looked the part as a man of God and was dressed in black with his clerical collar on full display. That could open doors where others may not be permitted.

The Church of Saint Lazarus was impressive with its bricks worn by the kiss of time. It was first built in the tenth century. Every inch and building block of the place was soaked in antiquity and reverence. Shepard took his time and absorbed the atmosphere and location, all of which looked ideal. There was plenty of space and what he could see would only enhance the provenance of the painting. Lazarus was immortalised. Of that there was no doubt, for in this building, constructed after his bones were removed to Constantinople, hung an untold mystery.

That wasn't the end of the story.

He is said to have lived for thirty more years and on his death, was buried here for the second and last time. This church, also called *The Church of Ayios Lazaros*, was built over his reputed (second) tomb.

In subsequent renovations of the church, on November 2, 1972, human remains were discovered in a marble sarcophagus under the altar. They were identified as part of the saint's relics – not all were removed to Constantinople, apparently.

So, he was still here in spirit and bone! Shepard's excitement grew. It was enough for him.

Also, there was a very impressive Byzantine museum located nearby, containing sacred and impressive relics. All these he saw as positive signs for a prosperous future.

Lazarus, in his time span, was said to have been appointed as the first Bishop of Kition, now Larnaca. It was magnificent, glorious, and fitted every aspect of what he had envisaged.

There were dates he could hang his miracles upon. On Lazarus Saturday, eight days before Easter, the icon of Saint Lazarus is paraded in a procession through the streets of Larnaca. Then, every seventeenth of December, the Catholic Feast of Saint Lazarus is celebrated. *Perfect!*

A few miracle cures and Lazarus would once more be raised from the dead!

Shepard decided he needed a place to rent or buy to use as his headquarters. A lengthy phone call back to Santa Fe and he reached Alphonse and Jeremiah, his acolytes who first told him of the Lazarus riddle.

He spoke to Alphonse. "I want you and Jeremiah out here to help me start moving forward with my plans. When can you get here?"

"Give us four or five days, Pastor."

The use of the word 'Pastor' caused him to wince. He would have to change that to 'Your Reverence.'

"I'm at the Grecian Park Hotel outside of Larnaca." As an afterthought, he added, "How's the recruitment drive going?"

"It's going well." Alphonse sounded enthusiastic. "We've been signing up over a hundred applicants each day, and there's no sign of it stopping – and from all around the world."

"Brilliant. I knew it was a good idea! I'll catch you guys later. Keep in touch."

A mood of euphoria rippled through him, but what he saw next caused it to vanish like writing in the sand.

It was a huge placard erected across a vast construction site.

CONSTRUCTION SITE IN PROGRESS FOR RODEO, LAR-
NACA'S FIRST CASINO.
ENJOY! WIN THOUSANDS AND MAYBE MILLIONS!

Courtesy of Las Vegas Inc. and sponsored by John D. Bower
Enterprises Inc.

Shepard felt the colour drain from his face. *Holy Shit! This is not happening!*

He read and reread it, but the sign did not change.

John D. Bower? My God! He's everywhere!

It was true, and there were workmen swarming in and out of the scaffolding, large trucks, vast piles of steel and bricks everywhere. The construction was in full swing.

Shepard went back to his hotel to give his plans more thought. With a Bower casino so close, it could be very dangerous.

CHAPTER 31

Maria – Condesa, and blessed person – awoke from a deep dream of peace and tranquillity. In part of the dream, she saw the shimmering sea. Quietness enveloped her. Then, she was standing in the cool depths of an ancient Byzantine church with a tall tower. She had no idea where she was, but she strived, with her intuition, to pinpoint her location. Around her were gold plated iconostasis and various objects of veneration. In deepest prayer, she could make out a woman, and without seeing her face, she knew it was Luciana.

No matter how she tried, she could not identify the location. She wondered why she was being shown this church. But she was certain that it was a significant clue.

It was time to talk to Brodie and Martha.

Garcia was experiencing a mental and emotional crisis, crashing around him akin to the walls of Jericho tumbling down. He'd been witness to a host of strange phenomena in his time, but what was happening around him beat all and sundry into a frothy mess. The thought hadn't escaped him that if he wrote of these events, his colleagues would think he'd lost the plot. He would be a laughing stock and could stand to lose his job.

He recalled Oscar Wilde's quote: "The truth is rarely pure and never simple."

With that in his mind, he knew he would not tell a lie and he could only tell it as it was. That was what he was good at, the truth, in all its guises.

At that moment, the Condesa Maria walked into the room and went straight to him.

"Ned." She gave him a rare smile. "I've had an obscure dream about a church. You've travelled extensively, and I was hoping that if I described what I saw, you might recognise it."

"I don't think that's likely, Condesa. I've always avoided them like the plague."

"Then you have surely missed something, Ned. That's a shame."

"After what I've seen of late, however, that's a situation that could change."

"Glad to hear that."

She found Brodie and Martha standing next to each other with puzzled expressions and looking at the paintings they had done. They were so absorbed they did not even greet her.

"Have you two been working together?"

"No," Martha replied, "but we managed to paint the same thing! It looks like a cave of some sort."

"This gets stranger. Do either of you know what it is?"

"Not a clue," Brodie said, shaking his head.

"I've been there. I know what it is."

"What? It's lost on us."

"It's the entrance to the Tomb of Lazarus, in Bethany, where he was raised from the dead. It's unmistakable and un-like anything I have ever seen."

"Oh God!" Brodie groaned. "Not again!" His head tilted back, and he raised him arms in supplication. "Come back, The White Horse of Uffington. All is forgiven!" He rolled his eyes as he brought his arms down.

"What is it trying to tell us?" Martha whispered, placing her hands around her cheeks in confusion.

Garcia moved between them and began taking photo-graphs on his mobile. "You sure you two haven't been prac-ticing this on the quiet?"

"Nice try, Ned, but not at all. Lazarus haunts me con-stantly. He never leaves me alone," Brodie replied.

"Well, that's the first thing they'll ask me if I print this. You can put money on that."

"Well," Maria said, "I'm now getting the impression that my dream is linked to all this – an ancient church with an un-known location, and now father and daughter, without knowing what the other is painting, both paint the entrance to the Tomb of Lazarus."

"Can I add something to this?"

The soft American accent of John D. Bower surprised them. In their puzzlement, he had been forgotten about. He had entered the room unnoticed and heard what they were saying.

There was an immediate silence and Brodie, instinctively,

stepped between him and the others, ready to protect them from him, if necessary.

"Relax." Bower sounded like a man about to drop off the edge of a precarious cliff. "I mean no harm."

"Leave him, Dad. I keep telling you ... he won't harm us. He's part of this whether we like it or not."

Brodie was taken aback by the sharpness of her reply. *My God, what sort of a daughter have I got?*

"You have something to show us haven't you, John?" Martha's use of his Christian name added to the surreal atmosphere that had descended on them all.

Bower gave a self-conscious smile. "Thank you ... Martha. Will you follow me? It's too large to carry in."

They moved behind him and went into the other room. His easel was positioned away from them.

His voice faltered. "Before I show you, and as you already know, this is not the first time that I seem to have been taken over by a force I can't control. I never planned to paint what I'm about to show you." He rubbed his face roughly, as if that would clear the confusion that threatened to engulf him. "You've all had similar events in your lives, and I've had two in quick succession. I will need your help with this and you may need mine in due course. All my life, I've lived a double role; heavy multi-billionaire casino owner yet living with a deep sense of dissatisfaction – hence my passion for art and unsolved mysteries in the world. What I've seen happening here is off the scale, and why I have been dragged into it, God only knows. But I promise you all, I will not harm you. I couldn't." He turned to a grim-looking Brodie. "I apologise for everything. Your daughter, Martha, when she first saw me, knew me at once ... and I have to confess that deep inside,

I knew her. She rode a white horse to reach me. It took her away from all that was safe in her life to bring her here, and you have all ridden on that beast in your time. I know that. I saw that too. Now ... look at this."

With care, he turned the painting around to face them all.

Larnaca, Cyprus
Grecian Park Hotel

I should have wasted him when I had the chance. He's bound to visit at some point in the future and any hint of my presence will have him pouncing like a vulture. Larnaca has to be the main place of focus – especially The Church of Saint Lazarus. What can I do?

Alphonse and Jeremiah were due soon. He would be needing a new weapon since he had to dispose of his Smith & Wesson before he boarded the plane. Make that a cache of weapons. He had to eliminate the threat of Bower.

His next problem was where to display the painting. It was unlikely that the current priest of the church would believe him if he told him the truth about the painting's provenance. Nothing short of a practical demonstration would achieve that.

He stretched out in his lounger, poured a healthy measure of Bourbon and stared out across the blueness of the Mediterranean. It wasn't time to get nervous. There was too much at stake and he didn't doubt that blood would spill somewhere along the way. He had no intention of it being his, and yes, he would have to employ some extra muscle.

CHAPTER 32

No one quite knew what they were looking at.
Bower moved to one side to let the light from the window fall on the painting. He looked somewhat apologetic.

"Before you ask," he said, "I don't know."

They were confronted with a blueness, a parade of what looked like palm trees, each surrounded by bluebells. The entire area was dominated by a tall, brownish-yellow tower structure, encompassed by what looked like a tripartite sanctuary. In the corner, painted in red, were the Latin words, *DEUS VULT* – meaning 'God Wills It.'

Garcia began taking shots of it. "It looks like a church."

"It's got to be the Med," Maria offered.

"It's a big place."

Martha and Brodie said nothing, but both were staring hard at the work.

Bluebells, yet again.

It was as if they were attempting to place themselves in

the location.

Martha shut her eyes. "There's a link between what we painted and what John has produced. We are being told something and we have to find out what it is."

"We, it seems, painted the Tomb of Lazarus. There has to be a connection," Brodie said to Bower.

"The Mediterranean Basin is a vast area and stretches to the Middle East. That picture could be one of many locations. It's typical of many churches in the region." Garcia said as he went around the easel, taking shots from different angles.

"We have to find one that is connected in some way to Lazarus."

Suddenly, Maria's face grew animated. "There's only one I know of. I wrote about it years ago, but I can't remember what it looks like. Can someone Google Lazarus and what happened to him after he fled Judea?"

There was a slight pause as they searched Google for the answer.

"What does it say?" Maria asked.

Garcia connected first. "It says he fled to Cyprus and lived there for thirty years or so and was made a Bishop. A unique achievement of having been buried twice. His bones were buried there and a church was erected on top of his tomb. Look, here's a picture of it." He held up the screen. "Behold, The Greek Orthodox Church of Saint Lazarus."

There was a communal gasp. Bower's painting looked identical in shape and structure.

He went pale.

"This is all getting stranger by the minute. Where in Cyprus is this church?"

"It's in Larnaca, near the port," Garcia replied.

Bower gave a sharp intake of breath, as if his heart was struck by a lightning bolt. To him, that's how it felt. He stretched out a hand for support.

Martha reached out and held him. "John, what's wrong?"

He couldn't utter a word. Disbelief was written all over his face.

"Tell us, please." Martha tilted his chin so she could look into his eyes.

Bower composed himself and stood straighter. Martha seemed to have a positive effect on him. After a few deep breaths, he looked at Martha.

"You know," he spoke softly, a bemused look on his face, "I have a vast collection of religious artefacts at home, and I know quite a lot about unexplained religious events, but this ... this has surpassed my imagination. I never would have conceived of this event happening. To me..."

"Why do you say that?"

He said nothing.

"Tell us, John. We have to know."

"I have recently invested heavily in a casino currently being built in Larnaca. Would you believe? It's the first in the Greek south. I am floored. It's one piece of synchronicity too many. Fate or God ... has really brought me here. *Deus Vult!* I know that now." Bower was surprised to feel relief after he said that, although his purpose was not yet clear.

"For your sake, Bower," Brodie couldn't bring himself to use his first name, "I hope it's not what I suspect it means. I've had that on my back for seventeen years, or more ... who can say?" He locked eyes with Maria, but she only shrugged her shoulders. "Now that we know what the message is," he continued, "we must consider a visit to Larnaca. It's telling us to go there."

"I agree, but first," said Maria, "we must get back to Guadamur, Abbot Louis and Luciana must be contacted and told of what we intend to do."

Brodie had a welter of emotions he kept to himself. Coupled with that, he had reservations about Maria and Martha embarking on what could be a perilous mission.

An hour later, they were on the road and starting their long journey back to Maria's home.

Guadamur

Abbot Louis had received their phone call and was deeply relieved to hear everyone was safe and would be returning soon. He had been of the sound opinion that no work of art was worth dying for. Maria had explained that they would tell him more on their return.

Luciana, for her part, had become increasingly devout and he wasn't surprised at that. It seemed perfectly natural and who wouldn't react in that way after what she had experienced? For himself, any lingering doubts he had about his faith and the road he had trod, evaporated. He now regarded the legend of the painting not as a legend to slaughter for, but a truth he would die for if he had to. That was how much what he had witnessed had impacted his life.

Stepping outside, he checked his watch. It would be several hours before they arrived, and Luciana had decided she would prepare them a meal to celebrate their safe return.

Outside, a blasting summer heat stifled everything alive or dead like a leaden mantle.

The previous evening, he had several troubling dreams, which left him wondering where he fitted in in the recent events. He had witnessed violence, a miraculous cure, and had been privy to information that even the Vatican had no knowledge of. Whatever, he would attempt to keep it that way. He knew that no matter how small his role was in this affair, he was meant to be here.

He heard a small cough behind him. It was Luciana, and in her slender hands was a jug and glass with ice-cold fruit juice.

"Father Abbot, it is too hot here. Get in the shade, sit down. This will cool you."

"You're very kind, Luciana, thank you but I will stay here. I need to think."

She turned and left, and he sat down and stared at the vista as Brodie and the Condesa had done all those years back. He implanted a prayer into his mind and closed his eyes. *Sweet Jesus, you know the secrets of my heart. I know so little but need to understand more. I am unworthy, but will you not show me?*

He repeated his request three times.

Before he finished, there came the sound of peaceful chanting all around him. He recognised parts of it from *The Way of the Cross.*

Pange, lingua, gloria
proelium certaminis
et super crucis trophaco…

Overriding this was a voice. "Your part in this is small,

but you preserved the secret well and this you will do until it is time for change…"

The Abbot held his breath in a welter of incredulity. He heard a flapping noise, and in his mind, he saw a black *pattée* embossed on a white flag. *Deus Vult!*

The spell broke and he fell to his knees. He was now certain of his role.

Brodie swung the vehicle into the parking area of Maria's home. Before they could get out, both Abbot Louis and Luciana rushed out to welcome them with drinks and food. Their greeting faltered when they saw who was with them. John D. Bower!

Brodie was quick to see their startled apprehension. "Father Abbot, Luciana, don't be concerned. I think this man is in the grip of what we all are. Something seems to have changed him, and I don't think it would take you too long to guess what it is."

They relaxed a bit, but Luciana still looked as nervous as a rabbit confronting a gun barrel.

"C'mon, you converts, let's eat and drink and discuss our plans." Brodie assumed control.

Everyone followed, although Bower appeared uncharacteristically subdued. He looked like a prisoner being led to a punishment cell.

While he was forthcoming, the Abbot appeared as if he was on another planet, with an odd glow in his eyes. He gave the impression that he barely heard the discussions on Cyprus and Larnaca. Martha looked at him closely and she deduced that he had an experience of some sort. She refrained from asking. If she had noticed, it was certain the others had also observed his far away manner.

Brodie was adamant that he wanted both women to remain in Guadamur whilst he and Bower were gone. After much argument – that it would be too much for her, and at her age, potentially dangerous – Maria relented and agreed to remain with Luciana.

That left Martha and the Abbot.

She was adamant. "I'm coming, whether you agree or not, Dad, even if I have to get a flight on my own. I will be there alongside you and there's no changing my mind."

He slapped at his head. "Sweet Jesus, you are as annoying. More so than your mother Ulla! Okay, you are coming with us. But I'm in charge, not you. Understood?"

"Understood." She gave him an innocent smile.

"That leaves just you, Father Abbot. What's it to be?"

A silence ensued like a monastery in prayer.

"Deus Vult, Brother Baez! Deus Vult, Broderick Ladro! I am with you. I swore an oath seventeen years ago to protect *The Raising of Lazarus* and I thank God I'm still beholden to that promise."

They embraced.

Maria wiped tears from her eyes.

Bower spent the rest of the evening contacting his various business interests in Vegas, and informing them that he was off to Cyprus to check on how his casino project was doing. It was partly true.

CHAPTER 33

I t was bad news. Well, depending on what side of the divide you were sitting in. Pastor Silas Shepard discovered that Cyprus had one of the lowest crime rates in Europe. Robberies and murders, of which there were very few, were chiefly the work of foreign nationals who had taken up residence on the island – often in the hope that they would not be found and extradited back to their country of origin.

Discreet enquiries in bars and less affluent parts of the city hadn't revealed much. He was looking for a couple of meatheads who didn't mind a session or two of rough stuff and could use a weapon or more. He wasn't sure when or how he would need them, but when Bower showed up, it would get nasty ... and Bower would want the painting. That was a certainty.

He had studied the financial reports and it appeared that Cyprus was running out of cash. The financial ratings agency, Standard and Poor's, had twice – in close succession – downgraded the credit rating of the country. Its coffers were running dry. With that in mind, he knew that with enough money on the table, he wouldn't find it too difficult to locate the sort of guys he was searching for.

A friendly bartender had told him that his best shot was the port of Paphos. Times had hit the place hard. Later, he checked it out. It was about 135 kilometres away, an hour and a half drive.

He hired a car for the day and drove down there. It was an uncluttered route and easy to park. He headed for Bar Street, the recommended location.

Jesus! What a tip! He counted at least nine smashed up, burnt out and closed bars. The place was littered with glass and stank. It was filthy. Surly youths and thugs loitered all over the place. He headed for *Flairs*, the cocktail bar which was supposed to be one of the few decent bars remaining open. It was, and there were many customers, which gave it a reassuring feel.

The music was loud, but looking outside, he guessed it needed to be. He ordered a Bourbon Manhattan, sat on a bar stool, and began to take stock of the customers and ambience. Nobody fitted the bill – too many tourists. Man One and George, although they threatened and roughed up people, were always dressed in suits. They were clean and in excellent shape, hard and tough as an ATM cash machine. That was what he was looking for.

One Manhattan later, he spotted them. Across the bar and in a secluded corner sat two men with half the island's gold reserves hanging off their wrists, fingers and neck chains. They wore slick suits and open necked shirts, and both had shaved heads that resembled Arnold Schwarzenegger's biceps.

This was not a time to be shy. He sauntered over towards them. "Hi guys. What are you drinking?"

"Who the fuck are you?" one of them asked.

"Are you some sort of faggot?" the other snarled.

This was music to Shepard's ears and he just hoped he hadn't made a mistake. They were perfect!

"Not at all. Just the opposite. I'm a business man with an interesting proposition." He leant forward. "Now, what's it to be?" He indicated the drinks.

He then called the waiter over and ordered another Manhattan and two vodka martinis.

He introduced himself as Silas Shepard, omitting the holy handle. "And who might you be?"

"We are from Latvia. My name is Bruno, and this is my friend Alexis."

They shook hands.

"What is you proposition, Mr. Shepard?"

"I need some persuasive help and I thought you two looked like the sort of people who could help me." Shepard very slowly began to outline what he needed from them. He omitted details like miracles and the potential of vast amounts of money coming in.

More joy. They had access to weapons. He needed one right away.

The next two hours were spent in deep discussion. They agreed on the fees and how it was to be paid. They would meet again in two days' time at his hotel where they would be booked for an unlimited stay. By then, Alphonse and Jeremiah would be on hand and commencing the publicity and organizational work. He needed access to the media.

Shepard was in no rush and drove sedately back to Larnaca and outwards to the hotel. He surmised that it had been a good morning's work. He had found two excellent heavies, former gun runners who wouldn't have looked out of place in Bower's heavy set up.

Inwardly, he was imagining his church going worldwide. He would have a pilgrimage site where all members and postulants would be obliged, once in their lives, to visit and worship. Larnaca would be that place. It had everything going for it and it wouldn't be too difficult to invent another holy or sacred place. He could even discover a relic or two in the future. The possibilities were rich with promise. *What's more, I don't even have to live here. L R H had a ship and crew and sailed wherever he fancied. Sounds ideal!*

The journey complete, he found Alphonse and Jeremiah at his hotel waiting when he arrived, bristling with laptops and files. Both were tall men with pinched, pale, and pious expressions, with the stench of missionary zeal about them. Shepard knew they were devoted to him. What they had become was due to him and his preaching.

That suited him fine.

They sat outside on the expansive porch patio, complete with sunshades, a large table and chairs. He'd already outlined what he wanted from them.

"What did you discover about the media here?

Alphonse spoke first. "The media set up is pretty much the same as any other free county in the world. We have the proposals and materials ready."

"Radio here," interrupted Jeremiah, "is listened to by ninety-three per cent of the population. That's a good place to start. The Cypriot Broadcasting Corporation heads the list with several other private stations getting in on the act. We need to target news channels, talk shows, and weekly event presentations. That shouldn't be difficult."

"Nice one, boys." Shepard began to salivate. "Okay, how about TV?"

"The mix follows the same lines, again a stew of state and private stations. They are news hungry here as not a lot happens locally. Again, with what we have on offer, they're going to be fighting over us."

"And the newspapers?"

Alphonse spoke. "The Cypriot Mail is the most and only widely read English language newspaper. The others, of which there are several, are in Greek. We'll find an interpreter or translator to work with us."

"So, you have this all covered. Very good. Now, what I want you two to grasp is that, what we do here will be a virtual template for what we're going to do on every other country and continent on this planet."

"God be praised." Jeremiah looked skywards, and Alphonse bowed his head.

My, haven't I trained them well? It's time to tell them.

"Alright, my faithful and trusted acolytes, I know you have an inkling about what this is all about, but I'm going to tell you the whole story as much as I know. At the end of it, if you can't get back to me with a suitable presentation that would drive people to our church, then you are not the men I thought you were, and my judgment can be considered suspect. Sit back and relax, this may take some time."

They removed their suit jackets, which they always wore. A zealous expression the Spanish Inquisition would have been proud of etched itself into both of their faces. Actions that would exalt the glory of God could only have His blessing.

Shepard's knowledge, whilst sketchy, began with the actual event and Annas Zevi's depiction of it, and of how the painting disappeared and was discovered during the Crusades. It had amazing properties to heal the sick and dying. He covered what he knew and how the information they had given him had led him to the Condesa of Toledo. He found out that the painting disintegrated at certain times but would then resurrect itself when a new artist was found. It seemed that the latest artist was still alive, and it was his version that had cured the Condesa. He omitted the name Brodie Ladro from his story. They need not know everything. He also left out the shootings and murders. They already had details of how the church would operate and its proposed structure. Everything was based on the miraculous painting of Lazarus.

They asked no questions and believed all that he told them.

"I have that painting here today, and I'm certain you would like to see it." It was like dangling a bone to a dog.

They gasped. "You have it here?"

"Yes. It's not that large. Wait here."

He went into the other bedroom, satisfied they were well and truly hooked. With the tale of an actual miracle occurring around the painting, a miracle witnessed by many, who wouldn't be? Everyone feared death. That's the concept that would make him rich beyond his wildest dreams.

Placing it before them, he peeled back the purple covering with care. "It will not look like what you might have imagined, I warn you."

He stood it before them and their reaction surprised him.

They went down on one knee, lowered their heads and muttered prayers. They were in the presence of an item touched by Christ himself. A religious icon. All things blessed by God were no less than perfection.

This is going better than I expected!

When they had finished their prayers, they looked up, their expressions like heavenly twins with the light of ecstasy shining from their eyes, matching their sensible, shiny, black leather shoes.

"God be praised. Christ be praised." Shepard, for one brief moment, felt inadequate. That was all he could think of to say. No need for more.

"Now that you have witnessed it first hand, you may photograph it and use it in our presentation material and PR shots. Spread the word. I'm going to leave you to get on with it. Your rooms are booked, and you can work there. Get back to me in twenty-four hours. Do you have any questions?"

"Just one," Jeremiah said. "Where did you find it?"

His lies fell from his mouth as easily as a windfall apple. "I saw it in a vision. I was led to it. It had been hanging on a wall of a hostel on the pilgrimage route to Santiago de Compostela Cathedral. I knew what it was as soon as I saw it. Our Lord directed my feet and the owner parted with it for a small sum of money. The woman, the Condesa, confirmed it as the same one that cured her. But I knew it was the right one because Christ had told me. How it got there, nobody knew."

"Amazing. Amazing," Jeremiah repeated.

"His return is nigh, and we are prepared. Thanks to you, your Reverence."

That sounded marvelous to Silas' ears. *Will they hurry up and vanish already? I need a smoke and a stiff drink. It's been a hard day.*

"Well, that's it for today, boys. I'll see you tomorrow. I shall be most interested to see what ideas you come up with. Before you go, take your photographs. I'm glad to see you have proper cameras, not mobile phones."

Five minutes and they were gone.

He breathed a sigh of relief. He transferred to the sun lounger, lit up a Lucky Strike, and poured out a four-finger shot of Bourbon. That way, he wouldn't have to pour again. It had been a good day.

CHAPTER 34

Bower sat alone, preferring not to mix with the others. All this was far too new for him. His other life called to him constantly. The visit to Cyprus would be crucial. He sensed that there, he would know which way his life was heading. To see his investment under construction would be a valuable insight as to how things were progressing. He wanted to gauge local reaction. He knew casinos attracted people from all directions and countries, especially if there was built-in accommodation and all the facilities one would expect from a five-star establishment. Whether this was what he wanted from life, he would have to find out.

Like the others, he had no inkling of what they would find there, and indeed, why they were going at all. The common denominator was the similarity of their paintings and the Lazarus link with Larnaca. It was a shot in the dark, but that didn't seem out of place with the whole scenario. They were in the clutches of an unseen power they would never comprehend. The recent events had shaken him, and his core beliefs in money and power had taken a severe hammering.

With his last phone call, he had asked his management how George was getting on, but nobody had seen or heard from him. He hadn't been in Vegas.

I guess he's quit. Who can blame him?

He finally decided to join the others. He wasn't keen on Brodie, and he guessed the feeling was mutual, but they were stuck with each other. Garcia was of no real consequence, but he didn't doubt the man's intelligence, especially as he now knew who he was.

The Abbot guy, he's nice enough but what the hell is he doing in this crazy set up? What's he going to do when we get there? The Condesa, well ... I'm glad she's not coming. She can be a pain in the ass. Besides, she's too old anyway and it could get messy if Shepard turns up. But why would Shepard turn up? He's got what he wants.

That left Martha.

What is it about her? How does she know what I think? I sense her presence in my mind all the time. Shit ... are we on some sort of fool's errand?

He went into the room and poured himself a scotch. Garcia waved a bottle of Drambuie at him. "Try a Rusty Nail before Luciana brings in the meal."

"Thanks, I'll check it out." He clattered ice cubes in the glass and poured in a couple of generous glugs of the liqueur before passing the bottle back to Garcia.

Looking around, he took stock of the others and himself, sensing his inappropriateness, like an alarm had gone off without being set to do so. There were so many unspoken words in the air – judgments tied together into a tight ball like the moment before a bridge collapses. Even Martha was closed to him. He guessed he'd been the topic of conversation.

"Have you decided when we're leaving, Brodie?" he asked, to break the stalemate.

"We reckon the day after tomorrow, we'll catch the midday flight to Larnaca. It'll be too much for us to drive back to Madrid tomorrow morning. Then, in between now and then, we have to sort out where we'll all be staying. With the state of our finances, it can't be anywhere fancy, and we can't stay too long. Some of us might need to share a room." He gave a sheepish grin. "What we'll do when we arrive is not yet certain. But knowing this group, we will be guided when we get there. I'd put money on it."

Bower, before speaking, took an ample mouthful of the Rusty Nail. "Hold it right there. Leave the booking arrangements to me. None of you interrupt me, please." He held up a hand as Brodie started to protest. "I insist on it and also the flight. I'm on a Magical Mystery Tour here, which I never asked to be part of, and in some way, I need to *feel* part of this. You see me as an outsider ... don't deny it. And I guess that's true to an extent. I've never been part of your world until now, so please, let me do my bit. There's no other way for me. Besides, that may be one of the reasons why I'm here. As you know, I'm loaded." He scanned the group, unknowingly waiting for their approval ... not only of his plans, but ... of him.

Nobody spoke as they looked at each other.

"That's settled then." Bower stood and raised his glass. He could no longer wait to be rejected. "To the animal that carried us here, The White Horse of Uffington. Deus Vult!

For a moment, there was an appreciative gasp. Then they all stood and repeated the toast.

Brodie said, "In some ways, you shame us, but all of us

here want you with us ... don't ask why. We don't know. Your offer is most welcome and gladly accepted."

As if on cue, Luciana appeared with spicy dishes of *Patatas Bravus* and a massive bowl of traditional *Paella*.

Larnaca, Cyprus
Two days later...

They had given Maria and Luciana an emotional farewell and promised to keep in touch. Hopefully, they'll be back soon. From there, the journey and the flight had gone without a hitch. Bower had booked them all into the Achilleos City Hotel, close to the city centre and a stone throw away from the Church of Saint Lazarus. From their balconies, they could see the port not far off and the tower of the church. It was as Bower had painted it back in Spain.

They had decided to meet in the bar area an hour later to discuss their next course of action.

Bower, in the meantime, had located the construction site. He had made several calls to inform the site foreman that he was in town and would be there to see their progress.

Brodie was outside his room, about to knock on the slightly open door, when he overheard Bower speaking to someone. It was only then that he realised what a dominant force Bower is – regardless of his current experiences.

"I don't want to hear no chicken shit excuses. If I do, asses are gonna be kicked and you will be looking for a new job. Do you hear me? Am I making myself clear? Κατανοητήbe?" There was a pause. "Good. You understood that well enough." He ended the call.

He saw Brodie nearby and guessed he must have overheard the conversation. He grinned. "No harm in keeping them on their toes. That's the only way I've ever known."

Brodie didn't know what to make of it and chose to ignore the remark. "Let's get to our meeting and discuss plans."

It was unanimously agreed they would all visit the church first and take it from there. They might see something or be shown something that would tell them why they were led to it.

The church was situated in its own square in the town centre. They stopped and gazed at it. Inwardly, each of them was on high alert, their senses attuned to every sight and sound, waiting for a sign. Abbot Louis was moved. Its Byzantine architecture was truly extraordinary. The baroque woodcarving and the old, covered iconostasis were without equal.

Martha said nothing, nor felt anything. She was preoccupied by a recurring thought of being astride The White Horse and riding over the church. A vision ... small maybe, but one she knew Bower was also experiencing. She turned to him and he had a faraway look in his eyes. There was nothing she could say or do but wait and see. She felt the wind blowing in her hair ... although there was none.

Brodie wanted to see the sarcophagus where Lazarus was entombed and in particular the inscription:

"Lazarus, four days dead and friend of Christ."

If there was to be any visions or messages, then surely there could be no better place than this.

They agreed that the interior was breathtakingly beautiful.

Brodie and the Abbott genuflected, both making the sign of the cross. Bower looked awkward and Martha was disinterested. Her focus was still out of this world. Her horse was traversing her through time and space – existing, yet at another level, didn't exist at all.

She sat in front of the venerated tomb with its inscription, aware of a flurry of wings and the ethereal brush of eternity around her. It's presence or non-presence was inexplicable, unknowable, and part of humanity in every way. People could see it, if only they would look.

Brodie noticed her condition and held the others back. He didn't have to ask. How many times over those past years had he had to endure similar states? He recognised what was happening. *Has she been chosen? Oh, my sweet Jesus, not her. I beg you ... no! Spare her. Take me again, if you must, but release her. I beseech you. She has done nothing wrong and deserves to have a life.*

Abbot Louis, Garcia and Bower looked concerned. Bower himself experienced sensations akin to electric shocks. *Deus Vult! Beauséant!* Those words flooded his mind and body. He stood still and accepted it, not knowing what was happening, apart from the fact that Martha looked as if she had been taken over in some mysterious manner.

They formed a semi-circle around her facing the sarcophagus, which had assumed a soft glow that rose to an intensity, before diminishing by degrees. To anybody watching, it would look like a Mad Hatter's revivalist meeting.

The strain on Martha's features began to lessen and she gradually returned to the present world. Her lids opened, revealing eyes that were possessed of a certainty, shining brighter than the stars. "Where have I been? Why are you all around me?"

"What did you see?" Brodie asked.

For a moment, she kept quiet, as if trying to piece together her journey. Her reply, at first hesitant, changed to a gush. "It was … I don't know how to express it. I don't know where I was taken. I was sitting on him."

"Siting on who?"

"It wasn't a person. It was The White Horse. Our very own white horse."

Brodie listened to his daughter with a gripping despair. It saddled him and rode off with his profound convictions that there was mercy and love in this world.

"Dad, don't look like that. I saw infinite love and beauty. I heard your plea, and know that somehow, we shall understand all this and triumph. Don't be afraid for me. I'm happy. No ill will come of this. I know it."

Brodie recalled the Condesa's remark. *Leave her. She is going beyond us.* He understood now how true that was.

"Let's get out of here before something else hits us," he said before gathering them all and pushing them towards the exit.

Garcia looked intrigued and had taken several shots with his Lumix camera. "What was that all about? That tomb thing was glowing, did you see it? Was it some sort of lighting system?"

Brodie found himself grinning. "Let's get coffee and we'll talk about it. C'mon, everybody out of here."

On the way to the square, Garcia, forever the journalist, brought a copy of the Cyprus Mail.

Martha's colour had returned and she was looking more like her normal self. Something had occurred back at the tomb, but she couldn't name it yet. The last thing she wanted to do was talk about it. She needed time to digest and reflect on what it might be.

They ordered coffee, except for Garcia who ordered an ice-cold beer. Nobody seemed to know what to say.

"Where do we go from here?" the Abbot finally asked what most of them was thinking.

"Well, we've been here barely five minutes and that happened. Isn't that enough for one day?" Bower was becoming more vocal. "Sorry, guys, I'm not sitting around here too long. Once this coffee is finished, I'm going to inspect my investments a bit further down this road, unless you have a better idea." He found it difficult to admit that whilst Martha was out of it, so had he ... but to a lesser extent. He had partially glimpsed what she had seen, but he was still stubbornly entrenched in denial although he allowed himself to experience it. His 'old' life still clung to his mind, deeply etched like murder on the guilty protesting their innocence.

"Good God!" Garcia suddenly exclaimed, his eyes wide as saucers.

They all stopped and looked at him.

"Look at this!" He had opened his newspaper to page three. "Bloody hell!" He stabbed at the page with his index finger as he read more of it. "This is all too much to believe, I tell you." He turned the paper around, so they could all see it.

Embedded centrally and dominating the page was a photograph of Brodie's work of art, *The Raising of Lazarus*. The strap line ran:

LARNACA:
MYSTERY PAINTING OF SAINT LAZARUS
REVEALED

Beneath the photograph ran a smaller line.

MIRACULOUS CURES CLAIMED BY FINDER

The anonymous discoverer of a painting of Lazarus (*above*) has claimed that it is capable of causing miraculous recoveries from all health and physical conditions. Among those cured is an ageing Spanish lady of noble birth, who fully recovered from terminal cancer.

The man who discovered it claims that Christ had visited him in a vision and was told to form a new church based on Christ's miracle in Bethany. Followers would be amongst those saved at the Second Coming, he claimed. He said that he was compelled to bring it to Cyprus since it was the resting place of the man Lazarus – a friend of Jesus and the first Bishop of the Island.

The formation of the Holy Church of Lazarus is now well underway in the USA, Europe and other parts of the world. The location of the painting is a closely guarded secret as there are rumours of a group of people attempting to steal it. When these dangers have passed, the painting will be displayed for all to see.

Editorial Comment: *If true, then this painting would be a sensation. A religious icon that would draw a bigger following then either*

Lourdes or the Shroud of Turin. If located on the Island, it would bring enormous economic benefits for everybody.

Everyone was shocked into silence.

"So, the douchebag is here after all." Bower thumped his fat fist hard on the table.

"That's why we've been brought here, I guess." Brodie looked thoughtful.

"He could be anywhere, but the report came from here. That would suggest he's around here somewhere and could even be watching us right now." Garcia pointed out.

"Let's not forget he's more than capable of murder. He must be dealt with extreme caution." Brodie struggled to be the voice of calm and reason.

"I'll twist his fucking head off!" Bower had reverted back to his original self. "We need to arm ourselves. If he spots us, I've no doubt he will dispose of us like old, used, snot tissues."

"We've nothing to bargain with either." Martha reminded them.

"Look," Brodie interrupted the conversation, "an announcement like that is deliberate. It's a net to catch fish and get the money rolling in. You can bet that in a day or two, we will see some more announcement around here. He's recruiting, and he will do this around the globe as he builds his church. Ned, you signed up for one of his courses. What gives?"

"They're weekend events designed to get you to join and begin to scale the pyramid structure – which gets more difficult and expensive the further up you go. The indoctrination and training will have all sorts of tests and psychological profiling. I don't think he has a headquarters as yet, but with the pace this is going ... it won't be long. He could set up major bases in most countries of Europe to start, and that includes this place which is a perfect place for the scam."

Bower pushed his chair away and stood up. "I'll see you guys later at the hotel. I've some work to sort out."

Bower looked around him with care. After what they'd learned, walking around could be dangerous. He had to leave them to it as the indecisiveness of it all made his head spin. It was a good time to pay a surprise visit to the site, which was about half a mile away. No doubt, they were rushing about trying to look busy since they knew he was in town. As he got closer, he could see the site and the cranes and lorries bustling about. Coming towards him were a couple of boys wearing delivery bags full of promotional leaflets they were handing out to passersby.

"Hello, Mister," one of them said as he thrust an A5 leaflet in the direction of Bower's hand, that with a mind of its own, reached out to take it. He didn't look at it but folded it up and placed it in his pocket.

Ten minutes later, he strode into the construction office. The site supervisor was there with his feet up on the desk and a beer in his hand. His ID tag named him as Yannis Magalos.

He looked up at Bower and bellowed, "Who the hell are you? How'd you get in here?"

For his answer, Bower sideswiped the beer from his hand and sent it crashing to the floor. "Well," he roared, "Κύριος

Yannis Magalos, I'm John D. Bower, the man funding this project. My investment doesn't include you lounging around in here and getting pissed at my expense. Get out and don't come back!" He kicked the chair from underneath Magalos, sending the man crashing to the floor. "Do you hear me?"

The man got up with fear written all over him.

Bower, without understanding why, came to a sudden halt. *Why am I behaving like this? It's outrageous.*

Magalos, visibly askance, made his way to exit.

"Stop right there." Bower held up his hand. "Sit back down and get on with your work. Next time, don't drink while you're on the site. Understood? Now, before you get to it, I've some questions to ask you."

Magalos, his hands still shaking, did as he was asked. Bower fired several questions at him about supplies, costs, and timelines. The man answered every question quickly and efficiently and was obviously well in control of the site, over-all. He knew his stuff.

"Well done," Bower said, patting him on the shoulder. Before he exited the confounded man's office, he turned. "My apologies."

Magalos gave a bewildered smile and nodded his head.

CHAPTER 35

S hepard had rented a small set of offices that gave him a clear view of the church and the central square. It was equipped with what every modern office would require. His two acolytes, Alphonse and Jeremiah were busy constructing websites and exploiting social media. So far, they had produced sets of promotional brochures and were in the throes of attempting to arrange a press conference. Leaflet distribution was underway across the island. The news worldwide continued to be encouraging, with fresh members daily and applications to enroll in the American programme and introductory courses. Shepard had mimicked the way Scientology was first introduced to the masses.

It was working. The news of the miraculous religious icon was spreading like wildfire.

His biggest concern was Bower. But his new heavies, Alexis and Bruno, were on hand to deal with him and any other troublemakers. They had also promised to supply him with a new Smith & Wesson, and other weaponry, if needed.

To date, *The Raising of Lazarus* hadn't performed any cures or healings. He only had the testimonies of the God Squad or Holy Bogies as he described the Condesa and her pals. A testimony plus a demonstration from Brodie or the Condesa would be invaluable. The only way that could be achieved would be by force and fear. He planned to capture anyone of them and pressure the others into giving a live testimony. After that, they would simply vanish from the face of the earth, very quietly, and go to the heaven they were always banging on about. *God be praised!*

He had a nagging conviction that what he wanted would happen on the island soon. Without a doubt, Bower would appear, especially with his casino under construction.

The painting was unwrapped and standing on the shelf of his personal office. *I don't like it. How that produces miracles is hard to believe.* The more he looked at it, the more he felt like it glowered at him. He turned away from it as it gave him a feeling of unease. He turned his attention to the street just below him.

The sun was at its zenith and the siesta lunch break had descended amongst the locals. The only people walking about were tourists. It was then amongst the small numbers crossing the street, one caused him to do a double take.

He spoke out loud. "Why ... look who God brought in." There was no mistaking the stocky man with the ambling walk making his way close to the office.

Shepard rushed out of the office and shouted, "Bruno and Alexis, follow me quick."

He sprinted down the small flight of stairs and out onto the street. The two men were close behind.

"What's the problem, Silas?"

"He's here and he's just upfront. We have to follow him to see where he's going. Quick, let's get moving. I don't want to lose him."

"Who is it?"

"It's Bower. That's him in the white slacks and floral shirt. If he's here, it's a good bet the others are."

"Shall we deal with him now or later?"

"Later. But make your way in front of him and get a good look at him for future reference. I want to know where he's staying. Once you've eyeballed him, get back behind him and go where he goes. At all costs, he mustn't see me. Go!"

Both men picked up the pace and strode close to Bower before overtaking him as casually as they could, making certain they got a good look. They stopped to look in a shop window to let him pass again.

He ambled past them and once sufficiently in front, they continued following him. Shepard remained further back.

Bower came to an unexpected halt to look into shops selling souvenirs. He paused for a few minutes, looking at various items, before moving on and turning off into a bar. He sat down at a cool table and ordered a cold beer.

I'm being followed. Bower's antenna had been on full alert ever since he left the site. He was an old hand at all the tricks and manoeuvres that accompanied criminality. The two meatballs who walked past him thought he hadn't noticed them. Stopping to look in a window gave the game away. It was too amateur. Two can play at that game. When he had suddenly stopped, he saw them pause, surprised and unsure of what to do next. *A sure giveaway.*

Bower drank his beer and waited. After only a few minutes, just as he suspected, they came into the bar and sat casually a reasonable distance away from him.

Who are they? They look Eastern European and not too friendly. He watched them through the bar's wall mirror. *Why would they be tracking me?* He smiled to himself. It was either a rival casino operator who wanted a slice of the pie or it was the slime ball, Shepard. Either one was possible, but nobody knew he was in town. In that case, it could only be Shepard. *My name is blasted all around the construction site and he must have seen it. He's expecting me and must have seen me, which means ... Shepard is in the vicinity.*

They need to know where I'm staying, was his first thought. There was no way he was going to lead them back to the Achilleos City Hotel. *They're in for a long afternoon.*

He ordered another beer, telling himself he may as well make the exercise as enjoyable as possible. At some point, he would to have to give them the slip.

As he passed the time, his thoughts went back to his experience at the bridge. That had started him on this strange journey. The White Horse, the blood and noise, and meeting Martha. He felt that they knew each other, not in this life, but some other.

She's a young girl but epitomizes every mystery I have ever read of. It's her that keeps me here. Nothing romantic, nothing sexual, but just ... just ... I don't know what to call it. Am I willing to accept this change that is being thrown at me? I could end up like Brodie for pity's sake and look at the state he's been in.

He noticed the thugs now sitting closer to him, like a pair

of hyenas waiting for the right moment to pounce.

He looked at his watch and his two beers had taken two hours. That was a record. Time to play the Pied Piper of Hamelin.

After paying the bill, Bower headed for the door and was not surprised when the two heavies did likewise. He failed to see an agitated-looking Shepard sitting in a bar across the road. Using the hotel as a central point, he began to traverse a half-mile radius, walking around to form a circle filled in with an X configuration … a tactic he'd learnt from old military manuals to confuse the enemy. It meant passing by the same spot several times, which creates confusion, and then at a certain point, vanish.

He set off.

Several times, he stopped to examine something, and he knew they must be getting frustrated. If they were professionals, they would know by now that he was on to them. He walked from north to south and saw another hotel on the way. Bower calmly stepped inside it. Sure enough, he saw them stop outside and write down the name of the hotel and then head back to wherever they came from. He never saw them meet up with a hot and perspiring Shepard.

Time for another cool beer. All that walking got him thirsty. He sat at the hotel's bar with a smirk on his face, put his hand in his pocket, and pulled out the folded leaflet. He'd forgotten about it. Bower read it slowly and gave a long slow whistle. "Holy Shit!"

It was an announcement of a presentation of the *Most Wondrous and Sacred Painting of the Blessed Saint Lazarus which had cured many illnesses, giving new life to the sick and dying around the world.* The date will be announced soon.

It showed a picture of Brodie's painting, and alongside it, a thumbnail shot of Shepard in a pious pose, eyes uplifted to heaven. The caption described him as the Chief Minister, The Most Reverend Silas Shepard of the Holy Church of Lazarus.

CHAPTER 36

Martha sat alone in the balcony of her hotel room. She was avoiding the others. She had spoken to Ulla and had given her details of everything that had transpired since their last conversation, except the murder of Man One and other violent episodes. She had reassured her mother of their safety, and that her father would be calling her in a while. She also omitted telling her of the vision she had experienced that morning. That would have put her mother into depression or panic, judging from the way her father, Brodie, had reacted. When the call was finished, she felt a deep sense of peace. But the unease had not totally left her.

All she wished for was to sink her fears and anxieties into the distant Troodos mountains – where they would be buried for eternity, out of everyone's reach. Her vision of the world had altered in a way few people experienced. The ancient ruins of the island had come to symbolize the impermanent nature of what we hold and love so dear. How could she relate that very personal experience to anybody?

Her vision that morning had been glorious, and for her, intensely moving. She had felt the brush of angel's wings and the soft breath of grace upon her. How could she relate that? Not that she thought she should. It was profoundly personal. What this episode had in store for her, she could not say.

She thought of Bower. He was an unidentified piece in this strange game. She had reached into his psyche and had found in him a deep yearning and a hidden sense of unrealized compassion. In her vision, she had sensed his struggle, his burning desire to know ... really know and understand what was, and the mysteries that invade our normal existence. There were, in many ways, great similarities between him and her father, Brodie. Their interests ran parallel, although they expressed them in vastly different ways.

Things were building to a peak, she sensed. Where it will all end was anyone's guess. That decision was out of her hands. Whatever it was, she knew she would have to accept it.

Brodie found himself nibbling at his fingernails, a habit he thought he had lost in his teens, which had resurfaced after all these years. He attributed it to the stress and strain he had to endure of late. His days as Brother Baez, the monk, were almost over. He'd served his penance well, sacrificing his own life, and loves, in the process. But he couldn't prevent the thought that Christ had suffered so much more. Such was the influence of a decade and more of monastic life. He'd now become uncertain whether he believed any of it anymore. He had loved the Brotherhood dearly, but come what may, he suspected that the time had arrived for him to say farewell to it all.

Underlying these thoughts and fears were his concerns for the fate of his daughter and of Ulla. The shock of meeting Martha had intensified his feelings that the cement of his monastic life was crumbling. It had held him together all these years but never removed from him his deep and intimate sadness. Running close to this, he was concerned for Maria. He would die rather than see her harmed in any way.

How close these events might be, there was no way of telling.

He had seen a man murdered and a woman shot but he had also seen a miracle. There were things in this world he would never understand, and the worst of these were the lengths men would go to gain money, power or whatever they thought they needed. Men like Silas Shepard, who would dress up to deceive and steal to achieve just that. Shepard had no idea what he was dealing with.

Brodie expected more bloodshed and mayhem from him, and he had weapons he wasn't afraid to use.

The painting had not, as yet, perished, so the time was not ripe for a new artist.

What of Bower?

He's an enigma. I sense he has no love for me, but that's his problem not mine. He seems to me like a man split in two ... wealthy beyond dreams but with a restless soul. A man looking for his true home.

A knock on the door caused him to start. Opening it, he was surprised to see Bower standing there looking hot and sweaty.

"Come in." He still found it difficult to use his Christian name. "You look as if you've been in a shower. Let's have a beer." He opened the fridge and pulled out a cold bottle of Keo. "Try that. What can I do for you?"

Bower related the events of the afternoon and what he had done to lose his trackers.

Brodie spoke. "It's getting worse. He's hiring muscle to back him up. If he can do that, he will get other things he wants, like guns. If he can recruit people like them, we are in worse danger than we imagined."

Bower took a long gulp. "Now, look at this." He handed him the leaflet.

Brodie read it through. "A clever bastard, isn't he? He's whipping up interest across the island and next, he will be on TV and the radio stations. He will repeat this across the globe. That's how Scientology started. What worries me is how he will convince his followers that the painting is authentic. He can't command it to perform, it's unpredictable."

"Let's wait for the first meeting. We'll know more about his schemes then. I don't think we'll have to wait long."

That evening, Abbot Louis had arranged to meet the Prelate of the Church of Saint Lazarus to discuss the leaflet and news-paper article. He understood clearly that their recent adventures were not to be mentioned. Garcia was shaping out his newspaper report. He was now considering turning it into a book and had prepared a list of questions for Brodie.

Martha accepted Bower's offer of an evening stroll, with perhaps a drink afterwards. He had thought it would, at last, give him a chance to talk to her alone.

The night air had cooled. Streets, restaurants and bars looked busy with flocks of tourists, all illuminated by a medley of streetlights and signs. As they walked along, Bower described the morning's events regarding the two men who had been following him.

She warmed to him as they spoke, and the more he did, the more it confirmed her understanding of him. They reached a point where the parade of bars was dwindling, and the lighting was less intense. One bar, seemingly constructed out of wood, beckoned. They took a table and a couple of seats.

Martha ordered a spritzer and Bower settled for a straight scotch. They sat there for a short time without saying anything. At last, Martha gave a little shrug, which seemed to acknowledge that they needed to say something to each other. She leant towards him.

"Where do you think this is all going to end, John?"

"I've no idea. I'm more confused than ever and you are the only one who seems capable of understanding me."

"Not so. Dad does too, more than anyone."

Bower gulped distractedly on his drink. Tears lurked mysteriously behind his eyes and his voice seemed to tremble as he spoke, but somehow, he retained control. "I don't know which way I'm supposed to jump. Everything I've ever known or worked for seems unimportant now – meaningless and about to fall apart. I'm not certain I want that. I worked long and hard to be where I am now. Anything else apart from this life scares me. I've never told anybody that before."

"Just let it be, John. Don't fight it. These dilemmas have their own way of sorting themselves out. Whatever you decide will be the right one for you."

"How do you know all this? You're only seventeen years old, yet you sound like some old wise woman. I sense you reading me like a book. It's unnerving."

"Thank my parents for that. They are remarkable. Let me tell you about them..."

For the next hour, she related Brodie and Ulla's dodgy background and the story of the painting and how it transformed their lives, and how Maria had shot and killed Throgmorton.

Bower's jaw hung open. "That changes everything. How wrong I was about you all."

It was only then she noticed that they were the only ones left in the bar. They still hadn't finished their second drinks. Bower looked up as the door swung open, and two bald men, dripping with gold chains and rings, barged in.

Bower went cold. "Martha, look at me, and do not turn around."

Too late, she already had, and immediately caught the eye of one of them.

"Hey look, Bruno, you have a fan!"

"It looks that way, Alexis, and just look at the guy she's with."

"What do you know? Yes, it's him. It looks like him."

"Bingo. Playtime! It's him alright."

They moved to both sides of their table. Bruno leered at Martha. "Out with Granddaddy or is he your sugar daddy?"

Martha bent her head, refusing to look or speak to him. Bower felt the other man's hands on his shoulders, as heavy as lead weight, before the man hauled him up by his shirt-front, lifting him as if he was as light as a puff of air.

"Who are you?" Martha's voice had raised an octave when she saw Bower dangling from the man's hands.

Bower struggled, without success, to free himself from the ox-like, steroid-fuelled ape who had hold of him. He failed, and a large, gold-ringed fist smashed into the side of his face. Pain shot up, but he made no sound. "They're those men I told you of earlier," he spoke from the side of his mouth. "They were following me."

Bruno yanked hard on Martha's hair, pulling her head and face backwards to look at the ceiling. Her mouth hung open and a gun appeared in his hand. He threw it across to Alexis, who caught it before smashing the butt onto Bower's head.

He still didn't make a sound.

"You gave us the slip earlier and I bet you thought how clever you were. Now, you're going to tell me exactly where you're staying and who's with you, but we aren't going to discuss that here, are we? No, we're not. We are all going for a little walk. Now, get up!"

Bruno pulled hard on Martha's hair, forcing her to her feet as Alexis dragged Bower towards the door.

"That's far enough, guys," a soft, low, American voice came from behind them. "Raise those hands now. One dodgy move and I'll feed your brains to the dogs. Now, drop that gun."

They heard a safety catch click. The gun was dropped.

"Move away slowly, and don't turn around. Head back the way you came and don't stop on the way."

As seasoned hoods, they knew whoever was behind them

wasn't making idle threats. They did as the man instructed.

Both Martha and Bower remained frozen to the spot, not daring to look. Bower could see Martha's face was as white and cold as a cameo.

The voice said, "You can turn around now."

Martha held on to Bower's arm.

They saw a smiling man putting away a gun, and they looked at each other in astonishment.

He picked up the discarded weapon and offered it to Bower. "I think you may need this, boss."

"Holy Mother ... it's you! George, by God! I'm so happy to see you, man!"

Martha's hand went up around her mouth, her eyes as large as a pinwheel and filled with tears.

"It's me alright, boss. Just didn't fancy a trip home, so I stayed close by. I followed you around and guessed that sooner or later you'd need help. I could see trouble coming and I was right."

His words came as a great relief to Martha. To her, he was a rescuing knight in shining armour. She felt like hugging him and declaring her friendship for life. She reached out to him and did just that. "I've never been so scared in my life! Thank you, George." She kissed him on the cheek.

Bower was jubilant. "You're a most welcome sight, George. We were in real trouble back there."

George looked embarrassed. "It's time we left here. Those mutton heads could be back with more firepower and we don't want a repetition. I've got something I can tell you."

CHAPTER 37

Father Ignatius, the priest in charge of the church, had been highly perturbed by the report he had read in the Cyprus Mail concerning the healing power of a painting of Saint Lazarus, which was said to be somewhere on the island.

A knock on his door announced the arrival of Abbot Louis from Spain. The Abbot was ushered in.

Father Ignatius rose, extended his hand and inclined his head towards the monk. "Abbot Louis, you are most welcome."

The greeting was returned.

For a short time, they talked about general church matters and international issues, until they reached the true reason for the meeting.

"You've seen the reports in the Cyprus Mail about this so called miraculous painting?" Father Ignatius asked.

"Indeed, we have had the same phenomena in Spain. There were reports of terminally ill people being cured." The

Abbot confirmed.

"Do you mean ... by this?" He jabbed his finger at the photograph in the paper.

The Abbot pretended to scrutinize the shot. "Well, it looks the same, but that's why I'm here ... to try and see if it is true or not."

"I heard that this Reverend Shepard wants to arrange a demonstration and a press conference. Do you know if that's true?"

"That's what I heard. I am also trying to pin this down. I would like to make a request, Father."

"What can I do for you?"

"If you ever talk to Reverend Shepard or one of his people, can you persuade them to conduct one of these events in this church? What place could be more appropriate than where our blessed saint was buried? Don't you agree?"

Father Ignatius sat back and considered the request. "I don't see why not. How do we get hold of the man?"

"I don't know. Nobody seems to know where he is, but I'm working on it. Of course, as soon as I know I'll inform you."

"It's agreed then. Personally, Abbot, I don't believe a word of it."

"That's what Thomas said. Look how wrong he was."

They both laughed, and a bottle of wine and two glasses were produced.

Shepard was less than pleased when he heard of the evening's mishap at the Larnaca bar. He had been a whisker away from getting six sacks of shit knocked out of Bower and taking the girl as hostage. A stranger, *who the fuck was that*, had robbed them of that chance. He had no idea who it was. He took refuge in the fact that Bower and his pals had to be lucky all the time – and he, only once. They were around here somewhere and sooner or later he would flush them out.

The hotel had conference facilities and he planned to invite the media from all over the island to attend. To do that, he had to make it attractive and worth their time. The media and journalists were a hard-bitten bunch, and the promise of food and drinks was one way of enticing them. Add the first-class facilities and they would be convinced this was not some cheap show. He settled for a capacity of one hundred and forty participants who would be served food, cocktails and an assortment of distractions, enough to tempt the Pope himself.

Alphonse and Jeremiah had drawn up a list of names spread across the entire media spectrum of TV, radio, magazines, newspapers, and various churches. It was well over the number he was aiming at, but not everybody would turn up. It would be a *by invitation only* event, and they wrapped it in a shroud of mystery and secrecy. It was classic promotional strategy. It rarely failed.

Brodie and the Abbot were horrified when they heard of the assault on Martha and Bower. The thought of what could have happened to her – beatings, torture, rape, and the list went on, was too dreadful to think of.

She seemed to have recovered and the presence of George, given his former role, caused them both to paradoxically feel reassured.

Martha had recovered from the ordeal and Brodie swore he would not let her out of his sight again, let alone allow her to walk around outside at night.

The more Brodie thought about it, the more he realised that he would kill any bastard who harmed her in any way. He found himself grinding his teeth and clenching his fists. When he last did that, he couldn't remember. If Ulla found out...

Garcia and the Abbot both turned away to look out of the window.

There was a knock on the door. It was Martha, plus Bower, and George who looked out of place.

They greeted each other, and Brodie rushed to give George a huge bear hug. "I would never have believed it possible, but we owe you a huge debt of gratitude, George."

"It's what I do. Forget it." He looked uncomfortable again. He was not used to being praised or gushed over.

Bower spoke. "George discovered we were coming here and had arrived before we did. He hasn't been idle while he's been here and reckoned we might need some help. Tell them what you found out, George."

George was clearly unused to being thrust into the limelight. He spoke almost in a mumble, so they had to lean forward to understand what he was going on about.

"I saw Shepard arrive and he booked into the Garden Bay Hotel, that's about twenty-five miles from here. He has two of his religious buddies with him and they are busy arranging a press conference and hopefully a demo at another date. I followed him one day to Paphos. It was there he found the two muscle men. From local gossip, they are known hoods, gunrunners and grifters. They come from some dump called Latvia, wherever that might be. I heard they are not to be messed with. Even the police give them a wide sidestep. Shepard must be funding them well for them to do his bidding, and it doesn't need a mind reader to know they will deliver what he wants. You are all in danger. I reckon if he gets his hands on one of you, he will use that to get juice out of that goddamned painting."

"So that's where he's holed up. Thanks, George, you've been a massive help. We owe you." Brodie shook him by the hand.

"Well, you can start thanking me by pouring me a drink," he quipped. His eyes gave a rare sparkle.

A large drink was poured and delivered.

The Abbot had been quietly listening, then he said, "I can't be part of violence and I know you now have two weapons. But that doesn't mean I won't support you. I went to see the priest in charge of the church and we agreed that once we know more, we will attempt to persuade Shepard to hold one of his demonstrations at the church. That would be an attractive offer for him, surely."

"That is a good idea, Father Abbot. If he bites, we'll be there."

"The problem now is, how do we keep away from him? If he can, he will take anyone of us, and then unless we are prepared to die, we will have to do what he asks." Martha remembered the thug's hand on her hair and shivered.

Brodie saw, and it brought home the fact that his daughter barely escaped Shepard's hired thugs. If George hadn't been there...

"I have a suggestion. You," Brodie pointed at Bower, "and you, George, let's go for a little ride. Don't leave anything behind."

They knew what he meant.

"Dad, you can't do this!" Martha knew exactly what he was intending.

"It's the only way." He put his arm around her. "I'll be back. I promise you."

She didn't know whether to believe him or not. Her mind was full of confusion and incomplete thoughts and vision. She clung to him like a python around its prey. "Dad, don't go. I beg you."

"Something has to be done and we can't sit here and let him play the tunes. You know that and so do I. Someone once said, 'attack is the best form of defense.' It's now time to put that to the test." He extracted himself from his daughter's arms, gave the Abbot a hug, shook Garcia's hand, and pulled Martha again in a tight embrace.

"*Deus Vult! Beauséant,*" she whispered, choking back tears.

"*Deus Vult,*" he responded.

The three men strode from the room.

CHAPTER 38

They sat in silence as they drove in the convertible with the top down.

Bower was aware of a new shift in his consciousness and attitude. Outside, the air felt soft, almost sweet, heightening his senses. The answer to his dilemma was already there for him, sitting there and fully developed in his head. As if lit by a lamp, he saw that it hadn't been arbitrary. It had been done in a series of signs, and it was telling him that he would be unable to sever the connection with Martha, Brodie, and the Condesa ... even if he had wanted to. Their journey gave him time to consider this.

Was *karma*, as he understood it, really the word he wanted to use to describe what's happening? It was one of those imported words that had become fashionable to use and cool in some circles. The more he thought about it, it described precisely what he had been struggling to say ever since he had come across Shepard. The word came closer than any other he could think of. There was nothing he could do about it. He was about to enter into a conflict with some unpleasant characters. It was inevitable. Casinos were no longer important.

He was being steered.

Before they came here, at the back of his mind, he had already accepted the proposition. He was now powerless to undo that or change direction. The die was cast, and he had to go through with it. There were no two answers, whether he liked it or not. The words *Deus Vult* were imprinted in his mind.

George broke his contemplation. "You okay there, boss? You looked kind of weird."

"I'm fine. How long, Brodie?"

"Another ten minutes, I guess. Once we've seen the place, we'll pull over and discuss."

It wasn't long before the structure came into sight. It was one of those smart five-star hotels specifically built near the sea, with its own swimming pools and all modern conveniences. It was popular for weddings and conferences.

"There it is, guys." Brodie pointed ahead.

"It's not unlike a couple I own," Bower said.

"We need to get in there and find out where Shepard is. He's not expecting us, and I want it kept that way. We don't know who he has in there with him, and in his turf, he could be very dangerous. You two got your guns?"

"We're locked and loaded."

"C'mon, let's do it."

The convertible crept forward and turned into the parking lot. Brodie killed the motor and for a minute, they sat in complete silence absorbing the situation. Brodie, as a signal, opened his door and the others followed suit. Within minutes, they had entered the hotel lobby and Brodie approached the desk.

Bower's recently discovered respect for Brodie solidified as he saw the natural manner in which he had taken charge of things. He was now feeling comfortable with him around and certain there would be few mistakes.

The smart receptionist, wearing a blue lightweight two-piece suit, asked Brodie if she could help.

"I'm Brother Baez from Spain and we're friends of Reverend Silas Shepard, here for a visit. Can you tell us what room he's in, please?"

She glanced at the register. "Ah, there he is. Room 416. Would you like me to call him to tell him you've arrived?"

"Goodness me, no. Thank you, but this is a surprise for him." He flashed a dazzling smile. "Does he have our other friends with him?"

"Not that I know of. You're his first visitors today. Okay, then. Just take the lift to the fourth floor. Have a good time."

"I'm sure we will. Thank you."

They moved to the elevator. "Nicely done, Brother." Bower was impressed.

The doors of the elevator slid open and they boarded it in total silence. George pressed button four and they ascended with the slightest of whirring sounds. Once it decelerated and came to a stop, they stepped out with caution.

"It looks like he's alone," Brodie whispered aloud, "but remember, he's no pushover and a cornered snake can be most aggressive and dangerous. Shepard's a low-bellied example. Let's go."

They stood outside the door of room 416. "You two out of sight on each side of the door and when I go in, you follow at the ready. Okay?"

"Affirmative," Bower felt a stab of adrenaline rushing through him.

✠

In his hotel room, Shepard approached the painting he had propped up against the wall. He was determined that somehow, he would elicit a response from it. But so far ... nothing. The only two people the painting had responded to was the high and mighty, snooty Condesa Maria and her subservient maid. They were out of reach at the moment ... but that could change. They were all here, it seemed. That girl at the bar was Martha. He wondered if the Condesa was with them too.

He leaned back on the sun lounge, smiled with a certain ironic pleasure, poured a hefty Bourbon, and lit up a Lucky Strike. Bower was a man who didn't fit in, but the precise nature of his imbalance aroused the sound of sad laughter. All that money and he still couldn't hack it. He was a joke that stopped short of the punch line, a vague sort of mirth that had no object. He was tired of theorizing about it. He should have killed him when he had the chance, but he hadn't taken it. Drawing hard on the cigarette, he then gulped another large mouthful of the golden liquid.

The buzz of the doorbell made him jump.

"Shit! Who can that be?" It could only be Bruno and Alexis or his two acolytes. Without checking the peephole, he unlocked the door and pulled it open.

"Jesus!"

One look at Brodie's face and Shepard quickly turned to get his pistol. Both George and Bower rushed in with guns pointing and both in a Weaver stance.

"Stop right there, Shepard!" Bower roared as George circled to the front of him with his gun pointing straight at Shepard's head.

Shepard froze and lifted his hands high as Brodie walked in with a broad smirk on his face. He saw Shepard's gun and holster hanging off a chair and picked it up. He slung it across his shoulders after removing his jacket.

"Wasn't expecting that, were you, Reverend? We've come to collect what's not yours. It reminds me of what I used to do a long time ago – liberating stolen works of art. It brings back old memories." In a flash, he thought of Ulla.

Scanning the room, Brodie spotted it sitting against the wall and resting on a broad mantelpiece. "You two, keep him covered. Don't let him make a move. I told you he could be dangerous. Cornered snakes always are."

He approached *The Raising of Lazarus* and couldn't deny the emotional surge that pulsated through him. It was like meeting a long, lost dear one – like meeting Martha for the first time. Like speaking to Ulla after all those years. He hadn't realised how deeply attached to it he had become. It was an outrage that it could be mauled and pawed at by the likes of this slimy, creepy Silas Shepard. A spark of anger ignited in him and he felt a strong compulsion to do harm to this man, who didn't think twice about gunning down anybody, male or female.

With great care, he retrieved the work and wrapped it in a sheet from an unused bed, before standing in front of Shepard. "It won't work for a thieving, murdering bastard like you. You just don't understand, do you? You are so thick you probably never will. I've given my life for this and I'm never going to simply sit down and let you play with it. Do you hear me? Never." At that moment, everyone thought Brodie looked like a righteous and determined avenging angel. "I got what I came for, but these two gentlemen are less than happy with you ... and with good reason. So, with that in mind, I'm going to step outside and let them have an in-depth discussion with you." He gave Shepard two taps on his cheeks and walked towards the door.

The implications of Brodie's words were easy to understand. The stench of fear oozed from Shepard, and he started to shake.

"Don't be too long, guys. I'll wait for you in the lobby bar area."

As Brodie closed the door, he heard George say, "You killed my friend."

It was fifteen minutes before they came into the bar. They looked no different from when they went in, apart from the perspiration hanging around their foreheads.

Brodie ordered three beers. "Did you have a good chat, guys?"

"It wasn't bad," Bower said. "I think we were persuasive and he decided that he'll stay indoors for a while. He's got some serious issues to think about."

"What do we do now?" George asked in his mumbling fashion.

"We go back to the hotel and make plans to defend ourselves. Be under no illusions, there will be attempts at reprisals. We may have to leave this place in a hurry. I guess right now, Shepard's press conference and witnessing demonstrations are on hold."

Brodie didn't know what to make of himself. Only a short while ago it seemed, he was in a cave in the desert, attempting to communicate with a God he was no longer certain he believed in. Now, here he was, participating in precarious activity and giving sanction to brutality.

What the hell? The slime ball deserved it.

The time to turn the other cheek had passed, and like Bower, Brodie's brain, his intellect and emotions, were being torn in opposite directions. He and Bower had developed a new respect for each other. Martha had told him of Bower's mental state and how she had detected tears in his eyes. He was a lost soul. Brodie could relate to that. Clearly there was more to the man than he had comprehended.

Undoubtedly, there were similarities in their makeup. He wondered if Bower knew of his life history...

An hour later, they were back at the Achilleos City Hotel and in their rooms, with the painting safe and secure. Martha and the Abbot had greeted them, amazed that they had the painting and were unharmed.

"What happened back there?" Martha demanded. "How did you get it? He couldn't have given to you."

"He did. There was nothing he could do. He seemed to think Lazarus was going to perform on command and we all know that's impossible. It makes up its own mind. We liberated it, as Ulla loved to say."

"Didn't he try and stop you? Where were his men?"

"He was alone. I also rescued this." He took off his jacket

to reveal the gun and holster.

"Dad!"

Brodie smiled. "Bower and George had a little chat with him while I made other arrangements in the bar."

Garcia had been furiously scribbling notes as they spoke. "He got roughed up then, did he?"

George made a rare comment. "He bumped into a few cupboards, I think."

Abbot Louis raised his eyes skywards and made the sign of the cross ... but kept silent.

"Now," Brodie spoke with urgency, "the painting has to be protected at all costs. Only we know its true power. Those meat cleavers will be looking for us soon and I wouldn't be surprised if they bring in more troops. Shepard is not going to let us get away with this. Not only will he want Lazarus, he will want revenge. The fate of his whole phoney church rests on this painting. Without it, he doesn't amount to a can of beans. People are following him for this reason alone. Suggestions?"

"I have to get back to the monastery, but I will do all that I can to assist you. Perhaps Lazarus should be returned to its hiding place?"

Martha looked at Bower and he returned the stare. They both had identical thoughts and knew it. *It's not over yet. Not by a wide margin.*

Brodie shook his head. "There's a lot more to come. The paint hasn't dried yet, and I fear it never will. I sense it's waiting for someone new. Don't ask me how I know that, but I just do. "

His heart was full of dread that the mantle would fall on his beloved daughter. That would kill him ... and it would kill

Ulla. Their lives would be finished.

Brodie turned to the Abbot. "Father Abbot, I want to go home so much but this millstone still hangs around my neck. Until it drops away, I can't leave. It's impossible."

"Dad, why is it impossible?"

"You don't understand, Martha." He looked around at them all. "None of you do, not even Maria although she has been closer to me than anybody else. It's my burden and I know it will not let me go, yet. We can't stay here, either. They will be looking for us and if they find us, it won't be pleasant. We have to go back to Spain. John, what are you going to do?"

"I need to talk to you privately. Can we do that? Now!" It wasn't a request, but a demand. His former self surfaced once again, and Bower's face looked grim, like a monk having a spiritual crisis.

CHAPTER 39

T hey stepped out to the balcony which was rife with the aroma of brilliantly coloured flowers; lavender and orange blossom. Brodie closed the sliding patio door behind him.

"Well, what do you want to say?"

"It's difficult to know where to start." Bower was beginning to relax.

"Try the beginning."

"Okay, but I'm not sure that I'm going to make a lot of sense. You know what I am, and I expect you have a low opinion of me."

"Not so much. The situation has changed a lot and I have formed a different viewpoint of you since my original dislike. We are all capable of change and I have seen that in you."

"I've felt that about you too. This whole affair started with me wanting to steal the painting and get into another mega money-making situation with that asshole Shepard running things. We would both have huge amounts of money and power. Now, here I am on the other side trying to prevent that from happening. You see, Brodie, now don't get me wrong here, your daughter changed all that. I sensed something very strange stir inside me as soon as she spoke to me and told you all that I wouldn't harm her or any of you. I was shaken that she acted like she knew me more than I knew myself. I know you've had a tempestuous struggle with that damned painting. She told me all about your past and your visions, and about you and her mother Ulla."

Brodie began to speak. "Now, just..."

"Shut up, will you?" Bower held up his hand and cut him short. "I haven't finished.

Brodie was taken aback. *What's got into him?*

"Nearly every day, I have been tempted to pick up the phone and book a seat to fly home, break the spell and forget about this mystical work of art and the legend that goes with it. Then I think of my *Book of Miracles* and the missing Lazarus plates, and it gets me thinking that I am connected to this whole affair. Ever since. The template was set for me when I brought that book, but how was I to know that? The days come and go, and I cannot remember a time in my life when I have been torn one way and then another. You see, Brodie, I'm changing, and I can't stop it. Little by little, I'm no longer the same. When I stop and accept it, I feel reassured ... but when I fight it, I feel lost and incomplete. The whole thing is a paradox. The closer I draw to you all, the more deeply entangled I become, yet weirdly ... the freer I feel. Martha, in some ways, is my mentor. Just as the Condesa Maria was yours. A short while ago, in that room, I felt her thoughts in my head and I know she sensed mine also. That morning, when she had that experience at the tomb, I was in some way taken with her, and I was shocked, shaken, but felt wondrous all at the same time. I'm telling you all this for as much as I struggle, Brodie ... I know I won't escape you." He paused, stared down at the ground, then back at Brodie who was staring straight at him. "I guess that's what I wanted to get off my chest."

"That's remarkable," Brodie spoke softly. "You are very honest and brave. I respect that. One word of advice ... hang on to that stroppy personality of yours. It's unique and belongs to you and no one else. It will serve you in good stead later. Welcome to *The Mad Hatter's Tea Party*, John. Don't fight it. It's much easier when you don't, believe me."

They shook hands.

He looked in the mirror and what he could barely see shocked him. He did not recognise himself. He looked as if he'd been hit by a tank.

His face had been altered. Both eyes were virtually shut, with massive purple and black bruising, and trickles of blood ran from the closed up corners. Large bumps of varying hues were dotted across his head and blood-streaked, swollen cheekbones. A knot of pain akin to a cancerous diamond sat in the middle of his head. His ribs, stomach and innards felt as if they had been kicked and ripped apart with red-hot splintered glass.

Pain.
Searing pain.
Nausea.

Vomit mixed with blood.

"Oh, God! Help me." He managed a guttural noise through a pair of lips the size of burnt sausages, as a bloody and viscous dribble of sick trickled down his bruised chin.

What have they done to me?

They hadn't been gentle and exacted every inch of malicious force they could muster. George had fashioned himself a new garrote and only Bower's interference had prevented him from using it.

What a fucking mess! This is going to take weeks to heal. That's the end of all my plans. Without the painting, the press conference would be pointless. I have nothing!

He swore that once he recovered, he would find them and rip their hearts out, and before feeding them to the ferals, he'd barbeque them first while one by one, they would have to watch until their turn came.

By God, I swear it. That painting belongs to my Holy Church of Lazarus and me, and I will have it.

He now needed to explain his predicament to both Alphonse and Jeremiah. He'd tell them he was set upon and the painting stolen from him, and that he knew where it could be, but the police must not be informed.

The two men he wanted to contact most were Alexis and Bruno. Some long-term planning was needed. But right now, he was experiencing too much pain to think straight, and it was going to be like this for a while.

Bent double, he hobbled to the land line, his foot a hive of agony. His cell phone was on the floor, shattered after that ape stamped on it.

The call was answered by Bruno and Shepard had difficulty getting him to understand who he was. Such was the pain in attempting to speak. The man eventually summed up the situation and assured him they were coming over.

CHAPTER 40

Guadamur
Two days later...

T hey had got away whilst they could. Again, Bower had taken care of all the arrangements and they had all come to appreciate Bower for his financial support. They had spent the last day in a degree of fear and trepidation, but nothing had occurred to menace or threaten them.

Now, back at the Condesa's home, the pressure had lifted, even though their location was not unknown to Shepard and that was still a cause for worry. There was no way Brodie or Garcia could leave the women alone. Abbot Louis was with them, but he would be leaving for the monastery soon.

That evening, as they ate a meal prepared by Luciana, the Abbot asked, "Would you like me to take Lazarus back to San

José de Nazaret?"

"That would put you and your monks at risk, and you don't deserve to have that hanging over you. On that score, I think not, Father Abbot," Brodie said, still using the polite and formal address. "It was my work and therefore it's my responsibility. You can't disagree with that."

"In one sense, yes ... and in another, no. We're all part of this and we belong to it no more or no less than you." Maria sounded strident as only she could.

"What do we do then?" Martha asked. "We stay here and wait until we're attacked? That will happen for sure."

"Shepard will not only want the painting, he'll want my guts hanging on the washing line." Bower added, although he did not look too concerned by what he said.

"And mine." George's words were laced with amusement.

Brodie looked thoughtful. What was going through his mind wasn't easy to figure. He opened his mind, but nothing was coming through. He would have to work this out on his own. He pushed his chair back and stood up.

"I need to think alone. Excuse me, I'll go to my room and see what I can decide."

"Don't be too long," said Martha.

"I won't."

Brodie stepped into his room and emitted a long sigh before sitting on the edge of the bed. *What am I to do now? I really have no idea.* The Lazarus painting was standing upright on the dressing table. He offered a prayer, which he hadn't done for some time – such was the state of his mind.

"God, you set me up for this and I haven't done too well.

Forgive me. Their lives are in peril and it's my entire fault. Show me what to do, I beg of you. If any more lives are to be lost, spare them and let it be mine. You've had me in suffrage for all these years, and the painting has and will cure many more. Let us be safe. We need not, nor deserve any more of this."

A thin ray of filtered sunlight flickered across the room, illuminating the area where the painting stood, impassive as always. A soft wind blew across the curtains.

The head of Christ turned and looked at Brodie, before the entire painting melted away into nothingness.

The Condesa Maria gave a start. She placed her hands on her head. A jolt went through her as if she had touched a live wire.

Bower cried out, *"Deus Vult!"* and had no idea why. He went down on one knee and bent his head low. He just had to. It was inexplicable.

Martha began to sob. "It's gone! It's gone!"

Abbot Louis looked startled and he felt the shift of something immense and unknowable pass through his entire being and life.

Garcia intuitively understood the enormity of what he was witnessing, as Luciana clung to him, sobbing…"He's gone. He's left us!"

CHAPTER 41

The sound of heaven resounded all around, and ahead stretched a long and lonely road arrayed with aged and weathered crucifixes, on which was hammered the forgotten and countless souls of those who had died for Him.

The rider wears their ancestral armour, the colours and the black cross pattée emblazoned upon a tabard of ancient Templars past.

The wind blows hard and there is rain in the air, as thunder begins its roll across the skies, lit by streaks of lightning. The rider has heard the call and knows it must be answered. The call is within the message.

Bells of heaven call to the rider, who, with head bent low, moves to where the sound is coming from. The voices of the angelic choirs sing, sending golden rays and dispersing the darkness of the world. The light descends and suffuses the rider... The Chosen One.

As it has always been and will be forever more.

A church appears bathed in a gentle healing light. The rider, like those that went before, is finally home. With outstretched hands, *the rider pushes open the door and when inside, sees that all is as was promised. The easel and paints are ready.*

A tear trickles down the rider's dusty cheek. The journey has been long but is now drawing to a close. The brushes glide swiftly and lovingly across the naked canvas. Body and form take shape. Life arises where there was once only death. The painting breathes as the rider accomplishes the role of artist.

Death has been escaped, and as it has always done, the eyes of Christ shine into those of The Chosen One. Lazarus lives again and in all humankind. The circle is complete. The vision is accomplished and hope for the world is renewed.

Brodie lurched back into the room looking like a man on fire.

"It's happened!" he shouted, "It's happened!" He was about to shout again but stopped short. Something had occurred. There was complete silence. Every one of them appeared transfixed and locked inside a private world of their own – wherein their own imaginations, hopes and fears abided. It was as if they hadn't heard him. He scanned the room. "What's been going on?"

No one spoke.

Brodie realised they had felt what had just happened. The miraculous event had communicated with all those involved, and they had felt and understood it. They appeared dazed.

Martha looked up, her eyes wet with tears. She stood and went to Bower who remained on one knee with his head bent. Putting out her arm, she hauled him up.

He looked shell-shocked. "Holy Mother, what was that?"

Turning to Brodie, she asked, "It's gone, hasn't it?"

"Yes," he replied flatly. "It's vanished to God knows where. Probably to that gallery which I alone have seen, wherein every painting ever done by the chosen artist since Annas Zevi, lives."

He watched the scene unfolding before him. Maria moved closer to Martha, as did the Abbot, Luciana and Garcia. She was surrounded as they all stared fixedly at him.

An awful thought began to form in his mind as it descended upon him like a sepulchral cloak. His hand went to his head. He went dizzy before he collapsed in a hunched up bundle on the floor.

Two days later...

Consciousness began to return and for the first time in two days, Brodie moved. He could discern the play of sunlight on his closed eyelids and thoughts began to stir. *Where am I?* He forced his eyes to open and take stock of where he was. It wasn't difficult. He was in bed at Maria's place, and staring down at him were the serene faces of both the Condesa and Martha.

He shook his head. "Why am I here? What happened?"

"You passed out on us. We had a doctor look you over and he said that if there was no improvement by tomorrow, we're to take you to the Hospital de Tavera in Toledo. He couldn't find anything wrong with you. All your vital signs and functions were perfectly normal. But he thought it would be best if you had a scan. How do you feel anyway?"

"I'm not sure. There doesn't seem to be anything amiss."

Maria pumped up his pillow.

"It's coming back now. That accursed picture, it vanished before my eyes, and you all knew when it happened. Didn't you? I didn't have to say a word." As he thought about it, a flood of despair assaulted him. He looked at Martha with eyes begging her to say no. "You've been chosen, haven't you?" He was willing her to deny it, to tell him he was crazy. But she didn't, and that compounded his misery.

"I'm joining the others outside." Martha looked unhappy as she turned and left the room.

He turned to Maria. "Maria, what do you do know? You must tell me. There is her mother to think of … poor Ulla. First me and then her daughter. She'll die when she finds out and if she does, I no longer want to live too."

"Don't worry about Ulla, Brodie. I know she calls Martha every day and she only tells her mother the good bits, believe me." She sat beside him and placed her hand on his arm. "There's something you should know."

"What's that?"

"We all had the same vision, all of us in that room, of the unrecognizable person in that church. So, it seems to me, either it's a collective choice, or the next artist hasn't been selected. But you, it seems, have been released as you so fervently asked."

"I didn't see anything, Maria, only Christ's eyes as he turned to me before the painting vanished! But it sounds almost the same as what I experienced all those years ago."

"Consider this, Brodie." Maria held his hand and squeezed

it. "The only people in that room capable of painting are John, Martha, and Abbot Louis, who I know is pretty handy with a brush. He has also been a guardian of your work since day one, up until the present time ... and he is in an ideal situation. If I was a gambler, I'd put my money on him."

"The continuum of elements never stops throughout time and space," Brodie muttered, not quite sure what he meant by that. The Condesa's assessment of the situation had helped calm him down a little. But until he knew for certain, he would never entirely settle. "Where are they all?"

"They're sitting outside, enjoying a drink. Would you like one?"

"I feel fine. I'll join you outside if you don't mind. Provided I can still walk." He swung his legs out and as he did, he realised they had undressed him before putting him to bed. *Oops!*

The Condesa Maria made a hasty exit.

Five minutes later, after putting on some fresh clothes and brushing his teeth, he emerged into the warm sun beneath the bougainvillea that covered the giant pergola. He got a round of applause and they lifted their glasses to him.

"Where the Abbot?" Brodie asked.

"He's in the chapel going through the office of the hour," the Condesa replied.

"What of Shepard and his thugs?" He directed his question to Bower.

"We haven't seen or heard anything from them yet. But give him time to recuperate and he'll find us sooner or later. Remember, he's been here once before."

"Who can forget it." Martha giggled.

Larnaca, Cyprus

Shepard knew that his two acolytes, Alphonse and Jeremiah, had done all they were capable of. With the painting gone and in his current condition, everything had been brought to a halt. Without it, the project was a dead dog. A fake painting at this stage, wouldn't do. It would be sussed in no time. He sent them home.

There were more important issues to attend to – like Bower and his jolly crew. He burnt for revenge on all of them. He still didn't know where they were, but he knew that once they had the painting, they wouldn't be hanging about. The most obvious place for them to go had to be to that crazy bitch's place in Guadamur, where she had fired her pistol at him.

With Alexis and Bruno as back up, things were going to get interesting. Pretty boy Bower, and his dumb stooge called George, were first on the list. He would wait for another week, then they would strike. He had the advantage. They wouldn't know when the attack would occur.

He could wait. He was good at waiting.

CHAPTER 42

**Guadamur
The next day...**

Bower paced up and down and guessed the party was
far from over. Moving backwards and forwards outside like a man who knew his final hour was upon
him, he plotted his next moves. He was sure that staying here
was the right thing to do. It was that or abandon the Condesa
to an uncertain, but no doubt, nasty future.

In spite of the peculiar events, the visions, and the vanishing work of art, he could not shrug off the feeling that there
was something else behind it all and that the entire panorama
of events had been constructed on purpose. An outside force
was beckoning him, and indeed ... Martha. They were being
led along, urged towards whatever was being clandestinely
planned.

Still, he had broken through something to reveal that change was possible if you surrendered to it. For the first time since he could recall, he was no longer standing where, before, he had feared to leave. This was a minor triumph, yet he was in no mood for patting himself on the back.

Looking back on his life, he felt that everything had been a waste of time. All his achievements, his money ... they all meant nothing. A colossal sadness edged into his thinking. He had little enthusiasm for the world of glittering Las Vegas or the spinning wheels of fortune of his casinos. Not so long ago he swaggered with a sense of his own power. Now, he was being tormented by self-doubt. He no longer knew, apart from Martha, who or what feeling to truly trust.

One day we are alive and the next we could be dead. I'm being carried along with no power or control. Nothing stays with me. Everything will die when I do, and death, in some way happens to me every minute of the day.

Even the paintings of Lazarus for all intents and purposes died at some point in time, as if their entire future had been mapped out.

But now there was a gap waiting to be filled.

Bower was caught up in intense introspection, and he wondered if he had been too hard on himself. There was a part of him that was growing steadily, that he was unaware of. He sensed that total redemption was possible and with that came hope, and what man would have the strength to resist the possibility of hope? A thought flickered through his mind, that like Lazarus, all men had the hope and possibility of resurrection. He knew that Martha would not deny that expression of boundless optimism.

With that, his mind cleared and all he could register was

a white blankness that caused him to close his eyes. Through it galloped The White Horse on which he was mounted and around the horse's mane was a garland of bluebells.

The vision went as quickly as it had appeared.

"Jesus!" he muttered out aloud. He needed to get away for a few hours or more.

He went back to the others and announced, "I have to go into Toledo this morning, to the bank, and arrange a funding transaction via The Wells Fargo Bank. They're located in Madrid but hopefully it can be sorted from Toledo. Also, I have to attend to some casino business. I won't be too long, and I'll keep the mobile switched on. I'm going to take my easel and paints, just in case I get inspired on the way back. You never know, I might find a field of irises or a farm garden with sunflowers!" His reference to Van Gogh was not unnoticed and prompted wry smiles from everyone, apart from George who hadn't a clue what he was talking about.

"I'll come with you, boss." George looked hopeful.

"No, you won't. I want this time to myself. You're staying here to watch over them."

Bower caught Martha's stare and he knew that she knew he was lying.

I just can't keep anything from her.

Martha stood up. "I'll give you a hand." She headed for the door and he followed.

Outside, she turned to him. "You're not going to the bank. Why did you lie?"

"I had to. I didn't know what else to say."

"I know what you saw because I saw it too. I was on the horse."

"You got that wrong, Martha, *I* was on the horse."

"What? We both can't be on it."

"Are we being told something? Is this a clue?"

"God only knows. We should be used to it by now. I also feel compelled to paint. It's too bad I can't come with you. Dad won't allow me to travel or even go out without him. I'll have to stay around here and see what I can come up with. There's something else I have to tell you." She stared into his eyes which had a haunted quality about them.

"What?"

"Abbot Louis."

"What about Abbot Louis?"

"He's become very quiet and has started drawing."

"That's goddamned weird. What's he drawing?"

"I'm not sure. He covers it up if I try to peek. He makes the excuse that he is no good compared to us and is shy. I found this in the waste bin." She reached into her pocket and produced a folded sheet of cartridge paper. With care, she placed it on the front of Bower's car and smoothed it out flat.

"Holy shit!"

"It takes some believing, doesn't it?"

Looking up at them, as a pencil drawing, was The White Horse of Uffington.

"We're not alone then."

"We can only wait and see."

She helped load his easel and stool into the car. "Don't go too far or too long. We may need you, as you know."

"I know, but this must be done. You know that."

"I know, and I have the same compulsion. We shall see what each of us produces." She squeezed his arm, turned and walked away.

Thirty minutes later, Martha stretched out her arms and legs and absorbed the warmth of the sun caressing her entirety. She wondered what she would paint. She set out her painting tools and checked that she had everything she needed. Her thoughts strayed to Ulla. She could not possibly reveal what was going on for it would drive her mother insane. She looked back at the events realising that the days came and went, and she had lost track of time. In her own quiet way, she had been steeling herself for this event. Not the violence about to erupt, but the culmination of what she had felt and seen in Uffington.

Be happy, for it is almost time.

Like the Condesa and Brodie had done so many times before her, Martha's gaze followed the contours of the distant hills that rippled and undulated across the backdrop as far as the eyes could see. She inhaled deeply, letting out the air in small sharp bursts. She imagined she was blowing away all her anxieties, her personal doubts and sadness into those distant hills and mountains, where they would be absorbed and buried until they bowed and withered away before the vast hand of eternity. She knew without a doubt that Maria's home, once a monastery was blessed with some ancient mystery – a mystery that had embraced her family. It was all around and had seeped into the very fabric – the stone walls, and the ground – it was built on.

She began to mix her paints, with no real idea of what she was about to do. The canvas was a mystery about to unfold.

The sun had risen higher on the blue and cloudless sky,

and for any artist, the light was a gift from heaven. Her brushes possessed a life and magic of their own over which she had little control.

Panels of darkness.

Panels of light.

Figures, first here, and then there, began formulating into a recognizable image.

She mopped at her brow. She lost all notion of time in a swirl of colours, light and shade. If something was not quite right, she would correct in any number of ways that artists are capable of.

Almost five hours later, she had finished. She stood back to evaluate what she had accomplished.

Her heart almost stopped.

During the time she had been painting, she had been locked off from what she was creating. But now... she could see.

Brodie and Garcia were busy making fortifications. At present, they had three guns plus a shotgun, and all phones were fully charged. A batch of sharpened hunting knives were deposited in hidden places that all would be familiar with. They also added one to their own personal weaponry. Garcia looked nervous and the Abbot refused to contribute on account of his religious vows. Brodie understood that their actions were no longer typical of monks. But what of the Templars? Were they not warrior monks? *Custodio Baez,* thought Brodie, was alive and well ... and still with him.

Heavy blocks attached to ropes were positioned in strategic doorways, and a barrier of razor wire – originally meant to discourage the odd wolf ravages that had once alarmed the region – were mounted across all entrances. Hidden behind this was a swinging pendulum of weights attached to a massive swathe of the same wire. It could be operated from a distance. They worked on their defences all day.

Trip wires were set up and the only danger was that they themselves would fall over them. Garcia tied temporary red ribbons on them to minimize the threat. The last thing they installed were two sets of double spotlights, in case of a night attack.

After exhausting all ideas, Brodie prepared barricades that would be erected once Bower returned. His ideas, he would have to admit, had come from an old film he had loved so much, *The Last of the Samurai.*

Dusting themselves down, they slumped into the chairs and let Luciana pour them two ice-cold beers. Brodie smiled to himself and chuckled. He saw Ned holding her hand and she seemed to like it. *How bloody nice. Good on 'em.*

Across the way, Martha appeared to have finished what she had been painting. He frowned. Painting around here was perilous. It had the possibility of unleashing dormant forces from ancient times. A tremor of fear passed through him. He remembered only too well his own experience with Lazarus and what it had done to him. Now that the painting has disappeared from this world, he knew there was a vacuum waiting to be filled.

He had begged for her not to pick up the mantle. For if she does, her life as she knew it would be finished – forever subordinate to the work she herself had created.

He stood, leaving Ned and Luciana together. With considerable trepidation, he walked over to his daughter.

She had seen him approaching and moved to meet him, blocking his way as if to prevent him from seeing what was on the canvas.

"Martha, it's no use keeping it from me. That in itself says it all, doesn't it?"

She looked up at him. His eyes were dark with a creeping sorrow, and in a few minutes, ten years had been added to his lived-in face.

"Please, Dad, no!"

He pushed her aside to inspect what she had done.

Encountering it was what he had expected and dreaded.

Before him, in bewildering flames of colour made of rich reds, blacks, whites and purples, stood the central figures of Christ with eyes ablaze, and a sitting figure in white wraps.

It was a new interpretation of *The Raising of Lazarus*.

"No, I begged you!" He reached out to sweep it away and destroy it, but Martha grabbed his arm, pulling it sharply downward and away from her work.

"No, Dad! No, you can't do that! I don't know what's happening and nor do you. Nothing is final ... nothing is settled! This means nothing yet. Believe me as you believed yourself once all those years back. Trust what I'm telling you. In some ways, Dad, you've been set free. I don't know my role here, but it's not only me. John's part of this too. Don't do anything, please, until he gets back."

Brodie didn't speak a word. He turned and walked away, leaving her confused and frightened. She felt cut off from him, lonely and full of fear. She covered her work with a small sheet. She barely noticed the sun's partial eclipse.

CHAPTER 43

T he bandages and strapping from around his body had been removed the previous day. It felt strange and almost breezy, but for Shepard, it was a good omen. He was on his way to recovery. The beating he endured had been brutal, savage, with a very real risk of leaving him permanently disabled in some way. In spite of the mishap, the mistake those two and their cohorts had made was to leave him alive. The alteration of his facial features and the devastation to his mental well-being were not forgivable issues. They would suffer once he got hold of them.

The beating had all but scuppered his plans for an upsurge in members, subscriptions and goodwill donations. He had vowed revenge, and in that transaction, to repossess the painting of Lazarus.

It would be true to say that Shepard was now deeply disturbed and dangerously delusional. He now believed his own lies and hyped-up nonsense. Within that distorted belief germinated the seed of a murderous and deeply disturbed individual, now bordering on the level of a psychopath.

Three days later, his breathing had become much easier. He called in Alexis and Bruno for a swift discussion. They booked a flight for the following day to Madrid. It was a long shot, but his investigations had found no trace or sound of them in Cyprus. He was convinced that they had fled the island as they now had the painting. What was to be gained by them remaining here and under obvious threat? Nothing.

Returning back to Spain had to be the logical choice. But where? The monastery where the painting was originally installed, or the converted monastery, the home of the crazy bitch Condesa? He would find out, but first, he would have to make sure they were no longer on the island. Then, he would decide.

It didn't take long.

There was no trace of them on the island.

It was time to return to Spain.

With that thought, he upped Alexis and Bruno's retainer fees, and booked a flight to Spain. His plans for the Holy Church of Lazarus were temporarily suspended.

Blood was what he wanted, and if the painting came with that, so much the better.

Thirty-six hours later, he was booked in at the Toledo hotel, Cigarral Bosque, located on a hill with superb views of the River Tajo. The views didn't interest him. A certain property down in Guadamur occupied his entire thinking.

The following morning, using two vehicles, he and his muscle men set off to Guadamur and to the home of the Condesa.

This was to be a reconnaissance mission. It was essential they were not spotted, because from this, he would draw up his future plans for them all. He was certain that they would be there. *That painting belongs to me and my church and nobody else. I need it and I must have it!*

It was not long before they were heading on the lonely track road that led to the Condesa's home. They came to a stop alongside a rocky outcrop, which concealed their presence but commanded a view of the place. Alexis and Bruno sheltered behind, out of sight, and Shepard trained his binoculars on the imposing structure. What he saw confirmed his suspicions. The parked cars were a giveaway.

He gave a start when he saw a figure. Focusing hard, he saw that it was Brodie. That confirmed it. They all had to be there with him. He watched for another half an hour and observed the Condesa and the Abbot moving about.

All was confirmed. He now had to withdraw and consolidate plans for an assault.

The previous day...

Bower drove away from the Condesa's home with no destination in mind. All he knew was that he felt compelled to get away for a while. He had become too involved in something larger and more mysterious than anything he had ever known. He needed some space.

He had a dream the previous evening. But whilst sensing

its importance, he had forgotten what it was about – apart from the emotions forgotten dreams often leave behind. This compelled his journey, which gave him the same feeling as his dream.

He avoided the main roads and settled for quieter back routes. He was an hour into his drive when he saw an escarpment with a view of the landscape, and deep into a wooded valley. It looked ideal and he doubted if he would discover anything better. It was isolated and as silent. Just the way he wanted.

Bower turned off the engine and for a minute or two, he sat still to absorb the silence. He got out of the car and looked around at the lonely beauty of the surrounds. He could smell the sweetness of the air, the smell of oranges and of pine and lavender. Never before had he noticed the intensity of it all. Now, he was prepared to suspend the constant garbage that trickled through his mind and accept – just accept and nothing else – the magnificence of the natural scene presented to him. For the first time since he could recall, he felt a degree of a rare and unusual sensation. It was called … peace.

Once he had absorbed the flavor of the surroundings, he unloaded his equipment, complete with bottles of water and a hip flask of scotch. What was in front of him told no lies and played no games. It was as it was … nothing less, nothing more. The truth of life, he thought, was far less simple than he would have liked it to be.

As he arranged his easel and canvas, unfolded the stool and sorted out his colours, Bower realised with certainty that this was just the beginning. He was struggling to let go of his grip on his past life. In the secret darkness of his soul, he knew there was a power that would give him the strength to open his heart to the world, but darkness surrounded him. He needed the darkness to be broken ... to be flooded with light.

To hope ... that required courage. But whether there was reason to hope was another question entirely. He was being given a second chance in life and he was powerless to resist the onward march of change.

Bower examined his palette. He had failed to clean it from the last time he had used it, but somehow it seemed unimportant and everything around him assumed the same unimportance. All was level and equal.

He mixed greens, reds, black and yellow, and began to dip his brush into the ensuing mix. He had no need to look or survey the complexities of what stretched out across the horizon in front of him. In an almost feverish haste, he began to apply paint to canvas. The odd car or lorry would pass by, but he never heard or saw them. If asked, he would have told you that neither could he see the canvas, nor did he care to do so.

It had its own life ... its own meaning. He was just the colourist.

The sun ascended high into the sky and what he failed to notice was that this was the day and the time that a partial eclipse of the sun was to occur.

The birds fell silent and not a breeze could be felt and not a leaf moved. The only audible sounds came from the panting breath of Bower and the sound his brushes made as they worked around the canvas.

The eclipse diminished, yet Bower had barely looked up. If he had noticed it, he gave no sign. His attentions were in another place, another time, and another dimension. Sweat began to drip from him, staining his white T-shirt with dark rings under the armpits, as if to pronounce his secret guilts.

Then abruptly, he came to a halt. It was finished.

Time had passed him by like a slow moving cloud and he hadn't even noticed.

He stood a few paces back to scrutinize what he had done.

At first, he couldn't make out the image presented before him. His eyes began to focus and then he saw it clearly. Lazarus was being raised from the dead and was standing looking out of the paint, and beside him, with a hand raised, stood the figure of Christ surrounded by his disciples. The expressions were challenging and almost scary, with a hint of El Greco around them. A bright sun shone light into the darkness of the tomb or cave.

Bower reached for his camera and took several shots of what he had achieved.

He sat back on the stool when suddenly, a violent pain bit into his head. Scissor-like pains were attempting to locate his brain. He bent his head down and grappled with the sensation as it flooded his entire head and then into his heart.

I'm having a heart attack!

There came one great and violent pulsation which racked his whole body and mind. He let out an agonised moan and then without any warning, the sensation vanished, as if someone had switched off a light bulb. The pain had gone.

He gasped momentarily to get his breath back.

Still bent double, he became aware of the warmth of the sun on his head and neck. He lifted his head to look at the sky and for a few moments, enjoyed the physical reassurance of the sun's rays. He returned his gaze back to his work.

Time stood still.

The canvas on his easel ... was now blank.

Brodie felt anger. As he hurried away from Martha he clenched and unclenched his fists several times in a blanket of angry frustration and bewilderment. *God, I curse you! You stole my life from me and yet, I have served you well. But you're not content with that, so now you have to steal my only child, who I barely know but love so deeply. How can you do that? How? I asked you to take me again, but no, you wanted someone new, someone fresh. I'd served my purpose. Leave my family and me alone. We've had enough of you. I curse you! Damn you!*

There was no vocal response.

He brushed away tears of anger, and as he did, a cold blast of air gushed through the room he was standing in. It blew over ornaments, sent curtains billowing, and papers cascading in all directions.

Brodie gasped. Maria, who was busy writing her next book, gave a small shriek and Garcia held on to his notebooks. The only person who had not noticed anything was George.

"What was that?" Abbot Louis looked concerned. He had been busy drawing but had somehow only been able to reproduce variations of the same image he originally started with, *The White Horse of Uffington.* All his finished pieces lay scattered across the room.

"It must have been something I said," Brodie grunted. "I'm going to my room for a short while."

Once on his own, he started to regret his actions with Martha and the way he'd attempted to trash her painting, and then turning his back on her to walk away. *Of all people, I should know there is nothing on earth she can do to stop what's go-*

ing on. I couldn't, so how the hell can she? I'm ashamed of my actions and my thoughts. What do I do now?

A deep tiredness, without warning, overcame him, prompting him to curl up on the bed. Before he could resist, and with one large gulp, he fell into a ferocious deep sleep.

Whirling, whirling and forever turning, coloured images played around in the corners of his mind. Drifting up through the kaleidoscope arose the face of Ulla, and next to it another face formed, and it was Martha, offering him the reins of The White Horse, as if to say, take and ride to wherever you wish. He tried to articulate but his mouth refused to open. It was as if his entire body had been turned to stone. The faces dissolved into the spinning rotation from which now appeared the unmistakable forms of Lazarus, created since the time of Annas Zevi, one after the other, through the years and the centuries, reaching out to Borgoña, Cortez, and then through to Ladro. Fourteen in total. They vanished like ghosts and a new picture was forming – but it remained indistinct, without form or recognizable features – before that too began to fade away.

Brodie, in his sleep, reached out to it, but it moved away from his grasp. In a moment, it was gone.

He spluttered into wakefulness. His head was full of a strange buzzing murmuring sound, like that of a hive of bees. While loud at first, it began to decrease back to normality.

He sat up and checked his watch. He'd been asleep for five minutes only. He recalled what he had just seen and hoped for a sudden epiphany, some sudden revelation of mystical knowledge that would tell him it was not Martha.

Come what may, he knew he had to speak with her. She hadn't deserved the fierceness of his angst. The idea of her taking over his role loomed up like a nemesis, a terrible dream. He felt an inner isolation as he listened to the silence around him. It didn't help, perhaps, that she had the biblical name of Martha.

This was the first time Martha had experienced distress and humiliation since she had arrived in Spain. As mature and confident as she was, she still had not encountered the full gambit of human emotions, life's trials and tribulations. In many ways, she remained a raw recruit to its ways. The sight of her newly discovered father turning his back on her and walking away had been deeply upsetting.

Amidst all this, she remembered her meeting with the Condesa and how all had developed from that point. The painting and its implications worried her. Martha knew that whatever happened, she must never forget who she was before all this started. She could easily lose herself to the mystery. It was real ... as real as the ground she could feel beneath her feet. Nothing, however, was clear. Who was she now? What would she become? What was her role in all of this? Will she live in the presence of some mystical painting that somehow had the ability to heal people? She had no answer. She wanted to speak to both Brodie and Bower.

Martha stood and turned around to look at her work, now standing serenely in the coolness of the shady bougainvillea draped overhead.

Brodie approached her, looking reproachful. "I'm so sorry." He held his arms open and for a moment, she hesitated. But her humanity compelled her and with a stifled sob, she embraced him. They stood together, flesh and blood, taking comfort to assuage their mutual sadness.

"Dad, whatever is going to happen, never ever push me away again. I need a dad right now. Please!"

"Martha, I promise you. Please forgive me. I shall forever be here for you. I promise."

"What's going to happen? Are those thugs coming back?"

"You can bet good money on it."

"Custer's Last Stand. eh?"

"I hope not. We are well prepared with some nasty surprises lined up." He was about to tell her about the dream but thought better of it. "I'm wondering what's going on in there." He pointed back to the house.

Maria was busy with her new book, and the Abbot was worried about his continued visions of The White Horse of Uffington. He couldn't seem to stop drawing it and what's more, he was keeping it a secret from everyone.

As for George, he was happy watching TV, even though it's in Spanish and he didn't understand a word of it.

Ned was busy typing on his laptop. He was writing a book out of the whole thing and reckoned it will knock Dan Brown off his perch once published.

"Do you know how long Bower, I mean John, is going to be?"

"Should be back anytime soon. I'm going to have another look at my painting to see if there are any clues in it," Martha said.

"Good idea. Let's look."

She turned and carefully removed the small white sheet.

Martha shrieked.

The painting had vanished! All that remained was her original blank canvas.

THE LAZARUS CONTINUUM

Brodie turned pale as he saw his worst fears demonstrated before his eyes.

CHAPTER 44

S hepard inhaled deeply on his cigarette and was pleased that his rib pains had subsided. He poured another hefty slug of Bourbon. Bruno and Alexis were with him but he didn't offer them one. They were getting paid enough to buy their own.

"Well, boys, how are we going to handle this? I need to know that they are all there and that we can grab the painting back. What do you suggest?" He looked at both of them in anticipation.

Bruno twisted a large, gold ring around his finger. "We need a hostage, one of the women. That's their weak spot. Once you have them, they will give you anything you ask for. Believe me, I've done this a few times in the past. It works every time."

It certainly does. Worked for me the last time.

"Okay, but I just don't want the painting. I want those bastard's balls on a plate. You understand what I'm saying?"

"Crystal clear, Mr. Shepard."

"Reverend Shepard, please, now that you know a lot more about me. What's the best time to go there?"

"When? It has to be when it starts to get dark. People are always confused at that time especially if they are not expecting trouble. But we will give them big trouble. A big surprise eh, Mr. Reverend?"

Shepard allowed himself a mordant smirk as he flicked a fingernail of ash into a jade ashtray. This was beginning to sound promising. *These guys are the types I would not care to meet down a dark alleyway.*

"I don't know where the painting is, but they wouldn't have come back without it. It has to be there somewhere, and you must find it."

"We'll search the whole house for it. If it's there, we'll find it."

"Once it's back in my hands, the whole world will know what it's capable of. Believe me!" Shepard paused and stroked his chin, staring out into nowhere land, before gulping back another swig of the golden liquid.

"Do you guys reckon we can get hold of one of the women?"

"If we can get close enough somehow, get in and out real quick, then the answer is yes. But we shouldn't try anything if the men are around. I think it would be a mistake to underestimate them. Just look at what they did to you."

"Okay, okay, knock it off, will you?" Shepard found that observation almost as painful as the physical damage he had suffered. "When do we do it?"

Alexis stood and moved to the window looking out on the panoramic views. "We need another good look at the place and locate all entrances, gates, windows and any weak points that will give us an advantage. You okay with that, Mr. Reverend?"

"Oh yes, I'm perfectly fine with that. It sound like a good plan. We'll set out tomorrow sometime. I'll let you know."

It took Bower at least a half hour to recover from the shock that what he had worked on so feverishly had simply vanished. *Someone must have stolen it when I wasn't looking!* In his heart, he knew that was not true. He had been there, awake, one hundred percent of the time. He remembered Brodie mentioning that all the paintings vanished at some point, but he had barely finished it and the paint was still wet! *Anyway, why should it vanish? I don't get it.*

He searched the whole area but there was nothing to see. In a state of complete bewilderment and frustration, he reloaded all his equipment and accessories back into the car and headed back to Guadamur and the Condesa's home.

As if on autopilot, he threaded his way through traffic until he reached the turn-off point. He gunned the car down the track as fast as he dared. He could barely wait to get there and tell them what had happened.

When he arrived, he saw that there was a difference in the way the place looked. To start with, there was a whole load of razor wire sitting with menace along the entrance gates. *That wasn't there before.* He gave the horn a prolonged blast, followed by two more in quick succession. Shortly after, George appeared with a toothy grin, looking lunkish and carrying his gun as he opened up the gate.

"Hi, boss. Had a good day? You better mind where you go. There are trip wires everywhere."

"Expecting visitors?"

"You could say that. We'll take the ribbons off the wires later in the night."

"Where are the others?

"In the sitting room. They've been waiting for you. I think something has happened."

"You can say that again, George!"

Bower walked in and was greeted by an array of sombre faces. He had no idea why. "What's wrong? You look like you're at a wake."

Maria spoke. "You could say that. Look, sit down. This will take some explaining."

He sat down, aware that what he had to say might also cause a stir.

"Martha," Maria said, "tell him."

"John, like you this morning, as you know, I was compelled to paint. I worked on a canvas for several hours, five altogether. When it was finished, it followed in dad's footsteps. It was The Raising of Lazarus." She paused. "I wasn't aware that I had painted it. I moved it into the shade and covered it with a cloth. Dad came to look at it but when we took off the covering, you are not going to believe this, there was nothing there! It had vanished. All that was left was a blank canvas without a dot of paint on it. It was as if I had never painted anything. I *did,* and dad saw it earlier and even got upset about it. Didn't you, Dad?"

"Yes, I did, and you know why. I don't want my daughter to live the kind of life I had led because of that painting. There's something I haven't told any of you before." He looked around and all eyes were riveted on him. Slowly and with care, not to omit any details, he narrated the sequence he saw in the dream, and the procession of all the paintings before they vanished from his vision. Of Lazarus since the first by Annas Zevi, and those that followed on in the bloodline of his legacy. That included the last known work by himself, Broderick Ladro. He had counted fourteen, including his own. A new picture began to form but before it was recognizable, it too vanished. "Why Martha's work vanished in front of us like that, I can offer no explanation."

Nobody spoke.

Abbot Louis looked awestruck. "This is God's work," he spoke out loud.

"Then he must be building quite a collection." Bower smiled judiciously before plunging in to tell his story. "That could be correct because he's got mine as well."

"What?"

"Like Martha I had a huge urge to paint something and I wanted to be away from people. I didn't go to a bank, that was just an excuse to get me out of here and away from you all. No disrespect meant."

Bower went on and explained what had happened – how he missed the partial eclipse of the sun, painted for hours, his attack of pain and then the total and unbelievable occurrence that his work had vanished and was nowhere to be found.

"It vanished just like mine?" Martha looked astonished,

"It looks that way."

"I don't understand any of this. Two paintings of the raising of Lazarus vanishing when the paint is not even dry? Why?" Martha exclaimed. She stood up and started to pace.

"God moves in mysterious ways," was the only thing the

Abbot could come up with.

Brodie cut through it all. "As Maria and I have always said, the painting has ways of looking after itself, and bearing that in mind, we can only leave it at that. What will be will most definitely be. Right now, we are here to protect Maria and her home, and now, we no longer have a painting to defend. If they come for us, they won't believe the painting had vanished and of course they'll think we've hidden it somewhere. It could rile Shepard up even more. George, I want you to show John what we have done to defend this place and you, John, take note of everything and where we have put things, like hidden knives. Also, between us, we have numerous farm implements that would make excellent weapons. These are now scattered around the property. You will see what they are; pitchforks, spades, axes, forks, crowbars, hammers, chisels, screwdrivers, and metal spikes. There are also buckets of water that can be used to deal with any fires, just in case. Joy of joys, we also discovered in the cupboard a couple of flares. They should brighten up the occasion. If they fail, we have the spotlights. Are you happy with that? By the way," he added as an afterthought, "I've rigged up a large steel drum with an iron pole. It's our alarm call should they decide to attack. This is what it sounds like." He stood back and swung the iron bar. BOOOOM! A thunderous sound reverberated around the entire area.

"Sound loud enough for you?"

They all nodded.

Brodie couldn't tell them, but he felt afraid. He was kicking himself for allowing Martha to be part of it. *Hardly the behaviour of a responsible parent.*

He let them discuss and arrange themselves into a watch

committee based on two-hour stretches throughout the twenty-four hours.

Something else was bothering him.

In his present condition, he had considered all the circumstances. He wondered why it was necessary to have a miraculous painting at all. What purpose did it serve? Shepard, in one way, had got it right in his intention to show it to the world, although the plan was deeply flawed by his lust for wealth and power. He thought the painting would pave the way for that.

Brodie finished the beer and surveyed the hills as he had when he first arrived here. They hadn't changed.

A crashing sensation powered through his head, causing him to buckle over. "Not again!" he shouted out as he clutched his head.

Deus Vult! Beauséant! Knights, flags, horses screaming, blood, noise, and steel clashing.

Bower who was sitting inside felt it too. He attempted to stand, but fell to the floor and clutched at the veins of his bulging temple

Beauséant! Ad maioram! Dei gloriam!

The clamour of battle. The clash of steel and the moans of dying and mutilated men.

Bower's cry caused consternation in the room and Maria rushed out to find Brodie and saw him similarly collapsed on the floor and looking deathly pale.

The Condesa took in the familiar scene. The clock had at last turned full circle. But it was strange that Bower was going through the same thing.

She cradled his head and spoke softly to him. "C'mon, Brodie, you're fine. You've been here before and there's no need to be afraid. You're going to be fine."

Martha came rushing through. "Maria..." She stopped. "Dad! Is he okay? What's happened? Maria..." Her look was imploring.

Maria remained calm. "Don't worry, Martha, we've seen this before. He'll be fine. Trust me. How's Mr. Bower?"

"He collapsed and looks like dad and was shouting out in Latin."

"Remarkable."

Martha knelt alongside Brodie who had opened his eyes and seemed to be recovering. "Dad, can you hear me?"

He didn't reply but began to cough.

She turned to Maria. "Why is this happening to them both at the same time?"

"That's a long story. They're going to be okay. Brodie will understand what's happened, but Bower, I think not. Your dad's going to have to explain it to him. I have to warn you, it's a battle cry. It looks like things are going to get tough. We are all going to have to work together."

Brodie sat up. "I heard what you were saying. Where's Bower?"

"Like you, he's recovering. Shall I bring him in?"

"When he's ready, and Martha, you stay here and listen. Do not speak."

It was ten minutes before Bower, still with an air of confusion about him, confronted Brodie. "So, okay, what was all that about?"

"Let's say it's an alarm bell."

"What does that mean?"

"It means things are developing fast and we are being

warned that danger approaches. By that, I mean Shepard and his crew."

Brodie went on to explain how he himself had experienced the self-same visions when he had first visited this place seventeen years ago. He explained the history of the building and its link with medieval times and how those links led him to the artist Cortez and the Condesa's search for a cure.

"It seems I was a conduit for the painting that had vanished, and I had been chosen for the next version. Before you say anything, don't … just listen. There is, at this moment in this world, no magical mystery painting. Let me just say, it's in another dimension. I've seen them all, every one of them, lined up and intact. Again, don't ask. The fact that your painting and Martha's took about the same time to complete and then both dissolved to God knows where, both at the same time, has a significant meaning. From what I have known and seen today, a page has been turned and a new chapter has begun. Strange events are about to descend on us and you will have to trust a voice inside you."

Brodie didn't know how he was so certain that Bower would experience such things. But with his painting vanishing, and his experience thirty minutes ago with the medieval world, he was prepared to put money on it. He hoped, but dared not mention, that the finger of fate would point at Bower and not in the direction of Martha. He didn't mean that unkindly, but reacted as only a parent could.

"You talk in riddles," Bower said.

"We shall see."

It was then that the Abbot and Garcia appeared.

Abbot Louis looked more relaxed this week than he had

been over the past months. "I am witnessing some very odd events since I've been here. This place is full of religious suggestion, I sense it in the air. If I didn't know better, I could swear on the bones of Saint Peter that I heard a voice whispering in my ear back there, when John was … ummm … shall we say, having a problem."

No more, please. Brodie bent his head and covered his eyes.

"It seems," said Bower, "it's turning into a common event around here. What did it say Father?"

"I'm not entirely sure, but it sounded like, 'fight fire with fire.'

"You sure it wasn't 'flight hire, hire flight?' Because that's what I wish I could do right now."

"Quite certain, sorry to say."

CHAPTER 45

It was 11.30 p.m. The 4x4's lights were switched off as they stopped near the Condesa's home. The vehicle was turned around for a fast exit and the engine off. At first, there was no sound, then the doors opened, and two figures alighted. It was Bruno and Alexis, dressed in black with balaclavas, and armed. Their flashlights were off as a thin moon and a cloudless night gave enough light for them to see sufficiently.

"Got everything?"

"Yep. All okay. Let's go."

Crouching low, they advanced towards the home. The ground beneath was sandy and interspersed with flinty stones and prickly shrubs. Bruno set a fast pace. This was a reconnoiter mission, and on his back, he had hung a drawing pad with a pencil attached. Sketches and diagrams would be essential if their future mission was to succeed. At least, there were no dogs to pick up their scent or security lights to bother them. It seemed everybody was inside or in bed.

They drew close to the walls and gates, and Bruno got his pad and began to sketch and write quick notes. What they both noticed was the appearance of the razor wire that topped all the walls and possible entry points.

They had been busy.

The main gate in the entrance was also heavily protected and all that wire would have to be rammed to gain entry. To go in that way would make them easy targets, as if in a turkey shoot, if they had weapons. Of that, there was no way of telling. It wouldn't be an option.

"This place is going to be more difficult than we thought, Alexis. It would be better in daylight."

"Then everybody would know who we are."

"We have false plates."

"Yes, and we don't know what security cameras she has in there. It looks like we'd have to go through the front gate. Every other surface is covered in wire."

They moved to the rear wall and there they saw something which raised their spirits. Behind the wall was a vast amount of earth that formed a natural slope, almost to the top of the wall.

"Get to the top of that and we're in."

"Yes, but we still have to get over that wire."

"They wouldn't have put that up if they didn't think we were coming."

"Seems that way. Let's complete the circuit."

"It's either the front gate or the back wall."

"Remember, we have grenades."

They continued around the property, still bent double and talking in whispers, their flashlights guiding them. All appeared quiet and not a sound could be heard.

Thirty minutes later, they made their way back to the 4x4.

✠

Every move they had made had been monitored. Bower was on first watch and he had spotted them almost at once. The moonlight wasn't only on their side. It shone for him as it did for them. At first, he was tempted to raise the alarm, but that would only let them know they were prepared for their arrival. Instead, he watched them. At times they disappeared from view but always reemerged further up. It was obvious they were giving the place a thorough once over.

He had no idea who they were, but that didn't matter. They were up to no good and he didn't doubt they were Shepard's hired meat. He'd have a lot to report in the morning. He listened hard and could just make out the sound of a vehicle starting up and moving off.

He checked his watch. Twelve-thirty. He had another hour to go. He moved up to the seat he had constructed against the wall with a viewing slit that allowed him to look out without being seen. There was also a wooly hat and a blanket to help keep out the cold.

There he sat.

The episode of the vanishing painting continued to fill his head. He hadn't admitted it to anybody, but it had freaked him out. It had scared him in a thrilling sort of way. The mysteries and unsolved riddles of theosophical, philosophical and religious lore had held him enthralled throughout his life. He, John D. Bower, was now in the middle of one. That was unbelievable. It was almost too far-fetched … but it wasn't. It was real. He had seen it with his own eyes. Luciana was there to be seen and not a trace of a bullet wound. The Condesa moving round like somebody thirty years younger was inexplicable. *The dreams and visions that stalk this place were like microscopes looking at the hidden occurrences in our souls.* This quote from Erich Fromm was an excellent analogy, well-suited to the ambience of the surroundings. Did he regret it? At first, he did. He resented it deeply. But as it continued, he had bent and accepted it.

He managed to stay awake and felt no cold. In fact, he felt an odd buoyancy. He had become part of something really important, and far removed from his Las Vegas life. His blood flowed fresh and alive and his thoughts had never been clearer. Bower had found happiness and he was unable to define it. It refused definition. It didn't need it. It was just as it was, crystal clear for all to see if they cared to look hard enough.

There was a cough behind him. Garcia stood there ready to take over the watch. He had a pissed off expression and looked and dressed as if he was about to embark on an artic expedition. Bower burst into unprecedented and spontaneous laughter. Anyone who knew him would have said they'd never heard him do that before. It was totally out of character. The unexpectedness of it caused his psoriasis to flare, which led him to vigorous bouts of scratching.

Bower told Garcia what he had seen and what had happened and that they had gone, and probably would not be back. But they must take no chances.

"We'll speak later, Ned." Bower clapped him on the shoulder and apart from his scratching, still had a grin on his face when he went off to bed.

That morning was once again blisteringly hot. The occupants of the Condesa's home at Guadamur were exhausted, their faces stretched with tension. Bower had related what he had seen on his watch, and the news had been greeted like a bomb had just landed.

"So, we are in for a scrap," a bleary-eyed Garcia spoke. "I saw nothing on my watch to worry about. The only way they can get here is through that track out there?"

"Yes, it's the only way in. But if they park their vehicle up behind those rocks, we won't see them." Maria pointed.

"That's correct," Bower added. "I didn't see a car, but when they left, I heard it start up."

Brodie looked thoughtful. "Maybe we should station a welcome for them at that point. They wouldn't be expecting that."

"Too risky. If you got shot or caught, we would be at their mercy, and I don't believe they have too much of that."

"All options have their hazards. For sure, we are out-gunned. We'll have to be more cunning, more devious and give them a false sense of security."

The Abbot sipped at his coffee, stood and glanced at his watch. He hadn't been able to stop thinking about what was happening in his life. He was now a million miles away from his cozy, cloistered, orderly, regulated life and routines. In comparison to what he was now in the middle of, it had all the potential of a painting by Hieronymus Bosch.

"I shall be taking over from Martha shortly. I'll go and see how she's getting on."

Martha watched the sun over the next hour in its endless climb into the morning sky. She had been on watch since six o'clock. It hadn't been as bad as she thought it would be. She found it restful, even peaceful. It gave her a chance to reconcile the recent events and analyse what might happen when Shepard and his men appeared.

After what she had learnt about them all, especially Brodie and Bower, Martha wondered, with an almost childlike horror, whether the epithet, evil, wicked or dishonest could be applied to them. They had done wrong ... this was true. There had been killings, and even her father was no stranger to that. Bower owned casinos and she was certain that he had pulled dodgy stunts in the past. In strict biblical terms, they both were doomed to fiery pits for all eternity. *What a load of crap. Life's just not like that, with a simplistic black and white label for every moral and immoral stance we take. Where do I fit in?*

She found it hard to understand how Brodie, her dad, once a devout monk, had so easily laid aside his monastic robes and vows and turned into this person who can devise potentially lethal traps. This was the worst she could think of them, but it didn't matter a jot. They were attempting to save lives, and this was the only way it could be done.

She shielded her eyes from the glare of the sun as she peered across the rocks and track that led back to the main highway.

She could make out a small cloud of dust that grew larger as it approached. Her first thought was to sound the alarm, but realised she could be overreacting. Using the binoculars

provided, she focused on the vehicle and made out the letter-
ing on the side. *Fernandez s.r.l.* Beneath that, *Meubles Para El
Hogar y La Oficina.*

It was a furniture delivery lorry. Maria must have ordered something. It pulled up ten metres short of the gate and
a tall man wearing denim overalls, a large hat and holding a
clipboard, jumped out. He saw Martha and gave her a cheery
wave before sliding open the side door. After a short rum-
mage, he pulled out a small crate, which was securely sealed.

The gate was locked and there was no way in for him, but
he shouted out to Martha.

"Hola, I have a delivery for a Condesa Maria de Toledo
and I need a signature."

For a moment, Martha hesitated, but it wouldn't do any
harm to open the gate and sign the delivery note. It would
save Maria from being disturbed. Using two hands, she struggled to draw the bolt back, but eventually it gave. She repeated it on the other bolt. It was easier, and now the gate
could be opened. She gave a slight pull and it swung silently
open towards her.

The man was smiling as he held out the crate. She took it
in both hands, placed it on the ground and went to sign the
docket. Instead of the expected pen to sign with, she found
herself staring at the barrel of a snub nosed pistol.

The colour drained from her face and her hand shot to her
mouth. "Oh, my God!"

"Yup." The man sneered. "Oh, my God, it is. Now put
down the crate and get in the back of the truck. If you think
this is a toy, you are dreaming, and I'll have no hesitation in
using it, pretty girl or not. Now, get in. Make it snappy ...
Move it!" He stabbed the barrel into her back, pointing where

she should go.

Martha, enveloped in fear and terror, froze. In robotic fashion, she started putting one foot in front of the other. On reaching the door, a large, rough hand propelled her into the opening, and the door was slammed shut.

Seconds later, the truck swung around in a swirling dust cloud and barreled out towards the direction it had come from.

Adjusting his steel-rimmed spectacles, his monastic bones creaked as he made his way out towards the gates where he knew Martha was ensconced. All the excitement and activity had worn him out. He wiped his brow as he made the sign of the cross.

The air had a coolness he enjoyed. Swinging around the corner of the room, he was startled to see the gate was open.

"What?" He called out loud, "Martha, where are you?" A stab of alarm rushed through him. He ran to the gate and looked all around. There was no sign of her in any direction. *What's happened to her! Dear God, no!* He looked one way and then another … nothing … not a sign of her. He turned and hurried back to the house. "It's Martha, I can't find her anywhere and the gates are wide open!"

Everybody rushed outside, led by Brodie.

The Abbot was right. There was no sign of her. The sudden silence was broken only by the sound of the gate creaking as it moved backward and forward in the slight breeze.

"She's been taken. They've got her." Brodie's jaw was set

hard and his eyes glittered with menace. "I will kill them. I swear to God, I'll kill them."

"Easy, Brother, easy," The Abbot's voice rose above the sobs from Luciana and the Condesa. He put his arm around Brodie's shoulder.

"Get off me, will you?" Brodie growled with a savage grimace. "I need to think."

The Abbot steppèd back, but at that moment, he felt inadequate and more than embarrassed.

"Hey, what's this?" Garcia pointed to the small crate on the ground. "We've been left a calling card."

Brodie snatched it off him and began to prise open the lid.

"Careful," Garcia said. "You don't know what's in there."

"There's only one way to find out." A few more tugs and pulls and the crate opened.

They all stopped and began to peer inside. A fetid smell arose.

"What is it?"

Brodie waved his hand under his nose but said nothing. He couldn't make out what he was looking at. He dipped his hand inside to pull the smelly object out and held it up. It dangled by its tail.

"Shit!" George shouted. "It's a rat."

It was a rat, a very large and decomposing rat. Pinned to its flank by a long, plastic spike or needle was a folded sheet of paper.

"Jesus," Brodie hissed as he pulled the pin out, threw it to the ground and unfolded the paper. As he read it, he turned pale and dropped to his knees. "No, God, why have you forsaken us?"

Bower grabbed the note from him. He read it out loud.

She could even end up dead,
Or at best lose her maidenhead.
The painting … I'm still waiting.
With sense, no need to mutilate,
Or gently slice away on her mamillate.

We'll be in touch.

"They can't mean that! Cut her nipples off?"

Brodie slumped to the ground and a stunned silence gripped them all.

CHAPTER 46

With difficulty, she opened her eyes. Her head was pounding and there was a strange sweet taste in her mouth. She had no idea where she was. When she moved, she realised she was tied by her wrists to the headboard rails of a bed.

The last thing she could remember was being pushed into the back of the lorry by a man with a gun, and then another man who was hidden inside had pulled her in and rammed some sort of cloth over her nose and mouth. Its smell reminded her of hospitals except she wasn't in one. She had been in a lorry full of cardboard boxes.

The realisation that she has been kidnapped struck her like a thunderbolt and her next thought was of Brodie and the effect that would have on him. She performed a mental check on herself. Starting from the top of her head, she worked her way down her body, attempting to sense any harm or violations. She found none. Apart from the headache, she was unscathed.

Lifting her head, she looked around the room. It was plain with a small table and chairs, tailored wardrobes and fittings. She could be anywhere ... and there wasn't a sound to be heard. Her heart raced ... she felt marooned and extremely lonely. She berated herself for letting this happen to her. Shepard will now use her to get the painting. The problem was ... there was no a painting. It had vanished into another place in time and space. But who would believe that?

Wriggling, she attempted to free her arms, but they were bound fast. She stopped struggling when the door opened, and Silas Shepard walked in, with two men she recognised as the men who had captured her. The same men from the bar when she had been out with Bower.

"Miss Martha." His voice washed over her, slithery with innuendo, like a snake about to strike. "Are we feeling comfortable enough?" He moved beside her and beckoned to Bruno who produced a pair of scissors. "This won't hurt one bit if you'll just keep still."

"What are you going to do?" Her voice quavered with fright.

"Proceed, Bruno."

Bruno said nothing. Leaning forward, he unbuttoned her blouse and with one swift movement of the scissors, removed a button. Next, he moved down to her slacks and again with another swift movement, cut away the front belt loop, which he held up like a trophy won at a contest.

"Last one next, Bruno."

Bruno smiled and ran his hand through her thick hair, making a soft murmuring sound as he did so. Grabbing a decent handful, he pulled it and snipped off a thick bunch, then turned and handed it to Shepard who was grinning like a

343

drunken monkey.

"These little items could do the trick." Shepard drilled his gaze into her. "Where are you keeping the painting?"

She tried to reply but her voice croaked and her throat felt sore. "I can hardly speak. I need water." She gave several raspy coughs.

He nodded at Alexis who went to the bathroom and came back with a glass of water. Bruno untied one of her hands.

She managed to sit up and gulp at the water before the glass was taken from her.

"Now answer my question."

"How would I know?" She realised that to tell him it had vanished would not be the wisest of answers.

"How wouldn't you know? You're very much an active member of those creeps. You are obviously lying and playing dumb. Let me just tell you this, in case you haven't grasped it in full. Your father has received a message from us giving him a clue of what we are going to do to you if he doesn't collaborate. Not very nice, I'm afraid, and a little messy. We'll send him these first." He held up the button, belt loop and clump of hair. "It's a wonder how such little things can focus the mind. Bruno, tie back her hand. We're leaving now, but I look forward to chatting with you later."

As Bruno tied back her wrists, she remembered reading about one of the methods the Great Houdini used to affect his escapes. When tied down with ropes or straitjackets, he gained wiggle room by enlarging his shoulders and chest and moving his arms slightly away from his body. She tensed her hand and wrist, making them slightly larger, and once the rope had been tied she relaxed them. Immediately, the bonds felt looser. She wasn't free, but there was now a good chance she could be if she was patient and persistent. She began her attempt.

Brodie was inconsolable, and the only person he could blame for the whole affair was himself, for not being firm enough with her and sending her home. Because of his failure, she was now in danger of rape and mutilation, and possibly death. He could save her life and give them the painting ... if they had it. It couldn't be done. Shepard would never believe it had disappeared.

He couldn't fake one either, that was just not possible. The others, including George, were equally upset, and were unable to comfort him. All he could do was wait for some sort of message from Shepard. *Surely this mad man can't mean to go on with this threat. He's supposed to be a man of God.* He could try and speak to Shepard, but as yet, he had no idea where he could be.

A shout from George who was stationed out by the gate, caused them to rush outside.

"What is it, George?" Brodie shouted.

"It looks like a motorbike and it's heading this way."

Brodie hauled himself to the top and shielding his eye, he saw the motorbike hammering towards them.

Brodie made sure his shoulder holster was in place, but a lone biker couldn't mean an assault of some sort. This was something else. With a roar, it came to a halt, and Brodie realised it was a Correos motorcycle courier from Toledo. He swung the gate open and rushed outside. He was handed a small box, which he signed for. There was no indication of where it had come from, but it was addressed to him. Fearing the worst, he pulled frantically to open it. The others gathered around, and all looked anxious.

Brodie lifted the lid and what he saw filled him with dismay. Sitting at the bottom of the box was a button, a belt loop, and more worrying, a handful of hair. He had no doubt they were Martha's. He tilted his head to the heavens and gave a small cry.

Maria spoke. "Look, there's a note of some sort in there." She pulled it out and opened it, and without reading it, handed it Brodie.

He took it from her and read it out loud. "As you see, here are some little keepsakes for you to remember her by, if worst comes to worst. It needn't be that way. Just surrender the painting to me and an exchange can be made. You will be called within the next forty-eight for the details. Before you think of going against my wishes, remember the note with my pet rat."

He looked around at them all. "What am I supposed to do? I don't have the painting, and nobody knows where it is. It's a catastrophe and it's my entire fault! I shall never forgive myself. What must she be going through?" He slapped his hand hard to his head.

The Abbot placed his arm around him and addressed him as Brother. "All is not lost. I am not a lot of use in these situations, but I can pray. I can also try and talk to him as he is supposed to be a man of God."

Brodie refrained from saying what was on his mind. *Fat lot of good. Prayers won't rescue her ... only direct action will do that. Man of God, my arse! He's a bloody psychopath.*

"Custodio Baez."

He turned to face her.

Maria's soft voice used the name only they knew between them. "You were Guardian of Lazarus and Christ's Holy Eyes. That has not been taken from you. I still sense your thoughts and deep sadness, but that is not the way forward now. Let us remember what we were and still are. It has to be the way of the warrior. The painting has gone to join its brothers. Where? Only you know. It cannot be retrieved. You suspect as I do that Martha or John will be a carrier of the burden, or even Abbot Louis. All past artists have had a chequered background. In biblical terms, they have all been sinners. Look at Cortez, look at us two. We killed people back then and you were a thief. Yet, the spotlight of God fell on us and more so you. I was healed, saved in more ways than one, although I killed Throgmorton. But you have suffered for me and everybody else who has been in contact with the legend."

"What are you trying to say?"

"I'm trying to say several things. If past history is anything to go by, the guardianship will fall on a sinner, I don't like that word, but it will have to do right now." She paused and lowered her head.

"Carry on."

"Martha hardly falls into that category. She's a normal girl with very exceptional gifts and talents. That White Horse, I suspect, is from where your home and heart is. I believe a complex plan has been afoot and it carried her out here so that you could return. It also carried Bower and Abbot Louis. I'm only making guesses, I cannot be certain, but I'm sure you understand what I'm hinting at."

"I see what you're suggesting, and I wish I could believe

it. But as long as she is a prisoner, I don't, and I won't."

"You are still Custodio, the warrior. You listened to him then and it's time to listen to him again."

"I haven't heard him since then. He's gone quiet on me."

"No. It's you refusing to listen. If you bend your ear hard enough, you will hear."

"I don't know what to do next."

"All we can do is sit and wait. We can't take the fight to him as we have no idea where he is. He will contact you and with any luck, he won't know the painting has gone."

"There has to be a way to get him here and to rescue Martha, but it will take some smart planning. We don't have a lot of time."

"Let's get inside and talk about it. If we can lure him here, with what we've rigged up, we'd have a better chance of dealing with him. Her safety is paramount and he can have all the paintings he wants for all I care."

They found the Abbot on his knees in prayer, Garcia pounding away on his laptop and George glued to the TV.

There was nothing else to do but sit and wait. The night would be long.

✠

Every so often the door would open and either Bruno or Alexis would check on her. Her attempt at the Houdini technique was still underway and her hand remained tied to the bed but was much looser now. If it ever got free, she would be able to release the other hand and escape.

Then what? She had no idea where she was being held or

where the men were in the building. If she managed to free herself, should she turn left? Right? She had no idea. From the low noise of traffic outside, she guessed she was probably in Toledo, and could find her way back to the hotel she had stayed in previously.

She had succeeded significantly in loosening her bond, but the last part refused to yield. An air of deep frustration descended over her as she let out a strangulated sob. It wasn't working.

The door opened again. This time it was Shepard, looking pleased with himself. "Well, my little Miss Martha, I thought it better to keep you up to date with what is happening, and from that, what your future might be. The little snippets we took from you were delivered to Guadamur for everyone there to digest. All we are asking for your safe return is that damned painting. If it gets difficult, we can always take more bits off you – like a finger, an ear, or your underwear. All these items, small they may be, can be wonderfully persuasive. I don't wish to alarm you, but I'm playing a waiting game and letting dear Daddy sweat. My church is waiting, but I can't keep them waiting too long. They want to see miracles, and miracles they shall have. What you don't know is that in that box you took from my driver, was a present. Do you want to know what it was?"

Martha shook her head and closed her eyes "No, I don't."

"I didn't think you would, but I'm going to tell you anyway. Are you ready for this? It was a big, decomposing and smelly rat to which I attached a rather touching verse. You won't like it, but I'm going to let you hear it anyway." He sat down on the bed, fished around in his pocket and removed a slip of paper, which he unfolded and silently read through.

"It's all about you, Martha. Here we go." He read it in a theatrical manner, waving his arm as his hand motioned like a slicing knife. He watched her horrified expression with glee. "Wasn't that fun, Martha?"

She didn't reply.

His jocular tone turned into a snarling spittle. "You stupid little bitch." He swung the back of his hand smartly across her cheek, sending her head reeling into a sideways lurch.

A rush of stinging pain shot through her face, and her eyes filled with tears that rolled down her face.

"You'll have plenty to say when it happens, when that knife gets closer and closer to your pretty bits and Bruno and Alexis take turns with you. I wonder if Daddy will cough up then, eh?"

"You're a complete animal," Martha spat out. What Brodie and Maria must be going through filled her with dismay. That verse, the dead rat, the barely concealed threats. She was being used as a pawn on a chess board, ready for sacrifice and even death.

I'm not ready for this. Please, let it not happen.

Without another word, Shepard left the room. When he called Brodie again, he wanted her there.

The door slammed with a sinister crash that epitomized her predicament. She recommenced on the binding, but it steadfastly refused to move that one inch more for her to be free.

CHAPTER 47

Time crawled by as if it had a massive weight on its back. No one knew what to say. Brodie paced up and down like a caged wild animal, waiting for the phone to ring. Even George looked uncomfortable and had taken to biting his nails and acting as butler, forever asking if anybody would like a drink.

Nothing happened that night, nor did the phone ring. Brodie had discussed what his response would be when Shepard called. Bower agreed, along with Maria, but they would be playing a dangerous game. There was no other way for them to rescue Martha safely.

Brodie couldn't sleep. When he did, it was in fits and starts of ten to fifteen minutes at a time. Every so often he would pour a splash of scotch. The only alcohol to cross his lips for over seventeen years was the communal wine of daily Mass. That had now gone to the dogs, and he had to admit to a slight feeling of guilt. Yet, the circumstances allowed for a discretional deviation from the norm. He no longer cared if the Abbot knew or not.

Amidst all the events, he could not fail to ask himself again why the two paintings Martha and Bower had done, had so miraculously vanished. Would they both, or one of them return? If so, which one? He was in no doubt that the three paintings vanishing more or less at the same time had significance.

In some ways, he no longer felt part of it. While he looked on, the mantle had been taken from him. So far, he was the last in line of the ancient and not so ancient artists that had gone before him, but now, he didn't want to pass it on if it was going to direct its intent on his daughter, Martha. There was also Ulla to think of. The current drama had been kept away from her, but sooner or later, she would know. She was far from stupid and could and would work out that things were amiss.

Brodie dozed on and off. It couldn't be called sleep. All through the early hours, he had fretted and willed the phone to ring for some news or information. He needed to talk to him and stage his plan. The cards were not all in Shepard's hands.

A lemony looking sun creeping over the edge of a dark horizon heralded the new morning. It looked insipid and lifeless and Martha could relate. She had been allowed to use the bathroom and once she returned, both Alexis and Bruno guided her into a kitchen area. She was given a plate of typical Spanish breakfast, consisting of churros and a mug of hot chocolate. As much as she was determined to resist the offering, she was hungry. Part of her understood now how a condemned man on death row must feel, eating his last meal. *Please God, don't let it be that.*

Neither men spoke. They had been instructed not to talk to her or ask her questions Shepard had said it was better for her to worry and fret. That made her more vulnerable, and the more so, the easier it would be to make a trade-off. Dear daddy would be prepared to die for her. But that wasn't the end of it. The man named George, and the slobby bum Bower, had to be dealt with – and dealt with severely up to the point of death, and beyond if needs be. To achieve this would need some careful planning, but he had already formulated a few ideas, and those he was about to discuss with his men. He saw that Martha had finished her breakfast.

"Get her out of here and tie her back to the bed, and then get back here fast. We have plans to discuss."

Martha was hauled back to the bedroom and thrown onto the bed. Her wrists were sore and chaffed from her attempts to escape. Again, she had tensed her wrists as they secured her to the bed and once the rope was tightened, she relaxed and felt a very small degree of movement from beneath. She resumed her wriggling and ignored the pain. *I have to get out of here!*

She guessed she'd be alone for some time.

The shrill tones of the telephone brought them all rushing into the room. Maria was first and picked it up. "Yes?" Her usual lofty manner was forgotten.

"Ah … it's you, the crazy Condesa. I don't want you. Get me Brodie."

Without another word, she handed the phone to an anxious Brodie.

"Brodie speaking."

"I want that painting in exchange for your daughter. Sound familiar? This is what I need you to do. You will go to this address." He gave him an address on the outskirts of the city. "When you arrive, stay in your car until I appear and tell you otherwise. Your daughter is here, a little uncomfortable but unharmed." There was a slight pause. "Oh, I forgot something. Aside from the painting, you need to bring your two new friends. Do you understand?"

Brodie took a long breath and hoped his voice would remain steady "I understand, but I don't think you do. Listen carefully, Shepard, for this is how it will be done. We are not coming to you or meeting you anywhere. The exchange would have to happen here. The painting will be yours once I have Martha back safe and sound." *I pray to God he buys this.* "I can see the wheels in your head turning, Shepard. You're wondering, why here? So, I'll be upfront with you. You know what my daughter means to me, and to convince you not to harm a hair on her head, we are willing to give you a demonstration. The Condesa has agreed to be a victim of a wound that you yourself may inflict. The painting of Lazarus will be used to heal her right there and then. You can then record it for all your followers to see. An intelligent man like you would understand that this can only be enacted within these walls. It cannot happen anywhere else. That's the proposition, which you must agree, is far better than you ever hoped for.

The painting will be yours, with incontrovertible evidence, but you must bring Martha with you. Think about it."

Shepard was silent for a long time before he replied, "Interesting, Brodie. I'm not giving you an immediate answer. I need to think it through. I'll get back to you very soon." There was a click and the phone went dead.

"Well?" Bower asked, and like the others, his expression was expectant.

"He hasn't said no, but in his plan, he wanted you and George to come along. I can guess why."

"You don't have to be a fortune teller."

"All we can do now is wait."

"How long? Do we know?

"No idea, but don't be surprised if he comes back with another proposition."

"In between this," Abbot Louis interjected, "I'll pray for her and I'll do that now. Can you all please join in? It will help."

Garcia rolled his eyes. But sitting on one of the most explosive stories he had ever handled, with reluctance, he stood, bowed his head, and along with the others, joined the Abbot in prayer.

CHAPTER 48

Martha could hear muffled voices from behind her door and guessed it was Bruno, Alexis and Shepard. That didn't interest her. She was almost free from the restraint on her right arm. If she could get free, the only way out for her would be the window. She hoped to God they didn't come back into the room. The restraint was now very loose, and she was able to flex her whole hand. Every movement slackened her bonds to a degree.

One final contorted twist and the loop came away and she pulled her hand free. *It worked! Can't hang about.* Now able to turn sideways, she quickly untied the tight knots around her other hand and wrist. One last tug and she was free.

She didn't hesitate and dashed to the box sash window and lifted it. *Definitely Toledo!* To the front, and in the distance, she could clearly see the cathedral. Confronting her was a drop to the ground of about ten feet. That was nothing. She hung both legs out and propelled herself forward to land with a solid thump on the grass below. She was unhurt. Immediately, she stood and began to run to the cathedral. She needed to contact the hotel she had originally booked into, *The Hotel Pedro Sanchez*. They had been very friendly, and she needed to use their phone to call Maria and Brodie.

She ran as fast as she could and began to recognise the area she was in. Looking behind her, she was expecting a chase, but there was nobody behind. Soon, she was in the main area and weaved in and out of the crowd until she reached the narrow street that led down to the hotel. Once outside, she took a deep breath, feeling conspicuous in her disheveled state, but this was no time for social niceties. She burst through the doors and was relieved to recognise the receptionist, who greeted her with a warm smile.

"*¡Hola! Te reconozco.*"

She recognised Martha, much to her relief.

Within minutes, Martha was using the hotel landline and speaking to Brodie.

"Holy Mary," Bruno shouted from the room. "She's gone!"

"What!" Shepard thundered, his voice sounding like an M1 Abrams tank. "What!" He smashed his fist into the door and burst into the room.

It was true, the room was empty. All he could see was a crumpled bed, a billowing curtain and a wide-open window. "I thought you fucking tied her up!" He continued roaring and smashing his fists into the walls and cupboards. His face resembled a bag of spanners.

He had lost his major bargaining chip and was now beside

himself with rage and fury.

"We did, we did, I don't know how she could have escaped. She couldn't move. We checked it several times." Bruno looked uncomfortable.

"You two Latvian morons have just caused a major clusterfuck!" He looked out of the window. "She could be anywhere and you're going to have to find her. If you don't, then we have a full-scale assault on our hands. Now get out and start looking! Go now!"

They dashed to the door, not knowing she had a fifteen-minute head start on them.

Shepard grabbed a bottle of Bourbon, poured a massive shot and slumped into a sofa to take a full throat of the golden liquor. His mind began to whirl. If they don't find her, that would change everything. He would have to take the painting by force.

There was no need to call Brodie now. He had nothing to bargain with.

Bower couldn't prevent the random images and thoughts that had begun to appear with increasing regularity into his mind. At first, he ignored them, but now their persistency was becoming annoying. He was concerned about Martha. He needed her. Only when she was about was he able to find some peace. He didn't like to mention it to Brodie in case it was only a wishful mental trick of some sort, but he had felt her presence and he *knew, knew with certainty*, that she was safe and unharmed by her ordeal. But to tell Brodie could give false hope.

In the background, he heard the sound of the phone ringing. He leapt from his chair and hurtled into the room.

Brodie had already snatched the phone. "Yes, Shepard." He tried to sound calm and reassured.

It wasn't Shepard. It was his daughter.

"Dad! I don't have time to explain, but I esc–"

"Martha!" He couldn't believe his ears.

"Yes, Dad, listen! I'm at The Hotel Pedro Sanchez. They don't know where I am, but they will be searching. Please, come and get me now! I'm getting desperate by the minute."

"I'm coming right now. Hang in there." He slammed the phone and turned to the others.

"It's her," he spoke in a rush. "Martha, she's managed to escape. I know where she is and I'm going there now." He turned, grabbed his car keys, and rushed off. They heard the gates open and the roar of the engine as he sped away.

"Our prayers have been answered." The Abbot made the sign of the cross. "God be praised."

Maria stared at Bower. "Are you okay, John?" She had noticed his odd expression. "Let's hope she will be back here soon."

"She will. And I think some very odd things could be happening," he said out of nowhere.

Maria stared at him hard, and for the first time, she was able to read him.

He looked at her with a wide expression as he felt her inside his head.

Deus Vult!

Beauséant!

They had heard each other and embraced.

Bower felt reassured. A door had been opened for him to join a very exclusive club.

CHAPTER 49

T hirty minutes later, the car screeched to a stop outside the hotel. Brodie ignored the parking restrictions, jumped out and rushed into the foyer. Martha was there and she rushed to him with arms wide open, before she burst into tears.

"Oh Dad, I thought I'd never see you again."

"Not a chance, but I thought the same about you. C'mon, no more tears. We can't stay here. They could be searching for you and I'm no match for those two heavies. Hurry now!"

He propelled her to the door and then into the waiting car. He had to get back to Guadamur before he could feel safe. He ignored the speed limits.

She briefly explained what had happened at the gates and the way she had been treated and tied up. They hadn't physically touched or harmed her, but she said she didn't know how long that would have lasted.

Brodie gripped the wheel hard and he knew in his heart he could do damage to people, kill people if he really had to, especially when it came to his daughter being threatened. *Custodio Baez* had never truly left him. He had a feeling that he would be visiting soon as Maria had recently suggested to him. This was to be the way of the warrior. There were no other cards to play.

"What's going to happen, Dad?"

"I don't know, but when he realises you're gone, he'll be furious."

"How's John?"

"Very quiet. There's something going on with him. From being a brash, flash humdinger of a casino owner and more, he's got introverted and often stayed away from us."

The rain, unusual for the time of year, began to lash down. Brodie slowed the speed. Old memories of car chases with him and Ulla being shot at filled his mind. To his surprise, he found that he missed it.

Alexis and Bruno came back empty handed to a foul tempered Shepard. He looked as tense as a man discovering he was standing on a land mine. He had also drunk too much Bourbon.

"You pair of arseholes. How the fuck did you let a slip of a girl get away? The damage is done now and nothing we can do will change that. No doubt she's back with that load of physic nutters at the crazy cow's hizzy. It's time for war and time to tool up. We have guns, ammos, two grenades, Zippos, and plenty of straw to burn. Also, we have thick army blankets to place across those wires if we have to. It's gonna get hot in that little oven and they'll know what a baked potato feels like when we've finished with them. The painting in our hands or not, that cozy bolt hole is going to look like a box of burnt out matches by the time we finish. Are you two apes up to this?"

An unspoken message passed between Bruno and Alexis.

Bruno said, "It's a big job, Mr. Reverend. We've surveyed the place and the only possible way in is around the back, where a mound reaches up to the top of the wall. There's one other thing..."

"What's that?"

"The painting."

"What about it?"

"If we get it, we want a fat bonus."

"I might have guessed you two would pull a stunt like this. What if I say no?"

"We walk away right now."

"You can't do that. Besides, I haven't paid you."

"You're about to."

Both men pulled out their guns before he had time to react. He didn't hesitate. "Okay, yes to a bonus." He held his hands up from outstretched arms. "How much?"

"One hundred thousand US dollars."

"That's ludicrous. I can't afford that." He heard the sound of safety catches flicking off. "Easy boys, easy." Sweat began breaking out all over his head and down his back.

"Well?" The pistols were now raised and pointing right at him.

"Agreed. I agree."

"Now, we want what you owe us up to now, and we mean

now. The bonus when the job's done, Okay?"

"Agreed. I'll get your fees right now. I'll be a minute."

They kept their guns ready to fire.

He soon returned with their cash, which he handed over, but with a silent promise to himself that he would get rid of them too, somehow.

After one final check on the equipment, they loaded them into the truck.

It was time to talk. They all gathered around the table, including George who had been busy fashioning a garrote. Luciana sat next to Garcia. Bower remained silent and kept his eyes on Maria and Martha. He felt a mystery emanating from them both, distinct and undulating. He had been deeply relieved to see her returned safely as had all the others. Garcia had quizzed her closely and made copious notes of everything she said. They were all agreed that she was a remarkable and a very courageous young woman.

During that questioning, Bower couldn't help asking the question to himself. *What will become of her? She doesn't seem to be of this world. It's like she's stepped out of my* Book of Miracles *back home. She would fit into that book with no trouble at all. The more I see her, the more I'm aware of her thoughts, and she mine. Is she from another dimension of time and space? Brodie's her dad, and he's had his moments too, and so has Maria and also the Abbot. Where do I fit in here? It's beyond me ... but I surrender to and accept whatever it is.*

Brodie's commanding voice brought him out of his reverie.

"We're not out of this yet. Expect an attack of some sort either from the weak spot at the rear or the front gate. There's no other way in. All the windows are barred. When Shepard gets it into his greedy, bony head that there is no painting, we can expect major fireworks. He would have spent a lot of money chasing a ghost." He glanced at Maria. "We've always known that the painting can protect itself." Maria smiled and nodded. Brodie slapped the table with both hands. "Okay, you all know where the weapons or tools are placed, along with the knives. The trip wires will be in place, as will my booby trap, flares, and water barrels. We have a total of five weapons and that includes the shotgun that Luciana so bravely demonstrated." He gestured towards her and there came a ripple of applause as she blushed bright red.

"So, all we can do now is wait and see. It's getting dark and I guess that's the time they would strike. Get some peace and quiet or whatever you want to do."

George went back to playing with the garrote in between watching the TV, before he went to guard the gate. Brodie, Martha and Maria went outside to watch the place, both back and front, although it wasn't dark enough for anything to happen.

Garcia stopped typing and relaxed with a Rusty Nail, with Luciana sitting as close to him as she dared.

Bower needed some rest and headed for his room. He opened the door and walked in. His easel was where he had left it, covered with an old white sheet. He looked around the room, then out the window and into the gathering gloom. He felt strangely uncomfortable. He couldn't work out what it was. It wasn't fear. He'd been in enough fights and scrapes in his time, bigger and larger than this one promised to be. Yes, he was worried. He'd grown to like the others downstairs and counted them as friends. But that's not what made him uneasy.

Stopping to pour a sizeable Scotch, he gave it a hefty swig, enjoying the hot burn down into his chest. He walked back to the easel, and for no real reason, pulled off the covering.

"Aaaah!" His glass dropped to the floor, shattering, while he stood there, dumfounded. Without warning, he began to shake, before he slumped to the floor beneath the gaze of his painting of Lazarus.

It had found its way home.

CHAPTER 50

Downstairs, Martha, Maria and Brodie were found sitting in the gathering gloom beneath the copious pergola, watching the rolling hills that had influenced two of them so long ago. Sitting further back, the Abbot was going through the office of Vespers. They could sense that he felt out of place, although it had been his choice to remain until the situation was resolved.

Tension hung like a suspended guillotine.

"What can we do now?" Maria looked apprehensive.

Brodie shrugged and looked out the winding track. "Nothing we can do apart from wait."

Martha begun twisting uncomfortably in her seat "Something's happened!" She held her head in her hands. "Noooooo!" She knelt to the floor.

Maria and Brodie looked at each other.

"Something is happening to her and for once, we're not part of it," Brodie snapped.

"I did say she was going beyond us." Maria knelt beside Martha. "Endure, my lovely girl, endure. We are with you ... don't resist."

Brodie paled, feeling helpless once again. He reached for Martha as she began to lean towards the floor, face down, her entire body quivering.

"I beg of you," he begged. "Hear my prayer, please!"

She was in a glorious hall glowing with the brilliance of many suns, but she was not blinded. The curvature of the walls that rose upwards formed a perfect circle suggestive of the Sistine Chapel.

There was no sound ... only an atmosphere of the deepest peace and love.

She, Bath Kol, the angel of divine prophecy, was at last back home. She had been away too long. Her predictions had all transpired, and would do so once more. She saw them around the walls, giving testimony to the triumph of life over death.

It began with the painting by Annas Zevi. His was the first depiction of The Raising of Lazarus which had spanned the ages — to Borgoña, Cortez, and to the latest, the work of Broderick Ladro. It glowed with light and magnificence ... the equal of all that came before it.

She had prophesied them all and there were many more to come. Empty frames as far as the eye could see hung alongside each other. She knew who the artist of the next work would be, before they were even born. That was her blessed domain, of which only she had knowledge.

She knew the next was finished and the artist had been chosen.

But it's allotted time span was God's will alone ... not hers. They could last months, years or centuries.

Her wings gave a gentle flutter as she glided to the empty frame next to Ladro's. A person stood with an easel and paints and was preparing to paint. Once ready, she placed her hand upon the canvas until it shimmered with a blue and golden light. When it was finished, she guided the person this way and that, revealing the whole time span of the universe, in all directions, so all doubts would cease.

And it was done.

"Martha, come back to us." Brodie recognised what was happening as he had once been there himself. He stroked her hair and held her unconscious body close to his. "My angel, come back." He wasn't aware of the irony of his expression.

"I've lost contact with her." Maria looked distraught. "What's happening?"

Martha's eyes fluttered several times before they opened, and she regained her sense of awareness.

"I'm okay." She rubbed her head and noticed the concerned gaze of her father and the Condesa." I really am. I've been on a journey you won't believe." She pulled herself into a sitting position and stared long and hard at Brodie. "Dad, oh Dad ... now I know. I know where you went. I saw what you saw. Your painting hangs with all the others. It was so amazing." She broke down in tears.

He tightened his grip on her to comfort her sobs and gave an enquiring look at Maria. Abbot Louis had now joined them.

Brodie continued to comfort her. "That's astonishing. Was there a painting after mine?"

"No," she spluttered. "There were empty frames as far as the eye could see. I was flying, almost as if I had become an angel."

Part of Brodie was relieved, another disturbed. He didn't doubt her experience based on his own back then.

"An angel you say?" The Abbot brimmed with interest.

"Not now, Father, please," Brodie snapped. He was frantic to know if she had any idea who the successor would be. "Did you, or do you sense that you are the next artist?"

Before she could speak, a large rolled-up canvas hit the table with a small thud.

"No, she's not," a voice boomed out around the patio. They had not seen his approach. It was John D. Bower with an expression on his face like a noble Roman statue, eyes gleaming.

"I am the one. Martha is my mentor. My painting is there to see. Look at it!" He pointed to the rolled canvas and Brodie laid it out on the table.

It was impressive. Reminiscent of William Blake. With clever juxtaposition of form and colour, it exuded power and the mystical energy that only the Raising of Lazarus could impart.

They gave a collective gasp.

"When I uncovered my easel, it was just there. After seeing it, I collapsed and heard those words over and over. *Deus Vult! Beauséant!* I was told to be ready by a being that looked like an angel of some sort, and help defend the work – to give my life if I must to protect it. I was shown all the past works including yours, Brodie. It was in this vast, shiny hall…"

"Stop there." Brodie held up his hand and looked at Martha. "Your stories are identical and you both collapsed, it seems, at the same time. Your angel, John, was Martha. Not as she is now, but in some mysterious way, in another form. She saw exactly what you did."

"As I said, Brodie, she is my mentor."

Martha looked up and sensed the enormous relief that her father was experiencing, and she was pleased for him. She stood, and with a hint of a smile, yet with a twinge of sorrow, she embraced Bower and held him tight. She was not surprised to see him weep, perhaps something he had never done in his entire life. From Brodie's experiences, she didn't doubt that he would be going through more.

She whispered, "No need for tears, John. We were meant to be part of this and only God knows why. All of us have been brought here and each of us, in our own way, serves a special purpose."

All went quiet and nobody knew what to say. Abbot Louis offered up another prayer, for he had seen a minor miracle being played out like some TV drama or film.

Maria spoke with caution, "This changes everything. Shepard knows what the Lazarus painting looks like and that's the only one he has any knowledge of. He's never going to believe our new version has any powers. He will think we're playing a game to save the painting he first saw."

"It has powers." Bower looked solemn. "Look." He pulled up his sleeves and the back of his shirt. There wasn't a mark on him. His lifelong psoriasis had vanished.

"God be praised." The Abbot fell to his knees.

Any lingering doubts they may have had, evaporated. Garcia, who had joined in to see what was happening, could only think that nobody was going to believe his report, let alone his book.

Brodie looked at them all. "Shepard will never accept it and he'll accuse us of having made a switch. But what he thinks doesn't matter. He's never going to get his hands on this wonder. What do you think, John?"

"I have no claim over it. It doesn't belong to me. It will need protection and care, like yours did, Brodie. I sense too, like you did, that my old life is over. Parts of me are trying to hang on to it, but it's slipping through my fingers. I can feel it and I don't feel ready for it."

Brodie thought back and recalled his own identical dilemmas and agonies. Bower still had a long journey ahead of him.

Their deliberations were interrupted by the booming sound of the alarm drum and a cry from George who was situated at the main gate. "We have visitors."

They all rushed to look. Barreling towards them in the distance, with headlights glowing, was the unmistakable outline of a Navara pickup truck. It drew closer and they didn't have to ask who it was.

"Right," shouted Brodie. "You all know what to do." He looked up at the dark sky and made sure the flares were nearby.

They all watched the truck as it switched on its full headlights. They were being surveyed.

"Stay down and keep out of sight," Brodie half shouted, "and dowse those lights."

The area was plunged into darkness.

The truck doors opened, and Shepard and the two others stepped out, all holding shotguns, dressed in black. Bruno and Alexis moved to the rear of the vehicle and swung down the tailgate. They reached in and pulled out bundles of straw, more guns, army blankets, and carried them around to the front.

Shepard stood straight and tall in front of the 4x4, shotgun across his chest and legs apart. "You know what we're here for, Brodie. You may have a chance, if you hand it over. You can't win this. We not only have the means to finish you all off, but we'll torch this place as well. God, I know, is on our side. What's it to be, Lazarus or the death of you all, including your pretty young daughter?"

For a moment, Brodie faltered. But then, he called out. "There is no painting, Shepard, whatever you think. It has vanished like all the others. A new one has taken its place."

Everybody was silent, listening to the shouted interchange.

"You must think I'm stupid to fall for that. You have it, I've seen it and held it, so you can't pass another off and pretend that a new version you painted yesterday has now got powers. Rubbish! You're trying very badly, Broderick Ladro. If you don't cough up, you and this cozy beehive will all be burnt to the ground.

"Ignore him, Dad, that's never going to happen." Martha gripped his arm. She gave him a tight smile and he saw her strength shine through.

"Go to hell, Shepard. Try your worst. We're ready for you."

"So be it," came the reply.

Shepard fired a round into the compound and signaled to the other two, who picked up the grenades and moved forward, only to be halted by bullets thudding into the ground directly in front of their advance. They retreated.

"Grenade! Let them have a grenade." Shepard was beside himself. He hadn't expected a show of force.

Bruno reached for his grenade, unpinned it, counted to three and threw it at the gates. It landed a few feet from the entrance and then exploded with an immense force, sending dirt and debris into the night sky. The gate survived but had been weakened when one hinge was blasted away.

The defenders were shocked. They couldn't survive if many more were to be thrown at them. But they had to stand firm.

Brodie had assumed total command. "John, over there, and get ready with the log swing and mind the trip wires."

Bower did as he was asked. A large heavy log had been mounted on a giant rope, and when swung, would zoom across like a lethal, silent, swinging pendulum.

"Abbot and Ned, take these pistols and go to the back wall. They may try that to get in. If I use this whistle," he held up a referee's whistle on a lanyard, "return immediately. This is what it sounds like." He gave it a powerful blow, and it emitted a high-pitched screech. Turning to the three ladies, he asked, "Where have you put John's painting?" They ducked low while he spoke, as a volley of shots bounced off the nearby woodwork.

"It's in the car, in case we need to get away," Maria shouted over the noise of gunshots.

"Martha, put these in your belt." He held up a pistol and a very lethal-looking knife. She tucked the knife out of sight in the back of her belt and the gun in the front. " You too, Luciana. The gun's loaded and ready to fire so be careful." *My God, what would Ulla think!* "Maria, you have your own pistol?"

"Yes."

"You know where the tools and knives are located?"

"Yes, I do."

"Good. Keep close to them." Brodie surveyed what was now the battleground. "I don't like the look of that straw they've piled up out there. It looks like they're preparing for a firework party! This should do the trick." He brandished one of the flare pistols. "I hope its sell-by date hasn't passed." Keeping low, he made his way back to George.

Short on many things George might have been, but he was a first-class marksman and was keeping the attackers back.

Brodie nudged him. "George, take this flare pistol. It's ready to fire. You see those straw bales there?" He pointed at them although they were barely visible in the evening gloom. "Do you reckon you could get a flare into them?"

"Is Santa Claus Father Christmas?" He grunted. "Give it here." He picked it up and aimed. "Now?"

"Yes, now!"

"I'm going to enjoy this." He pointed it through the small gap he was hiding behind and squeezed the trigger ... *WOOMP!*

There was a loud, rushing noise and the flare honed in on the centre bale, which exploded into a dangerous pyrotechnic display of a riotous colour of red.

"Yahoo! Bull's eye!" George shouted.

The bales had vanished in a storm of heat and flames, and the entire perimeter was lit up as bright as the noonday sun. The three attackers could be seen running behind the truck. They were now totally exposed.

✠

"Holy Shit!" Shepard screamed as his ace weapon went up in the fierce heat of the fiery blaze. "Those bastards are going to pay for that. Alexis, your grenade … at the gate, and don't miss it!"

Alexis fumbled around his waist and unclipped a grenade, held it in his hand, before ducking low and manoeuvering himself out of sight along the bottom of the wall. When he was certain he was in accurate throwing range, he abandoned caution, stood, dislodged the pin and lobbed the grenade straight at the gate, before turning around and throwing himself flat to the ground.

It exploded, and the blast brought the gate tumbling to the floor in a whirling mass of splinters and brickwork.

"We've got them," Shepard shouted. "They've got no defences now." He debated whether he should attack through the front or try getting over the wire at the rear of the building.

He decided to do the front. With all their guns firing, they rushed to the cover of the sidewalls and from there, and through the smoke, he could make out Brodie and the other asshole – one of the men who had made a mess of him.

His flare works for me as much as it does him. Thanks, Brodie! He took aim and fired. His shot was true.

George, his neck suddenly split wide open, collapsed in a fountain of blood before hitting the floor like a bag of wet cement.

"One down, one more to go!" Shepard oozed with malicious satisfaction.

Brodie was shocked. He crouched low and tried to reach George, but there was no point. He was dead before he hit the floor. *Dear God! Is this necessary?* His concern now was for the women and the remainder of his team. He gave several sharp blasts on the whistle. There was going to be no attack from the rear now that the gate had collapsed.

The Abbot looked deeply disturbed and breathless as they rushed back. He had decided he would not shoot, harm or kill any person. His allegiances to his vows were of the utmost importance to him. They were his solemn promise to God. He would, however, assist where permissible.

Garcia had read things similar to this in novels and had seen it in movies, but here he was, in the middle of a real live battle. He was scared. If he survived, he knew he had a major scoop – a bestselling book and a possible movie deal. The story was dynamite! He was determined to stay alive, come what may.

They found Brodie sheltering behind a large wooden post. "Down, you two, you're going to get killed standing up like that."

Bullets were whining and thudding through the air and into the woodwork.

"Look!" Brodie pointed to the prostrate body of George, oozing a soft flow of blood from his throat.

Stunned, they needed no second asking as they flung themselves to the ground.

Bower remained out of sight, but he had clear view of where

the ladies were positioned and had seen George go down. He felt responsible for his friend and of Man One. They had been loyal to him, and for what? He felt sorrow, but this was not the time or place for such sentiments. There would be another time for that. He knew where the Lazarus painting had been placed, and knew he would die if he had to, in order to protect it. For but a moment, he was staggered at that resolution and what had happened to him.

All had gone quiet by the gates.

He paused, Martha's face and presence flashed gently into his mind and she was riding The White Horse. He was no longer worried or startled by anything. He understood.

She was pointing, and his gaze followed. A mixture of monks and knights who had once dwelt in this ancient monastery, and bearing swords, moved in hypnotic fashion around its age-old structure. Their chant was a call to arms that had been part of the place since the Crusades.

In desert march or battle's flame
In fortress and in field
Our war cry is thy holy name...
Deus Vult!
Beauséant!

The medieval war cry was now part of him, and it was his honour to use it. He knew there could be no turning back. He had become the chosen one, the guardian of this most precious work. It could last a thousand years, or a day only. He had no way of knowing, nor did he have a map or compass to steer by.

He gripped the rope he was holding on to and balanced

the massive log, steadying himself for the expected assault.

Brodie fired the remaining flare into the night sky. Night was turned into day.

CHAPTER 51

S hepard gave the signal to attack, the light suited him as much as Brodie. All three moved in at speed, into the central area, guns blasting in all directions. Bullets spattered around the courtyard. In their charge, they hadn't been prepared for the trip wires. They had barely reached ten metres inside, before they were upended in a tangle of wire and their own feet.

Before Brodie could achieve anything, they picked themselves up, their weapons still in their hands.

"Let it go, John!" Brodie roared.

Bower responded with a mighty shout, *"Deus Vult!"* He pulled on the thick rope, and attached as a pendulum, the massive log swung at speed towards the three entangled men.

Shepard saw it coming. "Down!" he shouted.

Too late. It missed him but struck Alexis full in the middle of his back, sending him ten feet into the air with a broken shoulder blade. He screamed in agony as he hit the ground. Nobody went to his aid.

One bonus less. Shepard stayed close to the ground as the swinging log began its swooshing return journey past his head. He looked around and couldn't see where Bruno had gone. Things weren't going too well.

"You're beaten, Shepard. You've lost. Lay down your weapons." Brodie's voice echoed around the courtyard.

Shepard looked uncomfortable but still held on to his gun. Alexis was rolling in agony and Bruno had disappeared. His dream was fading before his eyes. Then, what he saw emerging from the shadows began to change everything.

Bruno emerged and held a very frightened Martha close, with a pistol to her head. In the commotion, he had slipped unseen around the building and found himself somehow behind her. He had surprised and overcome her, and at the same time, he managed to disarm the gun from her belt

"I think not, Brodie. Look again." Shepard pointed at the captive Martha.

Jesus, no! But it was true. Martha, his daughter was in deep peril ... again. He knew what was coming next. He was in danger of being hoisted by his own petard.

Shepard stepped over the wires to stand next to Bruno. He swung a shotgun from off his back and aimed it towards Brodie. "I could take you both here, right now, but that's too easy. There's something else I want, and you all know what that could be. So, everyone out there in the shadows, get here right now and stand next to Brodie. No sudden moves or tricks or her death will be on your own conscience. Do I make myself clear? C'mon, be quick about it and drop those tools." He blasted a shot into the air.

Axes, iron bars and shovels clattered to the ground.

✠

Bower's brain was racing. He knew Shepard would barter for the painting, but it wasn't the one he had originally stolen. That had vanished into that great hall somewhere. Shepard would also exact revenge on him, as he had done with George. He knew the danger, but the more he saw Martha at his mercy, the more enraged he began to feel. If it hadn't been for her gentle ways, he wouldn't have discovered all this. His fists tightened, and his jaw began its set.

Not yet. Not yet. It's too soon.

The Condesa's voice awoke in his mind and he looked over to her as she gave him a small nod. He was no longer amazed.

He turned to Shepard. "It is true, as Brodie has said. The work has vanished. There is now a new one in its place. I know it's hard for you to believe, but it's true."

"I owe you a gift, Bower, don't I? Before I leave here you will receive it in full." Shepard slammed the rifle butt into Bower's ribs.

Bower gave no sound as he slumped on one knee, clasping at his chest.

"That's just for starters." The next blow was aimed at the back of his neck, and Bower sprawled face down into the dirt.

"Hold it," Brodie shouted. "That's enough!"

Martha struggled to free herself, but Bruno was far too strong for her and the gun stayed to the side of her head.

"Shepard, why don't you just look at the painting? If we had the other one, we would have let you walk away with it. Do you really believe we would let any of us suffer like this if it wasn't true? But we don't have it. I swear to God, we don't."

Something in the way he spoke caused Shepard to stop and think. His brain could be seen working.

"How do I know it's got miraculous powers? Let me see it. Where is it?"

"It's in the back of the car. Here are the keys." Brodie lobbed them over.

"You." Shepard pointed to Garcia. "Open it."

Garcia did as he was asked, and the rolled-up canvas was still there.

"Spread it out."

He did, slowly and with great care, before securing it beneath two wooden struts of the pergola.

The red glow of the flare subdued and masked the colouring. Everybody stood motionless, as if they were about to witness a major event. Shepard had to agree that it looked superb. Better than the other one.

"Any evidence of its powers?"

"I have." Bower winced, attempting to mask a torso full of pain.

"You? How on earth could you possibly have anything to show? You're scum." He raised the rifle butt.

"No, wait," Martha shouted out. "It's true. Don't hit him. Let him tell you."

"My psoriasis ... you remember that? You commented on it once. I was always scratching. Well, the painting healed it. Look." He rolled up both sleeves and held out his arms. "See, blemish free. Now, look at my back." He pulled up his shirt and again, the skin underneath was clear and smooth. "You see?

"I see." Shepard paused and gave a smirk. "Modern day

medicine can achieve that. Now for the acid test, I've a better idea. Let me see your hand. Hold it out straight so I can see it."

Bower felt uneasy, but did as he was asked, and looked up at Shepard who had placed his shotgun down and replaced it with his Smith & Wesson.

"No, don't do it!" Bower looked on in horror as Shepard squeezed the trigger almost at point blank range, sending a bullet ripping through his hand, smashing bones and tendons apart in a sea of blood. Bower screamed in total agony. He passed out instantly, as everyone gasped in shocked disbelief.

"A modern-day crucifixion!" Shepard gloated as he looked around at them, revelling in the horror in their faces.

Nobody could speak.

Brodie attempted to reach him, but another shot hit the ground in front of his feet.

"Stay where you are and don't move. That goes for you all." He shouldered his pistol, picked up the shotgun and looked down at the writhing figure of Bower. "Well, he had that coming after what he did to me. Don't cry any tears for him. He's just scum."

Bower lay still, fainting from the shock.

"Mad cow, you there!" He pointed at Maria. "See to my man over there, will you?" He indicated the bent figure of Alexis. "Now, let's see that painting do its stuff."

Shepard stared at the painting and looked hard at both Lazarus and the figure of Christ. For a moment, he was transfixed, and if he had been drunk, he would have sworn that both the lips and eyes of Christ moved. *Impossible. The thing's a fake.* He went to Bruno who was still holding Martha, then turned and addressed Brodie, including all of them. "How much more can you take? How much more are you willing to take? I want that painting and I want it now. If I don't get it, you know what will start happening." He pulled at Martha. "It would be such a shame to lose her, wouldn't it?"

Brodie moved forward, still holding a gun.

"Drop it, Brodie. You are in no position to barter. Back off!"

Brodie put down the gun.

"But perhaps I am." A quiet voice behind him gave him cause for alarm.

It was Bower and he was standing ... unscathed and full of menace. He held up his hand and it was as it had always been.

There was no hole from the bullet Shepard had fired into it at close range.

Shepard's jaw dropped. He was rendered speechless, as was Bruno, who in his astonishment, let go of Martha. Her hand found the concealed knife, grabbed its hilt and without knowing where, backhanded a violent stab behind her. Where it penetrated she had no idea. She didn't look. Bruno gave a low, almost inaudible moan, and slumped to the dirt – his femoral artery cut. He would bleed to death within fifteen minutes.

Martha, still holding the knife, moved forward knowing she was free. She didn't give the dying man a second glance.

Shepard hadn't seen or heard. He was transfixed by Bower's hand. "No, this is not true. It's a trick." He blurted out incoherently. "Let's try again." He began to raise his gun, but he was too slow.

There was a sharp crack of a shot.

Shepard stood with a frozen expression of disbelief as he

felt his life force draining from him. The bullet went straight through his head. He keeled over sideways and hit the ground with a heavy thump.

The Condesa Maria Francisca de Toledo, stood imperious and impassive, holding her smoking silver revolver.

A silence fell on the compound like a heart that had ceased to function.

"I never did like him." She placed the gun back into her pocket.

CHAPTER 52

T he bodies were disposed of down the ancient and secretly concealed, massive, one hundred and fifty foot deep well that had accepted Throgmorton's body seventeen years ago. It had been constructed in medieval times for protection, and disposal of one's enemies, when necessary.

Apart from the Abbot, nobody had any qualms about it. They all swore to secrecy. He insisted on performing burial ceremonies for each of them.

The only surviving member of Shepard's crew was Alexis. They had picked him up – he could still walk – and dumped him into the driver's seat of the truck they had arrived in. They told him to vanish. He didn't disagree.

Two months later...

Ned Garcia had done it again. His exposé had finished off the already floundering Holy Church of Lazarus. It's founder, Pastor Silas Shepard, had vanished, and with him a considerable sum of money. Nobody knew his whereabouts or that of the money. It was rumoured that he had fled to the Polynesian islands somewhere. Of course, Garcia made sure the true circumstances were not revealed. He then published his book, a clever piece of 'faction' which was zooming up the best seller charts both in the USA and the UK.

Additionally, his personal loneliness would soon end. He'd taught Luciana how to mix a Rusty Nail to perfection. What more could a man ask for from his future bride?

Come the wedding, all his friends involved in the 'Lazarus' episode would be invited. It was a day he eagerly looked forward to.

Maria too had embarked on a new lease of life. She was so delighted with Luciana's news that she began making plans for the wedding reception and all the other issues that involved weddings. As a gift for them both, she had brought them a car that Garcia said he always wanted to own, an Aston Martin DB9. If that wasn't enough, in her will, she had bequeathed her Guadamur home to Luciana upon her death. What more could she do?

She had begun to write another book concerning the influence that miracles had on religious art, and how that impacted and influenced the observers. It was a subject that had now become very dear to her heart.

Alone at night, she would often stand and gaze upon the

distant hills, and in her loneliness, hear their call and take comfort in all the memories they held for her. She could ask for no more.

With sorrow, her mind would encompass Brodie whom she admired so much. He had given a great deal – a part of his life – and she felt she had given him so little. Meeting his daughter, Martha, in that remarkable fashion in Toledo's cathedral, had been a gift from heaven. Whether their story was finished, she had no know way of knowing. Only time would tell.

EPILOGUE

Sacramento, USA

He sat alone in the subdued lighting of his library. He hadn't been in there since that early meeting with Shepard. He still couldn't fully comprehend the enormity of what he had been through and witnessed. Nobody would believe him. But that didn't matter. He, John D. Bower, knew the truth of what had come to pass.

The effect of his healed hand on the Lazarus band had been profound – on him, most of all. When it happened, joy like he had never known had flooded through him. It had been astonishing. Now, his life had been changed forever. The paradoxes of his previous days had been erased. There were none remaining.

The mysteries would forever remain mysteries. *That is how it had always been and always will be,* he thought. His course had never been plainer. He now knew where he was going.

His painting, *The Raising of Lazarus,* had shone Christ's gaze upon him – as it had done since the first artist, Annas Zevi. He entrusted it back to Abbot Louis at the Monasterio de San José de Nazaret. It was the least he could do apart from earmarking a substantial amount of money for the monastery. Bower now had more cash and funds, and he did not know what to do with it. But there was no hurry, Abbot Louis would guide him. The life of a monk is not a rushed one. He had much to learn and his future was clearly set out for him.

The Raising of Lazarus would, as Brodie's work had been, be locked in a secret chapel. When the time is right, it will be displayed … so that it may serve its purpose.

How long that would be, nobody could say.

He reviewed the events around Shepard, his plans for a new church and the crookedness of it all, and it disgusted him that he could have *ever* wanted to be a part of it.

That young woman, Martha, had changed it all for him.

It had been instantaneous between them. It was as if she had been sent to guide him. That damned White Horse they had all ridden had brought them together. He knew he could never forget her – or any of them. They were now deeply ingrained into his being and that's the way he would always wish it to be.

There was one thing left to do.

He rolled the library steps to where he wanted, climbed, and reached out. It was still there where he had last put it. He pulled the *Book of Miracles* and carried it down to the table. He had promised it to the monastery. He had no more use for it.

Turning the pages with great care, he searched for the section with the missing Lazarus pictures. They were no longer missing. Staring up at him were the images of three paintings – and he recognised them all. Brodie's, Martha's – of that he was certain – and his own.

How did they get there? Of that question he had no answer. He could only believe in the miraculous once more.

For the second time in his life, he wept.

Uffington, UK

Ulla Stuart was on edge, very much so. At any minute, they would arrive at the door. The last couple of days had been spent cleaning up the spacious cottage, going from room to room with an array of buckets, mops and cleaning materials. The diffusers had been switched on in each room and she could say the house was as clean as a nun's convent.

Nerves were getting the better of her and she grabbed an extra-large brandy and took a big swig. That morning, she had taken extra care on her clothes and appearance. She wore tight blue trousers, and spinning around, she was pleased to see her figure was as it was many years back. She opted for an equally tight blouse, a couple of its buttons undone. *Just in case he's forgotten.* She had applied mascara, eyeliner and a soft pink lipstick. Silver pendant earrings hung sweetly from her ears. She felt ready.

From the phone calls she had received from Martha, and reading between the lines, she knew things had been happening. They always did when Brodie was about.

Looking out of the window at The White Horse, she lifted her glass to it.

"Here's to you, troublemaker."

A black taxi pulled up outside. *They're here!* She began to shake.

The first person out was Martha, looking as she did the day she left. The well-remembered form of Brodie emerged next. Ulla gasped. He looked older, but it was still unmistakably him. His walk and stance were the same old Brodie. He was smiling, and her heart leapt at the sight of it.

Martha walked to the door, but she beat her to it and flung it open, stepping out with wide open arms.

"Ma!" They embraced heavily before Ulla pulled away. Martha stood aside, and for the first time ever, witnessed her mother and her dad … together.

Not a word was spoken.

They stood silent, still, gazing deeply into each other's eyes. Tears rolled from Ulla's as he reached out awkwardly, as if unsure of how he should react and of her reaction to him. With a loud sob, she fell into his open and welcoming arms.

It had been a charged and highly emotional evening. The bond that had existed between her parents had never really left them even after all these years. It was so obvious. It caused Martha to think she was indeed blessed. They had been God's thieves. His raw humanity, and love for Ulla and herself shone through. *It wasn't all about perfection,* she thought. There existed faultlessness in the crack in a glass. The crack was in itself, perfect. Brodie and Ulla were cracks personified.

Faultless within the erroneous idea of imperfection.

Watching them together, she understood where she came from. She marvelled at their love for each other, which after so many years, remained as bright as the sun itself. It had never diminished. She could only feel the utmost pride and love for them both, and wished that one day, she would find it too.

Her thoughts turned to John. He now carried the burden her father had borne for so many years. He had volunteered to become a monastic under the kindly watch of Abbot Louis.

She loved him for being able to let go of what he had been. What was it she recognised in him when they first met? She knew she would never be able to name it. What was important now was that they had connected, and after a long struggle, Bower had finally learnt to truly open his heart.

John D. Bower's life, as he had known it … was finished. He was now Brother John, The Defender of the Risen Lazarus.

The role would never be a sinecure. More attempts to steal the painting and exploit its powers were inevitable.

Martha realised this and was happy that Brodie had been released from his guardianship.

For a young lady her age, she was quite remarkable. Ulla and Brodie both loved her with a fierce and consuming passion. She was now the brightest light in their lives.

The White Horse remained as it always had, the link that had connected them all. It had carried them equally with love and care and without favour. It had recognised Martha's spirit – naked and unashamed.

Of the bluebells, they still didn't know where they came from.

THE LAZARUS CONTINUUM

She sensed it was not over yet.

ACKNOWLEDGEMENTS

I wish to give special thanks to my editor, and book manager, Eeva Lancaster, and her team, for their hard work, perseverance and patience with a disorganised individual like me. Without that bond, all my books would not be possible.

Bestselling and multi-award-winning British author, Ken Fry, holds a university master's degree in Literature and has traveled around the world. The places and events are reflected in his stories and most of his tales are based on his own experiences.

He has extensive knowledge of the Art world, which he acquired while working as a Publisher in a major UK publishing house -- a wholly owned subsidiary of the HEARST Corp of the USA. In his thirteen years with the company, he worked within the Fine Arts and Antiques division of the organisation and controlled four major international titles.

He is now retired and devotes his full time to writing. He lives in the UK and shares his home with 'Dickens' his Shetland Sheepdog.

www.booksbykenfry.com

Connect with Ken Fry on Twitter:
@kenfry10

Made in the USA
Middletown, DE
30 June 2021